Wo-Sak,
The Frog God

Kel Lamplough

Table of Contents

PRELUDE

High above the metropolis, the stone steps of the Great Temple of Prophecy and Speculation soared into the royal blue sky. At the zenith stood a tall, lean man, rather gaunt. At his waist hung a skimpy loincloth fashioned out of the skin of a young slave girl. On his head was affixed the magnificent ceremonial headdress of the Super Oracle. The helmet was carved from the soft, light wood of a beach palm, decoratcd with the motley skins of deadly poisonous tree frogs. On top, multi-coloured feathers flopped and waved in the light breeze. At the fringe, high on the forehead, rows of tiny teeth swung higgledy-piggledy and at either side, just above the ears, two infants' skulls dangled, spare and bleached. Scarred with lacerations, the man's thickly veined arms and legs stretched out like a starfish. His hands trembled in silhouette, their thin, boney fingers splayed heavenward. His torso, layered in corrugated cuts and abrasions, glistened with silver coconut oil and his upturned face, drenched with the sweat of the topics, swallowed the full force of the sun.

Slowly, he turned away from the milling crowds below. He lowered his arms and picked up a knife. He then instructed a young boy to come forward. Steadily, without sentiment, Super Oracle placed the boy's hand, palm up, on the sacred block. The boy, holding a gaze

8

focused somewhere past the city above the teeming jungle, stood resolute and time, shirking the logic of inevitability, stood still. The Gods observed and the congregation held its breath.

Then, in a meticulous performance of practiced duty, the Priest carefully slashed into the child's tender flesh, raising the boy's hand into the air and draining the blood into a jade goblet. The boy didn't flinch, not one sound or movement. All was still, immutable.

The frozen moment lingered, then slowly melted as Super Oracle drank the thick, bloody offering. The boy swayed in the heat.

Now, Oracle slashed one long, scarlet gash across his own torso and commenced a chant in a loud growl of inhuman proportions. He gathered momentum, leaping this way and that, intoning the Gods and the heavens to come down and open up the truth to him. He slashed at his arms and legs, cutting his thighs and shoulders. He bayed as the blood oozed in glossy rivulets, and his abandoned wails rent the hot, toxic air at the top of the Temple.

"Let me see the light," he demanded. "Let me see the light."

He glared at the crowd, inviting them in to his frenzied recipe.

"Let him see the light," they shouted.

They called in unison repeating over and over.

"The Light. The light. Let him see the light."

The shaman, now under his own spell of incandescent trance, lurched forward, arms aloft. He yelled at the multitude, flings of spittle decorating the guttural invocations. Then, in a flurry of colour he swiveled, turned to the boy.

"I see it. I see it. The light. I see it. I see the light," he exclaimed.

His blasted eyeballs flickered in a frantic seizure as the orbs rolled up into his head. He let out a cry of orgiastic ecstasy. He took up the blade once more, and in a spiritual concentration, whirled sharply, snatching up the boy by his scalp. He tugged the head back and with clinical, savage precision, slit the throat from ear to ear. The crowd swooned.

A widening red gash appeared just below the jaw line. Then, a fountain of blood jetted out, and Super Oracle bathed in the gushing scarlet. His face, a pouring mask, glowed, blossoming in the glare of the sun, and his teeth sneered in the wet red veneer.

He luxuriated in the bloodbath, lathering his face in foamy spumes. As his audience bowed in awe, Super Oracle hurled the boy's dead body down the Temple steps. The child's parents, basking in the fulfilment of their dead son's sacrifice, rushed to the corpse. The mother, tears welling up in proud celebration, cradled her son's bloody head. She looked into his dry, dead eyes, and prayed for his young soul. The glory of the Gods around her maternal shoulders, she praised the universal deities that her son had been chosen. Her husband, a strong, powerful man stood erect, stoic, relishing the wonder of his boy's death. Together, the family posed in a magnificent tableaux of martyrdom.

Super Oracle glowered at the congealed masses.

"I have seen the light!"

Once more his eyes rolled into the top of his

head and his countenance distorted in brutal disfigurement. His sallow cheeks puffed in and out, desperate breaths coming in erratic gushes of air. He began to tremble and stagger about the top altar. looking for a foothold on the blood-sticky floor. As the trance deepened, the Priest yelled out in glorious profanities. Green bile dribbled down onto his bloody chest and sweltering, clearly in a state of transfiguration, he collapsed, heaving in a drizzling heap.

The horde surged forward in an urgent fever. Then, teetering, the man struggled to his feet, approached the front of the topmost altar platform and spewed out the purple ectoplasm of his possession. The crowd, berserk on bloodlust and spiritual fanaticism, roared out his name.

"Oracle. Oracle. Oracle."

In response to the swarming adulation, Super Oracle raised his arms calling for quiet, and a hush fell over the city. He spoke in guttural tones, his eyeballs dizzyingly tracing zigzag patterns in their sockets.

"We have sacrificed all our firstborn, and still we are dying," he started. "We have killed the products of our loins, yet still we are dying. We have done everything the Gods have asked of us . . . And still, we are dying."

His voice, in portentous crescendo, reached its apex of doom.

"We - are - dying!"

The multitude hung on his every word, and listened intently as he predicted disaster and universal catastrophe. The rhetoric echoed what all were thinking, but none had dared, until today, put into the spoken word.

Was this a divine punishment?

Had they not sacrificed enough virgins and slaves?

Should they perhaps sacrifice more of themselves in order to save their civilization?

Behind closed doors, they had all whispered these wild notions. But they all knew that there had to be a limit. They couldn't just keep on sacrificing themselves. That was insane. If they ripped out their own hearts, then who would survive to reap the harvest? No, this was something else. All signs pointed to the end of their world, and they knew it. But what could they do?

This was beyond the powers and understanding of the Super Oracle Priest. But he was too proud, and far too self-important, to admit that he had no idea why the drought continued. It had been going on for several years now, and the city was simply dying away.

"The heavens shall crack and the earth crumble. The air shall poison and . . ." for the first time in his life, he was lost for words.

It was over. No way out. They were all going to die.

PART ONE

In The Beginning

Long, long ago, in an ancient simplicity, there lived a small, tightly knit community of farmers and fishermen. They were pious, peaceful people and made no trouble for themselves, nor for their few and extremely distant neighbours. Life was pacific and worry-free, their serene existence attributed to the fact that the Gods, appreciating the virtue of their subjects, provided a tranquil environment in which to flourish. Offerings were made to the deities, simple things like fruit and flowers, and the husks of coconuts. Occasionally, a small, simple meal of maize and fish, or a dish of wild red-hot chili peppers would be left; and the beneficent Gods, happy with these simple gifts, responded with fulsome harvests, a plentiful supply of seafood and good, clean drinking water.

For as long as anyone could remember they had lived on the coast, and if paradise existed anywhere on earth, it was surely here. Each morning, warm, life-giving sunshine kissed the golden beach, the sand reflecting the heat in a haze of glory. Orange and yellow palms bowed in homage to the sun, their pink and purple fronds fanning in praise of the gilded orb. Glowing flowers dug deep to drink, then opened up their vibrant leaves to swallow the yellow rays, while roundly proud rainbow rocks soaked up the radiance and blushed, humming in the passion of a new day. Tiny wavelets chorused a gentle overture to the cresting turquoise surf beyond the reef, where whales, dolphins and luminous fish squirted in a diversion of games and illusions. And in the distance, an undulating horizon gave way to a light blue sky where a glittering cloud or two, unable to choose a purposeful destination, drifted, aimlessly.

Birds twittered a chirpy, welcoming song and the yawns of the waking people were quickly followed by smiles, as fires crackled and breakfast smells, crisp on the air, wafted on the gentle breeze coming off the glittering bay. Mothers cradled their hungry babies, fathers stretched and groaned happily in preparation for the day, and children laughed and played in the amber morning light. Day after day the sun rose, the people paid tribute to nature and their Gods, and the world turned on a blissful axis. And all was well in heaven on earth.

But one day, all this changed. For, one day, there was an event of such seismic proportions that for the first time in their lives, the people felt fear. The earth trembled, the sky grew grey, and coal and brimstone rained down. The people cried. Something had gone horribly wrong.

The force of the blast was immense. It blew the top off the world. It sent deep shockwaves through the core of the mountains, traversed the tropical jungles and funneled into the coast, exactly where the tribe lived. The earth shook and trembled. Birds fell silent, then took off in squawking battalions. Animals stampeded, roaring and snorting in panic.

The first the settlement knew about it was a very distant roar, an annoyed, heavenly grumbling. Then everything went dark and angry, and the people darted around in circles thinking that the end of the world was nigh. They looked skyward and wondered what was about to befall them. Ash and stone tumbled in clod heaps, and the simple people cried out in agonized, fearful sobs. They had never experienced trepidation before and did not know how to cope with this new emotion. They were terrified and knew not what to do.

What was this feeling?

Where did it come from?

What did it mean?

They had no answers, and as they screamed, some transfixed to the spot yelling at the sky, some concentrically dizzying themselves into frenzies of despair, their hearts cried to their Gods for help.

"Help us," they wailed "oh Gods of everlasting kindness."

"We pray you, guide us and help us," they shouted.

"Do not forsake us," they pleaded.

But the Gods did not respond.

Ash fogged down in thundering mass clouds, and huge angular rocks, pumice and the wreckage of the bowels of the earth, crashed to the ground in a deafening cacophony. Some sad, but lucky souls, uncomprehending faces upturned to the heavens, were killed outright, crushed and re-crushed, their skulls shattered beyond recognition by the massive, vomited boulders.

Others, hopelessly trying to escape, were brought down as they ran, a blow to the head, or grounded by the weight of hundreds and hundreds of stones. The gases and hellish ash choked and sapped the life out of all breathing creatures. And the bodies writhed in tortured agony as their oxygen starved lungs wheezed and gasped in pathetic attempts to grab the strangled air.

Eyes bulged, white and red, then dead and clogged with the grey of ash, dust and slag. Children screamed at their mothers, all suffocating in the dry, scorching hell horror, skin cooking, burning, frying, peeling as the heat seared through flesh and bone. Men cried terrible tears as they defiantly sheltered cowering wives and children. But as the blazing downpour raged, their strong arms smelted in the blistering salvoes. Families, melting together into unrecognizable mutations, cried in silent screeches.

The volcanic Armageddon destroyed everything.

It was the end of the world, and they knew it.

What had happened?

Who was doing this to them?

What had they done to deserve this?

They were puzzled and afraid.

It *was* the end of the world.

The Old Man, a Dog and a Box

One day a wandering old man of uncertain descent, entered the village of Suxx. He was quite short and skinny, dressed in a grubby ochre loincloth, and a rather ragged light green headband. He wore a pained, yet quizzical expression on his narrow, bony face and his eyebrows almost met above his long, sharp nose. His jug ears, thin and veined, stuck up like the chipped handles of a broken vase. His startling, obsidian-black eyes, sallow cheeks and high temples, gave him a somewhat intense look, and yet his face held an expression of some kind of happiness, giving him a magnetic, almost mystical aura. His hair was extremely long and very black, and this, along with his exceptionally dark brown, leathery skin drawn tightly across his small, angular frame, presented a rather starved attitude. Under his chin, suspended from a scraggy chicken's neck, hung several necklaces of high-grade, interwoven silver, each inlaid with uncut, semi-precious stones of various sizes. They caught the light, and sparkled and dazzled in the brilliant sunshine. A deep purple pendant, about the size of a small tangerine, dangled loosely at his famished chest and numerous multi-coloured bangles adorned each scrawny wrist. His fingers, long drawn-out affairs, glittered with pointed talons twittering in the hot air, and his arms, boney elbows almost at right angles to his torso, flapped lightly at his sides.

Shoeless, he stooped as he walked, but nonetheless managed to carry himself with a certain distinction, his deceptively strong, sparrow thin legs, clearly capable of carrying him for many, many miles. His feet shot out like girders, the toes, with their thick blackened nails, clawing into the dirt for balance and certain propulsion. All in all, the man had the threatening, yet somehow gently reassuring presence of an inquisitive, very hungry vulture. And strapped to his back, was a large, intricately carved, mahogany box.

Except that this wasn't quite true, at least, not all of it. Yes, he did have a big box on his back, and yes, it was intricately carved, and yes, he did wander into the village of Suxx. But he certainly did not look like a bird, much less a vulture. Yet, to the outside world he did resemble an avian scavenger, a sharp-clawed scrounger with a hooked nose and beady eyes . . . indeed, a vulture.

But the reality couldn't have been more different.

To begin with, his physique was dominated by a very large, and very round, fat head. And he was bald, but really bald, not a hair in sight. And short. He was *very* short. Also, he did not have eyebrows which almost met above a long sharp nose, because he had no nose, and he did not have any eyebrows - at all. And his ears did not stick up. They were too red, almost comical and too insignificant for that. His eyes were startling, this is true. But they were not obsidian-black. No. They were round, red buttons with golden pupils, lost in an expanse of podgy flesh.

His mouth, a downturned scarlet affair, did not invite conversation and he had no neck to speak of. His face, far from boney and narrow, did have a quizzical expression, but it was one more of misery, a confounded consternation. Despite this however, there was an extremely deep intelligence hiding beneath the features. His body was a compact, wavy thing, with sticky out arms and legs, all curves and soft lines. His feet, wide flappy things, were far too big for him, but did a great job of keeping his vertical posture. There were no bangles and beads, and no necklaces nor loincloth. He was as naked as the day he was born. But to the outside world, of course, he did look like a vulture.

He had, as companion, a black and white dog. Or, rather, silver and black, depending on the light and time of day, and the dog's mood. The dog had lost an eye in a bloody fight protecting his master, and he loped alongside him, with a bit of a limp, but a contentedly wagging tail. Intelligent, wise and full of interest in the world and its idiosyncrasies, the dog seemed to be grinning as it sniffed the ground, and occasionally looked up at his master.

"There's a good lad," said the old man, in his thin, gentle voice. "Keep up, and keep an eye out. There's a good lad."

The dog replied with a short sneeze, as if in understanding, and did indeed keep an eye out, just the one.

The two of them slowed to a meandering sidestep, taking in the village and wondering where everyone was. There were no people on the street. No children playing. No adults gossiping on corners. No activity of any kind.

"Strange," said the old man to himself.

And, as if understanding again, the dog stopped, sniffed the air and cocked an ear to the sky.

"Wonder where everyone is?"

It was then that the old man sensed, rather than saw, an ambulatory movement, a shuffling, a meandering listlessness. He felt the teeniest tremor of air, an insignificant vibration given importance by the fact that absolutely nothing was moving. The dog felt it too, and he gruffly raised a small, quite harmless, hackle.

"What's that then boy?" said the old man. "What's that then?"

The dog blinked, passed a long, angry red tongue over its lips,

and looked beyond the old man into the ruin of a dwelling. The old man followed the dog's gaze and saw, eerily drifting out of the rubble, what he perceived to be a family, shambling through the wreckage of what might have been their home. Wide, white-blank eyes gawped unintelligently. Hopeless open mouths vainly sucked for air, their hollow cheeks sagging, lifeless canvasses in a dry, indolent dessert ocean.

Their arms hung like the stiff, brittle boughs of a dying tree, their thin, reedy fingers jutting south, limp, ready to snap. Their grubby blue smocks, dusty shredded rags, dangled from skeletal frames struggling to find footing in the mess of destruction.

The dead troop snaked in an oblivious, icy file. They mutely wafted by, and the old man and his dog knew better than to interrupt the macabre procession. Shoulders sloping in avenues of dejection, the cadaverous party dumbly tripped through the rock rubble dust, aiming for an undisclosed destination.

The dog bobbed its head. The old man trained his squinting eyes on the dead parade. The family, mindless in their numb trudge, filed off along the road. The old man looked at the dog, thought of making a comment, but didn't bother. The dog swallowed, creased its mouth into a grim smile, then wagged its tail.

"Hmm," muttered the old man.

The dog looked up at him with its one eye, an unspoken exchange barely disturbing the air. They decided to follow the grim, sick cortege.

They continued to track the dire family along what the old man presumed to be the main street when, approaching a fork in the road he heard, very faintly in the distance, the sound of a solitary drum beat.

"Ah," he said to the dog, "life itself."

He and the dog set off tracking the family in the direction of the doleful thrum and thrum of the drum.

As he walked, passing by the destroyed dwellings, the collapsed roofs and caved-in walls of deserted buildings, and the piles of small boulders, rocks and stones, the old man thought to himself.

Great pity. And so grey. It must have been beautiful here, before.

Gone were the vibrant yellows, greens, reds and blues which usually adorned the houses of the coastal regions. It was now all so dull, and broken, and so, so, well . . . grey. Like a morgue. A dead place.

The old man stopped, turned and looked behind at the empty street.

"Great pity," he muttered. "Oh well."

He shrugged, and carried on.

21

It didn't take too long for the old man to come to the source of the drum and with it a sight that warmed his heart. Now he knew he was in the right place, and he knew that he could do well here. Ahead of him he saw a small group of people squatting on the ground, facing a mound of rubble. On the rubble stood a man. He was a bedraggled looking man with very short white hair, dark, heavy eyes and rounded shoulders. Dressed in a torn, dirt-red robe, he was mumbling and rocking from side to side. He had in his hand a smashed coconut husk, and, after a few seconds, raised it to the heavens and muttered some more. The assembled crowd joined in the chant, waving their arms in the air. The old man, looking at this, slowly shook his head.

"Pathetic," he said to himself. "Just pathetic."

The dog looked up at his master and agreed.

The old man narrowed his eyes and searched the group of people kneeling in the dust and rubbish. He couldn't see what he was looking for. He continued scanning the group, when a small movement caught his attention. Someone was getting up.

The old man smartly collected his thoughts and prepared for what was to come, for he knew what was to come. And indeed, within a short while what was to come, was heading straight for him.

"Alright, here we go," he said to the dog. "Keep an eye out."

And the dog did, indeed, keep an eye out . . . just the one.

Two men left the group and approached. Barefoot, they walked zombie-like, heedless of the rubble beneath their naked feet, perambulating in straight lines yet without much haste. Obviously interested in the newcomer, they were making an effort, either to welcome, or warn, or both. They were not very tall, and not especially large of frame. Dull, empty eyes stared through the old man as they approached, and he wondered if they were alive or dead.

They were dressed in the same torn robes as the man on the mound, but of dirt-green instead of the red, and their unkempt, rough-cut hair was powder grey, like the ground on which they walked. Ashen, pale skin hung from their boney arms and legs, and as the two men got closer, the old man could see that they were finding it hard to breathe. Their laboured chests gave away hardly any sign that they were, indeed, living creatures, but the almost inaudible rasping sound of air wheezing up through collapsed lungs, told the old man that what was approaching was not life as he understood it.

The faces held no particular expression, and the hollow eyes, drained of humanity, lay quite lifeless, set deep in the recesses of the cold, meaningless countenances.

The old man wondered at the vestige of human curiosity still flowing, however thinly, through the beings' veins. Clearly, they wanted to see who this stranger in their village was. Even in their desperate condition the two soulless men could not resist the power of the unknown, and so had left the group of sad devotees to investigate the newcomer.

The old man stood stark still as, unblinking, they slowly scanned him from top to bottom, digesting his rather peculiar state, and especially the large mahogany box strapped to his back.

One of them spoke.

"What do you want, old man?"

He had a flat, toneless voice and made no point of punctuating his words with gesture.

The old man smiled.

"Where are you from?" the other asked.

The old man smiled some more.

"I'm from over the rivers and mountains."

"Which river?"

"The one to the south."

"Where?"

"To the south."

"South?"

"Yes. The south. To the south," the old man insisted.

The larger of the two spoke up.

"There is no river to the south," he said flatly.

The old man looked at him for a moment as the drum beat sadly on in the background.

"Oh, but there is."

"No," said the bigger man, shaking his head. "There isn't. There's nothing."

"Oh there is. If you go far enough."

"I've never seen it."

"That's because you haven't been far enough," said the old man.

As if to add weight to his master's words the dog, now perhaps more silver than white, sidled up and sat down beside him, his one eye going from each to the other of the two grey men.

"What's in the box?" said the smaller one.

Ah ha, thought the old man, *it didn't take too long.*

"Ah, my box," he said aloud.

"Yes, what's in it?" asked the bigger one.

The old man stared at the two strangers.

"Do you think I can have some water please. I've travelled a long way and I'm rather thirsty."

The smaller of the two pointed to a well.

"There's plenty over there. But the water's dirty."

The old man made his way to the well.

"I'm sure it'll be fine. Thank you."

As he went, the two men noted the drawings running up and down the old man's calves. Each muscle was decorated by intricately designed mythical, legendary, or perhaps heavenly creatures of another world, certainly a world unfamiliar to the two dusty grey men in dusty grey rags.

"What are those?" said one.

"Don't know."

"Strange."

"Yes."

The old man drew some dirty water from the well, sniffed it and shrugged. He then undid the straps holding the box to his back, placed it on the ground, sat down, closed his eyes and fell asleep. The dog wagged its tail. It had a good feeling about the place. In fact, the feeling was so good that it had now turned completely silver, all hint of black having disappeared from its shaggy coat. Ever faithful, he sat beside his master. With his one eye he kept a vigil. His job was to guard and protect. And he did it well. He had the scars to prove it. He'd even lost an eye. The dog hardly ever slept, and the old man could rest peacefully.

The sun bore down, and the two men showed signs of neither pleasure nor discomfort at the hot rays. They simply stood there, next to the well, looking down at the man and the dog. They didn't speak, or move, until the fiery beams of the late afternoon began losing their heat.

They finally burst into activity, well as much as they could muster, and nodded to each other.

"I don't know who he is," said the small one.

"Neither do I," said the big one.

"Wonder what he wants?" said the small one.

"Don't know," said the big one.

"And the pictures."

"Yes."

"Yes."

Silence fell between them, and they seemed to have exhausted their conversation.

The beat of the drum still echoed in the background, and the chanting was as dull and lacking in intensity as earlier in the afternoon.

"Strange dog," said the big one, breaking the stillness.

"Yes," said the small one.

The men nodded again, then took as big a breath as they possibly could before making the effort to walk.

"Ready?" said the small one.

"Yes," said the big one, and with that they held hands and walked as steadily as they could.

Returned to the group, they sat down and joined in the chanting accompanied by the thrum and thrum of the drum.

"Wonder who he is?" said the big one

"Don't know," said the small one, and they both rocked to the rhythm of the drum.

They fell into a trance and dissolved into the group as they all melted into the dust and greyness of early evening.

The sun had almost set and the old man woke up to silence. There was no one about. The dog opened its eye, (for it had stolen a short nap), winked a couple of times, yawned, stretched and set about finding a tree. The old man helped himself to some dirty water from the well and looked about. No one. Not a thing moved and no one to be seen.

Just then, a young boy appeared from out of the dusky shadows.

"Hello," said the boy.

The old man, pleased to have some human company, raised his eyebrows into his deeply tanned, crinkly forehead, and gave the boy a hearty, "Hello" back.

"Who are you?" asked the boy confidently.

"I'm the old man from the south," said the old man from the south.

"The old man from the south?" repeated the boy.

"That's right," the old man said, nodding his head. "And who are you?" he asked.

"I'm Gamboa," the boy replied.

"Gamboa?" the old man repeated, with a knowing smile on his lips. "That's a fine name for a small boy."

"It was my father's name," said the boy, proudly. "And his father's before that, and his father's father's before that," added Gamboa.

"Gamboa," repeated the old man, ruminating. "Now I know I'm in the right place."

"What's in the box?" said Gamboa, showing a new curiosity.

"The box?"

"Yes."

The boy leaned closer to examine the box. He had never seen anything like it. Etched into the tough wood were the most incredible designs and pictures he had ever seen. On each side, and on the lid, were depictions of . . . well, he didn't have the words to describe them, really. What were those things? People? Animals? Flying creatures? And maybe even buildings? But not like any buildings he'd seen before. Certainly, there were sunny beach scenes he kind of recognized, and trees reminding him of his own village. But there were also dog-like beasts, and heads, coming out of the sand, and curly things going round in mad circles. Nothing seemed to be the right way round. It sent his head into a spin just looking at it all.

"Well," started the old man "there're lots of things. Would you like to see inside?

"Yes please," said Gamboa, with the enthusiasm of the young child he was.

"Alright. But first, you have to do something for me."

The boy looked puzzled.

"What?"

"Tell me something. Tell me something important."

"Like what?" asked the boy.

"Well, for instance: What happened here? Why is everything so grey? And the people. Why are they so dull?"

Gamboa scratched the back of his leg, bit his lip and forged an answer.

"We died," he said. "We all died."

"That explains it then," said the old man, frowning. "Death can kill a place indeed. Yes, death can kill a place."

"Can I see inside the box now?" asked Gamboa.

"Not just yet. There's one more thing," said the old man, rummaging under his belt. "Wait a moment."

Shifting his weight from one side to the other, the old man finally got hold of what he was looking for.

"First you must take this." And the old man gave Gamboa a small, jade vial.

"What is it?" said Gamboa.

"You'll see," said the old man. "Take the top off."

The boy did as he was told.

"Now, take a small sip. Not too much. Just enough to taste. Just

to wet your lips and taste."

"What is it?" the boy asked again.

"You'll see. Just take a sip."

The boy raised the small jar to his lips, tipped his head back and sipped.

"Not too much," said the old man, raising a wary hand.

He watched as the boy took the vial from his mouth, running his tongue along his lips.

"Hmm, tastes strange," said Gamboa.

"Yes," said the old man, with a twinkle in his eye.

"Almost like . . ." started Gamboa.

"Yes?"

"Well, like nothing I've ever tasted before," said Gamboa.

"That's right," said the old man. "Like nothing you've ever tasted before."

He smiled, and, taking the vial from the boy, said, "Now rest for a moment. Here, sit," and pointed to the floor, beside him. "Sit here for a while."

The boy sat.

A short time passed. Then another. And then something odd happened: time passed, and yet it didn't. It was as if everything was zipping by at a super-fast speed, yet in slow motion. Everything seemed, well, Gamboa didn't really know how it seemed, or how to describe it. As he sat there his mind became clear as a bell, then foggy again, then clear again. And then he noticed that he could hear the call of birds he had never heard before, and he could see the crawling of the tiniest insects that he had not seen before. He could smell the sweetest of flowers he had not smelled before. He looked from the grey, dusty square toward the setting sun, and he saw magnificent violet mountains, and great green lakes where before he had seen nothing. He could feel the beating of nature itself, and sense heavens and the universe beyond the horizon. A rainbow of twenty-seven different colours bled from the purple haze above a palm tree where nothing usually happened. Jaguars spoke and sang in rhyming couplets, telling their story of how they came into being. A trio of dolphins soared high up into the highest trees, resting to perch on delicate branches of yellow velvet. And turquoise snakes danced together and laughed and played games, sharing jokes and patting each other on their everlastingly long backs. Green dogs and orange cats romanced, and walked hand-in-hand by inky red rivers of honey, and stared into each other's diamond shaped eyes down by melon flavoured streams. He heard the passage of time, He could hear it, passing.

The boy tried to speak, but found his mouth rather dry.

"Would you like a drop of water?" the old man offered.

"Yes please."

"There," said the old man, passing him a cup from the well.

"But that water's dirty," said Gamboa.

"Perhaps," said the old man. "Try it."

The boy drank.

"Better?"

"Yes," said Gamboa, with a quizzical look on his face. "But that water's dirty. How come it tastes so delicious?"

"Never mind," said the old man. "Now, would you like to see inside the box?"

"Yes," said Gamboa.

And with that the old man leaned over, undid a catch and opened it up. The young boy peered inside and instantly his face lit up, and his eyes bulged in amazement. Another world beckoned, right there, before him.

"Wow," he said.

"Yes, wow," repeated the old man, widening his own eyes.

"Wow," said Gamboa again.

"Yes, wow," smiled the old man.

The boy made a move to put his hand inside the box but the old man quickly took him by the wrist.

"No," he said sharply "not like that. It's too dangerous. They'll kill you."

"Who? Who will kill me?" asked Gamboa.

The dog, sensing the danger, threw his head back and barked one short, sharp bark, and stood to attention, keeping his eye out in case of emergencies.

"What is it?" insisted the boy.

"You'll see,' replied the old man, a look of infinite patience crossing his face.

He licked his lips, sighed a bit of a sigh, gave the dog a knowing look in his one eye, then spoke in a stentorian voice.

"Gamboa, these are from the jungles and forests of the south. They are a gift from the Gods to us here on earth. They are the most precious gifts ever bestowed upon mere humans. They owe their very existence to one supreme God who created them, and gifted them to the world of mortals. They are to be treasured and guarded most carefully, for the Gods would have it that way. Their beauty knows no equal and they have reigned in the forests of the earth since time began. Brilliant and tantalizingly magnetic, they are yet the most poisonous creatures in the whole world. And I'm giving them to you."

He paused.

"One day, they will save your life."

Gamboa couldn't believe it.

"Me? You're giving them to me?" he said, incredulous. "Me?"

"Yes Gamboa, to you. You are now the guardian and I give them to you."

"But what are they?" asked Gamboa, bobbing his head, peering this way and that.

The old man ignored him.

"You must never touch them," he warned. "Never pick them up, nor play with them. Never. Do you understand?"

"But what are they?" pleaded the boy.

Again the old man ignored him.

"Do you understand?" he said firmly.

The boy turned away from the box, looked at the old man and nodded his head.

"Yes. I think so," he stammered.

"NO!" insisted the old man, shaking his head. "That's not good enough. You must NEVER touch them. Do . . . you . . . understand?"

The old man furrowed his brow and stared intensely at the young boy.

"Hmm?"

"Yes," said the boy, more decisively. "I understand."

"Good," said the old man. "Now. Let me introduce you."

Arguments

Suxx was abuzz with excitement as the Day of Reincarnation and Ultimate Sacrifice dawned. Festivities were to start at sunrise, building to a climax as the sun reached its zenith at mid-day. It was an annual event and all the inhabitants of the city were geared up for what promised to be a bumper day of sacrifice and rejuvenation. Every year the Temple Priests put on a festive show of pious, yet at the same time, raucous solicitude calling on the Gods to bless the city, bless the devotees and bless the harvest. This year there was an especial incantation and service for the falling of rain. Rain. It hadn't rained for several months now and the people of Suxx were getting more than a little worried by the drought: crops were dying. But, more importantly, the city's water tanks and reservoirs were running dry. Soon there would not be enough to sustain the city, and who knew what would happen then. Well, they'd probably die, was what most people thought.

It was some paradox that although they lived close to the shoreline of the salty gulf, and could see enough water to satisfy all their needs, it was, of course, undrinkable and the tribespeople were left in some quandary as to what they had done to anger the Gods. Where was the rain? *Just where was the rain?*

For several months the Temple Chiefs had been holding secret meetings. They talked about what to do and wracked their brains trying to come up with a solution to the problem.

Jaguar: "It's your fault."

Snake: "No it isn't."

Jaguar: "Yes it is."

Snake: "Why?"

Jaguar: "Why? Because you have angered the Gods."

Snack: "Rubbish!"

Jaguar: "Yes, you have angered the Gods. Yours is a false God and you have angered the great God of Universal Well-being, the Jaguar."

Snake: "Nonsense. The Jaguar means nothing..."

Jaguar: "Yes, you have fallen from grace with the Gods and now we are all being punished. The great God Jaguar is angered and is punishing us."

Snake: "It's YOUR faithless, ignorant rituals that are killing us. YOUR faithless mumbo-jumbo which has doomed us all to this dread fate."

Jaguar: "It's YOU who have condemned us to death. A dry death which the Gods have cast upon us. It is YOU..."

Snake: "You are the ones who have brought this down upon our heads with your disrespect for the Great Snake God..."

Jaguar: "Disrespect? Us? The Great Jaguar God's representatives on earth? We are the one true manifestation of the supernatural Jaguar universe, and it is *we* who will save our race from destruction, while you, you poisonous traitors, have brought us to this, this end of our world."

Snake: "You shall die for your words Jaguar. You shall die."

Jaguar: "Not before you - Snake."

And with that, hissing and snarling they lunged at each other across the fire, sending sparks and flames in all directions.

At that moment Gamboa jumped to his feet.

"Silence!" he roared.

He stared at the two men rolling in a tangle of fire.

"Silence, you fools. What are you, men or children? This is not the time to be beating each other over the head. We need solutions, not quarrels. Stop. Stop now!"

Gamboa, a huge man, had little trouble commanding respect. Muscular and athletic, he was renowned not only for his great physical strength and agility, but also his profound universal knowledge. He stood head and shoulders above his contemporaries, both physically and intellectually. He was the Chief Temple Frog Priest and as such ruled over, and was supported by, the people of Suxx. The Frogs were the masters of the city but had, at the same time, to engage in mediation with the Jaguar and Snake Priests, who made up the minority spiritual leadership.

At the best of times the relationship between the three was thorny, but now, with the drought straining patience to the limit, jangled nerves were being stretched to breaking point.

"You two, calm down. This will solve nothing," Gamboa said with authority.

"The Snakes are poisonous and will ruin us all," snarled the Jaguar Temple Priest.

"The Jaguars bring death to the city," hissed the Snake Priest.

"Shut up. Both of you," snapped Gamboa.

Gamboa looked down at the two men. They were here to debate and discuss, to try to find a solution to the water problem, and all they could do was argue. He was losing patience.

"Sit down." He glared at them as they both refused to move. "NOW!" he roared.

The two Temple Chiefs, realizing that Gamboa was about to strike, shied away from each other and reluctantly sat down, cross-legged either side of the fire.

"Now," started Gamboa calmly "can we get back to the business of water? There is no point in blaming each other. The problem is here, and it's here now. We have to do something."

He looked at the two men.

Silence.

"Well, anyone got a suggestion?"

Jaguar lifted his head.

"The Jaguars have always been respectful and made sacrifices to the Jaguar God. We have done all we can to protect our city and followers. There is no more we can do. We have religiously made the human sacrifices demanded, each family choosing one girl to be thrown into the Jaguar pit, their young virginal hearts cut out, offered in worship at the altar. We have eaten the flesh of our enemies and boiled their blood to be scattered on the fields. We have chanted with the dead and dying, carved up the diseased and fed their hearts to the ravens and dogs. We have done all this and still there is drought. We have done all we can."

He looked straight at the Snake Priest, challenging him to contradict his words. But the Snake Priest, containing his anger, had better sense than to start another fight.

Gamboa pondered Jaguar's words, then nodded to the Snake Priest.

"And you? What have you to say?"

"We have done all we can do," said the Snake Priest. "The Snakes are pious and respectful, and we have done everything in our power. Each month we sacrifice our youngest virgins and deliver them up to the Snake God. The hearts of the innocents we have taken out and wrapped in the skin of the dead and left them in the pits. We have never faltered in our duty to pay homage to our God. It is not *we* who have angered the Gods."

And with that he could not resist a sharp look at the Jaguar Priest.

"That's enough," interjected Gamboa. "There will be no more accusations here."

Jaguar, who had sat upright, leaned forward, and with piercing eyes stared at the Snake Priest.

Gamboa took a big breath and slowly shook his head.

"So, what can we do?"

He looked from one to the other of the men sitting on opposite sides of the fire. He continued.

"The Frogs have also done all we can. Each new moon we sacrifice slaves, tearing out their beating hearts, offering them up to the Frog God. The blood we drain and drink to bursting, and spread the shredded heart remains on the Frog altars of eternal flame. Every day we pray our mantras and bow down to the idols in our Temple. We fast and bleed our animals, smearing the blood on the faces of newborn children, and we light the midnight fires, brazing our enemies alive on the pyres, sending our incense up to the universal deities. More we cannot do. We have done all we can."

He rested, thinking deeply. Moments passed. He looked up.

"Clearly, we have not done enough," he said, shaking his head. "We have simply not done enough to please the Gods."

The fire crackled and each man sat in silence, pondering the future and what to do. The situation was critical, and not just because of the lack of rain. Each Temple Priest knew that the clansmen were getting impatient. There were rumours of mistrust, rebellion and insurrection. The people were losing faith in their leaders, and they simply had to come up with something. If not, who knew how long they could contain the unrest stirring in the city? And with that unrest their own positions would be threatened, and they certainly could not afford that. They had to think of something.

Jaguar, head bowed now, offered no ideas and sat brooding, aloof.

Snake was far away in his own thoughts and seemed to have no opinions or suggestions to offer.

Gamboa spoke.

"Is that the best you can do?" he said with a sneer.

Jaguar and Snake snapped to attention.

"It's all we have," said Snake.

"We can do no more," added Jaguar.

"But we must do more," insisted Gamboa. "It's down to us. We simply have to do more. We need rain and we have failed in our duties."

And with that he sprang to his feet, raised his head to the sky and thumped the air with his fist.

"We must do more. We must sacrifice more. Offer more. Bring more to the altars of our forefathers and pray for guidance in our devotions."

He looked down at the others.

"You, Snake, you have not done enough . . ."

"But . . ." interjected Snake.

"Don't interrupt! No. You have not done enough. You must make more sacrifices and spill more blood. The Gods' thirst remains unquenched and they need more blood. Only this way will they hear our prayer for rain."

He paused only slightly.

"Lest you feel that Snake alone is at fault, you, Jaguar . . ."

Jaguar looked startled.

"Me?" he blurted.

"Yes, *YOU*. Don't pretend to be so innocent. We both know better. You and your followers have clearly not fulfilled the sacrificial quota and should also do much more in an effort to solve our problem."

As if punctuating Gamboa's edict, the fire crackled and spat red embers into the night air, trailing rainbow sparks landing at Gamboa's feet.

He continued.

"As for the Frogs, we shall scale up the bloodletting. The Frog Gods *shall* be appeased, and they *shall* come to our rescue. We will be saved and we will have water. If we commit to this task we will overcome the drought. We will drink-in the waters of the divine universe, and swim in the heavenly pools of everlasting divinity. We will survive."

Jaguar and Snake looked at each other across the fire. There was little they could say. It was a desperate situation and they both knew that Gamboa, the Chief Temple Frog Priest, was right. They had to do more.

Slowly, they got to their feet.

"Go with the Gods," said Gamboa.

"Go with the Gods," responded Jaguar.

"Go with the Gods." repeated Snake.

And as Jaguar and Snake left, Gamboa took from under his belt, a small jade vial. Taking off the top, he lifted it to his lips and drank. Then he sat down by the fire and waited. Although now only embers, the fire threw out enough heat to keep him warm in the cooling air. After a while, he began to slowly rock from side to side, then he began to chant the ancient guttural incantation he had learned in his youth. His eyes went through the top of his head, and he was soon totally unaware of his surroundings. Time and space cavorted into a macabre tango of intrigue as his perception first tunneled, then land-scaped into vast canvasses of universal plains, beyond the realms of earth. He began to sweat. The liquid swirled through his veins, finding its inevitable way to his head and, diluting his brain, finally cut the elemental chord between the here and now, and the eternal beyond. Soon, the old familiar visions came rushing at him, in involuntary cascades of colour. The fabulous rainbow turned grey then red, then back to grey again and the earth trembled and the sky imploded as the ashes, and yet more ashes, fell to the ground. Fire turned to water, then back to fire again, and Gamboa, his limbs first rocks of granite, then invisibly light gossamer butterfly wings, began to transcend the concrete world of jungles and oceans. He soon found himself floating in clouds of tawny yellow, where birds spoke to him of troubled minds and galactic intrigue, rodents sang of heavenly harmony and divine intervention, insects choreographed operas of hope and confirmation, and, finally, there, what he had been looking for, the Frog God himself, smiling sublimely yet terrible in aspect, urging him to make the dreadful decision that he knew was waiting for him.

Meeting

"Now," said the old man, "are you ready?"

Gamboa turned his head.

"Yes, I'm ready."

"Good. Then let me introduce you."

Gamboa looked into the box again, and again his breath was taken away. For, inside, was another world, of trees and rivers, and lofty skies, and mountains and ponds. There were streams and valleys, and lush fields and knee-high grasses, and verdant pastures and limitless skies. Thick, knotted vines and glorious blossoms littered a forest floor, and incredible birds of all shapes and sizes nested and flew backwards and forwards across horizons. The box was alive.

"But how?"

The old man put a gnarled, but surprisingly well-manicured index finger to his lips.

"Shhhh," he whispered softly. "We don't want to alarm them."

He then, most quietly and carefully, picked up a small stick from the floor beside the well, and, with immense caution, meticulously lowered it into the box. Almost motionless, the stick made its way to a small, tropical tree, next to a small, tropical thicket, next to a small, tropical pond. The old man, calm and with nerves of steel, targeted a large brown leaf, recently fallen to the forest floor. He cautiously placed the stick under the leaf and, with minute, soundless movements, lifted it just a few inches.

As the tension grew, Gamboa's heart was ready to burst out of his chest, but he stayed still, stark, not even daring to imagine what was about to unfold. The old man started to hum very softly as he finally moved the leaf the last few millimetres, revealing the picture beneath. Placing the stick to one side, he silently smiled in satisfaction at the sight before him. Gamboa, as openmouthed as it was possible for a young boy to be, watched incredulous as his eyes, for the very first time, registered the awe and majesty of three superb, deadly poisonous dart frogs. Captured in a holy triptych of devastating beauty, the tiny frogs posed in studious aspect.

To the left, the smallest, dressed in glossy cardinal red, sat quietly nodding his head in great debate, eschewing the company of the physical for the ethereal mysticism of a universe beyond.

In the middle, boasting a rather wet turquoise, reposed a frog who was lost in a metaphysical reverie, demanding a lifetime's attention to detailed analysis of the origin of cosmic dust.

And on the right, sitting monumentally silent, was the third frog. By far the largest of the three, by a good half centimetre, his speckled red and white skin bloated in and out in minute inflations as he breathed deeply. His eyes firmly glued shut, he was oblivious of the world's whizzing by at breakneck speed, leaving him to review and revise his own peculiar version of heavenly events.

It was almost impossible *not* to pick them up. They were simply wonderfully beautiful. They were small and petite, and so at peace it was hard to believe that they could kill without raising a finger. No wonder the old man had told Gamboa that he must never touch them.

As if their natural beauty were not impressive enough, another miracle of the universe was about to unveil itself. Without even opening its eyes the largest, the red and white speckled dart frog, the most poisonous frog in the entire world, if not the entire universe, opened its mouth and began to speak.

"Gamboa," it said, in a mellow, commanding voice, "you and your people are dead. You have died because you have failed to see the true Gods. You have died because you have worshipped a false God, a God who no longer helps and protects you. For hundreds, if not thousands of years you have been true to a mocking God, one who has finally deserted you."

Gamboa stared in amazement at the brilliant frog.

It carried on.

"There is only one way you can survive and this is to deny your past and serve the true Gods, who alone can resurrect your people and lead you back to life. You must abandon all other Gods and worship the supreme Gods. You must worship the Frog Gods."

Gamboa felt a surge of expectancy and lowered his head further into the box.

"You must put away your childish idolatry and infantile gifts of fruit and flowers, and make sacrifices of human souls and the flesh of your fellow human beings. You must offer up blood to the Frog Gods who, in return, will restore you and grant you everlasting life in the Frog Kingdom. This you must do, Gamboa, if you want to save your people."

The little frog stopped and seemed to be listening to an inner voice before he carried on.

"The Frog Gods want it all Gamboa; the eyes and the tongues, the skin and the bones, the fingers and toes and lungs and brains and the organs and souls and hearts . . . they want the hearts; the very hearts, the beating, bloody hearts of humans. Only then, and then only, will you live, Gamboa."

With that, the tiny, florescent spotted frog, opened its eyes, closed them again, considered saying something else but thought better of it and disappeared into the camouflage of the leaf.

"But who are you?" asked Gamboa, almost in despair. "Who are you?"

The old man patted him on the arm.

"He's gone."

"But who is he?"

"He's the Frog Gods' messenger," said the old man. "He is the poison dart frog of the south and he has come to give you a message."

"But why me?"

Another smile creased the old man's lips.

"Ah well, that would take some time to explain," he said.

And before Gamboa knew it, the old man had replaced the leaf, snapped shut the box, called for his dog and set off walking straight towards a tree.

"Wait!" called Gamboa. "Wait a minute."

"I've done all I can," said the old man. "My job is finished."

And with a wave of his hand he and the dog walked right up to the tree and went straight through it, as if it were mist, never to appear on the other side. All that was left was the box.

At that, Gamboa's head switched off, and he fell into a very deep sleep from which he awoke days later. He could remember many things, but there were also lots of details he could not immediately bring to mind. He did, however, awake to find himself feeling stronger and healthier. He felt somehow newer and refreshed, and although he didn't know how, he knew he was ready to seek out the bloody beating hearts of his fellow human beings which would bring back to life his dead village. Of this, more than anything else in his young life, he was absolutely certain.

As he sat there, head empty, yet filled with the hope of a new beginning, he felt, in the palm of his hand, the vial. The vial. Now, how did that get there? He smiled to himself, a confident, grown-up smile a man would use when he knows something is finally going his way.

The vial. Wow, the old man really did make things happen. He was growing up, and he felt brilliant.

Sacrifice

Out of the cold, grey ashes of the volcano, grew a new beginning, a fresh chapter in the life of the tribes-people. A new hope had arrived and with it, the chance of survival. Slowly, they began to put their lost lives back together, and haul themselves out from under the morass of physical and emotional distress. Life took on a purpose which they thought they had lost. Indeed, many thought that up to the terrible moment of the awful grey day which engulfed them, they had not really been living at all, that they had only been existing, playing at life, with the simplicity of children. Offering the Gods fruit and vegetables soon became thought of as infantile and useless. How could they have lived their lives in such ignorance, such darkness? The light, in which they once thought they had lived, now seemed, on reflection, to have been nothing but a dull, misty flicker of misguided futility; a game, a trifle, a childish torchlight existence just waiting to be extinguished and come crashing down around their ears. And of course, crash down it had. The Gods had been angry, dissatisfied with their pathetic efforts, till eventually, they had lost patience with them, and sent the thundering, deadly torment, a blistering grey hell pouring down on them. They had been punished and reminded that they were mere mortals, who needed to mend their ways.

But the road to recovery and enlightenment had not been easy. After the old man had left, Gamboa didn't really know what to do. After all, he was just a young boy, what could he do? Who would listen to him? How could he possibly influence the people and tell the elders that they needed to "mend their ways"? He had no say in affairs, nor, if he was really honest, did he have the courage to speak up anyway. He was just a child.

No, it was not going to be easy for Gamboa. Nothing had ever been easy for him. His short life had seemed such a hardship and hardly worth the effort. He didn't have any friends and his family was nonexistent. His parents, long gone, had died when he was but two weeks old. His father, a fisherman, had one day been caught by a freak storm and drowned, his dugout canoe being capsized and catapulted to the bottom of the bay. His mother, on hearing the terrible news, immediately dropped the baby, ran out of the house, sloshed into the water and swam to the spot where she thought she might find her husband. She swam and swam, and dived and dived, down into the depths, only to find that she could not actually swim at all. She drowned. The tragedy shook the village, and each family offered to take-in Gamboa for several months at a time. This worked well for a few years. But Gamboa eventually ended up living by himself on the fringe of the town. Orphaned, and alone, he was regarded as an outsider, with a reputation for being an oddball, and the other children were quite wary of him. In fact, their parents told them not to have much to do with him at all, as he was perhaps unpredictable and not really quite like them. This didn't bother Gamboa too much, and he survived quite happily submerged in his own world. But of course, that didn't help him in his new found quest of trying to convince the townspeople that if they wanted to live, then they had to change their ways, start killing people and rip out their beating hearts.

No, it was not going to be easy at all.

And besides, where were they going to find these beating hearts? They could hardly be expected to execute themselves - could they?

He was puzzled. But he took strength in the knowledge that he had been chosen by the old man, and, in the added fact that he now had the box. The box. Yes, he was now guardian of the box, no matter that he, Gamboa had always been a rather quiet, aloof boy, he had been chosen and he had the box. Also, he didn't actually feel alone anymore. He kind of felt that somehow, he didn't know how, the old man was sort of, well, with him. He didn't understand it and was left a tad puzzled by the feeling. But, deep down, he knew that he was no longer alone in the world, that something had changed. He didn't know exactly what or why, but things were definitely not what they used to be.

And so, with this in mind, he set about his task of converting the population of his small, ashen town.

At first, no one wanted to hear him. Of course.

"What do you want?" they would say in the monotones of the dead.

"I, I, need t' to t' tell you something," he stammered.

"What?" they would drone.

"W . . . w . . . well," he tried, not really sure how to say that they had to change their life style and start tearing out the bleeding hearts of the living.

"What is it?" the dead voices asked.

"Well . . ." Gamboa would start without real intention.

"What?"

"It's . . ."

"What?"

Silence.

People would shake their grey heads, dust and pumice flying like dandruff. The more sympathetic villagers would perhaps attempt a dead, grey smile and even a ghostly condescending pat on the shoulder.

"Poor Gamboa," they would say, in dead unison. "Poor little Gamboa," turn around, and silently be about their dead business.

And off he would go, head down, dejected, not quite having built up enough courage to preach his new tidings. He would go home to his shed made of palm leaves and dead trees, caress the box, occasionally open up the lid and peer inside. This always gave him comfort, and renewed his courage, and the following day he would go out again in an effort to preach his new gospel. But always he would go home having failed to get anywhere in his mission.

After several days of this, he one evening opened up his box and searched out the little frog, the red and white speckled frog, which had spoken to him when the old man first introduced them to each other. It took a while for him the find the tiny frog, as he was camouflaged, reposing against a curling, pale yellow and russet leaf, ready to fall from a tree. The miniature amphibian sat very still and quiet, apparently not even watching the world go by. Gamboa pursed his lips and sat in deep thought.

"What shall I do? What on earth shall I do? Nobody wants to listen to me. No one's interested. It's hopeless."

He rather dejectedly sat chewing the inside of his mouth, thinking the whole thing a waste of time. A few crickets clicked away in the distance, and inside the box a flock of flamingos took off, heading in the direction of the setting sun. The box glowed in the darkness of the shed, and Gamboa's face reflected the light, giving his complexion a flushed, buttery hue. He was down in his boots, but the box gave him some comfort. But not enough. Nothing was happening and he quickly, and perhaps, even a little bad temperedly, shut the lid. This was soon followed by the closing of his eyes as he lay down with his head on the makeshift pillow of grasses. He tried to empty his mind and made an effort to think of nothing in particular, least of all, his failure to deliver the message to the people. He *was* a failure. He was just a child. It was hopeless. There was nothing for it but to admit defeat.

After several aborted attempts, he finally cleared his head, and had succeeded in achieving the blank page on which he could paint a good night's sleep when, on to the paper, was sketched a voice.

"A voice? How can you sketch a voice?" he asked himself.

He opened his eyes. Well, actually he didn't open them, because he couldn't. They were sealed. Tight shut. And no matter what he did, he just couldn't open them. Panic set in as he thought he'd been made blind, and immediately thought of the one-eyed dog.

He was using his fingers in a frenzied fidget, pulling his lids this way and that, when the voice picture spoke to him.

"Gamboa," it said, confidently.

He froze.

"Gamboa!" it said, more insistently.

Gamboa stopped what he was doing, and found himself eye to eye with a very small, red creature, which he recognized as the frog from the box. It was tiny, no more than three centimeters in length, and sat in the middle of his mental landscape, looking straight at him.

"Hello," it said in a rather snappy, high-pitched voice, filled with authority.

Gamboa didn't know what to say. His eyes were sealed and he was trapped in a confrontation with a scarlet frog in his head.

"You don't have to say anything," said the frog. "Just listen."

Preparing itself for the task ahead, the frog flashed a sticky, lithe, green and mustard tongue over its thin cherry lips, took a big breath (as big as he could for a tiny frog) and launched into his speech.

"Now, listen to me," he said, commandingly, pausing ever so slightly for effect. "Are you listening?"

It was all Gamboa could do to nod his head.

"Good," said the frog. "You have been chosen. You. Yes, YOU!"

He pointed a long, knobby finger at Gamboa's forehead.

"Do you understand that?" he said more quietly, and rather more confidentially. "It's YOU. Not somebody else who doesn't understand the importance of this, but YOU! You are the Chosen One, who has been picked out of all the others to deliver the message to set the people on the road to salvation. To prepare them for the holy path of righteousness."

The little frog spread out his little arms embracing Gamboa's mental horizons. He continued.

"They must follow you and do as you tell them, or else they will never regain life. The living purgatory they now endure, will last for eternity if they do not. Do you hear me? They will all remain dead."

He paused again, his globular eyes piercing Gamboa's.

"It is your mission, no, *duty*, to lead these people. They MUST be converted. They must follow the path to blood sacrifice or else there is no future. No future!" He stopped to swallow. "Now, in the morning, go down to the meeting place and preach. Preach I tell you. Deliver the word of salvation, the message of life and redemption. Tell them what they have to do. It's *your* calling, *your* own particular path to Godliness. You must do this. They will never come back to life if you don't. No food, no water, no crops. Nothing. The grey death will continue into infinity."

And with that, the burgundy frog (for he had now changed colour slightly with all the excitement) erased himself from Gamboa's cerebral sketchpad, and disappeared.

In that instant, Gamboa's eyes flew open and the darkness bled into his pupils.

"Wow!" he exclaimed.

He sat bolt upright and gasped for breath.

"Wow!" he blasted out to the empty night.

"What was that?"

He didn't know what to call it at the time, of course, but Gamboa had just had his second religious experience. And it left him feeling exhilarated, and totally exhausted at the same time.

"Wow!" he exploded again in a gush of hot air.

And with that, he lay down, turned over and fell fast asleep.

*

In the morning, the sun came up as usual pouring in like daggers through the gaps in the sides of his crude shelter. One sharp sunray tickled his nose, waking him up with a sneeze. He shook his head, and even before he fully opened his eyes he could smell the new day, with its promise of rejuvenation and fulfillment. It was a brand new morn of opportunity, and he, Gamboa, the Chosen One, had been charged with saving the world. He got to his feet and, with the vigour of a true evangelist, began to sing the praises of the universe.

Stepping outside, he scanned the grey horizon, the grey trees, the stubbly grey grass and the sad, grey, broken-down shanties of the distant village. Debris and dust still covered everything and he saw the washed-out, ash-drab people, as dots in the midst of a destroyed existence wandering, aimless and lost. They needed him. He knew that now. They needed his guidance.

He gathered up his newfound courage and went to the meeting place, stood on the mound of rubble and began to speak. He spoke with the mystical tones of a heavenly flute, then the strident blasts of a trumpet, then the booming glissandos of brassy trombones and finally, in an ecstasy of promise, the sheer echoes of angels. His voice floated on pink and pale blue waves of luscious taffeta, drifting into every broken dwelling, every bleached field and every wretched ear. He found he could speak words which he'd never used in his life, ever, and express himself in volumes of newfangled catechisms, which took root in every individual soul who had been magnetically drawn to hear him. He felt he had the whole population in the palms of his youthful, playfully hypnotic hands.

They came from the worthless, burnt out fields and crushed cindered ruins of the simple dwellings. They rose up, grime covered, from under the piles of rubble and earth, coughing and choking and staggering like underworld corpses, treading a path to his feet. They came and sat and listened to the prophet. They didn't know why, or how, but they found themselves mesmerized by this messiah, and not only *heard* the word, but *understood* it, and swallowed every syllable, every nuance and idea.

His words echoed, and carved out deep furrows of comprehension in his audience, who nodded sagely in agreement with his every divine deliverance. Gamboa spoke of the grey, the grey which had come from the sky, from the Gods. The grey, which had destroyed their homes, their crops, their water and was taking their very lives. The grey, which even now, as they sat listening to him, was eating away their souls. He spoke of the destruction and the living death, the living death they were all doomed to. He talked about life before the calamity, telling them that the innocent naivety, which saw them offering up gifts of fruit and maize and yes, even coconuts, had angered the Gods and that they needed to abandon their childish habits and grow up. The Gods needed more than bananas and melons and fruit and nuts. They were angry, and had visited this destruction upon them as punishment. It was time to change.

Then, as the sun peeped above the shoreline palms, and spread its fingers inland warming the barren air, he turned to the source and fruit of life itself. Blood. How blood, and only blood, could save them.

"It is blood," he said in his honey voice "and only blood that will deliver us from the evil of the living death we face. Only blood will restore life to the dead."

There was deathly quiet now.

"We have to spill blood in order to live, to survive this terror which has befallen us. The Gods demand we change our ways and follow them on the paths of sacrifice. We must spill blood in order to live."

Now one or two heads very slowly nodded. Their eyes were still blank, but the idea was registering, and Gamboa knew he was on his way to victory. He felt the presence of the old man and the small red frog in his head. He was not alone now, and he felt a wave of triumph starting to wash over him.

He dived in and went to the crux of the matter, raising for the first time the notion of live human sacrifice. He spoke of blood, and crops, and water and fish, and offering up virgins and the beating hearts of innocents. The crowd sat silent, but knew what the boy said made sense.

Of course blood will save them. It was obvious. Blood!

He enthralled the crowd with promises of plenty, and then, as if dropping seeds into fertile ground, he subtly suggested that if they followed him, and did as *he* said, they will enjoy an everlasting life in the heavens above, and live forever, keeping company with the Gods for eternity.

It was wonderful, terrific. He was the savior, the leader of men beyond all men. He surveyed his new flock and his heart flooded with pride and hope, the hope of a new flourishing forever with he, Gamboa, the ostracized orphan boy, as their trailblazing champion.

He stood tall, and with velvet eyes, welcomed his congregation into his fold. He had taken the first grand step towards immortality.

There was, however, one small problem, which Gamboa, being a clever young lad, had foreseen but to which he had no answer: as the Great Grey had left everyone virtually dead, how were they to find fresh blood to offer up to the Frog God? He didn't exactly freeze, but his euphoria at having overcome the first steps to infinity, cooled off in the tepid calm of practical consideration.

As the assembly broke up, the robotic dead drifting off in crude directionless lines, Gamboa sat and thought.

"Fresh blood. Where on earth am I going to get fresh blood from?"

He thought some more, and some more, and then went for a walk. He walked along the beach and back again.

"Where am I going to get fresh blood from?" he kept asking himself, over and over again.

He went for another walk, this time inland towards the thick jungle that went on for ages and ages, and into which, very few people ever ventured, for here lived the restless spirits of the dead trees and the rotting bodies of animals left in between Heaven and the underworld. But he wasn't bothered by that now. He had to find a solution, and onward he walked without fear or dread.

Eventually, he came to a pond. He was thirsty so got to his knees, bending down over the water. But just as he was about to take-in his first mouthful, he saw, there, a little off to his right, at the bottom of the pond, a whole village. Yes, a village. A complete village with lanes, and paths, and dwellings, and shelters and an open meeting place, just like the one in his own village. Except this one was not grey and ruined, and broken and filled with the dying and the dead. This village was alive.

Gamboa stared in disbelief into the deep, still waters.

"How is this possible?" he said out loud. "How?"

He frowned, long and hard into the water until his own reflection eventually stared back at him. And as he looked at his face, he saw it twist and transform, morph into something hideous then quite charming, then clearly recognizable. The eyes bulged and the mouth widened. His arms elongated. The whole shape now resembled not a human, but that of an amphibian. And he found he was now not looking into his *own* face, but straight into the large, round red eyes of a red and yellow speckled frog.

"Hello, Gamboa,' it said.

Gamboa didn't know what to say.

"Don't look so surprised," said the frog. "I am you and you are me," he added, a minor chortle sneaking into his deeply expressive voice.

"Don't be alarmed."

The frog launched its tongue and slapped up a water boatman skipping its way across the surface of the pool.

"Yummy," said the frog. "I haven't had breakfast yet and this is just splendid. Are you hungry?" he asked jovially.

Gamboa could only manage a shake of his head.

"What's that?" said the frog, raising its nonexistent eyebrows.

Gamboa shook his head more vigorously, adding a nervous, "No."

"Oh well. You're missing out on a grand meal. These fresh-water ponds are simply brilliant for live meat. Brilliant!"

"Oh, right," said Gamboa, hardly believing what was happening.

"You should always start the day with a good breakfast," said the frog. "Most important meal of the day. Everybody knows that."

He licked his lips with a loud smack and smiled. Open-mouthed Gamboa simply stared straight ahead.

"Anyway," the frog carried on "down to business. You need blood, don't you?"

Gamboa managed a nod.

"Right," said the frog. "Blood," and winked.

He seemed to think a bit then blurted out.

"Well, there's only one thing for it. You see this village here," pointing to a spot well below him on the other side of the pond. "See this?"

Gamboa said nothing.

"Hey! I asked you a question. You listening?"

"Err yes. Yes. I'm listening."

"Well?"

"Well what?"

"Do you see this? This village, here?" he pointed again to the other side of the pond.

"Yes," offered Gamboa, a little hesitantly.

"Good. Well, there's your answer."

"Where?" said Gamboa.

"There," said the frog, emphatically.

"What, the village?"

"Yes, the village."

"But how . . .?"

"Young man, use your head. The village has people in it and those people are alive."

He grinned from ear to ear, except of course, he didn't really have any ears to speak of, so he kind of grinned from shoulder blade to shoulder blade.

"So?" asked Gamboa, really not getting to grips with the topic.

"So, bird brain, go and get them and bring them back here."

"What for?" asked Gamboa.

"Heavens above! I'm beginning to think we chose the wrong boy for this mission. Blood. Right? You need blood. They," he said pointing a padded middle finger, "are alive. Go get them, bring them back here and get their blood. Cripes, it's hardly inventing the wheel."

"The what?"

"The wheel . . . Oh never mind, forget it. Look, just go to the village, grab a few people and bring them back here. Alright?"

Gamboa's face gave away his consternation.

"But there aren't any villages around here," he said.

"Yes there are."

"No there aren't."

"Yes there are."

"Where?"

The frog glanced sideways at the village under the water.

Gamboa finally got the message.

"I'm not getting in there," he protested. "I'll drown. My Mum and Dad drowned and I'm not keen on following them to a watery grave thanks very much."

The frog tut-tutted, shaking his yellowish head.

"You don't have much faith, do you?"

"Faith?"

"Yeah, you know, faith. Belief in yourself. And others."

"What d'you mean?"

"Look, you've been chosen . . ." he paused a second, then added rather impatiently "I thought we'd been into this already?"

"Hmm," offered Gamboa, not quite so confidently.

Somewhat puzzled but resigned, the frog took his time, humphed and arghed a bit, breathed in a big, big breath, shook his head yet again, and carried on.

"Well, never mind," he said slowly. "It's too late now. You're the Chosen One."

He softened his approach.

"You know, *you* can do anything you put your mind to. You just need to trust yourself. Now, look at this village here, under the water. All you have to do is dive down into the depths, choose a victim, preferably one with lots of flesh, pull him out, alive, and take him back to your place. And, hey presto, fresh blood."

Gamboa looked at the frog.

"I can't swim," he said.

"What?"

"I can't swim."

"Nonsense, of course you can."

"No, I can't."

"Yes you can."

"No I can't."

"You can."

"No . . . I . . . can't!" insisted Gamboa.

The yellow headed, red speckled frog, knitted its invisible eyebrows and gave Gamboa a withering look.

Pause.

"There is another possibility, of course," it said.

"What's that?" enquired Gamboa, not altogether enthusiastic.

"You could get a couple of villagers together, head north through the coconut grove, cross the roaring river estuary (at low tide, of course, because you can't swim), climb the sheer glossy cliff face of the impossibly high, high-plateau, trek through the caustic mud of the mystic marshland, weave a passage into, and out of, the terrors of the poisonously infested forest and then . . ."

He stopped.

"What?" asked Gamboa, still not enthusiastic.

"Raid the next village."

"What village?" said Gamboa, confused

"The village through the coconuts, on the other side of the river, up the cliff face, through the mud and the infested forest. That village," insisted the frog with growing impatience.

"There's a village there?"

"Of course."

"I've never heard of it."

"Well, it's there."

"Are you sure?"

"Of course I'm sure!"

"I've never heard of it."

"For goodness sake!" exclaimed the little frog.

"I've just told you: have a little faith."

And with that, the frog, even though as a forest floor dweller not such a great swimmer, disappeared in a mini whirlpool of swirling tidal waves, and Gamboa found himself alone at the water's edge.

"Wow!" he said, almost relieved to be rid of the frog. "You mean there are other people here as well as us?"

And with that, his enthusiasm certainly boiled, then roared then exploded in a torrent of excitement. He had his answer. He would save his village. He would get the blood he needed and the world as he knew it would be saved from the Great Grey and the death and the destruction, and he would live forever.

"WOW!"

Commencement

No one could remember how it all started. Not really. For what seemed like forever the rituals had been carried out, and as long as the weather remained clement, the rains regular, the crops full and wholesome, then the rationale or logic of human sacrifice was never brought into question. It clearly worked.

That the world consisted of more than one peaceful coastal village had never really been an issue for the inhabitants of the small, isolated Suxx community. Collectively, they had lived in solitude and never had reason to contact any outsiders. Indeed, they didn't even consider the possibility of an outside world. Their universe, up until the Great Grey, had been so tranquil that they didn't even have a word for outsider, or neighbour.

But the volcanic Great Grey had devastated them. Their belief in the simple deities of their youth, had been aborted. Their Gods had abandoned them. They desperately needed a new path: a new path to life. They needed a new God. They had worshipped false Gods and been punished for it. The Great Grey had come and destroyed a whole belief system. Their naive faith of thousands of years had failed.

But they had a saviour, a boy man-God who had promised them salvation, if they would but follow him and do as he preached. They had in Gamboa, walking alongside them, an earthly representative of the Gods.

Only Gamboa, only he had the vision to lead them to everlasting life and prosperity.

First, however, they would need to swallow their fears of the outside world and travel north. To begin with, the villagers were not keen on the idea of such a great trek, but Gamboa, by now a charismatic and most persuasive youth, eventually formed a raiding party of twelve men who would make the risky trip. After several days they achieved their goal and found the promised village. True enough, here it was, just as Gamboa said it would be. And, true enough, there were people who, just like them, lived and breathed the air of the world, except that they were not grey and ashen, but alive with passion and love. And beating hearts.

It wasn't easy, of course. The hike through difficult terrain was fraught with complicated hazards, and the initial raid on the encampment itself demanded skills alien to the people of Suxx. They were a peaceful folk, and had no tradition of warfare and violence. As a result, they were clumsy, and almost apologetic in the first encounter. Also, it must be said that the innocent victims were as mystified as the bandits themselves, as they too, were, at heart, a harmless, peace-loving people, unfamiliar with physical threat. They were so easy to catch, at first.

The initial confrontation was cordial. The new villagers greeted the Suxx raiders with no little wonder, smiles and open arms. The men, smilingly welcoming the intruders, did not realize what their fate would be, and so were easily shackled and taken off without putting up much of a fight. The women were next, and they battled as only mothers and daughters would. But, now that the majority of the men were already gone, they stood no chance against the surprise attacks. Then, inevitably, the invaders took the children. This was easy, as they trudged along scampering and yelping after their mothers who, manacled, screamed dreadful, lost cries.

Then came the actual sacrifices. Just who was going to do this? And how were they going to do it? It's one thing to capture a victim, quite another to tear into his flesh and rip out the heart.

Inevitably, there was only one person who was in any kind of position to take up this mantle of responsibility, Gamboa. As young as he was, he had to corral the courage of his convictions, and if not exactly relish the task, then at least, with some minor gusto, try his best to satisfy the Gods' hunger by detaching the heart from the various in-and-out valves, without actually fainting. Like most newcomers to any trade, he was keen to get the hang of it quickly, not just in the interests of efficiency, but also in the hope of a little self-promotion. After all, he was the Chosen One, and it was he who had to set an example.

Well, of course, there were the first botched attempts. Ineffective incisions, wrong angles and blind rummaging around under rib cages. All this did little to boost young Gamboa's confidence. He wasn't sure what was beating, pulsing or simply dying on the spot. Hacking away into a soft belly with a jagged, seven-inch stone flint, was a bit of a hit and miss affair. The shivering, frightened victim, rescue or reprieve nowhere in sight, writhed and panicked, horrified. It wasn't easy. Eventually, though, like everything else in life, practice made perfect, and the thumping hearts were extracted with great aplomb, and, it might be said, expert efficiency.

Despite his calling, Gamboa, nevertheless, felt a tad awkward facing his victims. He would avoid eye contact. He couldn't bear to look into the desperate faces, the hopelessness, the terrified blank incomprehension. He took solace in the fact that his mission was a Godly, spiritual directive, and that he alone was responsible for the salvation of his people. But the desperate pleading in the desperate eyes made him feel uncomfortable. And so, he came up with the idea of promoting an anonymity, a way of detaching himself, attempting to annul the possibility of intimacy with the victim.

Perhaps out of embarrassment, but also heavily influenced by a growing sense of occasion, Gamboa started to wear a mask. At first, this was a simple affair, the bark of a tree roughly hewn to size. This then developed into something more elaborate, and he decorated the crude disguise, daubing it with bright pigments, yet with a gruesome aspect. Over time, a clearly defined art form manifested itself and the mask was adorned with feathers, skins and bones and the features of animals.

An appreciation of showmanship blossomed, and Gamboa realized the importance of spectacle. His people wanted something to look at, as well as believe in. Ceremonies became an explosion of colour, and headdresses, fantastic cloaks and daggers of brilliant ornamental yet practical value, were expertly crafted, contributing to the overall effect of spiritual and Godly celebration. The carnival atmosphere spilled over onto the victims themselves, and they were decorated, or had their hair arranged, perhaps even plaited, in shapes and tones worthy of sacrifice in the name of the Gods.

Over time, out of the desire to meet the demands of the deities, and a general upsurge in things cultural, the people of Suxx saw various rituals and customs grow out of these sacrifices, and preparations took on ever more intricate, ceremonial detail.

And in the town centre, the old earthen mound, now long gone, had grown into a huge edifice with steps leading up to the top where, at the zenith, the sacrifices were carried out. Closer proximity to the Gods made for a better reception, and the more likelihood of a successful ceremony. The altar at the top was beautifully carved with images of snakes, jaguars and of course, frogs. The frog took pride of place, and it was the frog that looked down on the people of the city casting a caring, yet threatening eye over the populous.

Special feast days and celebrations were established. There were also rigorous procedures of how, where and when certain blood-sacrifices were made. The ancients had long ago worked out the winter and summer equinoxes, and there grew up an idea that at these auspicious times of the year, only virgins were to be slaughtered, as the people deemed it necessary for the Gods to be offered pure, untainted blood.

On other occasions, for example after a big storm, or if neighbouring tribes had been uncooperative fighting back rather too strenuously, it was only men over fifteen years of age who were offered up, as these were seen as stronger, virile and more acceptable to a capricious God. Women, and the very young, were generally only sacrificed if there was a decline in the supply of the prime bloodlines of virgins and young men of the warrior class.

It soon became custom to decapitate victims once the hearts had been struck out, the heads stuck on poles about the feet of the Temple steps. This was a value added extra, designed by the Temple Chiefs who, over the years, had now developed their own peculiar systems and practices. The obsidian knives, essential tools of the trade, had to be blessed each full moon, and the night before a ceremony, washed in the urine of a young girl. This would guarantee a good harvest and plenty of rain. Equally, the victims were well prepared for their deaths. They were starved of food, so that upon evisceration there wouldn't be bits of undigested banana or maize or fish flying about. The ancients certainly did not want a mess on the steps of the Temple. Only blood.

Music also took off during this keen developmental phase, and there grew out of the carnage, a new respect for the rhythms of life, with drums and flutes echoing the sound of the seas and the beating of the waves, and the wind in the trees, and the crashing thunder in the heavens. The ceremonies would build to their fantastic climaxes, accompanied by a full symphony of woodwind and stretched skin, boom-swooning, screeching and thrashing out in unison, a frenzied rhythm. Each victim was hailed by blasting, crash-splashes of sound, as the hearts were presented to the crowds below. There were no tunes to speak of, just an incredible, vibrant cacophony of celebration.

And, just like at any other party, there was food and drink. Fresh fruit, fish, maize pancakes and roasted pig were sold on makeshift stalls along the road leading to the Temple, and as the victims passed, they were spattered with the blood of chickens, goats and pigs. Menstruating women mischievously sold their own blood to gullible devotees, who wished a tighter grip on salvation, and the underclass, the lost, the void and dispossessed, scavenged for scraps in the mayhem.

With a bourgeoning religion there was an explosion of urban development, and soon many Temples were soaring high into the clear, blue skies, aiming to get as close as possible to the Gods. Suxx began to prosper, and crops grew and harvests blossomed. Clearly the Gods were exceptionally happy, and the rains came and went, and with them the sight of annual renewal and rejuvenation. Everyone was happy, and as the years rolled by, the village grew, from a small collection of badly made wooden shacks, to a flourishing town with a busy, blustering heart. Then a glorious city, with supremely well-constructed structures, Temples and sturdy stone houses, and irrigation and prosperity worthy of a real, advanced society. All was great and wonderful. The blood flowed, and Suxx became the leading light of civilization in the region. The people of Suxx were feared and bowed down to. And gradually, there grew up a warrior class and a priestly class, and scholars and architects and designers and craftsmen of all kinds. Teachings and textiles of brilliant colours began to appear, and the city of Suxx was beautified with fine carvings and buildings.

And all this they achieved without even the slightest suggestion of a wheel.

But in Suxx, not everyone went along with the idea of Frogs being in charge. There were other factions in the community. These rivaled the Frog fraternity, and Gamboa had to work hard to keep his privileged position. There were those who looked at the world through very different eyes, and they saw how snakes, jaguars, scorpions and crocodiles ruled their own kingdoms. Out of this grew separate ways of worshipping these various animals. Some, like the Monkey sect, fell by the wayside very early on. Monkeys were considered far too untrustworthy, cunning yet playful, and thus held no threat, and ultimately little attraction for a people demanding more menace from their idols. There were clubs formed where villagers could worship ants, and fish, and turtles, but these also, along with the simians, didn't really make the grade, and were ultimately subsumed under other, greater deities.

74

The most enduring of all these lesser sects, however, were the Snake and Jaguar groups, who fought hard for recognition, and occasionally challenged the Temple Frog Priests for domination. But over time, Gamboa and his supporters convinced the population of the superiority of the Frogs, and eventually even the hard line Jaguar members, although loath to admit it, were a poor second best to the Frog clan. The Snake set, also never really posed a serious challenge to Gamboa's leadership, and they, too, ultimately bowed down to his authority. The Temples of the Snake and Jaguar, whilst imposing, were smaller and artistically less impressive than those of the Frog Temples. The carvings on the Frog Temple pyramids tended to be more intricate, and of a higher quality than others, and, as competition grew to create the tallest structures, Gamboa and the Frog followers conjured up the best materials, and contracted the best architects, to make sure their religious edifices were superior to all their competitors'. The higher the Temple, the more power implied, and the highest Temple of all, was that of the Frogs.

Gamboa and his fellow Priests held the majority seats, and it was their festivities and their sacrifices, which were held in the greatest esteem in the growing community. The blood on the Frog Temple steps always ran red and long, from the heady heights of the altar, down to the huge supporting foundation stones, many metres below.

As customs and traditions developed, and the vigour of sacrifice took over, it became apparent that there was a movement fermenting which would change the nature of sacrifice forever.

Although having as their God the Frog, Jaguar or Snake, the ancients knew that life's central driving force was the sun, and that without the sun, there was no

75

real life. And so many young people were now considering offering *themselves* as blood sacrifices, in order to not only ensure prosperity for the community, but also book themselves a ticket in the afterlife; their place in the sun, so to speak. As this notion took off, hundreds and then thousands saw the opportunity to offer up their hearts, to open the doors to Godliness and everlasting life. This did not conflict with the worshipping of the Frog, Jaguar and Snake deities, but added an extra dimension to an already busy schedule of daily idol worship. The shamans encouraged sacrifice within families, but there was a pecking order, and the first born of each family were prohibited from offering up their hearts, as it was they who were to inherit their fathers' birthright.

Other family members could join in the euphoria of blood spillage, but there were limits, and Gamboa was very quick to make sure his Frog sect did not get too carried away with this habit of self-sacrifice, otherwise his power base would soon be shaved away. So, he continued to make organized raids on other, now even more distant, villages, the circle of attacks growing ever bigger and bigger as the power of the ancient tribe grew.

Decades, then centuries and millennia passed, and Gamboa became the universal Frog God's representative on earth. He was immortal. He never aged. He never stooped, faltered or fell. He matured but was always the eternal youth: tall, strong, handsome and very brave. He really was the Chosen One.

*

And so began the dreadful human sacrifices demanded by the Frog Gods, in return for which, they would protect Gamboa and his people. Although at first reluctant, the villagers were eventually persuaded by Gamboa, and selecting victims became, if not exactly a pleasure, then certainly not a burden. In the end, the killing and sacrifice became a joyous, if somewhat bloody affair, and victims were plentiful. Scouting, or hunting parties, went far and wide in search of suitable human offerings, and the tribe soon racked up an awesome reputation for as far as the eye could see, and many miles beyond.

Over time, the rituals had taken-on a festive atmosphere, and they made great spectator viewing. The ripping out of hearts and the flinging down the Temple steps of the headless corpses became a highlight of the calendar. Life was good, the blood ran freely and thickly, and the Frog Gods were pleased. Very pleased.

Until one year, in one epoch, the rains decided not to come . . .

Example

Gamboa sat in darkness. He was in the small anteroom of the high altar at the top of the Temple. Here was stored his festival costume, his headdress of feathers, his necklaces, bangles and bracelets, and the ceremonial blades which were kept sharp and brilliantly shiny. Acrid incense burned in thick clouds, and there clung to the air years of death. It was here that he prepared himself for the ceremonies; where he prayed to the great Frog God for guidance, for the strength to help him through the endless bloody ordeals. In the musty den he knelt before a dais, on which images of his God sat quietly, dominating his thoughts. In the silence, he bent down, kowtowing, forehead kissing the ground. He begged to be directed in his zealous endeavors to serve.

On shelves at one end of the room, rested, one on top of the other, the skulls of young victims. They stared down at Gamboa as he knelt in supplication. Their hollow eyes had seen this ritual many times and their taciturn mouths, naked jaws clashed shut, held a mute silence.

Gamboa muttered the incantations of a lifetime's worship and, raising his head every now and then, stared into the eyes of the central image above him, the stone, green jade carving of the Frog God himself, whose soulless gaze mesmerized Gamboa with a hopeful dread.

In the final stages of his preparations, he took from his waistband a vial. He upended the contents into his mouth, and within minutes was transported beyond the confines of the dank, humid chamber. He coursed rivers and valleys, weaved through forests and crossed plains. He soared over mountains and oceans, and blasted through star systems and galaxies, traversing countless unknown satellite worlds to a universe of soft pastel imaginations, where he saw there, tremendous in his majesty, the magnificent Frog God himself, his God, the supreme Frog God. The God he loved and worshipped with unequivocal devotion. The God for whom, he would do anything: *Wo-sak*

Gamboa stood atop the Temple steps and surveyed his people. He spoke.

"Frog-clansmen, listen to me. Listen to your leader."

He raised his muscular arms, gold clanging, semiprecious stones flashing in the sunlight.

"Listen," he shouted.

The milling crowd, a nervous expectation settling over them, fell silent. Gamboa looked down, the whites of his eyes beginning to clot with wriggling, scarlet spider veins, his brain on fire. His chest heaved.

"We are facing the biggest challenge of our lives. We are facing the future of our existence. We are facing the possibility of annihilation and destruction, the destruction of our families, our homes, our city, our empire. We are facing the end of everything we have ever known. Yes," he said, "we are facing the apocalypse."

Punctuating his words, a gust of wind sent scurries of dry earth, dust and grit swirling into the parched, fetid air. Seeing this as a heavenly sign, Gamboa forged on.

"Our world, clansmen, is dying!"

The crowd surged forward with shouts and wails of despair.

Once again he called for silence, turning left and right to make sure he embraced all the Frog Temple followers.

"Clansmen, clansmen, you must remain calm. You must not panic."

He raised his voice to new levels and it echoed around the city.

"Listen to me," he demanded. "Hear what I have to say."

But the crowd crushed and churned in its anxiety and fear. The young, the weak and the elderly faltered and gave way to the power of the multitude. Faces, screwed up in pain and trepidation, glared in horror at the words they had feared to hear. The mood turned, a terror clouding the huge assembly.

Gamboa leapt about in his desperate bid to maintain order, his headdress bobbing around in a riot of shapes and colours, gaudy feathers flying in silhouette against an electric tropical blue.

"Do not be afraid," he screamed. "Do not despair. Listen to me. Listen."

His face contorted into a gullied grimace and he reached out to the Gods for divine inspiration. It came in folds and waves, cascades and avalanches of sound penetrating his very being. Then, with one bellow, one almighty belch of power, Gamboa tore into every ear and soul of every person there in the city. He expelled an utterance so deep, so profound it shook the core of the world and drilled deep into the hearts of his followers, projecting them into the promise of living salvation. A huge, fluorescent eagle, vibrant in its rainbow coat, a portent of hope and belief, flew in scrolls high overhead and Gamboa, with every beat of his exploding heart, felt a surge of power, a renewed ascendency urging him on to drive his message home, a supreme dominance worthy only of the Chosen One.

He had them.

He knew.

Beneath him, the mass of humanity heaved as one, in unison inhaling the pungent, toxic message from their leader. The colossal figure of Gamboa towered over his domain.

"I have words for you from the Temple Frog God himself, the Great *Wo-sak*. These words come from the inner sanctuary, the Temple of Heavenly Creation and Divine Sacrifice. *You*," and he pointed down to the masses beneath, "you are the true believers, and you have the power within you to help change the inevitable and the eternal. *You* have that power. You are Frog Temple worshippers and it is *you* who hold, in the palms of your hands, our destiny."

His bloodshot eyes rolled heavenward, and Gamboa searched his spirit for the words he had to deliver. He looked around again from one to another, picking on this or that particular face to drive his point home. He took-in the multitude beneath, and realized that what he was about to ask of them was the absolute test of devotion.

There was to be no mistaking *this* message.

"We are dying. We have no water. Our wells, once bottomless fountains, are but hollow, burnt out holes in the ground. Our reservoirs, once endless lakes and pools of life-giving fresh water, are dried up beds of crumbling dust. Our crops, once rich and bountiful, now stand wretched, withering. Our animals, sick and shriveled, skeletons, stare, hopelessly dead or dying. But worst of all, we ourselves are now starving without food or water. We are at the end. This is the end."

Where before mayhem had greeted him, now an unearthly silence overcame the city as Gamboa spoke. The drums were dead. Children and dogs, their cries muzzled, panted in what little breeze flapped the crispy leaves on strangulated trees.

"But the great *Wo-sak* has spoken," Gamboa continued in a more upbeat tone of encouragement "and he knows our peril. He has spoken to me. Yes, clansmen, he has given me the vision, the undeniable spectre of redemption. He has given me the sign, the route, nay the map for our salvation. It is a path which calls on all our determination to see the end of our woes. It is the ultimate act of devotion, of allegiance to our Frog God, to *Wo-sak*. Only this pathway will save us. Only this act will lead us to life, glory and paradise."

Gamboa was in full sway, and now he called for his wife, Tsok, and only child Chatlan, to climb the Temple steps. He stretched out an arm towards his family.

"Come, wife. Come, and bring our child. Bring our child to the Temple and let us lead the way to salvation."

The drums began to beat, a dull thump at first, growing in tempo and volume with each step taken by Gamboa's wife and son.

The crowd, sweaty in the noonday sun, stood in quiet expectation, as Tsok and Chatlan reached the top of the steps.

As the vial's message surged through his body, Gamboa swooned in tune to his own internal rhythmic dance. The relentless beating of the drums sent blast waves of hot air up the steps swirling around the high altar. Gamboa could now see only one thing, a blood red sky inviting him to a blood red Heaven of divine, everlasting life.

"Where is he? Where's my son?" he said.

"Father," said Chatlan, "I'm here."

"My son," exclaimed Gamboa, as he embraced the young boy. "My son."

The boy, admiration and love fixed on his face, stared up at Gamboa.

"Father," he said.

The boy's naivety could not be measured, and as he proudly stood there next to his father, he had no idea what was to befall him. Tsok, a quick-witted, intelligent woman, was painfully cognizant of what was about to happen, and violently broke her silence.

"Gamboa," she said, begging her husband "you don't have to do this. He's your son. He's all we have. He's our only child. Gamboa. Please, listen."

"Silence!" shouted Gamboa. "We have no alternative. We must offer-up our own bloodline in order to be saved."

The child froze, the dawn of understanding crossing his young face.

"But Gamboa, he's our only son," pleaded Tsok.

"He must die," exclaimed Gamboa, who then looked at the crowd and shouted at the top of his voice. "All first born boys must die. All first born boys *must* die."

The crowd gasped, and many mothers enclosed their children in cloaks in desperate, distracted attempts to hide them.

"All first born boys must die," Gamboa repeated. "*Wo-sak* has spoken. It is the only way we shall live. All first born boys must die!"

Chatlan struggled to free himself, but he was helpless in his father's powerful grip.

The boy yelled.

"Mother."

"Chatlan," screamed Tsok.

But before she could move, Gamboa picked up the boy, slammed him onto the altar, and plunged a knife into his slender stomach. Blood flooded in a thick glistening torrent over the stone, oozing a hot red treacle towards the steps.

The crowd shrieked in disbelief as Gamboa, his glazed bullfrog eyes stark in the roasting heat, ripped out his own son's heart, the sticky muscle glistening as it caught the rays of the golden sun.

Tsok, paralyzed in horror, bayed, agonized, her howling wails wrenching the soul of the city. She fell to her knees, then sprawled, face down in her son's blood. She writhed and rolled in the incredulity of the awfulness. Her tears, massive and torrential, came in a tidal wave. She felt herself melted, diluted and finally invisible as she gave in to the blackness that overwhelmed her.

Gamboa, oblivious, mindless to the reality of the moment, charged on in his petitions.

"With this heart," he shouted above the roar of the crowd "I, Gamboa, Chief Temple Frog Priest offer the great *Wo-sak* appeasement. I offer my son, my own flesh and blood. I offer his heart, his beating heart. My own son I give as a blood offering. This offering I make to our God *Wo-sak*, that he may forgive us and deliver us from the drought blighting our people."

Holding his son's young heart on high, Gamboa saluted the crowd, and the crowd, in return, swirled in anxious anticipation, their leader's oratory reaching new heights.

"Give us rain, oh God. Give us rain that we may live and prosper and serve you. Give us rain that we may continue to worship you and hold you in reverence for eternity. This I ask you in supplication and humility. This I ask you as your servant. Oh great Frog God *Wo-sak*, give us rain."

Arms out-stretched, the blood now dripping in slow globes from the dead heart, Gamboa looked down from on high and challenged the throng.

"I call on you all," he said "to follow me to the feet of the almighty Frog God, beg for forgiveness and offer up the hearts of your first born sons."

He threw his head back embracing his universe.

"I call on you all to sacrifice your sons."

With that, he picked up the blade again, and in two expert slashes, hacked off his son's head and hurled it down the steps. It bounced and thudded, finally looping into the crowd, who scattered as it landed with wide, incredulous dead eyes.

The drums roared out a primitive, pulsating beat then suddenly stopped, the rhythm of the day interrupted. Gamboa stood breathless, his body drenched in perspiration. His head, filled with thunderbolts of clarity then confusion, rocked unevenly, an erratic metronome wagging fitfully under the cloudless sky. In his blurred, myopic vision, he didn't even notice Tsok, his wife, lying there, soaked in their son's blood.

He turned away from the crowd, dived into the blackness of the anteroom and fell into a mournful trance, his son's still heart glued to his wet, twitching fingers.

Outside, there was chaos. Fathers grabbed sons who cried out in disbelief. Mothers clawed and begged. A mad scramble ensued as fanatical parents fought over their children. But upwards they went, the firstborn of every family, up towards the altar, manic termites dragged to the zenith of a bloody citadel. The mothers clung together as they watched their sons hauled to their deaths, and were powerless as the fanatical surge took over.

Soon the cries became even louder as the first boys were torn apart, their bleeding hearts beating their last in the brilliant sunshine. Mothers shrieked as heads rolled and twisted in somersaults rocketing, tumbling then smashing into a scarlet, starry-eyed pyramid of decapitation. Fathers called on *Wo-sak* to bless them, release them from the famine and drought which was blighting their city. And they mourned not the loss of their sons, for they knew the Gods had demanded the sacrifice, and they had seen Gamboa, their eternal leader, kill his very own son on these very same steps.

The blood ran in rivers down the Temple and mothers cried in helpless, scorching screams.

And inside the anteroom Gamboa sat blindly, motionless, silently observed by the bleached skulls ranged on the mini altar. The incense swirled and mushroomed, and *Wo-sak*, the great Frog God, impassive, stared down at his beloved disciple.

Failure

As a youngster, Xzirqutz Xzirqutz had watched and observed. He had stood in the crowd at the feet of the Temple watching the eviscerations and beheadings, and, along with the other children, marveled at the fountains of blood streaming down from the heights of the steep steps. Rapt, he traced the bouncing heads lolloping down, gathering speed as they crashed into a thumping pile, the thrilled congregation shouting in sycophantic bloodlust. On a good day, a twizzling artery would spatter him, gushing red, and he would relish the baptism, smearing the hot blood over his skinny chest. He looked forward to the ceremonies, and as each new day of sacrifice drew near, he would perk up, a fresh sparkle glittering in his young eyes. He loved the ceremonies, and thoroughly enjoyed the carnival atmosphere and spectacle of the processions. The whole city would come out to revel in the celebrations, and he marveled at the line of sacrificial victims as they were paraded through the city. The stars of the show, however, were the Priests, and Xzirqutz Xzirqutz was always mesmerized by their terrific costumes, proudly displayed headdresses, amulets, bracelets and finery. The Priests were his heroes, and he dreamt of someday becoming one.

As he turned into adolescence, he became a rather single-minded young man, quite driven, but without, of course, the measured control of adulthood. He did, though, apply himself to his ambition and was determined to make his mark in the world. As a boy, he used to hang around the bottom of the Temple steps offering to tidy up after the marathon sacrifices, rolling the severed heads into small pyramids and generally helping wash blood off the masonry. He often got in the way, but generally he worked with a seriousness worthy of the tasks, impressing the Priests with his application and devotion. Eventually, he was invited further up the steps, to polish the stonework and help prepare for minor ceremonies. He made a point of always being on time and, never complaining, soon became a permanent fixture, eventually recruited to help escort the victims to the top of the Temple.

He had a natural flare for the job, and he savored wrestling reluctant slaves and virgins to the top altar, keeping the victims under control by the careful application of jabs to the ribs with sharp sticks, and blows to the head with a cudgel, made from the hard wood of the cocobolo tree.

He was growing into a strong young man, and soon caught the eye of the upper echelons of the Temple hierarchy. Like most of his contemporaries, he had thick, black hair, smooth, deeply tanned skin and a long narrow nose. But what drew attention to him was the look in his eyes, the intensity, the self-belief, and, perhaps, an as yet not obviously detectable disdain for authority. He had impertinence, a treacly stripe of defiance just below the surface, which singled him out from the rest. The Temple Priests were impressed by Xzirqutz Xzirqutz, his attention to detail and fortitude, and not only tolerated him, but prepared to nurture his enthusiasm, grooming him for a future position.

Eventually, inevitably, Xzirqutz Xzirqutz was noticed by Gamboa, Chief Temple Frog Priest, who encouraged the teenager to take a more active role in the ceremonial sacrifices.

Gamboa commissioned Xzirqutz Xzirqutz as a Temple assistant, whose job it was to hand him the sacrificial knife, and be responsible for the upkeep of the blade. This Xzirqutz Xzirqutz did with great care, until one day, atop the Temple of Heavenly Creation and Divine Sacrifice, Gamboa invited the young apprentice to plunge the knife into the body of an aged slave, who was too weak to offer resistance and had simply lain down to die.

Xzirqutz Xzirqutz couldn't believe it; here he was living out his dream. Standing next to Gamboa at the high altar his pulse raced, his heart thumped with the beat of the drums below, and his palms ran sweaty. He could barely contain his excitement as there, at the zenith of the principal Temple, he, Xzirqutz Xzirqutz, was offered his official public blood initiation. His mind raced and his soul sang.

But his legs felt like tree trunks, his feet massive boulders. He couldn't move. Small rills of sweat trickled down his armpits and he began to feel not just nervous, but apprehensive, even afraid. He had seen this done thousands of times and dreamed of it all his young life, and here he was, on the threshold. Yet his head wasn't right, his balance thrown by the quivering heat of the day. He had been there all afternoon, standing in the sun, and he felt weak, and now, suddenly unable to move. Sick and panicky, a nauseous quavering flooded his senses. He couldn't move. He couldn't do it. He simply couldn't do it.

In that eternal moment he drifted off into the horizon, the hazy green of the tropical jungle sucking him in and he froze, an icicle deliberately melting, diminishing in the heat haze. He was a boy, a useless, insignificant little boy, who had no right to be there. An imposter. He could feel the eyes of the entire empire zooming in on him, and the pressure to perform was getting the better of his crumbling confidence. He sensed the mounting anticipation of the Priests and he shrank, his poise draining with the dissolving ice of his soul.

How could he have been so foolish as to think he could be one of them? How could he have deceived himself so? He was a nobody, a child, a paltry cheat, a sham.

Xzirqutz Xzirqutz, his bottom lip quivering, managed one short step backwards, before a hand pushed him forward.

"The blade. Take the blade," a voice said sternly.

He looked up and silhouetted against the immense sky Gamboa's figure loomed over him.

"The blade," repeated the Chief Temple Priest.

Xzirqutz Xzirqutz swallowed, his dry throat rasping. He stood on the precipice, the edge of his own ambition. He didn't move.

"Take the knife," insisted Gamboa impatiently, scarcely hiding his irritation. "Take the knife. Do it. Now."

Xzirqutz Xzirqutz visibly shrank. But from somewhere deep within him he felt a swell, a surge of bitter decision and he snatched up the knife. Barley thinking what he was doing, he skewered the old man, driving the blade into his withered, scrawny chest. It seared between the ribs ripping through his heart, killing him instantly.

Gamboa was furious.

"What, are you stupid?" he said, eyes flashing. "Have you been watching? Have you learned nothing?"

Pushing the boy to one side, the Chief Temple Frog Priest snatched away the knife and carved a slash just under the ribs of the dead man. He reached in and yanked out the heart. With trembling fingers, he faked its beating, raised it to the adoring multitude below, and forced a triumphant smile across his lips. The crowd roared and applauded, and praised the Gods, chanting rhythmic mantras to the Frog mosaics on the Temple walls.

"Idiot," snapped Gamboa.

"Forgive me master. Forgive me," Xzirqutz Xzirqutz pleaded.

"Fool. Get out of here."

"But master . . ."

"Get out of here. Go now," blasted Gamboa.

Xzirqutz Xzirqutz didn't move. He stood transfixed, a masque of horror plastered on his young countenance.

Gamboa towered over him.

"I said, get out of here."

Zxirqutz Zxirqutz started to mutter, but an associate Priest stepped in and escorted him away.

"You'd better leave, now" he said.

The young man hung his head in shame. He trudged miserably towards to edge of the high altar, then on to the side-steps leading down to the back of the Temple. With every humiliating step, his heart wept, his wretched soul aching. He was furious with himself. He had lost his big chance. He half turned. If only he could go back and . . . But it was too late. The damage had been done. He'd failed. His dream was over. How could he have been so stupid? Fighting back the tears he finally rushed down the steps.

*

The small, tightly patterned emerald leaf, trembled imperceptibly. The supremely well-camouflaged caterpillar, clinging to the underside, lost its grip and tumbled through the foliage onto the jungle floor, where it curled up into a scroll. Other leaves began to shiver, and in a tentatively growing crescendo, a small eddy of warm air shook ferns and the stems of green verdant fronds into an orchestration of malcontent. The swift waft of air developed into a current, a flurry, then a draught as the invisible eddy, inbred on its own momentum, grew into a light breeze. The breeze found itself gusting into a wind, then a coiling squall twisting in a determined confusion. The young tornado funneled its swirling eye upwards and gathered a threatening pace, pulling plants, bushes and saplings in its wake. Upwards it stormed, roaring a gale, a hurricane of anger. It soared into the sky, swirling a torrent of fury at the heavens. The black, spinning chimney yelled out a ferocious cry of wrath, and fired silver forks across the sapphire skies and a crack of thunder, juddering the earth's foundations. In the distant city, the people cowered in dread and wailed in fear. Then, in a blink, it was gone.

Later that night, as he lay in the open air, the stars winking overhead, Zxirqutz Zxirqutz lay exhausted, collapsed in a troubled, deep sleep.

And away in the jungle the caterpillar, gently shaken awake by the primitive melodies of the forest, unfurled itself, and hunchbacked its way into the darkness, and the uncertainty of the night.

Equivocation & Eternity

Annihilation beckoned. Gamboa understood perfectly well what was really going to happen, and so warned everyone to prepare for impending doom.

Super Oracle Frog Priest, a devout man who assisted Gamboa in the sacrifices, realized, all too late, that their efforts were to no avail and that catastrophe lay in wait. He'd tried addressing the masses, but found himself struggling for words as the enormity of the devastation hit him between the eyes. As he had stood at the top of the Temple steps, Super Oracle Frog Priest floundered and spluttered, as he realized that not even his powerful, firebrand deliveries, could avert the disaster facing them all. He had simply told them they were going to die. What use was that? He had no words of hope, no solutions, no magic cure and he had felt all too humanly hopeless in the face of such calamity. After his theatrical antiques at the top of the Temple weeks ago, he had simply faded away into the collective memory-loss of the dying nation.

Sadly, the bloody efforts of all the Temple Priests failed. Everybody died. At least, everyone outside the Temples, for the Priests had their own secret supply of water. But now, even they had enough only for a few days at best. The smell of decay and rotting bodies was foul and the Priests, having once been at the pinnacle of the ancient society, found themselves facing extermination. Their wives, children, mistresses and slaves were all dead, and it was only a matter of time before they, too, perished.

As he walked the deserted streets, Gamboa pondered the possibilities. He looked at the dregs of his kingdom and gritted his teeth.

"I'm not going to die like a dog," he said to himself. "I am a Chief Temple Frog Priest and I will survive. I, Gamboa of the Temple of Heavenly Creation and Divine Sacrifice, say it is my destiny to rule forever and not perish. I will survive!"

He considered it his right to lead and live forever. There was, however, simply no water. What could he do? The box was no good; he'd tried that and been none the wiser. The last time he'd looked in it he couldn't even find the frogs, let alone be privy to their council. Disappointed, and utterly lost for ideas, he had taken the box back to the old well in the square, and left it, sitting mute and useless. The frogs had had their day and were now abandoned.

He passed corpses, the empty shells of what were once his subjects. Bones littered the highways and dogs hunted in packs, scavenging on the scraps of humanity. He threw a couple of stones at a snarling, frantic stray which threatened with gritted, yellow teeth. Rats had free rein to chew, gnaw and gulp down whatever they could, and Gamboa kicked out in a rush as a score of vermin capered out of a doorway. Yelling, he sent them squealing as he launched them into the air, tumbling into the dirt.

"My empire," he screamed. "Mine!"

But it wasn't. Not anymore.

He sauntered on, the futility of the situation fueling his awful mood of hopelessness and despair.

It was hot. Boiling hot. And dry. As dry as the Hell in which he was certain he was doomed to spend eternity. He was a Frog Priest. Hell? How was that possible? He shrugged and grimaced in ridicule of his lost soul.

"A Frog Priest," he said out loud to no one. He smiled ruefully; a smile filled with irony and no small sense of self-pity. He shrugged heavily and sighed.

He made his way to the foot of the Temple steps and began to climb. His weary legs ploughed a tough furrow up the steep ascent, and with each step his heart grew heavier. He had seen the beginnings of this empire centuries ago. He had been there at the beginning. The very start of the whole business. Was it all for nothing? All coming to this terrible end, after everything he'd achieved?

His mind cast back to his small beginnings. He'd never known his family, but he'd always felt some close affinity with his mother, even though he had no mental picture of her. Sometimes he would sense an aura about him, especially when he felt anxious or undervalued. A cold, yet comforting essence would occasionally swirl about his frame, and he would have a sensation of being watched, followed, at times even guided as if by a protective spirit.

He thought he felt his father's presence now and then, but he had no image to take comfort in. He'd been too young when his parents had died and so had no visual reference. Did he miss them? Had he missed them over the years? He'd been on his own so long that it really didn't matter anymore, and yet he genuinely did feel that they were there, somewhere in his life, wandering in the background, ready to pick him up when he stumbled or fell.

Where are you now? he thought.

As he neared the top of the Temple, he considered all the girls, young woman and wives he had known over the years. He'd sired half the population of the township years ago, so that even today, when he looked about, he thought he saw his own reflection in the eyes of passersby. A fleeting grin creased his lips as he recalled the countless children who'd called him Father. He really was the father of the empire, in more ways than one.

Inevitably, he considered his all-time love, Tsok, his last, and only, truly great love. *Wow*, he thought, *what a mess I made of that!* He thought of their only child, Chatlan. His heart sank, and a dark cloud shrouded him in misery. *All for nothing,* he said. *Nothing.*

He reached the top. The great expanse of the city stretched about him. Magnificent. Or it had been. It now began to look tired and with empty streets, he knew it wouldn't be long till the forests took back what was once theirs. His reign, his kingdom, would suffer the indifference of neglect. It would be consigned to abandonment and oblivion, like it had never happened.

He'd simply borrowed time and space, and now the earth was taking it back. He'd never owned it. It was never his.

He sat down and drifted off into a reverie, his head weighed down with the despondency of imminent defeat. The dying world offered no hope of salvation and Gamboa, wallowing in despair, shed a quiet tear. Then he lay on the stones and slept.

After a short while, disturbed by the faint, weeping bark of a dog, he woke, got up and wandered down the Temple steps into the square. He looked back up at the huge edifice towering above him. How things had changed. He shook his head. It all seemed so long ago.

He walked down the main thoroughfare, past the dead and the dying, through the stench of decay and starved cadavers littering the street. This was Hell on earth. Gamboa recalled the days of the Great Grey. He was the only one who could remember those days. All had passed on many centuries ago. Only he carried the gene of remembrance of that apocalyptic time. The Great Grey. He almost smiled. How simple it had been back then. How clear and ordinary. How uncomplicated and straightforward. In his nostalgia for the simplicity of life, he did smile - eventually. But then the images of the ash and the destruction brought him back to the present, and the death associated with each traumatic event.

The Great Grey. The drought. Why had it all gone wrong?

He walked on by the piles of rotting, skeletal carcasses. And in the blistering sunshine everywhere was dry, as dry as could be. A fetid, rank smell invaded his senses. He could barely breathe. He carried on, until finally coming to the end of the urban sprawl, the end of the city and the beginning of the wilderness. He laughed out loud. He had lived here once. Right here on this spot. He wondered if the pond was still there, the pond where he had seen one of his first visions. But of course, that was a silly idea. How could there be any water now, after months and years of drought? No, there would be no water. Still, he ventured to where he recalled the water should have been. No sign, of course. Not even an indentation. All gone, probably a very long time ago. He flopped down.

How could this have happened? How could this be? Hadn't he done everything he'd been told? Had not the old man's instructions been followed to the letter? The old man; he pictured him in his mind's eye. So old, and so . . . *So weird,* he muttered. And the dog. Now that was weird. A one-eyed dog. And a really odd shape, just weird, a weird tail. And silver. Gamboa's face puzzled over the memory.

He thought of the box. He remembered wanting to reach down into it, and the old man snapping to attention, stopping him.

"Not like that. It's too dangerous. They'll kill you."

He'd remembered this advice for years and years as, on many an occasion, he had opened the box and stared in wonder at the contents.

"They'll kill you."

Oh yes, he remembered those words very well indeed.

He had been entranced by the box and the tiny frogs inside, so small and yet so powerful.

"They'll kill you."

That was all so long ago now. So long ago.

He picked up a stone and threw it at the space where the water should have been, the old man's words drifting in and out of earshot.

"It's too dangerous. They'll kill you."

Well, he was certainly dying now, that's for sure. He looked around at the powdery earth, the plants, desperate and crisp. No birds flew overhead, no weeds frilled the edges of the pond. The fish were all gone. All gone.

He rubbed his hands together, locked his fingers, rested his chin on his knuckles and considered his life. It had been good. *Very* good, he decided. He'd been around for many, many years so he couldn't really complain. And he'd also spent most of his life as Chief Temple Frog Priest, and not many could boast that. No, he thought carefully, it had been a good life. Well, actually, much better than that: it had been great! And now?

Well, it didn't really bear thinking about, but his mind still wandered through the years, good and bad, the errors made, fortunes won, lands conquered. Yes, it had been good all right, but ultimately, it all boiled down to this one defining moment. The end.

He chewed the inside of his cheek and wheezed a snort of dejected acceptance. The end.

No breeze blew. No birdsong decorated the air. Nothing stirred.

It was as if life itself had been sucked out of the earth. Time did not exist and his mind meandered gently from people to places, and finally, events.

Eventually, inevitably, he again came to thinking about his wife. She was wonderful. Kind, generous, soft and attractive in a way none of his other wives over the centuries had been. Her love came in infinite, unconditional terms of affection and understanding, and she was, of course, the mother of his son.

His son. He sighed. Had it all been worth it? Had he made the right decision? He tried pushing this thought to one side but it came crashing through the gate of his consciousness to replay in full, terrific technicolour:

He came to lying in the anteroom, the fusty air still sour about his shoulders. His head ached. He rose groggily to his feet. He ventured outside. The darkness, painted silver by a full moon, could not disguise the smell of fresh meat and blood. It hit him full in the face before he took a step forward, slipped on the greasy stones around the bloody altar, and launched headlong toward the edge of the platform steps. He just managed to cling on, to wedge himself against the wall, managing to avoid plunging headfirst down the monument to the ground. His head spun but his mind was clearing.

"I must get home," he said out loud. "Home."

Crablike, he negotiated the steps and descended to the square where the bodies of scores of young boys lay wretched, headless on the bare earth. Defiled, crushed and ragged, their hearts were strewn about the base of the Temple, and over to one side lay a heap of eyeless heads, the flies feasting even at this late hour.

He made his way past the gore and followed the road back to his house. As he neared the door his heart beat fast, for he remembered his wife's screaming, imploring him not to kill their son. He dreaded entering. He prepared himself and practiced some placatory remarks, which he hoped against hope would satisfy his wife.

Like most men, he thought a few words of explanation would suffice, and though there might be

102

some hours of silence to endure, ultimately a balanced peace would reign.

"I mean," he thought to himself "I had to do it. We were all going to die otherwise."

Yes, all would be well, he reassured himself.

He pushed open the heavy, wooden gate. Not a servant in sight. All must be asleep, not even the night watchman standing guard. Gamboa bristled. Where were the guards? Heads would roll in the morning.

He crossed the courtyard, quietly edging his way towards his private quarters and the secluded bedroom beyond. Parting the heavy curtaining, Gamboa peered inside. He could see, clearly outlined below the simple, textile cover, the form of his wife and her head facing the wall, resting on the pillow. He smiled. He felt quite relieved to see her and his heart settled down a little. His wife. He looked at her sleeping, hardly moving. So peaceful. So very quiet. He loved her very much. Yes, she'll understand. Of course she will. She's the wife of the Chief Temple Frog Priest, of course she'll understand. Everything will be fine.

And with that, he quietly entered, removed his loincloth and crept under the sheet. Yes, all will be fine. He turned on his side, inhaling the intoxicating aromas of primrose and coconut oil massaged into his wife's thick, long black hair. He lay there quite still.

"I love you," he whispered.

In the quiet, he realized just how lucky he was. She was a wonderful woman, and she'd been at his side for some years now. But to him, she remained the beautiful young girl he had known since she was a child. The daughter of a fellow Temple Priest, he had got to know her as a youngster, and watched her develop into a fine, adolescent woman. Coming of age, she was always laughing and had a smile ready for any occasion. He couldn't resist her. She was charming, playful, great fun and simply delightful company. He soon fell madly in love and marriage the inevitable outcome. In no time at all, a son was born, and they were perfectly happy. They were the envy of the tribe and his lovely young wife thrilled his friends and the hierarchy at the Temple. She was loving and fiercely loyal, standing by him through thick and thin. Theirs was a great marriage, and he felt proud, so very proud indeed. But now, lying next to her, he realized that perhaps he had over stepped the mark, and his wife needed all the love and affection he could muster to make things better.

He inched towards her, sliding his arm around her slim waist as he snuggled closer.

"Darling," he said, very gently. "I love you."

They had had arguments in the past, and he knew that he would have to be loving, tender and understanding. His attentions normally paid off with her turning to face him, forgiveness just a minute away. But tonight she didn't move.

"Tsok, come on. Please."

He moved his hand up towards her small breast, and it was then, in that deadly, lifeless microsecond that he knew. He KNEW!

A murderous pause framed the deafening silence, as time, deep-frozen as under a mountain of arctic ice, glued itself to eternity.

"What's this?" he said aloud, feeling the sticky, damp wetness against the palm of his hand. "What the devil . . .?"

In a surge of energy, he tore back the sheet. His mind blew into a trillion atoms of disbelief.

"No," the word hardly escaping his lips.

"No," he said louder, shaking his head in denial.

"Noo," he repeated, the volume increasing with his incredulity.

"NOOO!" he finally screamed at the top of his voice.

He shot to his feet, naked in the pale light, glaring at the bed. Eyebrows in a tight knot of terror, his face contorted into a mask of petrified confusion as his roaring eyes simply could not believe what they saw. His wife, now bereft of the shroud, lay prostrate, unmoving and covered in blood, her torso glistening in the moonlight fetching in through the open window. His breath caught, his appalled senses incapable of taking it all in.

"Noooo!" he screamed yet again.

Taking a step closer, looking down at his wife's desecrated body, he bent over, tears already stinging his terror struck eyes. He reached for her hair, her face, her soft skin and long dead love, and as he did so further horror took him to the profoundest depths of despair, as his wife's head, now clearly seen detached from her body, rolled off the pillow and rocked to a silent stop in the middle of the mattress, her dry, dead-eye stare piercing his soul.

105

Unable to breathe, he reeled back from the bedside, realizing the magnitude of the atrocity before him. He tore his eyes from his wife's gutless gaze and scanned the torso, a butcher's cargo of blood and gore. He gagged. From the base of the ribcage, the skin had been peeled back, the thin, sparse ribs thrashed apart and where her heart was supposed to be, a black, brazen cavity jeered at him. Sacrifice! Human sacrifice. In his own house. His own bed. His wife. His own wife!

He was sick. Even all his experience could not prepare him for this horror. He vomited and vomited and broke down into a billion pieces of heartache. How could this be? How could this have happened? What was this, in his own bed, his own house? His wife, his lovely young wife, dead, sacrificed in his own bed?

The horror and sacrilege was unimaginable, and yet here it was, staring him straight in the face. He cried out again, in a howling torrent of rage and despair. Then he slumped in a heap against the wall, a deafening roar splitting his head wide open.

"Why? Why have you done this?" he cried out in agony, his heart wrenching in a pit of unbelievable pain and anguish.

"Why?" he screamed out.

By now, candle light had appeared in various parts of the house as servants, hearing the commotion, ran around in circles aware that something terrible had happened. One rushed into the bedroom and was just about to say something when Gamboa, furious and destroyed at the same time, cried savagely at him to get out.

"Get out of here! Get out! Out, out! Get out!" he yelled at the top of his voice.

106

Gasping for air, he stared at the dreadful bed. He started to shake. His hands trembled and his body quaked as his blasted mind raced to comprehend the scope of the scene. Despair, hopelessness, regret, fear, loathing and utter desolation flooded his shattered emotions, and he detonated into an explosion of angry, rivers of grief.

But even in that wretched moment, his head cleared and he saw what this was. Through his anger and grief and fury, he realized that this wasn't just a sacrifice. It was also something else.

A new, dark, white heat came over him. WHO? Who had done this? Who could have done such a thing? A sacrifice? No, this was murder . . . murder, in his own house.

*

He stared at the empty space. No water. All gone. No water, no life, no point. It was all a waste of time. His wife and son were dead, and it was only a matter of time till he joined them. He sat despondent on the dusty bank. How had it come to this? So sad. So utterly, utterly sad. He didn't understand. He rubbed his tired eyes shifting his position in the hard earth. No, he simply didn't understand, any of it. He sighed for the umpteenth time.

It had been several months since his wife's death, and he had never really come to terms with it. The shock had been tremendous. But, perhaps worse than the shock of seeing his wife mutilated in their own bed, was the fact that he still did not understand *why*? And even more to the point, *who*? Surely his wife had been an innocent victim? What could she have possibly done to warrant being killed? She was loved by her family, adored by everyone. Why, and how, could this have happened? Still, months later he had no clues. No one to blame and punish.

Immediately after the death, the Temple Priests had formed an investigation, and scoured the city looking for potential culprits, but nothing valid came to the surface. There were the usual ne'er-do-wells brought up for questioning, and summarily executed, despite their innocence, but apart from that there were no leads. At least nothing substantial, nothing that could be proven. There was simply no hard evidence to pursue. Gamboa and his advisers were convinced it had been some kind of conspiracy involving rival groups, and he systematically tore through the other Temples in his pursuit of his enemies. Suspicion naturally fell on the Snakes and Jaguars, and Gamboa was convinced it was one of these two houses who had killed his wife. For a long time, there had been animosity between various Temple groups, and Gamboa was very aware that his support was by no means unanimous. He knew that there was always someone, somewhere, who fancied his chances at taking control of the city, and that they would take any steps to unsettle his rule and depose him. But killing his wife was a mean, cowardly act, and he would be ruthless in his retribution when the murderers were exposed. He spoke to all leaders of all the Temples in an effort to root out the culprits. But whoever they were, they had covered their tracks very well indeed, and he was left none the wiser for his efforts.

The Temple Priests had been just as puzzled as Gamboa, for they understood, or, at least tried to understand, his pain, and wanted to help. But weeks of investigation revealed nothing, no solution to the mystery and, as time passed and the drought grew worse, people were dying and the Temple Priests, and even Gamboa himself, gave up trying to solve a mystery which soon no one would even be alive to remember.

He threw a stone into the nonexistent water. He sighed. Glumly, he lay back. He stared up at the cloudless skies, his head a vacuum. A lone, black silhouette drifted across the emptiness. It grew bigger. Gamboa squinted as the solitary shape swirled in descending curlicues, tracing imaginary geometric patterns in the blue. As it came closer, Gamboa determined the clear outline of an eagle, its colours and designs, symmetrically linear dots and dashes, brilliantly decorating the avian wings and body. Its tail, a fan of kaleidoscopic translucence, tweaked and tilted, adjusting the giant bird's trajectory. Majestically, it swooshed over Gamboa's head in a rush of breeze. The rainbow colours almost blinded Gamboa, but he felt the bird's large penetrating eyes pierce his consciousness. It glided up and away towards the horizon, over the lifeless trees, and was gone.

Strange, he thought. *How very strange.* He'd seen this image before, but he couldn't quite place it. The dots, the dashes, the swirling circles and menace, yet with a message of hope. Now, where had he seen it before? His face twisted into puzzled creases as he trawled his memory. Then it hit him. The box. Of course. The box. The old man's box. The carvings. The images. The engravings on the box. The pictures. They were real. They were real!

A snort of quasi enlightenment escaped his lips, and he wondered how he hadn't realized this before. The box. He smiled.

But it didn't last. He was still dying and the world would still disappear. He felt at his side for the vial. Now *that* was a mystery he would never get to grips with. It never emptied. Never! He took up the container and poured the contents into his mouth.

How very, *very* strange. It was all very strange. And he drifted off.

When he awoke, he got up, groggy in the afternoon sunshine, brushed off the dust and started back for the city. He was exhausted, and the heat was taking its toll on his weary senses. He sighed, shoulders round, dejected.

As the dried up shrubs, dead plants and desperate trees stuck up brittle and crusty under the harsh rays, he managed one last thread of sensible thought - the box. He had been to the box many times over the last few weeks, but had closed the lid after finding no solutions to the tribe's problems. No water, meant: no water. They had done everything possible and they were staring death straight between the eyes. Each time he had opened the lid, nothing came to him. The frogs were there, but they said nothing, or nothing of value at any rate; nothing he could pin his hopes on. One day, he'd poked around with a stick and found them slumbering under a leaf, as usual, but all they said when nudged awake was, "One day, we'll save your life," and then nodded off again.

Hopeless. It was hopeless. The frogs were hopeless and he'd lost confidence in them. Their powers had faded and they were now defunct. The world they inhabited inside the box still flourished, but any words of wisdom or advice were now unforthcoming. In the end he left the box in the square where the old man had met him. It no longer served and, in his opinion, deserved to be abandoned. His last, coherent sentiment, as he prepared for the trek back to the city, and death, was one of thanks but ultimate disappointment, as the box and its contents had finally let him down.

It was deathly quiet. Not a thing budged. He kicked a stone, watched it roll away. Then another. Then another and with each rolling stone his one last contemplation took off. The thought grew. It sprouted a fragrant sapling of chance expectation. It flourished and blossomed into a thick perfumed bush of hope, and, ultimately, a magnificent tree of faith and courage. Its huge boughs embraced and unsealed Gamboa's now limitless imagination. He stopped, dead in his tracks. The bird. How strange. The vial. Where had he just been? What had happened?

A curious consternation threw a shadow over his face and slowly, mystically, a dawn of understanding evicted the doubts and fears of recent months as he teetered on the edge of a terrific comprehension. He was a God, or at least the next best thing here on earth. He was the great Frog God *Wo-sak's* representative, and he held the key, the magic to unlock the door. There was a way. There was. The frogs!

Gamboa, tingling with electric inspiration, considered the outrageous possibility staring him in the face. He spoke to the putrid air.

"The old man said that one day the frogs will save my life. He did say that. I remember him saying that. Yes, he distinctly said the frogs will one day save my life. *'One day they will save your life.'* Yes, he said that."

Gamboa felt a rush of energy, an earthquake deep in his gut.

"Of course, the frogs!"

The only creatures with any possible way to survive drought were the frogs, for they are the great survivors. The old man. Bless the old man, thought Gamboa, the ancient, old man. And the dog. The weird, weird dog. How beautiful the dog was, really.

"The frogs. Yes, the frogs," he yelled.

For the first time in weeks, his tired eyes lit up and he felt a spring of optimism watering his parched soul. The frogs! How come he hadn't seen it before? The frogs, of course. It was a wild, crazy idea but he knew, he just *knew* it would work. He was a God, of course it would work!

The astonishing realization slapped him a stinging welt across the face: the only way for him to survive was . . . to actually become a frog himself.

"I am a Temple Frog Priest and I will survive," he declared, arms aloft. "It is my destiny to survive. I am a Chief Temple Frog Priest. I am a God."

Of course, he knew what he was thinking was insane and made no logical sense. But he also knew very well what he had to do. Out of his brains with excitement he jumped up and down like a child.

"One day they will save your life," he shouted out. "One day they will save your life," he hollered. "Of course, the frogs!"

*

Gamboa couldn't wait to get back to the city and tell his fellow Priests about his revelation. Despite his thirst and hunger, he positively raced along the deserted streets. Jubilant, he gasped for victorious air as he reached the steps of the Temple, and called out as loud as his roaring lungs would allow. Slowly, the other Priests appeared, wondering what could possibly be the source and meaning of such commotion. Gamboa could hardly contain himself.

"The frogs," he said, panting heavily. "The frogs."

The Priests gawped.

"The frogs," repeated Gamboa, insistently.

"What about them?" offered one Priest, unimpressed by Gamboa's enthusiasm.

"They will live."

"The frogs?"

"Yes, the frogs."

"Live?"

"Yes."

"How?" asked the Priest, his interest only slightly piqued.

"They will burrow themselves into the ground and wait for the rains. That way, they will survive and outlive the rest of the dying world. The frogs are the answer."

A young, rather earnest Priest put in.

"All very well, Gamboa, if you're a frog."

As grave as the situation was, there were still one or two who managed a sartorial smile at this. But one older, wiser Priest, clearly close to death, inclined his head and asked weakly, "Gamboa, what are you saying?"

Gamboa looked at the old Priest.

"We should do what the frogs do," he replied. "Bury ourselves and wait for water." He paused, looking around the group. "We should do the same as the frogs."

"But how?" asked another Priest. "How can we do that?"

Gamboa, taking out the sacrificial blade from his belt, said in a voice leaving no room for contradiction, "Like this."

And with that, right there and then, he took a great gulp of air and raised his arm aloft. The other Priests stood wide-eyed in horrible anticipation.

"No," said the old Priest, staggering forward in a vain attempt to stop him. "No Gamboa. Don't!"

But it was too late. In a second, Gamboa had slashed at his thighs and seared off whole chunks of his muscular torso. Blood squirted in showers, and he felt the wonderful pain of freedom and salvation. He hacked at his flesh, unswerving in his determination to carve himself into the image, the very image, of the Gods he worshipped.

He sheared his legs, honing them into fine, tapered limbs, at the ends his feet, slender and smooth. He lopped off his ears and slashed at his nose and distended his tongue, pulling it to a luxuriously suckered point. Then he cut and chopped at his fingers, stretching and snapping each joint into lean, elongated dislocations. He twisted his spine into cracks and groans and he jerked and jolted the hinges of his body. He stooped and crawled, in a frog-like hunch.

In a tentative step, he gritted his teeth, grimacing as each movement, each unspeakable stutter challenged his resolve.

"This will work," he told himself through clenched jaws. "This will work. I *will* rise from the dead and I *will* rule forever."

His eyes bulged, and his mouth, now a red gaping chasm, dribbled goo and phlegm as he struggled with the torment of physical revolution.

The other Priests, motionless, gasped in amazement. Flesh and maw flew through the air and the mighty Gamboa, leader of a once tremendous empire, reduced himself to the size of a small rock. The remains of their Chief lay scattered about, and a lone dog came sniffing the air. The old Priest shook his head. He'd thought he'd seen it all - before today.

Silence.

A voice then reached into the inner sanctum of each Priest's head, a mesmeric, commanding, hypnotic voice, Gamboa's.

"Come with me," he said "and live forever. Follow me and have everlasting life."

The Priests slowly turned one to another, some frowning, others muttering in consternation. Who was speaking? Whose voice was in their heads?

Of course, they didn't know that they were all hearing the same voice, but they could tell by the reaction of the group that something was going on.

The old Priest was first to speak.

"Gamboa?" he said tentatively. "Is that you?"

The other Priests turned as one to look down at the small, bloody shape on the floor.

"Yes. It's me," said the voice. "You must follow me if you want to live. You must do as I do if you want everlasting life. It is the only way we are going to survive this calamity. You must become the image of the great *Wo-sak*."

The old Priest responded.

"But Gamboa, you ask too much. How can we do this? What you ask is impossible. We cannot do this."

The bloody amphibian didn't move, but the voice replied.

"Old man, you must have faith. You must put your faith in the Frog God, for he will save you. I have been directed by the Gods to do this, as they have a greater plan for me, and you. Only this way can we live and follow our destiny. It is there for us to take, but we must take it now, before it is too late."

The Priests were not sure of any of this, but one bright young man spoke up.

"What choice do we have? We're going to die anyway. What else can we do?"

Others chipped in.

"It's a trick. Gamboa is tricking us with his witchcraft. It's not possible. How can he do this? It's a trick." And they scoffed at the idea of hacking themselves into the shape of a frog.

The old Priest, however, was wiser.

"I have known Gamboa all my life, and he has always been fair and direct. He is a great leader, and it was he, in antiquity, who delivered us from the Great Grey. Gamboa, he did this, no one else. It is Gamboa who saved us. He is the living God here on earth. He is the light and the truth. I will follow him."

With that, the old Priest took out his knife and prepared to make the first cut.

"Wait!" cried another. "You cannot do this on your own. I will come with you. I will follow you. We can do this together, and, as one, we will follow Gamboa to the everlasting truth of eternal happiness."

He also took out his knife, and prepared to make the cuts.

"I too, will come," cried another. "For we have nothing here and he is right, Gamboa has been our leader for centuries, and he cannot be wrong. We must follow him."

After these words, all the other Priests swore to follow Gamboa and prepared to make the cuts. But there was one, however, a slightly built young man with fine features and thoughtful eyes, who cast a doubt on proceedings.

"What if he's wrong?" he said.

"Wrong?"

"Yes, wrong. What if he's wrong?"

The youthful Priest scanned the faces of his colleagues.

"He's a living God, we are mortal. What if he's wrong and we all bleed to death. What then?"

"Then we die," said the old Priest.

"Die?"

"Yes, die. We're all going to die anyway," said the old man. "Of that, you can be certain."

The young Priest just looked at the ground, lost in doubt.

"You must have faith," said the old man, taking up a blade.

"Faith. Here, take this. Your faith will carry you through. This is but a test. Have faith in Gamboa and the Gods. Here, take it."

The young Priest, struggling to keep the fear out of his voice, raised his head and spoke.

"I can't. I can't do it. It's too much for me. I'm too afraid. I don't have that much faith. I'm sorry," and he turned away heading towards the steps of the Temple.

One or two shouted after him but the old Priest bade them leave him alone.

"He's made up his mind," he said. "Let him be."

Then, mustering all his strength, the revered old Priest struck the knife straight through his biceps, his calves, then his stomach and shoulders. He rapidly shaved and scraped away at his scrawny frame, until he had nothing left but the shape and image of a small frog, about the size of a pear. The other Priests wasted no time in slicing, cutting and hacking at their own flesh, and the blood poured and the meat exploded in all directions.

And the Priests became images of *Wo-sak*, the Frog God they worshipped.

It was truly remarkable, and the Frog Priests now communed with each other on a plain ethereal, and divine, leaving the earth far behind as they joined their leader.

"Welcome, brothers," announced Gamboa. "This is our new clan and we will return to the earth and we will live forever. Now, follow me."

Shadowed by his entourage of Priests, Gamboa crawled toward the empty space where the pond used to be, on the edge of the city. There, he sniffed out the best spot to start his digging. The soft pads of his grazed fingers bled as he scraped his way through the tough, earthy crust of the dried up pond. Eventually, he found what he was looking for, a mud frog, resting gently in a hollowed-out burrow. Ancient, primeval instinct had somehow led the frog to hidden moisture in underground clay deposits, dampened by dew. The frog was now quietly meditating, musing, seeing out the drought, waiting for the rains. It was a miracle.

Gamboa managed to squeeze past the hibernating frog, and settle down in the clammy sediment. It was dark. He began his incantations. He prayed to *Wo-sak*, the God for whom he had killed so many. To whom he had devoted his whole life. He prayed to the God who had fostered, protected and nurtured him as a young boy. He loved his God, the Frog God. He had torn out the hearts of so many innocent people and drank the blood of so many victims, all in service of the one true God.

If his existence had meant anything at all, then at least he should be spared and given life after the great drought. He had turned his sacrificial knife on himself, tearing at his own flesh. Now, surely, *surely*, the supreme omniscient *Wo-sak* would recognize this sacrifice, and save him. Faith. His faith would see him through.

The Frog Priests of the Temple of Heavenly Creation and Divine Sacrifice, dug long and deep into the land of their forefathers. The rock hard soil, unforgiving and mean, forced the frogs to draw on all their reserves of energy. But eventually, they forged themselves living tombs out of the dead earth. Exhausted, they breathed-in their last tiny lung-full of air, and began to sleep for a very, very, long time.

Gamboa, his incantations over, was silent now. Hushed still in his murky crypt, he expelled his last sentient breath, and fell into a deep unconsciousness, from which it would be over a thousand years before he awoke.

PART TWO

Jaxxa

As a young boy, Jaxxa had enjoyed the ceremonies in Suxx. He loved the spectacle, the costumes, music, dance, and thumping drums. He could sense the symbiotic relationship between the hearts, the drumbeat and the heady mesmeric rituals of human sacrifice.

His mother had taken him to the ceremonies as a baby, and so, from an early age, he was accustomed to the blood feasts and the gore. He remembered being in awe of the heads raining down the steps, and the grim expressions on the disembodied faces as they bounced down from the altar. The closer you got to the steps, the more chance there was of being splashed by the blood. This thrilled Jaxxa, and, as he grew up, he would always manage to squeeze his way to the front to get a better view, increasing his chances of getting blood showered. His mother wasn't too bothered by this preoccupation, and in fact, actually encouraged him, as she saw it as a way of her son taking a step closer to Godliness.

Jaxxa's father, a middle ranking Temple Priest, assisted Gamboa at the top of the Temple steps. He would stand next to the altar, preparing and handing over to the Chief Temple Frog Priest, the ceremonial, obsidian knives. Occasionally, he would be given the job of sacrificing slaves, but the more valuable, the more honourable offerings of virgins, would always be Gamboa's. This left Jaxxa's father feeling rather second rate, and it rankled, there lying beneath his supportive exterior a hidden, very unpleasant man. His frustration tended to cloud his judgment, at times diminishing his devotion to the job. He never failed in his duty, but his attitude was sometimes a little negative. But he worked hard not to let his disappointments show, especially on festive days, when he would execute all his tasks with a precision veiling his antagonisms. Privately, however, he was a volcano waiting to erupt.

One fateful day after a long session of sacrifice, Jaxxa's father reached his breaking point. As a man he felt unfulfilled, and his dark soul, unhappy at what it considered to be a failed lifetime of second class servitude, exploded in a blaze of violence. His frustrations boiled over, and Jaxxa's life changed forever.

"Why?" he demanded taking another draft of maize wine. "Why not me? Why not? Why do I always get the filthy slaves? The waste nobody else wants? Why me?"

He took another mouthful from the coconut shell.

"Why . . .?" he repeated. "Answer me that!"

Jaxxa's mother cowered in the corner. She had seen all this before, and each time she grew more afraid. There was a terrible ferocity in her husband, which she knew she could not control and physically, of course, she was no match for. In the past he had lashed out at her, and she had pretended some domestic accident to cover up the shame of bruising. She tried her best to protect her children. The neighbours knew what was going on. The walls weren't that thick.

"But you are a Temple Priest," she offered.

"Shut up! What do you know?" he shouted. "Nothing. You're just a woman. You know nothing," and with that he poured himself another shell of wine.

She knew what was coming. It was going to hurt but there was nothing she could do. Her husband was ruler of his house, and if he wanted to beat her then he would, and that was that. She braced for the attack. But this time, she was surprised as her husband sat quietly on the floor, brooding. Usually, he would rave on about the injustice of it all, and then gradually work himself into an intense frenzy, which would inevitably result in brutality. She knew what was in store and resigned herself.

But it didn't come. Not this time. This time, he sat on in silence. He just sat there. What was going on? This was not like her husband. What *was* going on?

In so many ways this was worse, much worse than the beating she came to expect, as she couldn't predict what was about to happen, and felt lost where the rules had been torn up. But, perhaps, she did know, and just decided to take no notice, as she could do very little about it anyway. She, in her turn, said nothing and sat, head bowed, waiting.

The explosion, when it did come, took her completely by surprise. In one ejaculation of energy, her husband bounded up off the floor, leapt to the other side of the room where she was seated, grabbed her by her long, raven hair, and yanked her to her feet. She gave out a weak, defiant murmur. This was it, she thought, it's a beating, blood and pain for days.

But she was wrong. She was so wrong.

With his free hand he pulled open the wooden door and dragged her outside. It was late, the streets deserted. She was just about to scream into the black night, when she felt the full force of a smacking fist. Her front teeth flew into the darkness. She was kicked and punched, then trawled and wrenched by the hair through the city. She could see the Temple looming in the silvery twilight and she wondered what on earth was going on. Then it dawned on her, as her naked feet bumped up the steep steps, her ankles bruising and battering on the stones. He was taking her to the top of the Temple. To the altar!

She tried to scream but the pain was too much. Her head snatched back and her face smashed into the steps. Through swollen eyes, she saw the city getting smaller and smaller.

No, she thought to herself, *not this. Not now. My children. I'm not a slave. He can't sacrifice me. He can't do this.*

But her thoughts were heard by no one. She called on all the Gods to help her. With a scarlet, bloody gurgle, she invoked the Frog God *Wo-sak*, whom she loved and served. She called on her ancestors. She prayed with all her heart and through a demolished, splashing red mouth, begged her husband to stop.

It was no use.

She made an oath of blessing for her children and as she faced the final moments, she prayed her son would avenge her death and kill his father. This she prayed for with all her might as she saw, for the first and only time, the panorama of the darkened city. And in that stupid, moonlit moment, she thought the metropolis looked fantastic. Fantastic!

Her husband raised his eyes to the heavens and also swore his own private oath. Then, with one hand holding his wife on the sacrificial stone, with the other he slashed at the stomach, then dug out the heart from her now listless body; for she had given up. She had offered herself to *Wo-sak* and not fought anymore. For one dreadful moment, she saw her own heart, beating, held up by her husband for the Gods to see. She saw the blood running down his arms and the wild look in his furious eyes.

"This is for you. You," she heard him say. "For you, *Wo-sak*. For you."

This is for my children, thought Jaxxa's mother, and in the final act of the terrible night, she prayed that Jaxxa and his sister would somehow survive.

Her head pulled back, revealing a slender neck, Jaxxa's mother never saw her husband raise the knife. Nor did she cringe in pain as the blade sliced through her throat, severing sinew and bone sending her sickeningly mutilated face head over heels. Nor did she live the final, tumbling decent down the steps into the morass of heads below. She missed that.

But her son didn't. Quietly, Jaxxa sat at the foot of the steps and gazed in total horror as his mother's head came hurtling down towards him; his mother, his beloved mother. She had protected him, guarded him, nurtured him and given him everything. Her mad, bloody eyes whipped around in hoola-hoops of crazy turmoil and the final thud, as the head thumped into the pile, made Jaxxa jump.

"Mother," he said. "Mother."

And then, in a hotchpotch of legs and arms, his mother's body came slamming down from the top, mangled, dislocated. It too, finally came to rest in a jumble of other corpses, and Jaxxa froze as the exposed fragments of vein and artery pumped blood in a lunar, grey-scarlet geyser. His mother.

In that moment Jaxxa made an oath: "One day, father, I will kill you."

And with that, the six-year-old turned around and went back to the house where his sister lay sleeping.

Journeys

The Earth fell silent. The wind disappeared, clouds vanished and forever and ever as far as the eye could see, rivers ran dry. Animals and birds fled the skies and fields, and the plains and valleys were desolate. The universe held no record of human activity, save the silent, deserted buildings of the ancient civilization.

They had worshipped the good and the holy with the fruit of the Earth, and had failed in their efforts.

They had worshipped the good and the holy with the blood of their enemies, and had failed in their efforts.

They had sacrificed their own offspring, hewn down, like unwanted saplings of a scorched earth, and still they had failed in their efforts. And now the dry, crumbling soil held the last remaining vestiges of life itself. The regal leaders of the proud, the feared and mighty Suxx empire, lay buried for history itself to forget. An unremorseful silence was all that ghosted through the avenues and alleys of the once great city. Devastation and punishment had, once again, been meted out by the Gods. The blood, the sacrifice, the pain and torture had failed.

The only hope of salvation lay beneath the bleak earth. The only way the bloodline could continue was for the Chosen One, Gamboa, to be resurrected with his fellow Temple Frog Priests. But there was no guarantee that they would survive the eternities they might have to wait, interned, dormant under the Earth's crust.

Days, weeks and months, passed. Then years and years, and decades and centuries, till time itself dissolved the notion that the great empire had ever existed. Even the land, parched, wretched, had forgotten the frogs beneath the ground. But there they lay, unbidden by nature to do anything other than bide their time waiting . . . waiting . . . waiting . . .

*

Out at sea, beneath the great ocean, deep down under the dark waters, there lay a turbulent world of fiery lava oozing out of the planet. Earth's broiling core was struggling to contain itself. And as the frogs lay in their sandy graves, senseless of the universe, way beyond the coral reef, which had framed their city for hundreds and thousands of years, in one cataclysmic expression of untrammeled emotion the Earth shifted, giving out a tremendous belch of lava and molten rock. The volcanic quake throttled the shaking planet, conveying booming shudders from the yawning epicentre to the icy towering peaks of the highest mountains. The eruption sucked in trillions of gallons of water, evacuating seashores and emptying coastlines for thousands of miles.

The rush, followed by silence on deserted beaches, held nature in limbo, as all life stopped breathing for those moments that stretched into minutes, then hours. The lull, giving false hope of reprieve, was broken by a distant thunder. Water. The sizzling ocean had hawked up a terrifying tsunami of vast dimensions. It started as a swell, then a plateau, then an impenetrable wall measuring hundreds of metres high. As it gathered speed, all sea-life and the flotsam of millions of years were drawn in, dragged into its formidable wake. The watery leviathan rose to its full height, and in one almighty roar came sweeping down onto the coast. In its path, unsuspecting, lay the abandoned city of Suxx.

The universe of water smashed its way onto the beaches and, at alarming speed, headed inland. It dug up the dead trees and furrowed canals, and surged through what was left of the deserted city, destroying everything in its path. It cursed down ancient roads and alleyways, flattening civic buildings and deserted homes. Only the great Temples could withstand the deluge, but even they suffered, as the power of the tsunami's bore hurtled on past the urban complex, seeking out the burnt-out jungle beyond. Eventually, the surge found itself at the edge of a dried-up pond on the edge of the city.

The water's tongues dug deep into the dead soil. They unearthed a sleeping prey, a precious, dormant prey, which had been lying in wait for hundreds and hundreds of years.

The water drilled down, snaking and twisting, then funneled upwards, a geyser seeking out unsuspecting quarry. The frogs, in a murky subterranean whirlwind of soaking mud, stirred, jolted awake in the shifting, churning swamp, cloudy eyes mired by silt and the sleepy dust of a thousand years. Shock gave way to panic and chaos, then wrenching pandemonium as the frogs' senses rocketed from suspended death, to a desperate, almighty struggle for survival. Heart rates exploding, the little frogs gasped and wheezed in the asphyxiating wet quagmire, coughing out lung-fulls of sludgy, suffocating morass.

Idle for so long, their voices gagged in the bedlam and they lurched in a frenzied, sickening torque, pitched helter-skelter like sodden chaff. Thrown into the world they had abandoned for centuries, the Priests goggled, wide-eyed, then squinted at the dazzling hues, the shrill blue and golden shards of the brilliant day.

With a rush, the gushing jet spouted Gamboa and the Temple Priests way up into the spray-filled crystal air, where they hung, suspended, fully conscious of the explosive realization of this new dawn. Liberated, the Priests reached out, rapturously clawing at the heavens, in relief and ecstasy mouthing wordless praises, sung to the vanquishing Gods who had delivered them from the obscurity of their earthy tombs.

Then, a mighty whooshing sent them hurtling towards the coastline and the open sea. The water was being sucked out again, vacuumed back toward the immense, wet wilderness. Out in the deep, another earthquake had erupted.

In the spinning confusion, Gamboa and the Temple Frog Priests were at once thrilled, yet dazed, by the turmoil. Powerless in the face of the currents, they were swept out miles into the ocean. The frogs stood no chance against the supremacy of the open waters and tossed about like matchwood. Helpless against the tide, Gamboa and the other frogs desperately sought refuge by clinging to an uprooted tree as it pitched in the cresting waves.

New ocean rollers now began to take over the receding wall, and the frogs found themselves totally lost, as land first held a spot on the distant horizon, then disappeared as they dipped down into the wallowing troughs. Latched on to the trunk, the Priests danced a perilous waltz. The merry-go-round of water swirled, then heaved and peaked, then lulled and gurgled, and spun them through a thick mist of cold, salty spray.

And it was at the base of one of these dizzying helter-skelters that the frogs felt a fresh surge of power, an energy driving them upwards, above the gravitational pull of the trough. They were lifted, tree and all, a commanding motion driving them away from the crashing waters, towards the steadily rolling waves and the open ocean. Gamboa, gulping down life-saving chunks of superbly clear air, sat heaving, mindful, wary of the change. He stiffened, motionless. They were moving not *with* the water, but *across* it, and they were, incredibly as it seemed, being transported independently of any tide or current.

How can this be? he thought to himself. He was about to call out to the others when, from the alcoves of his sleepy memory, he recalled the maritime legends of his people. He remembered how the old fishermen talked of the mysteries of the sea, and how, in times of trouble, maids of the ocean and dolphins, even whales, had come to the rescue of men lost in peril. As a child, he had sat around camp fires, listening to men speaking of great storms and thunderous tempests and how, out of the darkest, most treacherous of seas, there came to their rescue creatures who carried them to the safety of calm waters. Although he had never seen these creatures for himself, he knew they were there, and he believed in their powers. Indeed, there were many great carvings and illustrations of these creatures on the Temples and palaces of the city.

Now, as he hung tightly to the tree trunk, he was fully aware that he and his fellow Priests, were being carried by a magical, unknown force, carefully sweeping them along, across the water. He was in awe of the

131

mighty power of the sea, but found himself confident that all would now be well.

Deep inside him the tension burst, and in the unexpected calm of the ocean, he raised his head to the heavens, closed his aching eyes and praised and thanked his God, *Wo-sak*, that he had been saved. His countenance a euphoric etching of triumph, he croaked and growled, spat and crackled, cleared his throat and found his voice. He howled in relief, exalting the one true God who had delivered him to safety. His soul was on fire.

The stars twinkled overhead, and the heavens beckoned. A whiplash of asteroids flashed earthbound and the massive carousel of undulating ocean reflected the cosmic Gods' silver light. No clouds clouded the sky. No evidence of mankind littered the water or air. This was the world at its most wonderful.

There was no sound save for the regular lashing of water as their gentle up and down and up and down glided them eastwards.

The exhausted frogs, mesmerized by the rocking-horse motion, were lulled into a happy, bottomless dream world. One or two snored or moaned in their sleep, but all rested, slumbering, spent after their tumultuous day.

The ancient Temple Priests had all carved themselves into small frogs and been buried alive. The stress on their bodies had been enormous. But they had survived, thus far. Who knew what lay ahead? What dangers? What chaos or new hope? But for the moment they were safe, and they had Gamboa to thank. He had saved them all. It was his inspiration that had salvaged the ragged remains of their civilization, and they were all grateful. Gamboa was their true, living God on Earth, and they would remain faithful to him, forever.

*

As leader, Gamboa took his responsibilities most seriously and as the others slept, he sat reflecting, legs tucked under his now small, neat body. What an incredible day it had been. After all this time, to be hurled into the present and saved by such a mighty force. It didn't bear scrutiny, for if he analyzed it too much, then he would not believe it, and think the whole thing a dream. Here he was in the middle of the ocean, no idea what the future held, nor where he was going. A grin creased his lips.

"Smiling?"

Gamboa started. "What?"

"Smiling. You're smiling."

"Oh yes," he said. "Smiling." He laughed.

He'd been joined by the only true friend he'd ever had. Jaxxa, a fellow Temple Priest, made himself comfortable.

"Something funny?" he asked.

"No, not really. Well, actually," he continued after a second or two, "only the whole thing."

"Yes. It's a lot to get your head round."

"Hmm."

"Can't sleep?" asked Jaxxa.

"No. Brain won't stop. You know how it is."

"Oh yes. I know."

They both breathed quietly and neither spoke for a minute. The water lapped and the balmy air caressed their tired bodies.

"You did it," said Jaxxa.

"Hmm."

"You did it. Without you, we would all be dead."

"Not me. The Gods," said Gamboa. "Wo-sak. He did it, not me."

"But it was you who put His plan into action. You, Gamboa, you."

Gamboa said nothing but stared out across the water. Jaxxa knew his leader to be a modest man, and so didn't push it any further. Then he, too, gazed at the horizon and considered what might lie ahead.

"Scary isn't it."

"Yes," said Gamboa. "It is a bit."

He didn't waver in his inspection of the water and with his following words took Jaxxa by surprise.

"Do you miss your family?"

This knocked Jaxxa off balance. Gamboa knew he had no family. Why would he ask such a question?

"My family?"

"Yes. Your family."

"Don't really think about it much."

"You should," said Gamboa.

Jaxxa had never spoken to Gamboa about his family. All the years they had known each other, the silent code between them which dictated that family matters were not up for discussion, had never been broken. He didn't really know what to say.

Jaxxa knew that Gamboa had lost his mother and father many, many centuries ago, and, of course, he also knew about his wife and child. They had never talked about it, and he was wondering where this conversation was really headed.

"Tell me about your sister," said Gamboa.

Jaxxa now felt very uncomfortable. He didn't usually speak about his sister, and over the years she had become a silent memory, a closed tomb he never opened in public.

"My sister?" he asked, taken aback.

"Yes, your sister. Tell me about her."

"Well," exhaled Jaxxa, not really knowing where to start "she was my sister. That's it."

"No it isn't. You know it isn't," replied Gamboa. "You never talk about her. Tell me."

"Not much to tell, really," Jaxxa offered guardedly.

"Don't be so defensive Jaxxa. Here we are in the middle of the ocean. We don't know where we're going, or even if we'll survive. Tell me about your sister. I want to know."

Jaxxa took a gulp of air. "Well . . . if you insist."

Gamboa smiled encouragingly. "Yes, I insist."

135

A sharp, strong breeze coursed across the vast, open space of the ocean, and Jaxxa shivered a little as he began to tell the story.

Withdrawing into himself, his discomfort hard to disguise, he recalled the terrible night years ago when, in a rage, his father had dragged his mother to the top of the Temple steps and killed her. He stopped. He relived his mother's dreadful pain as she was hauled up the steps, and the awful sight of her petrified face tumbling down from on high as Jaxxa, a little boy, watched in horror. Then he told Gamboa how his mother, in a vision, had visited him, urging him to kill his father in revenge.

"I can see why you haven't talked about it," said Gamboa.

"Yes, it's not easy," replied Jaxxa.

They looked out over the undulating water, each lost in his own thoughts.

Then Gamboa asked gently, "What happened to your sister?"

After the slightest of pauses, Jaxxa said, "I'm not really sure."

Gamboa looked at his friend.

"What d'you mean?"

Jaxxa returned the gaze, but said nothing.

"What happened, Jaxxa? Finish the story. What happened?"

With that, Jaxxa turned back to the sea, fixed on a point far away and carried on.

136

"She died. Or at least, I think she died. I'm not really sure." He paused. "She was lovely." He smiled with the memories. "She was great. A great, lovely little sister. Everybody adored her. She was just like mother; had her eyes, her hair and her smile. She was mother's child, not father's. She had nothing of him."

He gathered his thoughts. He described how, one summer solstice long ago, he and his sister had been to the Temple to celebrate, and how, that evening, their mother's restless spirit had visited, urging him to kill their father.

He went on to tell Gamboa of the terrible revenge slaying, the pride he had felt at carrying out his mother's biding, and how he had felt the power of the tribe and the spirit of *Wo-sak* surging through his veins. He held his head high, and Jaxxa narrowed his eyes in the ocean currents as he told his story.

He paused.

Gamboa could tell there was something else, some untold truth he was holding back.

"And your sister?" he asked.

Jaxxa sighed. Pain flitted across his face and left a patina of regret and shame.

"I didn't mean to do it," he said. "I didn't mean to hit her so hard. It was just instinct. She was in the way, and my mother was shouting at me to kill him. What could I do? I just had to kill him. And my sister got in the way. She just got in the way. What could I do?"

He stopped again.

Gamboa said gently, "You killed her?"

"No, not really. Well, maybe. Perhaps . . . It was a few days later. She'd been sick and resting in bed. She was very quiet; hardly spoke a word for days. A neighbour came in and helped out, but largely I was on my own with her."

He stopped, lost in his private thoughts. Gamboa left the silence alone, allowing Jaxxa time to control his emotions.

"Did she try to stop you?"

"What?"

"Your sister. Did she try to stop you?" Gamboa repeated.

Jaxxa drew the biggest breath of his life.

"That's something I've never understood. I don't even know what she was doing there in the first place."

He looked directly at Gamboa.

"Why was she in our father's bed? What was she doing there?" He shook his head. "I'll never understand."

"You don't have to," explained Gamboa. "You don't have to know everything. Some things are . . . well, they just *are*, and you leave them alone."

Jaxxa's lips tightened in a stiff line. "Maybe. Maybe," he said.

Silence sat between them but there was a shared intimacy drawing them closer.

"So?" said Gamboa.

"So what?"

"What happened?"

"Ah. Well . . ." Jaxxa drifted again and Gamboa could see that this was difficult for this friend, but he didn't interrupt.

"She died. In the end. Or at least I *think* so. I'm not really sure. See, the thing is, she just disappeared. I don't how or why. One minute she was there, and the next she was gone. Gone. Just gone."

Gamboa frowned, but offered nothing.

Jaxxa continued. "There was a fire, you see. The house caught fire. I never found out the cause but it burned down, the house and everything in it. Everything." He stopped, not for effect but in pain at the memory. "She was still in the house, my sister. I'd been out. It was late morning and I was coming back when I heard shouts, then I saw the smoke. I ran as fast as I could. People were running around in circles trying to put out the fire, but it was no good. The place was an inferno. I made for the door but neighbours held me back. I screamed for my sister but it was useless. Nothing could have lived through that."

Just then a meteor shower rained down, and they both raised their heads.

"The Gods are listening," said Gamboa.

"Hmm," was all Jaxxa could manage. He carried on. "We all watched as the fire raged. We managed to stop it spreading but our house was burnt to the ground, gutted, just charcoal embers. Eventually, I made my way through the debris. I expected to find something grotesque. But after a time sorting through the ashes, I realized that there was no body. No remains. Nothing."

He looked at his friend.

139

"There was no body, Gamboa. Nothing. No evidence of any kind that she'd been there. At first I was elated, and thought she'd escaped. I looked everywhere, scoured the city, but no one had seen her. There was no trace of her anywhere. She'd disappeared, vanished. It was as if she'd never existed. No body. Nothing. How could that be?"

Gamboa nodded, but offered no words of comfort or understanding. What could he say?

"How can there be no body?" asked Jaxxa.

Gamboa had no answers. But as he looked deep into his friend's eyes he saw the truth, the *real* truth; the truth that Jaxxa could never tell. He saw the knife and the long black hair, and the young girl's soft, silky skin. He saw her pain, the anguish and despair, her empty eyes as she raised the knife to her throat and cut the long fatal gash across her neck. She dug deep, as far as her strength would allow. Then she lay back on the bed and bled and bled . . . to death. The blood ran, a heavy river spreading over the pillow and onto the thin sheets where lay her brother, sleeping soundly by her side. She trembled and shook one last earthly gesture, then vanished. Disappeared. Gone forever.

For a long time, they stayed looking out over the water. Finally, the silence was broken.

"I know," said Gamboa. "I know. I understand. It's alright. It's alright now." And he put a comforting arm about his friend's shoulder.

*

140

Days, then weeks passed. They were desperately hungry, but every now and then a wayward fish would flop and flap itself onto the log, and the frogs would pounce on it and feed themselves full on its flesh. At other times, lost swarms of insects zoomed close to the tree trunk and the frogs flashed their tongues, picking off the stragglers. And, gradually, they began to feel the cold. Yes, it was getting colder. And the days shorter.

Of course, Gamboa had often pondered the big issues of the universe, and night after night, as he stared at the stars, he recalled the time many, many years ago he had met the old man and his one-eyed dog. *Where are you now?* he thought to himself. *Where are you, old man?*

Invariably, a shooting star exploded across the sky dragging Gamboa's attention with it. And in those glorious astrological moments, he realized that he was not alone, he was never alone, and never would be. He was the Chosen One and he, and only he, would lead his people to safety; whether the days were colder or shorter, made no difference to his pilgrimage of hope and salvation. They had survived the great drought, the Great Grey and now he would survive this. He was the Chosen One and he would survive. Oh yes, he, Gamboa of the mighty Suxx, would survive.

*

Just as the water had resurrected the frogs from their parched burial ground, so it lifted and carried away a rather ornate, old box which had been left, abandoned. Fierce waves launched it out to sea, the frothy breakers

141

rushing it in sporadic bursts of speed over the crests of white-capped rollers. As it ventured further and further out into the ocean, the water gradually became colder and colder. The days grew shorter as the temperature dropped. Inside the object, however, the sun rose as usual, and the sky persisted in its purple haze. The orange and ochre hues, turning inky blue as the golden sun set, cast an acid stain from one horizon to the other, and the occupants knew nothing of where they were, or what the watery world outside had in store for them.

For several months they bobbed along with storms coming and going, interspersed with calm days, when nothing seemed to be happening at all. A lone albatross, way off course, once landed for a rest then took off again. But other than this, the days passed without incident.

Eventually, the box came to a standstill, thuddering gently as it hit land. It wedged itself into a knob of beach on a sandy cove, and gradually made a home for itself deep in the pebbly sand. Inside, the flamingoes and frogs had no idea where they were, but there they lived, for years and years in peace and tranquility, almost forever and forever. Except that they had no notion of forever, and so each day they simply passed the time of day passing the time of day.

*

They had been travelling for several weeks now, and when the intrepid frogs spotted the corrugated coastline, icicling its way out of the moist horizon, they gathered at the front of the trunk to see the Promised

Land. Pulses quickened, and they leaned all over each other trying to get a better view.

"Looks grey," said one.

"And wet," said another.

"Cold," chimed in several together.

Cold, wet and grey. The frogs weren't impressed. They were, however, glad to see landfall after so many weeks at sea. But just as they were resigning themselves to docking on the miserable looking landscape, the trunk took a sharp left and carved a trough parallel to the shoreline. They travelled north, until a strong current took them east again. Then strong winds turned them right, and they hugged a misty coastline in a southerly direction.

At times losing sight of land, the frogs were alternatively afraid, then heartened, as a rugged shoreline would ghost into view through thick, wet fog. For several days they drifted, enduring choppy seas, but managing to avoid angry gales and storms. Eventually, they caught site of a flat, yellowish-brown beach. After so many weeks bobbing up and down on fathomless waters, they were most keen to set foot on land. But it was a false dawn, as onward they journeyed, still ploughing into the unknown, the wind taking them now closer, now further away, from the shore.

Then, quite alarmingly, they felt a surge of water beneath them. They had been caught by a tidal wave, a rush of drilling water going home. Riding high on the bore, they feared they might be heading to the edge of the world and held on tight, expecting a mega-drop into a big black hole. Before they knew it, however, the frogs were passing two flat headlands on their way inland. Now, their fears were somewhat assuaged by the sight of marshland and slowly undulating fields. Copse after copse of tree outcrops littered the skyline, and wild, pink and pale blue flowers, poked out their delicate heads from thick tufts of bushes and prickly thorn hedge. The frogs stared in great excitement as they sucked in freshwater air. Looking down into the river, they could see loads of fish and the thought of a meal not soaked in sea salt brought juices to their tiny mouths.

Then, with a pitched lurch and shocking jolt, the tree suddenly veered right, heading straight for the shore. The frogs gripped tightly, knowing that they were in for a rough landing. Just how rough they had no idea, as, waiting for them, was a mud trap, a huge hole in the riverbed where it met the shoreline. And it was into this that the little frogs were violently hurled as the tree hit a jagged rock. It bounced way up into the air and landed in the gaping cavity as the swirling water, first drowning the space, then sucking itself out, left the frogs exposed to the world. They yelled and screamed in panic and dread. And they stretched and strained their sticky fingers and toes in pathetic efforts to stay afloat on the log. But it was no use. They were powerless in the face of nature. Flung, lobbed into the air, the frogs rained down in vomiting blobs of despair, and plopped and spattered into the void of the riverbed.

Next, with an almighty slap and slobber, a gargantuan flap of brackish mud poured in over them, a wet, cement grave. A grave so deep, so thickly glued and buttressed against the world that it formed a prison, a tomb from which they could not flee.

Submerged under massive dollops of grey mud-slime, the little frogs had no chance of escape, and they gasped as the grim reality hit them. They had been buried alive - again.

And it was here they stayed for hundreds of years, once more sleeping, hibernating, unconsciously waiting for the right time to rise. To rise and rule the world.

Awakenings

Years passed. Decades. Then centuries and millennia. The frogs slept on, encased in their muddy grave.

After their mega-oceanic crossing they were exhausted, and simply did not have the strength to fight back. They slumbered on in unconscious hibernation, unaware of the passage of time and the events unfolding above their heads.

They missed wolves, bears, the animism of pre-civilization.

They missed the ancient Britons, their dead language and paganism.

They missed stone circles, the Druids and Stonehenge.

They missed the Romans, the invasion and the rise of London.

They missed Boadicea, the uprising and defiant sacrifice.

They missed the Saxons and their banditry.

They missed the Vikings, the new names for the days of the week.

They missed the Normans and a new language.

They missed the Tudors, the Stewarts, the uprisings and repressions, civil war, the religious rancor and the deadly, deadly, Black Death.

They missed wars, more wars, and even more wars. And they missed the Renaissance, the Enlightenment, and the explosion of science.

The circumnavigation of the world, and the intrepid golden age of discovery, all passed into history whilst the frogs lay dreamless beneath the earth.

Slavery, greed and guilt passed unnoticed.

Chaucer, Shakespeare, and even Newton, all came and went without so much as a nod from the frogs.

They missed global expansion and the big bang British Empire, the beginnings of the industrial revolution and the ascent of London as the world's financial powerhouse.

They missed it all in their wet darkness.

In ignorance and peace, the frogs slept. And could have gone on sleeping forever. Except that one summer, one earth-shattering summer, with the warhorse in decline, motorized destruction a short train ride away, mechanical flight threatening to take off and great big metal tubs traversing the world's oceans, everything changed, forever.

*

In late August 1883, London stewed in its usual pollution. The Thames, filled with its regular quota of filth, flowed, as ever, towards the Essex coast, the river's estuary and the North Sea beyond. And the frogs, unaware of life overhead, slept the sleep of the dead, the river watering their sloppy grave. Their solitude, however, was, one night, violently disturbed, as yet again their lives were rocked by traumatic, uncontrollable natural events. The silence of their mud and silt tomb was jolted into life by a thundering tremor. A tremor so profound, it shifted the whole marshland at the edges of the river. It tilted the banks, so that water gushed one way then another as gravity itself vacillated, not between the heavens and the core of the earth, but somewhere at a lateral angle, sending everything haywire on a dizzy merry-go-round of chaos.

Nature, for a brief moment, stood still, contemplating the shift in the great order of things, then shook, with a ferocity previously unknown to man. The world echoed of its primitive origins. The raw power of the earth, forever instrumental in its very creation, once again displayed its all-conquering ability to destroy what it had crafted in the first place. Dull reverberations were replaced by jolts and mighty bangs. Memories of distant rumbles became real events of fear, as the earth decided to expunge itself of its collected gore. In one, violent explosion, the most violent detonation ever recorded in human history, the planet screamed out its anger and blew its roof apart. The Indonesian island of Krakatoa, off the coasts of Java and Sumatra, was chosen as the vent for the livid expression of the earth's fury. On 27th August there was a titanic explosion heard 3,000 miles away in the Indian Ocean. Thirty-metre-high tsunamis were witnessed, and over 36,000 people died. Millions of tons of sulfur were released into the atmosphere, and there followed a calamitous volcanic winter, which reduced world temperatures for five years. Clouds of

148

pumice and volcanic ash rocketed from the site, the effects of the blast being felt worldwide.

As the explosive shockwave quickly gathered pace, its power began rooting underground around the earth. It passed through the Indian Ocean, up to the deserts of the Middle East and across Europe. It traversed the empty spaces of the Atlantic. It thundered across the North American continent, the Pacific, through Asia and back again to its origin on the other side of the world. Then on, again, and again in an endless circumnavigation of destruction.

The earth *did* move. And the frogs *did* awaken. And they stirred with trepidation. *What was happening? Where were they? How did they get here?*

As the mud slid, slithering beneath and around them, these and other questions rattled through their heads in the darkness. Then, as the full weight of the massive explosion rocked the planet, they were lifted, in one almighty upward thunderbolt, out of the solitude of centuries and into the new world. They gasped, and heaved huge piles of fresh air, and their barren lungs did cartwheels of joyous celebration as they inhaled, for the first time in centuries, the air of the sentient world. Shaking off the sloth of inactivity, they motored their limbs as they realized that they had little time before the mud came crashing down on them, and they would be lost again - perhaps forever.

They leapt and jumped to their freedom, and headed for the only thing they recognized in the strange new territory into which they had been vomited: the green of the riverside grasses. Desperately grabbing onto whatever they could, they fought for their lives as their world hiccupped, lurched and slopped about, rendering them drunk on the banks of the rushing Thames.

149

Gamboa found his voice and screamed at the others.

"This way! Over here!! This way!!!"

The frogs heard him, then saw what he was pointing at. They followed, leaped high into the air and with terrified expressions focused on a landing place. A rock, lodged in the riverbank, stood proud of the mud, a beacon of hope, survival, if they could but reach it.

As the mud swilled, each frog fought for his life. But one of them, smaller and perhaps not quite so strong, misjudged his jump and landed, splat, in the brown cement-like mire. He yelled piteously, his arms and legs working overtime, the pull of the water sucking him into the slime. He was being dragged under, and the frogs watched in silent horror, as the gluttonous mud swallowed him whole. Gamboa, heedless of his own safety, took a massive gulp of air and dived back into the morass.

"Don't!" the others screamed. "It's no good. You'll die."

Too late, Gamboa was gone, and he too, dissolved under the gooey mass.

"He'll die," one screamed.

"Gamboa," they cried. "Gamboa."

But he was gone, vanished under the gluey torrent. The water rushed in and the mud lay invisible under the tidal wave.

"Gamboa. Gamboa," they screamed at the top of their voices. But it was futile.

The little frogs, frantic for safety, turned away and slogged doggedly inland. They knew it was no use.

150

Gamboa was gone. The force of the mud and water was too strong even for their fearless leader. The fabulous Gamboa of the Suxx empire was gone. In a final heroic act, he'd been devoured by an ignoble, viscous brown slush.

No time to mourn, the frogs crawled away from the water's edge. They shivered in grief and despair. No-one spoke. After all they'd been through, Gamboa was gone. Gone.

A voice piped up.

"We better make a move. It's dangerous here."

They all agreed. Not one ventured to offer up a rescue plan. It was useless. Even Jaxxa realized just what a hopeless case it was.

"Come on," he said. "Let's go."

They turned away, each one deep in thought. It was over. The new life promised by their Chief Temple Priest would have to be discovered without him.

A roaring wind blew the grasses horizontal. Thick, heavy clouds pressed down on the sad troupe of frogs as they tripped over clods and roots. Then, out of the deathly chaos and mournful grey, they heard the faintest echo of a voice they all recognized.

"Help."

It was Gamboa. He had caught hold of the ailing lost frog, and was trying with every ounce of strength he had to drag him to the safety of the rock.

"Help!" he shouted again. After centuries locked underground, he was weak and losing the battle.

The frogs raced back. In a flash, Jaxxa leaped to his friend's aid, diving into the waters. He grabbed hold of Gamboa's arm, kicking and pulling in a valiant effort to reach the rock. Grit and sand blinded him but he instinctively pulled for the shore, towing with all his might. The frogs heaved and pushed against the current, and then with one, final, colossal effort, all three lurched to the safety of the protruding stone. But it wasn't over yet. A great wave came crashing down on them. They held on fast, and, as the water subsided with the whoosh of the tide, the trio of frogs saw their opportunity and leaped to the riverbank. Gasping for breath, they crawled toward the other frogs and were met with the knowing smiles of a great victory. They'd made it.

They did not know it, of course, but they had been asleep for centuries and they had awoken in a brand new world. A world of which they had no knowledge, and even less understanding. It was nineteenth century England, and the late dawn of scientific discovery. It was going to be tough. Very tough!

*

With Gamboa at their head, the frogs set off across the marshy ground. They had no idea where they were and no idea where they were headed, but reflex led them away from the fast flowing river inland, towards a clump of trees and bushes, which seemed to offer some protection.

Although it was August, the frogs felt the cold of a north European summer, and despite their years underground, their human instinct kicked in, and they shivered in the cooling breezes. But that was the least of their troubles. It was to get even colder as the volcanic winter set in. The Krakatoa explosion triggered a universal drop in temperatures, and clouds of sulfur, and ash and pumice, floated around the atmosphere for several years. The planet was wounded and the frogs were none-the-wiser as to how, or why, this was happening.

For the moment, they plodded on and every now and then they came across pools of water, at which they stopped and drank.

"At least we won't die of thirst," said one.

"No," said another as he took great swigs from the pond. "Not much chance of that here."

Gamboa was listening closely, and thought quietly that his decision had been right. The dreadful option of carving themselves into frogs had worked. But then again, he considered, why should it *not* have worked, he was, after all, Chief Temple Frog Priest, and he did have a direct link with the Gods. He had been inspired and here they all were, living proof of his divine right to rule and lead what was left of his people.

"No. We will never thirst here," he said, raising his head from the water. "This is the Promised Land." And he looked at the others, who exchanged glances, then raised their heads to the heavens and offered up thanks to the great *Wo-sak*.

"We will never thirst again," said Gamboa.

He paused, looking at the remains of his empire.

"Come," he said kindly "let us explore this new land. Let us find a new home."

And off they set, together, in search of food and shelter, and a new beginning.

*

Gamboa led his people towards what he hoped would be safety and the relative peace of a new, foreign land. They were alive and they had been given a second chance. They were grateful, and so rested in the knowledge that, for the moment, all was well in the world. They found they could eat and drink, and generally feel comfortable, even though it was a little cold for their liking.

Of course, being frogs, their food options were limited to what they could find in the marshland's waterlogged ditches and ponds. As small amphibians, they could eat varieties of meat, but initially chose to stick to insects. There were lots of these, and they feasted as they made their way through the grasses, flashing their tongues here and there at the flying, buzzing things, which they didn't recognize but guessed, rightly, to be frog food.

Their curiosity was not tempted by the flowing river, nor the distant sounds of habitation they could hear far, far away; strange sounds as of grinding rocks and great hurly burly, a chaos not of their own world, but alien, and not altogether welcoming.

They nervously clung together in their novel world, taking-in the environment and what it had to offer. There was shelter from the wind, and the rain didn't bother them too much, but after a while they noticed a strange darkness converging on their new home. Dusky, grey-white clouds, rolled in from the east, and they noticed that it was becoming difficult to breath. Then, gradually, the earth became covered in light sheets of grey ash. The fallout had arrived.

After the blast from the volcano, clouds of ash winged their way across the globe, arriving even in the south east of England. For as far as the eye could see, the land was white and grey, and the frogs wondered what they were in for. Only Gamboa understood what it was, or at least, wasn't afraid of it. For he had seen this many, many years ago, when the old man, his dog and a box had arrived in the village of Suxx. He snatched his breath and gasped, *The box. Oh, the box.*

Instantly his head ached at the thought of it. The box. Where was the box? What had become of it? In the chaos and despair of the final moments, he had left it behind. It was an easy decision, as he had no idea how he was going to transport it, so had left it, sitting forlorn by the well. There was nothing else he could have done. The box. The frogs. The whole universe enclosed in that small space. All gone.

He felt guilty. But what could he have done? How was he supposed to carry a box that size on his small frog back? That was impossible. No, he had done the only thing he could have done, leave the box behind. There had been no choice. He sighed and swallowed, hard. The tension between his shoulders eased slightly and it was with mixed feelings of melancholy and joy that he smiled to himself as, traveling back in time, he remembered the first fabulous moment of discovery, his initial glimpse into the new, unbelievable universe inside the old man's gift. Wow . . . it was wonderful. A whole new world. And the frogs. The frogs were magnificent. He'd never seen anything like them. How they glowed and shimmered, almost translucent in the golden light of the box. It was a miracle. A miracle he'd left behind.

Regret gave way to resignation, and, with it, he accepted the sadness of a great loss. It had gone. It was too late. He could do nothing about it. There was no need to dwell on what he couldn't change. It was over. He would just have to live with it.

He looked up at the cement sky and the falling ash, and recalled the Great Grey and the death associated with it. It seemed as if a cycle was repeating itself, a universal cycle of events which he didn't fully understand. All he knew was that this new land was not entirely different from the old one, as it too suffered from the same Great Grey.

The sun, in a losing battle, tried its best to shine through a haze of cloudy dust, and Gamboa, now in a moment of quiet reflection, thought back to his childhood. *The Great Grey,* he thought to himself. *Yes, I remember that. The Great Grey.* A sense of sad, yet satisfied nostalgia overcame him, and his mind went centuries back to his infancy, his lost parents, his role in the history of his people and how he had been instrumental in the fostering of sacrifice. Had he really done all that, all those years ago?

He laughed quizzically. How had he lived for so long? It was then that he remembered the vial. The vial. Where *was* the vial? He had tied it around his waist when he buried himself underground, but it was nowhere to be seen now. Where was it? It must have come off during the escape from the mud. He had to find it.

"I must go back and find it," he said.

It took only a flash of instinct to retrace his steps as he set off towards the river. Threading his way over clumps of grass and around pools of dark water, he eventually came to the river's edge. The tide was out. He scoured the shoreline where they had landed, and found the now totally exposed, lifesaving rock.

He was incredibly lucky for there, next to it, sticking up out of the mucky sand was the thong, the leather strap he used to tie the vial to his waist. He hopped down and gave it a tug. It was stuck. He tugged harder, and up came the vial, still attached. The vial. It had been the vial that had kept him alive for thousands of years, its elixir connecting him to the divine Gods, separating him from the mortality of the other Priests who, unlike Gamboa, were trapped in their temporal bodies. Although worshipped as demi-Gods on earth, the other Temple Priests were not eternal, and without the vial, Gamboa would eventually die, just like them.

Thank God he'd found it. But, as he looked at it, to his utter horror, he saw that the top had come undone. As eternal as its contents were, the liquid could surely never have survived in the mud and water? He raised it to his lips, his mouth. Nothing. The priceless elixir had spilled out, lost forever. It was useless. All gone. Empty. Gone forever.

"No," he shouted at the heavens. "No."

He was furious with himself. How could he have been so stupid? He needed the vial. It was his link, the connection with the Frog Gods and *Wo-sak*. How was he going to survive without it? He screamed at the ebbing water's indifference and cursed as he'd never cursed before. He hurled the vial far into the river and clenched his fists, damning himself for his stupidity.

"What am I going to do?" he cried. "What *am* I going to do?"

He stood silently in the gloom of the fading grey sun, and dusk began to set-in proper. His heart was heavy. After the euphoria of the rescue and leading his fellow Priests to safety, he now felt the weight of the world about his shoulders. He had lost the one thing above all that he needed to survive. First the box, and now this. He shook his head in despair. How was he going to survive?

His stomach churned, twisted with anger and frustration, and he challenged the sky to fall further, to finish him off. A distant rumble flattered in reply.

At that moment, an ink-black raven passed overhead. It circled once and swooped down to land on the isolated rock. It cocked its head to one side, then the other. Then it blinked. The raven looked at Gamboa. Gamboa looked at the raven. It squawked its distinctive squawk and then incredibly, as another far away rumble fractured the silence, it turned into a blindingly magnificent rainbow bird.

Gamboa squinted, shielding his eyes. Then miraculously, he felt the secret recesses of his head opening as, to his astonishment, the bird spoke.

"Utopium, Limehouse. Ask for the Wolfman."

"What?" said Gamboa, taken aback.

"You heard," said the bird. "Utopium, at Limehouse. Ask for the Wolfman," and with a squealing cry, it flew up into the gathering darkness heading east, towards the gloomy estuary beyond the horizon.

"What do you mean?" shouted Gamboa. "What do you mean?"

But the rainbow bird was now as black as night, and gone.

What did it mean, Utopium, at Limehouse? What did it mean? Gamboa stood, perplexed. *And the Wolfman? Who's the Wolfman?*

He waited a moment or two, then turned away from the river. He headed back to where the other frogs were now settling down for the night.

What did it mean? Gamboa was not unintelligent, but he simply didn't understand. Limehouse? Wolfman? Just what on earth was that supposed to mean?

"What's that all about?" he asked himself out loud. But, of course, he had no answers.

*

Days passed. After their initial excitement at having been reborn into a new world, the frogs quickly began to despair as the food lost its attraction. Although relatively easy to catch, insects and water-borne prey tasted horrible, and the frogs also discovered that the water they were drinking was not actually fresh. At first, after the centuries underground, any food and water was welcome, but now, having found their feet, they realized that what they were eating and drinking was, in fact, disgusting. Within a short time, they all fell sick, vomiting and suffering incredible stomach cramps, swollen tummies and the most awful headaches. The source of their discomfiture was not hard to explain: they had, of course, been partaking of the products of the most polluted river on the entire planet, the late nineteenth century River Thames.

159

The Idyll

The Essex Marshes, to the east of London, were a safe haven from the bedlam of the sprawling city with its gangs of violent thieves, pimps, gin houses and opium dens. In fact, one could say that, so close to a huge metropolis like London, the Essex Marshes were a miracle of nature. True, the great Thames waterway usually hummed with the to-ing and fro-ing of barges and cargo ships bound for all corners of the world, but the marshes, set back from the main watery thoroughfare, were generally of a quieter solitude. A sanctuary for wading birds, small amphibious reptiles and mammals of many kinds, wildlife thrived in these more often than not waterlogged flatlands, where most humans, uninvited by nature, seldom ventured.

But that is not to say that the area was uninhabited. There were many small settlements, and at that time of great social and economic upheaval, the towns and hamlets of Essex proved most resilient. One such village was that of Mucking. This community of hardy individuals, occupying land long ago invaded and occupied by Saxons, in what may mistakenly be described as the dark ages, lies to the east of Tilbury, on the northern banks of the Thames. It is a place of strategical significance, sitting as it does at the mouth of the river's estuary, in close proximity to the maritime highway connecting London with, at that time, the British empire. Over the years, many a weary sailor was grateful to see the yellow beams of Mucking's coastal lighthouse, welcoming him home to safety and loved ones after an epic, universal journey. It was, indeed, a busy place in the mid-nineteenth century and the people of Mucking, affectionately known as Muckers, enjoyed a hardworking, quite carefree, if not altogether luxurious, existence. Barges plied the shallow shore-side waters, whilst at high tide, huge ocean-going ships majestically made their way up river towards the docks and warehouses of the East India Company. Mucking's small, mediaeval church, surrounded by shops and houses, gave the appearance of some serenity, and locals, working in various trades and crafts, made sure of the upkeep of their village. The neat, church graveyard was hardly overflowing with tombstones, and a healthy, if somewhat guarded religious outlook shrouded the hamlet in pious protection.

Life for Muckers wasn't easy, but artisans and agricultural labourers were hardworking, and did more than simply scratch out a living. They worked the land as best they could, and produced goods and services worthy of a much larger, perhaps more advanced, community.

But not all Muckers enjoyed prosperity, however meager. There were those for whom survival meant fishing, and catching eels, and trundling down to Mucking Mud Flats, a short walk eastwards, grubbing for shellfish at low tide. Life for these Muckers was indeed a struggle. Living abreast of the marshes however, was certainly better than slavishly wasting away in a factory, or begging on the streets in the grime and filth of a rapidly industrializing London. And besides, the local community pulled through in times of shortage, and there was a heartfelt spirit of camaraderie in the village.

The marshes were a thing of beauty really, and many an artist had been drawn there to paint and lay down for posterity the peaceful embrace of where the fresh water Thames meets the salty North Sea. The solitude and attraction were, though, one summer's night, shattered, as an event of singular supernatural dimensions produced a chain of events that would change things forever. The lines separating the real, factual world of the century's scientific revolution, were about to be blurred, and fractured, as natural selection itself took on a frightening detour on its everlasting journey.

Things were about to change forever, not only in Essex, but London and the whole of the western world.

Pollution

At that time, things were afoot of which the frogs were completely unaware: physiological changes taking place that the frogs wouldn't even understand. Living where they did, on the edge of a great industrializing metropolis in nineteenth century Europe, they were ignorant of how their habitat was undergoing such rapid, uncontrolled change. On a daily basis, factories and mines, and great urban sprawls, were pouring gallons and gallons and gallons of sewage, industrial waste and domestic refuse, into the very water system, which, since Roman times, had been the life-blood of the city. Gases, grease and oil, toxic sulfur, zinc and mercury and just about every harmful product known to man, were literally being dumped into London's waterways. These pollutants had no trouble finding their way into the drinking water, before finally ending up in the North Sea. But on their eastward journey, the contaminants also did an excellent job of poisoning the Essex Marshes, and all the wetland habitats on which wildlife, in and around the River Thames, depended.

One particular factory on the banks of the river, at Greenwich, was even producing explosives of such a deadly nature that one day, the whole place simply self-combusted, blew up and destroyed the area for miles around. This sent millions of particles into the water, and killed off whatever remaining fish populations there were in that part of the river. Blast furnaces and smelting works all deposited waste into the waterway while humans, too late before common sense kicked in, sent huge barges of excrement up-stream to fertilize the very crops they were later to eat. The river was a dying, open sewer and where salmon, trout and the tiny fresh-water stickleback use to thrive, now there was only a stenching sludge, which not even the daily tide could wash away. In their pursuit of wealth through industrialization, Londoners were slowly killing their own city. The smell was horrendous, and only those fortunate enough to have the wherewithal to escape, did so.

Although diluted a little, by the time the polluted water found its way to the marshlands of the Thames estuary, it was acrid poison to the frogs. Originally feasting on insects, a number of more adventurous frogs had quickly graduated to eating grubs and newts. One or two had been catching small snakes and bite-sized rodents, and generally they had all advanced to a carnivorous diet, which included smaller amphibians or even larger prey.

However, because of the effluence and the poisonous toxins in the water, the frogs now found themselves in a desperate situation, for when they did catch an insect, corner a water vole, small rat or some such game, the meat was horribly infected and tasted vile. There was simply not enough fresh food for them. They were starving.

It was this crisis that triggered a deep-rooted survival instinct, harkening back to the days of their ancient civilization. They needed blood, this time not just in sacrifice, but also as a lifeline, an elixir. They needed an infusion of plasma to heal their sickly bodies. Deep down in their psyche, lay the magical wonderland and intellect of the frog kingdom, which they, as humans transformed into amphibians, could now tap in to. Thinking both as frogs, and human beings, they realized

165

that they not only needed a good source of nutritious food but, far more importantly, fresh blood. Blood was the key to survival. As revered Temple Priests they also knew that the best blood was to be found in humans. They needed human blood. But how were they going to get it? In silent quandary the frogs mulled over this conundrum, but there seemed no solution.

Then, one day, one cool summer's morning, very early before the sun had risen above the melancholy horizon, the answer arrived on their doorstep. And they knew, they knew right then, right there, in this strange land, this land of long wet summer days, and cold dark winters, that their destiny was to be fulfilled.

The Holy Innocents

Sam Golightly, and his wife Mary, had been living in Mucking for as long as they could remember. They had known each other since childhood, and had grown up playing along the banks of the River Thames, learning, indirectly, how to cope with life on the wetlands. Their parents had been Muckers, as had and their parents before them. They could, in fact, trace their family line back to a distant point in time which no-one alive could remember. And so it was, that life amid the marshes was in their blood. They knew little else, and although it was a tough existence, it was the only life they did know. Mucking was their home. Having been born there, they didn't recognize hardships and never really saw life as a struggle. It was just how it was. Many-a-time, as children, Sam and Mary would race down to Mucking Flats to play hide and seek, although it was a challenge to find somewhere to hide in such a flat, stark place. But therein lay the fun of it, and they loved the openness.

As teenagers, they had inevitably fallen madly in love, and eventually got married. Their families were very happy, and they all looked forward to the birth of children, and a prosperous future. Or, at least, as prosperous a future as good fortune, or otherwise, would allow.

Time passed, and Sam, by now a muscular, yet thin man in his late twenties, counted himself lucky to be blessed with a good wife, good health and two lovely children, Agnes and Simon, both of whom helped

167

deliver a welcome dollop of contentment into the daily life of the small family. Mary, a pretty young woman with blond hair and of a merry disposition, kept their home as neat and tidy as possible, whilst her husband did his best to provide for his little family. Each day he would get up before sunrise and make his way down to the mudflats, searching out eels, oysters and other shellfish. Three times a week, he would walk to the ancient town of Tilbury, selling his wares to the dockworkers on the quayside. On a good day, he would manage to sell everything and make his way home armed with provisions for his family, a smile on his face and a few pence in his pocket. But, oftentimes, Sam's luck was out, and he would go home with nothing. Down, but undaunted, Sam would arrive at his ramshackle house on the edge of the village, to find his wife and children waiting for him, and Mary would miraculously manage to cook-up a heart-warming dish out of their meager supplies. Sam and Mary would sit contented in the knowledge that tomorrow would bring better fortune.

Situated on the fringe of Mucking village, their house was of simple construction and lay in the lea of the only rising ground for miles around. Just how these lumps of geographical anomaly came about was a matter for some local conjecture. One traditional tale, which held little water as far as most residents were concerned, suggested that the mounds were a prehistoric graveyard, made up of wooly mammoth skin and bone. Another, perhaps more realistic idea, was that the hillocks were thrown up by an as yet undiagnosed gaseous force, creating a welcome respite from the unimaginative flatness. But by far the most popular, and agreeable idea, with which most Muckers were content, was that the mounts were a deliberately crafted beauty spot designed by God, and gifted to the Thames estuary in a promise to provide solace in times of flood and watery peril. A peaceable people, Muckers felt comfortable with this notion, and slept soundly at night in the knowledge that God was on their side.

Made largely out of scrounged timber and driftwood, the Golightly's house consisted of two rooms only: one for the children to sleep in, and one for Sam and his wife, which also served as living room and kitchen. Their possessions were crude and sparse, but nonetheless homely, and Sam was proud of the way Mary kept everything spic-n-span.

The Golightly's was a Christian home, and displayed proudly over the fireplace was their single, most cherished possession: a brilliant, but rather intense, portrait of the Virgin Mary. Framed by flowers and set against a striking cross and a clear blue sky, with one or two glittering, fluffy white clouds, the Madonna's golden face, modestly inclined, smiled beatifically. She took on the woes of the world, and Sam and Mary prayed to her with earnest, open hearts. Nightly they confessed their sins, and asked for forgiveness and protection. The Virgin's benign smile comforted Sam and Mary, and they rested content that their children lay embraced by angels, in the arms of the Redeemer's mother.

The family counted their blessings. They owned very few possessions, but what they did have, they treasured, and looked after most carefully. A simple crucifix, carved from the smoothly gnarled timbers of an abandoned row boat, was nailed to the main joist supporting the roof. This hallowed icon, of little monetary value, represented the belief they had in the resurrection and everlasting life in the hereafter. As such Sam and Mary saw the carving as a symbol of their spiritual fortune, and could not imagine an earthly life without it. The simple crucifix was a priceless possession. There were no clocks, fine porcelain or ornaments of any great value, and they owned only one book worthy of mention, a fairly worn copy of illustrated Bible stories. This had been in Mary's family for many years, and she remembered, as a child, listening to her mother reading from it. Now, each night, she would read to her own children, Agnes and Simon. This she would do as Sam sat dozing in the big, threadbare chair by the fireside. Eventually, the children fast asleep, Sam and Mary would go to bed in the corner of the living room and dream, tired but humming a tune of happiness as their children slept and they, contentedly, snuggled up together.

One day, Sam had been up very early in the morning and managed to catch a fine selection of fat, juicy eels and a whole basket-full of shellfish, including some especially succulent oysters. As he had slugged through the marshland-mud, he'd noticed a number of frogs jumping and leaping around. There was nothing particularly unusual about seeing frogs, and indeed, on occasions, when food was rare, he would catch one or two and offer them up to Mary for cooking. She wasn't too excited by this, but realized that frogs' legs were considered a delicacy in some parts of the world, and so if they were hungry, they had better just swallow their disgust, and get on with it.

Anyway, as the little frogs plopped about and swam, and generally scuttled around, Sam felt a really nasty sting at his ankle. This, again, wasn't so unusual as there were all sorts of creatures living in the flats. But this was less a sting and more of a bite really.

Yes, he thought to himself, *most definitely, a bite.*

170

Ow! And there it was again. Oh yes, clearly, a bite.

He smartly moved away, found a little patch of dry land and examined his leg. And sure enough, there, just above the ankle, he found the distinctive, telltale puncture holes of several bites, and trickles of blood. Yes, bites and blood.

Hmm, he thought to himself, *how very odd.*

But Sam was a tough bloke, and he was happy with his full basket of eels and oysters. So, setting his sights on the tall, distant masts of ships in Tilbury docks, he plodded on.

Later that evening, after a long day's work selling his wares, he came home, dropped half a chicken and a loaf of bread on the table, and, as a really special treat, presented his beloved Mary with a small pat of butter and a parcel of cheese. It was indeed a special day for the family, and they all ate their fill.

As his wife settled the children down with their Bible stories, Sam had a look at his leg. Yes, there they were, small, bite-sized punctures just above his ankle. They didn't particularly hurt, but it was out of the ordinary. He hadn't really seen anything like it before. But as he wasn't in pain he didn't mention it to Mary and began to doze in front of the fire, as usual. Soon, Agnes and Simon sound asleep, he and his wife were also in bed, and all was well with the universe as they dreamed sweet dreams.

The moon was full, and quietly shed its beams across the marshes. A light breeze came east west from the flats, and with it, the odd silver cloud drifting aimlessly. There was a rare squawking now and then, as a bird, startled off its nest, would break the silence and fly off into the midnight-blue distance. As the tide turned, small wavelets lapped the shores and the mudflats sank beneath the water for the night.

And, with the rise of the water, came the rise of the frogs. Their little bodies, thirsting for more blood, harboured the germs of transformation, an initiation, a small, seemingly insignificant conversion. It commenced with one molecule, one chromosome, then one profound supernatural atom of an altered state. Sam's blood had awoken, deep in the frogs' veins, a primeval gene, which, since time immemorial, had lain dormant, quiescent, awaiting the spark of divine intervention. The frogs were turning.

*

Keeping one step ahead of the rising waters, the little frogs jumped and leapt from reed to reed and pond to pond. They were fresh water frogs, and didn't like the daily invasion of the salty North Sea rushing into their habitat. Their instinct was to find higher ground, ride out the growing tide, and then, later, wander back down to the flats once the water had abated. Tonight, however, the frogs had a different agenda. They were not simply looking for higher ground, but a new source of sustenance: blood!

For a couple of years now, ever since arriving in Essex, the frogs had been living a quiet, rather frustrated life. They had kept themselves to themselves but had, nonetheless, felt that things weren't quite right. They were, after all, magical Temple Frog Priests. They had saved their very existence through making the ultimate sacrifice. They had turned themselves into the very objects of their Priestly adoration. They had become frogs themselves. They came from proud bloodlines and yet here they were, living not the life of Gods on earth, but the blighted existence of plain old marshland frogs. This had to change. And change it would, but not in the way any of them might have foreseen.

Blood

Sam, his wife Mary, and the children, slept peacefully in their simple home on the marshes. It had been a successful day for Sam, and the chicken, bread and cheese had been a most welcome addition to their usual diet of eel, fried or boiled. As they slept, they knew nothing of the stirrings outside on the mudflats.

The frogs gathered and set off in the direction of the isolated house. Silently, they surrounded and entrapped the family in their crude home. Cautiously at first, they encircled the simple habitat, approaching from downwind so as not to disturb any domestic animals. Then, one by one, they sought out gaps and holes through which they could sneak in. It wasn't too difficult to squeeze through under the door, or between the cracks in the window ledges, and soon, they were inside. Adrenaline and natural hunting skills kicking in, the frogs crawled silently towards the bed where Mary lay wrapped in Sam's arms.

The full moon surveyed the earth, and held its breath as it watched the atrocity unfold beneath its blue-steel luminescence. The wind refused to disturb its midnight slumbering, and the torpid air stifled any gasps it may have been tempted to make.

It was death time on the marshes.

Nature was being challenged and the elements cursed their inability to compete. Whatever was happening was part of nature, yet separate from the

174

eternal way of things. The frogs, an affront to the natural order of universal balance, were a freakish, rogue anomaly and earth, fire and water, held back any interruptions likely to interfere. There was evil conquest in the offing and nature stood nervous on the sidelines, waiting.

The frogs, bolder by the second, found themselves uncontrollably lusting for blood. Their metabolisms were changing. If they'd had the patience to look into a passing pond or shallow pool, they would have seen the physiological changes for themselves: covetousness in their eyes, a brutish craving in their bearing and, most profound of all, two upper canine teeth now protruding like sharp pearls, their glazed lustre catching the moonlight. They were turning.

The collections of human blood, poisons, potions and factory effluence were working their horrid magic, and the frogs, powerless to prevent their transition into nocturnal bloodsuckers, craved the warm, thick blood of humans. Their teeth grew elongated into spears, sharpened to the finest points able to pierce the toughest of skins, and their eyesight, now telescopic, developed a night vision able to seek out prey in the bleakest and darkest of corners. But perhaps even more extraordinary, was their newfound ability to move at lightning speed, covering short distances in the blink of an eye. They could shift and shove, disappear and reappear in a flash, a mockery of the laws of physics. They were becoming superpowers of nature.

One by one the frogs climbed onto the bed where Sam and Mary slept. The amphibians switched into kill mode and made for the throats. Their teeth, sharp daggers, posed before plunging into the inviting white flesh, and each wide-eyed frog, fevered in primeval rapture, salivated, hissing a jungle cry. Then

175

with a single, silent clarion call the frogs stretched forward, opened their mouths, and drove their teeth deep into the velvet necks of their unsuspecting victims. They drank and drank, draining the poor lost souls. Turn-taking to satiate their incredible thirst, the frogs eventually collapsed, exhausted, bloated, swollen stomachs distended, their stretched bladders ballooning with fresh blood. Spent, they fell into a gorged, dreamless sleep.

But not all slept. Gamboa, awake and alert, was aware of another presence in the house. He felt a spirit, a quintessence of purity, alluring, irresistibly magnetic. Instinctively he crawled off the bed and made his way to a simple wooden door. He squeezed through the opening and there, in the murky light, he could just make out the undulating form of two small bodies curled up tight under a thin, puffy eiderdown. He crept forward. Slowly he mounted the bed. As he inched onto the pillow he saw his prey, his prize, Agnes and Simon, eyes closed, lost in their own blameless world. They slept with unimpeachable beauty and Gamboa knew, he just knew, that this was his chance. He leaned forward and quietly, with a guile practised over thousands of guiltless years, slaughtered the innocent children. He steered his hungry teeth into the infant flesh and drank from each child. With every mouthful he felt renewed, rejuvenated.

An energy riffled through his body, and the years of buried purgatory dissolved as he felt the transformation take hold. His brain reeled and a torrent of rebirth swamped his expanding physique. In a deluge of revolution, Gamboa's electrified form gasped for air and he staggered outside.

The steely night currents kissed his skin and he panted and buckled, crushed by the excruciating warp. His head, pulsating with the surrogate blood, spun out of control and his heart screamed in agony till finally, shattered, he passed out.

In the house, the Virgin Mary, abandoned above the cold, empty fireplace, looked down on the massacre. Heartbroken, she stoically shed a tear in salutary benediction, a fountain drip of remorse and helplessness running down her face. The Madonna was melting, the furnace of evil too much for her. She lowered her head and wept.

The moon, bowing in through a window, lowered its head in a hoary cloud while outside, a short step to the south, the mighty river as it turned tide with a lingering sigh, stopped breathing.

In the dead moment, a small gust of air broke ranks, stirring up trouble under the eaves of the ramshackle house. A stern, draughty breeze caught the sad curtains wafting them into flags of surrender and suddenly, with a fanfare of deafening silence, a new manifestation arose, an awesome spirit demanding attention.

Wracked with pain, Gamboa lurched about, staggering, unable to control himself. Every muscle and tendon screeched in agony as the torque twisted and distorted, perverting the contours of his physique. His tightening skin sobbed red as he morphed. His spine cracked and his joints snapped as he elongated, transmuting back to human form. In his chest the clavicle and sternum belched out agonized cries, while the swelling pelvis punched electric shocks through his groin. His arms hung useless at his sides, as first the humerus, then the radius and ulna bones, lengthened, creaking under the near breaking skin. His legs buckled beneath him. The thigh and shinbones grew long and large, and his feet and hands juggled the tiny wild metatarsals, which collided, miniature asteroids shooting pain up and down his limbs. Every sinew and bone ached and screamed in defiance of the revolution being demanded of his body. Each joint and ligament was stretched, tortured by the mutinous transfiguration.

His brain bubbled, gurgling in its expansion and the skull creaked with the exploded dimension. His eyes, a whirligig duet of kaleidoscopic colours, spun round like dizzying, hysterically woozy cogs. His tongue shot out red and purple while his teeth gnawed through his gums in a blue terror.

As he got to his feet, his green amphibian skin buzzed with frenzied squiggles, and he felt a surge of power shock through his frame. Strong and defiant, he stood, erect, an almost man, returned from the dark of the past. Recognizably human in form, he flexed his neck this way and that, then hunched his shoulders and clenched and unclenched his fists. He earthed his toes in the soft turf of the marshland, then walked. He tentatively put one foot in front of the other. He balanced and turned, and through a grimace his spirit rose.

He licked his lips, the red and purple tongue flashing over the pointed canines. He was almost there. He could feel it. He, Gamboa of Suxx, was almost there.

The frogs, their round, fat bellies bursting with the luscious crimson blood, awoke. They looked up at the door. They blinked. They could hardly believe their eyes. There, silhouetted in the moonlight was Gamboa, his formidable shape all-conquering. A single rivulet of scarlet cruised down his chin.

He looked at the frogs, triumph in his eyes. He had made it. He had crossed the fantastic chasm, his reward stupendous. He was restored to his human form. He stood over six feet tall, massively handsome in the

178

pale light. He breathed deeply and his smooth olive skin, almost translucent, shone with a renewed brilliance not seen for hundreds and hundreds of years. The human blood, the blood of the innocents, had done its job.

Owning the moment, he crossed the miles and oceans, and recalled his ancestry, the golden sands and the green, verdant jungle of his homeland. He could see the Temple mounds, the altars, the mighty throngs of people at his feet. He pictured the blades, the blood sacrifices and the beating hearts. The blood. The blood.

He looked heavenward and praised the Frog Gods for this divine deliverance. He closed his eyes and threw up the ancient incantations and rededicated his soul to *Wo-sak*.

He had travelled a cosmic journey and now here he was, anew, Lord of his tribe. He had saved them, his people, his tribe of followers. They had shown faith in him and it had been rewarded. He smiled gloriously and held his head aloft, muttering the prayers and invocations of the Temple. And as he did so, a river of understanding flowed through him, a river of enlightenment, a river flooding him with the language of the new world into which he had been thrust. The Frog Gods were preparing him. Preparing him for a world so different from the one he had left long ago.

His skull swam with visions, innovative words and tongues. A brand new vocabulary catapulted Gamboa's grasp of the physical universe into the nineteenth century, and he found himself host to a vast collection of fresh, exciting understandings which sloshed around in his head, opening up a new consciousness gushing with the clarity of comprehension. His expanding cognizance of new horizons in physical sciences, the arts, humanities and historical perspectives had him reeling in the spirit of invention and discovery, and Gamboa's imagination flooded with possibilities. His eyes glistened as the whole gamut of innovations in mathematics, physics, chemistry and biology roared, clamouring for his attention and studied considerations. Architecture, engineering, design and great works of classical art poured into his head, and his soul sang, mesmerized, teetering on the brink of ecstasy as fabulous music, wonderful novels, lyrical poetry and the deliberate cogitations of great minds rushed into his brain. And with this knowledge came a meditative, fuller insight into his place in the world, and where he had come from. His thousands of years piled up before him, a colossal mountain of religious, philosophical and practical experience, its foundations firmly rooted in prehistory. He saw the forming of the continents and the crunching plates shoving sea beds high into the sky. He saw deserts as forests and mountains as valleys, rivers as dewdrops and oceans as ponds. Volcanoes launched Earth's bile miles into the atmosphere and he saw the Great Grey, ashen and red hot, scalding his world and he understood, in a finality of amazed perception, the beginnings and endings of life.

His enlightenment was thorough and complete. The Gods had fed him everything he would need. He gave thanks for the life-giving blood he had so readily drank. He addressed his tribe.

"Drink," he instructed. "Drink and be transformed. The blood of life is there to take. Drink and be renewed as *Wo-sak* intended. Drink. DRINK!"

The frogs turned to the whitening corpses.

"No, not there," Gamboa shouted. "Not the adults."

180

Intensity burned his words.

"The children. You must drink the blood of the children, the innocents. It is they who hold the key. The children. The virgins!"

Gamboa broiled exultant as he led the frogs into the small bedroom where Simon and Agnes lay.

"Drink. The blood of these children will transform you."

The little frogs, encouraged by their master's words, lapped up the blood of the innocents, and soon they too were morphing back into humans. Backbones straightened, fingers fattened, their tiny pads and suckers melding into people digits. And legs, no longer amphibian springboards, stood firmly erect beneath sturdy bodies with arms, shoulders and necks, boldly reclaiming the physiques.

Torsos, muscular and athletic, announced to the world that the Priests were back. Eyes narrowed, becoming the familiar almonds of the indigenous people, and their skin and hair shone with the natural oils of their tropical homeland. Repossessed features, so long buried in the wide-eyed frog faces, proudly proclaimed their return.

The Temple Frog Priests glared at each other in amazement. They had done it. By the Gods, they had done it. No, they corrected. Gamboa had done it. It was Gamboa who had achieved the impossible.

Proudly, unalarmed by his nakedness, Gamboa challenged fate and defied its inevitability. He raised his arms to the heavens. He called on his ancestors to recognize his greatness, his undeniable supremacy. He had defied mortality. His was the ultimate victory of life over death. He had transported across his universe to claim his rightful station as supreme Chief Temple Frog Priest - next to Godliness.

Settling In

Early in the nineteenth century, the British empire, thriving on the profits of slavery, attracted all manner of privateers, economic gamblers and poachers. Some were earnest, perhaps even honest. Others were just well-meaning. But they all took risks. And amongst these risk-takers, there were some simply bent on making a shilling or two at everyone else's expense. These prospectors were determined to cash-in on England's international hegemony. Many speculators made fortunes while others who had begged, borrowed or ultimately stolen money to invest, ended up broke. Prosperity bloomed in the capital and huge houses, monuments and mansions were built all over London. The banks of the Thames were not spared this opulent display and sparkling gems, testaments to hard work, wise investment, sheer good luck or criminal activity, sprang up with increasing regularity.

One such diamond was Wetheringdon Hall, a grand Georgian affair built to withstand not just the poor British weather, but also invasion and pestilence. The owner, one Sydney Grenville Wetheringdon had predicted, quite rightly, that London would indeed expand, and he'd had the foresight to commission an excellent architect to design and construct a fine, sturdy house, near to where the busy Tilbury docks were to be developed.

Unfortunately, Wetheringdon, a confirmed bachelor who'd been big in pig iron, was not built of the same stuff, and he fell to London's second great cholera pandemic in the early 1830s. The mansion house had just been newly kitted out and freshly furnished, when the cholera hit, and the esteemed Sydney Grenville Wetheringdon joined the dead at Gravesend. On his untimely demise, the house and grounds on the marshland and empty fields around Tilbury, to the east of the City, were left unattended, falling into overgrown, abandoned disarray.

*

The Priests spent the next two days at the Golightly's house. They judged themselves safe there for a day or two, but knew that to avoid discovery, they really had to move. And so, early in the morning, dressed in Sam's simple, and rather tight-fitting clothes, Gamboa set off on his own to scour the countryside for suitable premises. He had no great expectations but trusted in *Wo-sak* to provide for him and his band of followers. He needed to get a decent view of the land so, as he walked away from the house, down the path and past the small pond, he went up the hill for a better vantage point from which to scan this new territory. As he ascended the mount, he saw to the south the river in which he had nearly drowned. Tall masts of great big ships glided up and down the water and he was amazed at their size. How they didn't topple over was a magical phenomenon the Gods had prepared him for, but still, as he was confronted by this modern wonder, he couldn't help but be impressed. To the west he noticed a weighty greying of the sky, a murkiness of unnatural colour, a smoky kind of opaqueness which puzzled him. He searched in his new found treasure trove of information and realized that this must be the city, London, the fantastic metropolis, the capital and head of a huge empire stretching around the world.

He stared at the distant greatness, and as he gazed he felt a keening of his senses, a narrowing of his vision, focused yet expansive at the same time. Sharp, scissor explosions of dark, dangerous colours speared his head and his eyes squinted in vibrant primary quadraphonic hues. Spinning in nauseous mini rainbow orbits, Gamboa's pupils swam in a spectral montage of squiggles, and the clutter of ages was swept away as he saw an innovative, different panorama, a fresh vista of his new world.

He felt his Frog God, *Wosak,* in his head, in his soul, speaking to him, a willing and persuasive mentor presenting him with a clear revelation. The God enabled Gamboa to see beyond the rural landscape, beneath the grey, and into the city itself. He saw towers and keeps, steeples and spires, and bridges and roads and avenues, the monuments and thoroughfares of industry. He saw magnificent buildings and palaces, huge dazzling houses and gardens verdant and flush, and the splash and splendor of regally grand parades. He saw majestic squares with statues of the dead and glorious, glistening, erect and proud, standing next to austere testimonials, tributes thrown up in serious celebration of military campaigns.

Then he saw factories and factories and even more factories, and the smoke and the dirt and the grime. And the people. He saw lots and lots of people. And through it all he saw the possibilities. The potential. The wonderful prospect at his feet. And he knew. He just knew. *But not now* he said to himself. *Not now, Gamboa. You must be patient.*

185

And with that, his vision of London evaporated and he was back on the little hillock. Except that he wasn't back, at least not completely. *Wo-sak* hadn't finished yet, and presented Gamboa with another vision. A clear blueprint, an explicit visual narrative describing a house. Not just any old house, but a mansion. A great manor and estate, overgrown and abandoned not too far away in a forgotten field, secreted behind hundreds of trees and the iron railings of an ageless quest for security. And Gamboa, warmed by the thrill of opportunity, smiled, nodding his head in satisfaction.

The owner may not have survived to enjoy the splendor of his dream house, but the ancient Temple Frog Priests of a forgotten empire gave daily thanks to him, and their Frog God, of course, for his posthumous beneficence. For, set apart from the rest of humanity, Sydney Grenville Wetheringdon's, Wetheringdon Hall, was just what they were looking for.

They said goodbye to Sam and Mary Golightly's house, and set up stall in the supremely well-appointed Wetheringdon Hall. Before leaving, Gamboa went into the children's bedroom. He had killed countless children over the years, but none so crucial to his own survival as these two innocents. He stood quietly at the foot of the compact bed.

"Thank you," he said, slowly nodding his noble head. "Thank you."

Their little dead bodies were silently perfect. Eyes closed with tiny dark lashes still, unquivering in their eternal repose, their round faces extoled a serene patina of everlasting tranquility, as if they knew. As if they knew they had been part of *Wos-ak's* plan: the saving of Gamboa and his people.

186

Theirs was a death worth dying. It was a sacrifice paid in blood to redeem the tribe's lost years in the wilderness of time; to restore the lost empire and resurrect Gamboa as supreme leader, and the Frog God's representative on earth. The children would go down in the tribe's history as heavenly spirits, harbingers of fulfilment, revered forever as messengers of the Gods.

Gamboa took a step forward, leaned down and did what he had never before done in his entire life. He lowered his head and kissed the sacrificed children.

"Thank you," he said once more, and left.

In their deaths the living would prosper, and in their magnificence Gamboa knew in his heart, they would be granted a special place in the hereafter.

On his way out, he noticed something he hadn't seen before, a rather curious piece of wood hanging from a beam in the living room. He reached up and took it down. It was a cross, simply made but clearly a cross in shape. On one side was a man, rather crudely etched, but a man nonetheless. He toyed with it, turning it over in his hands. It was just a piece of wood in the shape of a cross with a man on it. But it did hold some attraction for him. As he was about to pop it in his pocket, he thought better of it. He was a Chief Temple Frog Priest, for goodness sake, not a pilfering thief. He shook his head and left.

*

The imposing gates and protective walls kept the curious at bay. As a billet, there was plenty of communal

187

space and the numerous rooms provided lots of individual privacy. To the Frog Priests' delight, on close inspection, they discovered that the derelict manor delivered up countless closets and cupboards, bursting with gentlemen's clothing.

Apparently Wetheringdon, in his hey-day, had been a bit of a dandy, and enjoyed the finer things of life. He had commissioned a tailor to cut him an entirely new wardrobe, which on his death, had simply been left, forgotten. The Priests, of course, leapt at the opportunity of trying on every set of breeches, trousers and underpants, and although ill-fitting, not to mention a little dated, emerged decked out in almost fashionable cotton shirts, not quite the latest in Victorian tailored suits, and classic, though hardly trendy, fine, glossy footwear. Custom-made cufflinks and clips, gold collar studs and silver fob watches, acquainted themselves with other accessories and the Priests swaggered about in new silk scarves like gallants.

With their profoundly altered circumstances, their eating habits also changed. No longer happy to feed on the scraps of filth in the river, in their search for fresh meat, they soon made regular sorties into the local villages and hamlets. Blood was now their sole dietary requirement, and a pattern soon emerged. Each new moon they would raid the most vulnerable looking communities, picking-off their victims whilst they slept. Typically, they worked in twos or threes, hunting out a target, assessing the potential rewards then attack after midnight when all were asleep. They soon realized that the most fruitful yields were to be had from the young, healthy infants, who had yet to be totally infected by the contaminated waters of the Thames. And the Priests, used to child sacrifice, had no lingering doubts of conscience about their rights to kill off the children of England.

And so, for a year or more, the fraternity of Temple Priests enjoyed their secret existence, eating and sleeping, sleeping and eating. In daylight hours they tended to shut themselves off from the outside world, eager to resurrect and appreciate their own, highly specialized company. Forays into the mundane world of regular humans inevitably fell into the fixed, celestial cycle of the stars. They soon learned the northern hemisphere's cosmic map, adjusted to the vagaries of the seasons, and fell into a rhythm of feeding and sacrifice.

Between times, they would sit in calm reflection, often chatting about the good old times, nostalgically recalling the sunshine, the clear blue skies, and, of course, their previous lives as Temple Frog Priests. They availed themselves of Wetheringdon's extensive wine cellar, and regularly toasted their deceased host. Raising a glass to herald the new dawn, the Temple Priests, confident in their superiority, sank back in the plush leather sofas and blithely drank from the rich bottles of claret, left to air on ornately carved rosewood tables.

Sitting around the heavy marble fireplace in the great hall, a roaring blaze throwing up red and orange glows, the Priests exchanged stories and anecdotes, reviving the great days of glory long since gone.

Late one evening, a Priest who had been an assistant to Gamboa in the other life, burst out laughing and guffawed. Wrapped up in his reveries he had obviously remembered a funny incident well worth the belly laugh. Encouraged to share his memory, he related the moment a young Apprentice had killed, outright, an old man who lay benignly prostrate on the sacrificial stone.

"It was his lucky day," he said. "This young'un took the blade and put it straight through the ol' boy's heart. Killed him dead as a door nail. Bang."

They all cackled and hooted, and Gamboa smiled to himself as he recalled the day. How he had pretended that the heart was still beating, lifting it high and twitching it with his fingers in a fake tremor of life.

"Yes," he chuckled. "It was all a bit of a mess. Wonder what happened to that young lad?"

"Don't know," said Jaxxa. "But he sure made a mess of things that day." And they all roared.

One of the Priests, a vibrant man with a self-assured, yet crafty disposition, grinned and snickered along with the rest, but deep down he scorched in pain, as the acid of humiliation burnt through his gut. He had managed to keep the story quiet for so many years, disguising his identity and rising through the ranks of the Temple Priesthood. And, as he sat there, he felt the heat of his indignation mounting, his resentment feeding the dishonour and devastation he had felt as a young man. He had suffered greatly as his family and friends had not been slow to show their disappointment in his failure to qualify as a Temple Priest. The shame and mockery he'd endured as he'd been drummed out of the Temple, still ate away at his ego.

Ridiculed and scorned, as a failed Apprentice he had found it hard to find any place in society. He went from one miserable job to another, eventually finding himself rubbing shoulders with the outcastes, the diseased, the sickly and disfigured. After weeks of opprobrium, he found work lumbering the piles of headless corpses to the open graveyard on the outskirts of the city, where vultures and rats fed on the carrion. It was a soul-destroying existence, and the disgust he felt towards the Temple Priests flourished with every mutilated body he humped on his back.

The Apprentice toiled day after day, hulking the dead. The stench of decay filled his nostrils, and it was rare indeed that he slept without rancor boiling in his heart.

One night, unable to close his eyes, he rose, walked to the stinking pits and sat staring, his mind a canvass of bitterness. A dog, fat and hungry, was biting itself, lost in its search for an annoying flea. The Apprentice looked at the dog. He was almost envious. It had a ready supply of food, it didn't have to worry about getting a job, and, most likely, it had status and respect in its own community.

"Wish I was a dog," he said out loud.

The dog stopped chewing itself and looked up.

"What are you looking at?" said the Apprentice.

The dog sat motionless, then, clearly unimpressed by the Apprentice, turned its attentions to a rather attractive round-face. It had lodged itself between the decomposing legs of an old woman. He started on the eyes, licking, nibbling, sucking and slurping, and finally, via the sockets, chewed through to the brain. It then moved down to the lips, munching on the juicy curvatures, chomping away until the exposed, naked teeth, set in a dead pearly white grin.

The Apprentice began to think. Somewhere, deep down, a germ, a seed, a tiny sprout of an idea was forging its way up through the trivial uselessness of his everyday trials, beginning to flower into a fully-fledged plan of action. He sat up. The scheme was taking over, gathering speed and scale.

"What if . . .?" he said. "What if I . . .?"

He stood up. He knew. He knew exactly what he had to do. The dog had given him the perfect idea and it was obvious, so obvious what he had to do.

"Oh, you dog, you," he said. "You lovely, lovely dog."

And he went for a walk.

*

Slicing off a face is not nearly as difficult, or as painful, as one might think. As long as the blade is sharp enough, then a clean carve can be effected, and the whole facial-skin-flap lifted off in one handy piece. A plentiful intake of cactus juice does help, of course, and one simply must have the appropriate herbal medications to assist the healing process. The Apprentice knew this, and, as he sat there, his severed face a gritty mess in the dirt and sand at his feet, he massaged a syrupy jungle salve into the exposed raw meat and bone where his face used to be.

On a broad, bright green frond, lay his new face. It was quite a handsome face and, as luck would have it, it too, had come off in one piece, saving him the inconvenient trouble of patching it up. He would, then, have a splendid, scar-free new countenance, something to be proud of.

He looked down at the pathetic Priest he had kidnapped, hands tied behind his back, writhing in pain on the ground, a faceless horror story.

"Thanks for volunteering," said the Apprentice, cheerfully, a red and white clacking grin lighting up the maw of his skull. "All be over soon. Just wanted you to see me. Well, see *you* that is . . . Oh, you know what I mean."

But of course, the Priest didn't know what he meant, as, without lips, the young man's words were incomprehensible.

The Apprentice lifted the mask and fitted it. Snug, with only the merest suggestion of a drip, the new face slotted into the foreign undulations almost perfectly. The cactus-avocado-and-papaya unguent did its trick, and the Apprentice carefully smoothed out the creases and cracks, using a fern to mop up any gooey emissions that may have escaped the continuous seam around the edges. He had deliberately cut the Priest's face right under the chin, and up to the ears, meticulously following the hairline, so that onlookers would not see the join. He thought he'd done a pretty good job.

With some satisfaction, and only a modicum of discomfort brought on by a stinging sensation around the eyes, he shifted his attention to the tormented Priest and addressed him.

"So, how d'you like it?"

The Priest's faceless head was, by this time, covered in flies, and a rat was gnawing on his cheekbone, a barely audible grinding accompanying the grunts and anguished cries of the desperate man.

"I think it suits me. What d'you think?"

The rat chewed some more.

"Tell you what," he said, testing out a smile "can't wait to see your wife. Hey, she'll be thrilled, what with the new body and all. She'll probably think you've just been working out. It'll all be fine, don't you worry," and he winked.

And with that, he took the flint knife and drove it straight into the Priest's eye, twisting it as it skewered into the brain.

"There," he said "all over."

The transplant took some time to heal, and the Apprentice was careful to hide away for several weeks before making his public appearance. He wanted to ensure that not only had the scars healed, but also enough time had lapsed between the disappearance of the kidnapped Priest and his own entrance. This would give people's memories plenty of time to forget the details and nuances of the vacant Priest's physique and character, thus making the new manifestation more easily acceptable.

The Temple Priest, whose identity he had stolen, was quite a high-ranking cleric, responsible for sacrifices at one of the mid-range Temples in the city. He was a quiet, family man, who took his responsibilities seriously, and was known to Gamboa and the other top Temple Priests as a reliable, if not exactly sparkling, minister of sacrifice. This suited the Apprentice perfectly, as he did not want to draw attention to himself, but rather simply enjoy the kudos of Priesthood, then worry about promotion later. He was ambitious, but also realized that he had to be patient.

He had no trouble fooling the general populace, but his victim's family was another matter. He had to work hard with the wife. Convinced that he'd been off on a secret adventure with another woman, she was, after the initial shock of seeing him alive, unconvinced by his story: that he had been lost in the jungle for a couple of months.

"Lost?"

"Yes."

"In the jungle?"

"Yes."

"Do I look like an idiot?"

"What?"

"An idiot. Do I look like an idiot?"

"No, of course not." *Wow, is this what married life is like*? he thought to himself.

"Who is she?"

"Who?"

"Who? You know."

"No."

"Who is she?"

"Who are you talking about?"

"What are you, seven years old? Do you expect me to believe that a grown man can get lost in the jungle, then, months later, come back looking ten years younger with the body of an athlete?"

It had been difficult. But he stuck to his story and ultimately his "wife" dropped the anger and just gave him the silent treatment.

He had claimed that the muscles and generally younger physique were the result of trekking and keeping himself fit for his homecoming. Somehow, he managed to get away with it, but his adopted wife was never completely convinced, and she would follow him about the city, spying, in the hope of catching him with that "other woman".

He didn't mind this though, after all, he'd got what he wanted. He was a Temple Frog Priest, finally achieving his ambition of mortal divinity. He'd made it.

As a Temple Priest, over the next eighteen months or so, he started to introduce some rudimentary elements of showmanship. On ceremonial occasions he would tease the hosts of worshippers, entertaining them with his surgical dexterity and legerdemain. He saw a knife not as a weapon, but as a somewhat fetching instrument of charm and diversion, there to assist him in amusing and engaging the mob. Warming-up his audience for the main event, he would raise the blade high above his head, bringing it down stabbing at imaginary victims in a mock evisceration, a murderous pantomime of slaughter. Twisting and gyrating, he'd leap in the air, coming to earth in a flourish of feathers and bones, his headdress wobbling tantalizingly askew. The jade shards of his necklace jangling and clashing in the blazing sun, he would gnash his teeth, then arrogantly thrust his head back, arms akimbo, in an adoring gesture of supplication to the glorious Gods.

The Apprentice, his humiliating lesson never too far away from his thoughts, acknowledged the crowd's thunderous applause, milked every ounce out of each sacrifice and made sure never to make the mistake of killing a victim outright. He stretched out the initial stomach incisions, carefully slicing, taking his time to open up the wound, and after each thrust he would stop, making absolutely sure that he was not about to hit any major organ. Between each cut, he addressed the

196

congregation, calling for their prayers and altar offerings whilst the victim, held fast, lay bleeding.

His victims were not too pleased. Word soon got around that if you wanted a swift dispatch to the safety of the heavenly sanctuary, then there was one Temple that should be avoided at all costs.

Of course, the crowd was not there to see torture. No indeed. They were there to worship, and pay homage to the Gods. But, at the same time, they appreciated the artistry, the dexterity and charisma of the Apprentice. He would, for example, parade the beating heart, flamboyantly juggle it, and toss it from one hand to the other, finally presenting it to the devotees with swagger and panache. He chatted to the head after decapitation, wishing it the best of luck in the afterlife. He would give the cheek a paternal pinch, fling the head into the appreciative crowd, and if he had managed to land it exactly where he had indicated, punch the air in delight. He also made a point of extending the torso's sausage entrails before sending the headless corpse bouncing down the steps. The audience, thrilled, roared in holy delight.

Priest, entertainer and sportsman, the Apprentice's reputation grew, and come sacrifice season, his small Temple rapidly became the place to be seen. Inevitably, his success drew the attention of the Temple hierarchy, and soon he was invited to the top table, slicing with the best of them, Gamboa included.

Years came and went, and the recognition he had craved adorned his shoulders. He really had made it. But he never forgot the trauma of his youth and the shame of his lost years down among the corpses. His soul was tarnished with the disgrace he kept hidden away, and if one looked really closely, but *really* closely, a rare and horrible truth could be seen in his eyes. He wasn't a Priest, and he wasn't pious. Unconvincing in his religious devotion, he was but a born murderer. He killed not for the glory of the Gods, but for the glory of the Apprentice.

*

As he sat in the shadows of the blazing fire, his face lit up by the orangey red flames, he laughed along with the others. He slapped his thigh and joked, and knowingly wagged his head up and down as each Priest kicked in with another jibe at the youngster who had made a fool of himself. But deep down, the Apprentice still smarted at the memory, and he felt the ridicule as brutally today as ever he had. His anonymity secured, he looked at the other Priests with rancour in his heart. He really didn't like them. He thought them conceited and self-righteous, a crew of privileged, pompous aristocrats dealt a good deal at birth and didn't know what it was like to struggle, to fight to get to the top. He hated them all. But he was clever, way too clever for them, ever to let his real feelings out of the box. He sat. He smiled. And inside, he seethed.

Visitation

Weeks and months went by, and the Priests settled into the comfortable routine of a landed, and bloody, gentry. Behind the huge walls and railings, they were secure in the knowledge that they could do whatever they wanted, without drawing unnecessary attention. This was fine as far as daily activities went, but it was the monthly feeding cycle that presented problems. They needed nourishment. They needed blood. This was unavoidable.

Their feeding pattern coincided with the full moon each month, and, of necessity, they had to venture out into the local communities. They were smart enough, however, to realize that they couldn't just keep popping out to the local villages and shop around for the best blood. This would soon attract the attention they were determined to avoid. The nocturnal ravaging of small populations would have been a magnet for busybodies, and this had to be averted at all costs. So they ventured very long distances, far away from Wetheringdon, travelling to destinations spread out over hundreds of miles in order to keep their bloody activities scattered, and therefore less noticeable.

In the early days, they would go out together as a large group, but they soon abandoned this idea, as feeding thirteen together in one sitting was impractical. They organized themselves into smaller, more manageable units, who went out on compact raids, silently sneaking in and out of communities without being seen. Patterns developed over time, and soon they were able to identify targets where the danger of discovery was much less likely. Isolated farms and smallholdings were popular, and although there was more choice in towns and large villages, they avoided these as being too dangerous.

Mini allegiances developed, and the Priests sorted themselves into various small hunting parties. Already trained in the art of execution and disembowelment, they were certainly not squeamish, but they found that digging their teeth into a victim's flesh was a much more personal event then extracting hearts, and at first they found the proximity to victims as they sucked at their necks, if not discomforting, then certainly a little awkward. In time, they got used to it, though, and found that, with practice, they could detach themselves from the physicality of the act, and enjoy the feeding event with little or no inelegance or vulgarity.

Of particular interest were the young, the innocent children from whom they could extract the best, untainted blood. But as they wandered the English countryside, they realized that one day, inevitably, supplies would run out and they would have to venture into the big city, London. They had mixed feelings about this as it was a huge, foreign metropolis. But, as Gamboa kept reminding them, they were the Temple Frog Priests of Suxx, and knew in their hearts that they could overcome any and all obstacles in their quest for survival.

Gamboa himself grew accustomed to hunting on his own. He enjoyed the solitary stalking, prowling in the darkness. There was, deep within him, a primordial instinct of self-preservation, and if that meant to hunt and kill, then that is what he would do. But he wanted to do it on his own. His motives were mixed, but he felt that mainly he needed an independence and freedom not available to him at Wetheringdon. He needed a break from being a leader. He needed time to himself. He saw the opportunity, and took it.

As a boy, he had led the raids on distant neighbouring tribes for the initial sacrifices, and so he was no a stranger to attacking aggression. But that was many, many centuries ago, and had required a different set of attributes. Now he was on his own. And he found he was no natural predator. He had to work hard to learn the demanding skills of his new trade. And this he preferred to do in his own company. He wasn't familiar with sneaking around in the middle of the night, crawling into private, domestic recesses. It was against his nature to lurk in the darkness, but if he wanted to live, then he had to adapt to his new circumstances. He certainly wasn't afraid of the dark, but neither was he used to operating in the shadowlands of humanity.

He was much more comfortable with a very public display of human sacrifice. But he couldn't simply barge down a door, march into someone's home and drink the blood of the first child he saw. He had to be much subtler than that. He forced himself to be more secretive, furtive. It took time and guile, and he came to understand that it may not have been a natural skill of his to hunt and prey on the innocent. But in time, and lots of practice, Gamboa realized that he was actually very good at it.

As he honed his talents, it became apparent to him that it was the thrill of the hunt, as much as the kill itself, that gave him enormous satisfaction, and that his whole existence had led him to this point in his life. He had a God given right to survive and one way or another, he was going to enjoy it. It was as if the Gods had prepared another coming of age, another rite of passage for their earthly vassal. And there was no way Chief

Temple Frog Priest Gamboa of Suxx, was going to disappoint.

It took him a while to adjust. He didn't exactly have a troubled conscience about what he was doing, but it did cross his mind that, in a way, it was rather selfish. After all, the thousands and thousands and thousands of victims sacrificed in the Temples of Suxx, had been delivered up to the Gods for the collective good of everyone, and yet here he was, devouring children in a case of self-survival. But he consoled himself with the fact that without him, the tribe would be lost and the empire gone forever, without any prospect of resurrection. He had to kill, to live this new life as *Wosak* intended. And if that meant the blood of children, then he had no problems with it.

But one night, as he hunted and fed, alone, Gamboa's life changed forever.

*

Numbed into ecstasy, he knelt, greedily drinking at the neck of a young boy whose parents lay ravaged, blood-soaked in the next room. The child's sister, dead, stared with empty eyes at the ceiling. Her body, newly stiff with the veneer of mortality, knew nothing of the spirit now claiming her soulless corpse. A cool stillness settled on the room and it became colder, as a vapour, a misty haze, swirled and rose up from the dead girl's chest. Starting out as a needle-thin smoke flute, it fanned out, up into a cone, circling, rotating, and then flattened out into a cloudy cocoon, within which vague outlines could just be discerned, suspended in the puffy web.

"Gamboa," a voice said.

He stopped feeding.

"Gamboa," the voice said again, more firmly.

He wiped his mouth. He knew this was a voice from the past. He recognized it straight away. But it couldn't be, could it?

"It's me."

Gamboa's face contorted into a grimace of bewilderment and some pain. He knew what he didn't want to admit, for the memories had been safely locked away, and with them the voices and pictures of his past.

"Gamboa," the voice repeated, insistently. "It's *me*."

He slowly turned his head. A smoggy film now covered the dead girl's body, and there, above the deflating torso, was an image. No, not an image, but a very real, physical entity. And the entity spilt in two. And there, very clearly, he saw his son. Gamboa's heart leapt. But who, or what, was that with him? Its silvery curves carved dotted red troughs in the chill air and faces, elongated lime green in a spherical bubble, mocked at him, laughing in cynical heckles, jeering with snide facial asides. And from the centre, a dead red stare tore into him. Then he knew. He saw. He knew it was the spirit of his dead wife, Tsok.

It was Gamboa's wife and child. They hovered over the spent cadaver of the little girl, his son holding his mother's hand, a benign smile on his face. He looked at his father and opened his mouth to speak, but instead of words, a deluge of blood gushed out, a red river in spate. It twisted and eddied and whirl-pooled, and whopped up angry waves, and consumed Gamboa in its intensity. He was lifted and tossed, and brought up and down like unwanted flotsam then beaten, floundering, tide after tide, an unstoppable crimson inundation washing over him.

Gamboa caught the anger in his son's eyes, the searing hatred and revulsion as he bore through his father's despairing look. A roaring avalanche of drums then tore through the small room, with a cacophony of screaming souls splitting the air in screeches of anguish. And above all this, above the chaos and mayhem, his son's voice suddenly exploded.

"Enough!"

Silence.

His son looked at him.

"Still killing children?"

It was now that Gamboa saw the empty space where the boy's heart should have been, a gaping hole, a ragged, torn vacuum. His son glowered as he glided, stalked, circumnavigated, a predator about to pounce.

Gamboa couldn't speak, and even if he could have found his voice he didn't know what to say. Close to the ceiling, his son continued to drift in circles, never taking his eyes off his father.

Tsok ruptured the silence.

"You broke my heart."

Gamboa held her gaze, and he longed to reach out to her, but he knew it was far too little, far, far too late.

Tsok took her son's hand and together they spiraled in a whipped miasma of fog, descended into the young girl's heart, and disappeared.

Gamboa, alone and shaken, wept.

Retribution

The once powerful aristocrats, aliens in an alien world, adapted quickly, and remarkably well, to their new circumstances. Recovering from the traumas of burial, transshipment, then burial again, they saw how their faith in their God had rewarded them with life everlasting; how they had been granted a new existence. Through bloody substantiation, they had been granted eternity, a God-like status only temporary in their own old world. The blood of the innocents had done its job, and the Priests were now living life eternal here on earth. Their leader was right. They had been delivered from the drought, as he said they would be, just as their ancestors had been delivered from the Great Grey of antiquity. They were meant to survive, to rule. To dominate. They all saw the potential. The power at their fingertips. They wanted to rule again.

And Jaxxa was no different from his fellow Priests. He was eager to climb the steps, to ascend, to wear the mantle of supremacy. He was glad for this new beginning, this new hope. But his head was filled with the past and he, more than any of his compatriots, realized that no matter where he ended up, his past would always be there, taunting, poking him with the stick of uncertainty and conscience. As he lay on his bed at Wetheringdon, his mind traversed the titanic oceans of time and space, and every night he relived the terror of his childhood:

Temple Frog Priest Jaxxa was very used to blood. In fact, in his exalted position as a Priest, he often drank a cup or two during sacrificial sessions. Not only that, but after tearing open the chest of a victim, he was also fond of biting chunks out of a beating heart before flinging it to the crowd below. He relished the juicy, red-raw organ and seeing it as one of the perks of the job, had no qualms about partaking, often, and with enormous satisfaction. This did not make him someone to be feared, however. In fact, quite the contrary, for, as people would often say, "Jaxxa? Oh, he's a real gentleman."

And, true enough, Jaxxa was, a real gentleman. In fact, most who knew him were impressed with his quiet demeanor and rather charismatic features. He spoke well and had excellent table manners. He was a responsible man who was not averse to shedding affection on others, and was certainly regarded as intelligent, kind and generous of spirit. Indeed, he could afford to be, for it was Jaxxa, along with Gamboa, who was responsible for the sacrificial deaths of thousands upon thousands of virgins and slaves. This privileged position allowed him to live quite a luxurious life, and he had his own coterie of slaves, which he looked after very well. He had a big house, with a large, quiet garden and entertained if not lavishly, then certainly with a flare not exhibited by the common man. For Jaxxa, life wasn't too bad at all.

But Jaxxa's childhood had not been too easy. After the death of his mother, he and his sister had lived a life in the shadows, afraid their father would ultimately take out his frustrations on them. Yet, strangely, their father had become aloof, passive and almost unaware of his children. It occurred to Jaxxa that after killing his wife, his father had accepted his appointed lot, and that

207

the sacrifice of Jaxxa's mother had atoned for his failure to rise to chief of . . . well, chief of nothing. Either way, the siblings spent the rest of their childhood in relative safety, and, despite having lost their mother so early on in life, developed into rather balanced young people.

Jaxxa enjoyed looking after his little sister, and would play with her for hours, giving away no clues as to the trauma that had hit him several years ago, when he saw his father kill his mother on the steps of the Temple. Sometimes days would go by, even weeks, and Jaxxa himself would forget his vow to kill his father.

But although the living had forgotten about revenge, the dead were far from restful, and the spirits did not sleep peacefully knowing that justice was still undone.

It was approaching dusk on the day of a summer solstice mega death ceremony, and the city thronged with people. A festive but increasingly weary air, laden with the smell of blood, filled the late afternoon sunshine as hundreds of heads rolled, and scorched hearts smoldered on the open, consecrated fires. The crowds, intoxicated by the pious savagery, swayed, sang in wretched chorus and beat drums calling on the Gods to bless the earth, bless the harvest and deliver them a fruitful, holy fertility.

As a Temple Priest, Jaxxa's father had been at the altar table, helping with the butchery. All day he had sharpened knives, held down victims, hurled headless torsos down the steps and made sure there was a ready supply of fresh meat. It had been a long day. Now, as the end was in sight, he was tiring and ready to go home. The last victim stood trembling, speechless. She had been captured from a rival village far away, and the poor thing had been at the end of a very long queue, stretching for a mile or so to the edge of the city. She had heard the screams of the other victims, seen their headless bodies discarded, and trembled as the shouts and wails of the crowd filled her soul with dread. She stood, rooted, hypnotized into a deathly, vacant stare.

Jaxxa's father grabbed the girl by the wrist and thrust her forward, toward the altar. She was just one more of the hundreds who had been killed that day. Just one more body.

The crowd roared a final, somewhat fatigued salute. The blade rose. The heart beat its last, and it was all over. The end of the day.

As the ceremony closed, Jaxxa's father bade farewell to Gamboa and made his way home through the teeming streets. Blood-stained faces contorted in and out of focus, and drunken drummers beat out a sad retreat from the foot of the Temple. The festivities were over, and although people were still in a frenzied mood, the blood party really was over, and the alleyways and paths eventually became silent as the spirits of the afterlife took over the dark places. The streets quickly emptied, and the sun was all but set. The ancients didn't like nighttime, and they kept their doors firmly closed to keep the goodness in, and the evil out.

On arrival at his house, Jaxxa's father made straight for the wine gourds and, with a raging thirst, downed first one drink, then another, and another after that. He burped, sat down on the floor and drifted into thoughtless reverie. Another ceremony. Another day over. More blood. He drank some more. Then some more, and it was with some determination that he drank even more. Then he fell into a deep, drunken stupor.

Jaxxa and his sister had been at the Temple steps for most of the afternoon, and when things had wrapped up, not wanting to be out in the dark, they went home. When their father arrived, they sat silently in their small bedroom, watching him through the doorway. Apart from the rhythmic snoring, it soon became deathly quiet, only the sad howling of an odd dog or two breaking the peacefulness of the city's streets.

Jaxxa looked at his sister, and told her to get into bed. She did so and wrapped herself up in the thickly woven cover. He looked at her small shape.

"I love you," he said, and kissed her cheek.

Curled up like a kitten, she looked back at him and through huge, dark eyes, their mother's, said, "I love you too."

He smiled. He really did love her.

She closed her eyes, and was soon off into her own little world, and Jaxxa sat on the edge of the bed wondering. He seemed to have so much on his plate. So much to do. So much responsibility. Was she really alright, he wondered? Had he been doing a good job bringing her up?

Since their mother's death, his father had been worse than useless, and it had been Jaxxa who had stepped into his mother's shoes looking after his sister. It hadn't been easy but he tried his best, and although he didn't know it, townspeople were quietly saying he was doing a good job.

He sighed quietly, and noticed how quickly his sister fell fast asleep, her small fame lifting up and down with her steady breathing. The day had been exciting and the festivities exhausting. She needed to sleep now.

It was then, in the still moment, that he felt if not exactly an uncomfortable presence about his shoulders, then certainly something that made him rather wary. A coldness perhaps, borne on a draught through the open space of the small window. He felt cool and yet warm, then cool again. Strange. He was just about to shrug it off, when a voice broke into the confines of the room.

"Jaxxa."

He looked around.

"Jaxxa," it said again, softly, yet demanding.

He didn't understand. He looked around some more.

"Jaxxa. It's me, your mother."

"Mother?" he said, astounded.

"Yes, Jaxxa. Your mother."

"But how?"

"Here, Jaxxa, here," and the voice pulled him towards a tiny shard of smashed jade on the floor, caught in the moonlight opposite the window.

"Here, over here," the voice called again.

Jaxxa rose from the bed. He walked over to where the glint of light reflected, sharp, like a splinter.

"Mother?" he said, incredulous.

"Yes Jaxxa. It's me."

"But how?"

"Never mind that."

"But Mother . . ."

"No time for questions, my dear," said his mother. "You have business to do. Tonight."

"What do you mean?"

"Tonight."

"What, tonight?"

There was the slightest of pauses.

"Tonight, Jaxxa, you must kill your father."

A giant boulder, a rock, a mountain, an avalanche of fear hit Jaxxa in the chest. Kill his father? It wasn't that he had forgotten his vow, it was just that he hadn't thought about it for a while. Kill his father? Yes, actually, on reflection, he had forgotten.

"Mother," he said.

"Yes," she replied.

"I need your help."

"I shall help. But first, come."

And with that a sparkling, golden mist smoked up out of the jade, gathered in a whirling column, took on human form and headed towards the door.

"Come," his mother's voice instructed.

He couldn't believe it, but Jaxxa followed his mother's lead and walked soundlessly through the door.

"Where are we going?"

"You'll see," his mother said.

She took him through the now dead streets. Up ahead he could see the Temple, looming in the silver light.

"Where are we going?" he repeated.

"Be patient," his mother said.

"Are we going to the Temple?"

The misty shape stopped and the voice softened.

"Trust me, my son. You must have faith."

The luminescent apparition gathered itself into a form more concrete and placed an ultra-light hand on Jaxxa's shoulder.

"Come," his mother said.

She turned and Jaxxa followed. They soon found themselves at the bottom of the Temple.

"Here," she said to her son, "let's climb."

And together they began to ascend the ancient stone steps. It was a tough climb, but the air was moist and comfortably cool after the steamy heat of the day. The giant steps were sticky with the blood of the dead, and it wasn't easy getting to the top. But they managed, and finally rested close to the altar where the stone bowl still held the hearts of one or two souls. It smelled of death.

Jaxxa's mother, in silhouette, now stood clearly identified in the mild rays of the Moon. What was left of the mist created a golden halo about her head.

"Mother," said Jaxxa.

"My son," she replied, and embraced him with the warm love that only a mother can give. "My son," she whispered again, gently.

Jaxxa began to shed tears and his young, teenage body shook with the terrible pleasure of seeing his mother again.

"Mother," he managed, sobbing.

213

"I know," she said, holding him closer.

Glued in their embrace, they stood like statues at the top of the Temple, the world at their feet, eternal heavens above them. Time stretched into the forever of the infinite stars, and the embers of the last fires sent faint wisps of smoke into the clear sky. This moment would become etched on the young man's heart, and carried with him for the rest of his days. He clung to his mother as if his life depended on it.

She broke first.

"Look," she said, releasing him, "the city. Magnificent isn't it. All the people of the world live here."

Jaxxa looked down at where his mother pointed.

"Yes," he said.

She went on. "The centre of the world. The very heart of the world."

She paused.

She took Jaxxa's face between her soft, silken hands.

"The heart of the world. And this is where your father killed me. He tore out my heart, severed my head and threw me away. It wasn't a sacrifice, Jaxxa. It was murder. He murdered me Jaxxa. You must kill him in return. He must not be allowed to get away with it. You MUST kill him. I will help you."

She stared straight into her son's eyes and bore deep into his youthful spirit.

"Kill him, Jaxxa, tonight. Tonight as he sleeps. Kill him."

214

She took him by the shoulders.

"Today, it is five years since my murder, and my tortured soul has been circling the universe waiting for revenge. You will kill your father, tonight."

Jaxxa stared into his mother's eyes.

"Mother, you must help me," he said. "Help me do this. I cannot do this alone. I need your help."

"I am with you," she said, and the golden mist reappeared, swirling, comforting her son's trembling body.

"Do not be afraid," his mother said. "I am here. I shall help you. Do not be afraid."

Jaxxa shivered.

"Mother?" he said.

"Yes, son."

"Is it right to do this?"

Tsok's face, a picture of resignation, softened enough to betray her fears for her son's strength and resolution.

"Yes son. It is right."

Jaxxa swallowed hard and fingered at the gathering mantel about his shoulders.

"Mother?"

"Yes, son."

"You will help me, won't you?"

"Yes son, I will help you."

"Good," said Jaxxa and he stood up.

215

There was seldom any movement once darkness fell over the city, for the citizens were afraid of the haunting spirits, which sang in the lanes and alleyways crisscrossing the main thoroughfares. As Jaxxa climbed down the steps he could see, still burning here and there, odd, random lights, but they were far away. Anyone looking out from that distance couldn't possibly have been able to see him. Neither he nor his mother had said a word once the decision had been made. They walked on in silence.

Finally, they arrived at the house. Jaxxa girded himself. Even though he had seen many sacrifices and even witnessed the death and mutilation of this own mother, it was quite another thing to actually kill with one's own hands. He faltered at the doorway.

"I am with you," said his mother.

He looked at her.

"Go on. I am here, Jaxxa. I am here," she said.

He entered and noticed that his father had moved. He was no longer drunk on the floor, but lying prostrate on the bed. In the flickering candlelight he saw the flint knife, usually in his father's waistband, lying invitingly beside the bed. His hand shaking, he picked it up and moved closer. Unexpectedly, there was movement on the other side of the straw mattress, and he saw there the figure of a young girl. For one moment he wavered in his courage, and thought of fleeing, but then the girl sat up. She knew someone was there. She blinked twice and then stared into Jaxxa's eyes. He was held transfixed. He couldn't believe it. He was staring straight into the eyes of his own sister. He took a step back. His foot knocked over a gourd at the side of the

216

bed. *The clattering woke his father who saw the blade, and in an instant lunged his drunk, lumping body at his son. Jaxxa, a surge of blood-rush exploding in his head, in a flash plunged the knife into his father's fat, naked stomach. At the same time, he pulled left and right and ripped a huge gash across the abdomen. Blood shot out in a scarlet fountain. His father stared aghast at the sight of his own knife, in his own son's hands, in his own stomach.*

In a grey-red gush, the yards of intestines unfolded onto the bed. To Jaxxa's utter astonishment, his sister threw herself across her father in a vain attempt to stop the evisceration. Jaxxa gasped in disbelief.

She was about to shout and opened her mouth to raise the alarm. As she did so Jaxxa dived forward, and in his panic, struck her across the head. The blade's handle knocking her out cold.

"Finish it," said his mother. "Finish the job."

"What do you mean?" asked Jaxxa, confused.

"The heart, Jaxxa. Finish it."

"But what about my sister?"

"She will be fine. Just finish the job," said his mother, without a shred of concern for her daughter. "Finish it, Jaxxa. The heart. Dig out the heart. I must see the heart."

"I . . . I can't do it," stumbled Jaxxa. "I can't do it."

"Yes, you can," insisted his mother. "You can and you will. I MUST see the heart."

Jaxxa hesitated.

217

"Do it," shouted his mother. "Do it now."

Jaxxa looked from his mother to his father.

"But he's not dead."

His mother scoffed.

"Did he care when he tore out my heart? Do it! Now."

Jaxxa gathered all his strength. His nerves flew about the room, his mind a bewildered blur. How could he tear out his own father's heart? And yet.

"Do it, Jaxxa," his mother threatened.

He looked at his mother, and above all the panic and terror of the moment, he saw that the golden orb, her glistening halo of hope and so much love, had disappeared. In its place hung, hovering, an eternal flame of an eternal fire, burning red, orange and scarlet, reaching up through the roof and out into the heavens. The sky, glowing fiery yellow, roared, a purple furnace. He caught his mother's face beneath the inferno, and turned to stone.

There, in the pulsing coals, he saw not Tsok, his beloved mother, but a grotesque death mask, its florid eyes shooting flames and hot ash in a blaze of blackening purple. Into this Hellish inferno, from behind the barbed teeth, was released a squirming, hissing snake, its acid spittle scalding the air.

Jaxxa froze.

"Mother?" he gasped.

"Do it," the voice croaked. "Do it now."

Jaxxa, terrified, drew back.

218

"Do it. NOW! I order you," the hideous vision cackled.

Lost, his head spinning out of control, the young boy stared in disbelief.

"DO IT NOW!" the vision yelled.

Jaxxa, recoiled.

"NOW. DO IT NOW!"

Tears welled up in Jaxxa's eyes as he gazed in disbelief at his mother. His soul burst in pain. How can this be? How can this be?

"Jaxxa, you must do this. You must release me from this vile curse. You must do this now, or I will be forever condemned."

Through stinging tears he looked at his wretched mother then, driven by fear and love, Jaxxa took a step back towards the bed, summoned all his inner strength and launched his fist up into his father's torso. He reached under the rib cage, found the beating heart and tugged with all his might. He pulled and pulled, but it wouldn't release. Then he struck with the knife, up into the chest, and cut away everything he could feel. The heart gave way. He yanked it out, dripping, beating in his wet hands.

Gasping for breath, he held it up to the heavens, as he had seen his father do many, many times. Beneath him the body stopped jerking, and Jaxxa stared at the deadness on the scarlet bed. His father. He had killed him. He had taken out his heart and killed him, his own father.

He looked at his mother, expecting some praise or comfort, or an expression of gratification and finality.

219

But instead of seeing the shape and form of the earthly being which had brought him into the world, all he saw was a golden haze, a mist, an apparition, an intangible glowing corona slowly diminishing in size.

"Mother?" he said earnestly. "Mother?"

"Thank you, Jaxxa," said the voice. "Thank you."

"Mother . . ."

"I shall always be with you, Jaxxa. Always. Remember that."

And the halo was gone, shrunken into a tiny, golden orb, which shot up through the ceiling and out into space.

"Mother," whispered Jaxxa. "I love you."

He walked, as steadily as he could, back to the Temple. Then, just as he had with his mother, he climbed. On reaching the top he held aloft the heart, uttered an incantation, and lowered the blood red organ to his young lips. He opened his mouth and bit as hard as he could. It was tough, chewy, but he was determined. His father had killed his mother.

He needed to do this. He swallowed, and heaved in some disgust, but then he took another bite, then another, and then another, till, in the end, there was none left. He had eaten his father's heart. It was over. Finished. Done.

Lice

Life at Wetheringdon was secure, and the Priests were safe in the knowledge that they could live out their lives in peace. They had come to terms with their new status and it didn't take long for set routines to become entrenched. They slept. They feasted. They slept some more. They had plenty of time for reflection, and many of them spent hours and days just drifting in and out of the reality which faced them. They dreamed of their past lives and wondered at their new-found eternity. They had joined the ranks of the infinite, and were now wedded to perpetuity. One or two found this a little daunting, but they were reassured by Gamboa that all would be fine.

"It'll be fine," he'd say, stretching out his arms, smiling a confident, splendid smile. "Look at me."

This was usually enough to allay any, or at least most fears they had about longevity, and they, too, would smile, ultimately relishing the thought of being eternal.

But of course, they weren't all young. Several of the twelve Priests were actually quite old. They were old men when the drought had hit, and, having little to live for anyway, it was they who'd had the least qualms about slicing themselves up. When they looked in the mirror, they saw not a youthful, vibrant man, with a fabulous eternity in front of him, but an endless continuum of years in old age.

They were afraid and not too excited by this prospect. But, after a time, it became apparent that they were all becoming stronger, younger, vigorous men with healthy outlooks. The life giving blood diet was restoring them to vitality. It was amazing.

One evening as Jaxxa sat mesmerized by a dying fire, he pondered this phenomenon. *Incredible,* he said to himself. *Absolutely incredible.* He considered the fact that they now only drank blood, and the fact that they needed only blood to survive. This was an amazing feature of their new life. And then, in his head, with one thing leading to another, he ended up recalling how he and the Chief Temple Frog Priest Gamboa, had first met and become friends. It had nothing to do with blood, but a great deal to do with head lice. Yes, head lice.

After the death of his family, Jaxxa led a very quiet life. He'd seen his mother brutally murdered. He'd slain his own father in revenge. He'd seen his sister kill herself. This catalogue of slaughter took its toll on the young boy, and he was traumatized beyond reason. He was haunted, especially by the death of his beloved little sister. In nightmares he saw the knife scythe across her tiny neck, and he'd wake up dripping in sweat which he saw as blood oozing out of his own skin. He still couldn't work out exactly why she'd done it, and he'd spend ages and ages ruminating on the motives behind her suicide. He was sensitive to the fact that his sister had lost her mother and father . . . but so had he, and he hadn't killed himself. He reflected on the night he slew their father. His sister had been there. In the bed. He didn't understand. Would he ever? Why had she killed herself? A taboo subject in the lore of his ancient tribe, Jaxxa had no one to talk to about it, and so became withdrawn, insular.

222

He kept himself to himself. He became moody, and brooded away the daylight hours in a copse outside the city. This went on for several months and he lost touch with all his friends. He'd been a popular boy but now, bereft of his family, he became morose, and ever so slightly, well, odd. He didn't eat well and lost weight, wasting away to almost nothing in a matter of days. He kept alive by occasionally eating grass and sucking on the shells of small, red beetles, which left an acrid taste in his mouth, as well as making his breath stink. For water, he licked the dew off the leaves first thing in the morning. He was becoming quite feral.

He began to talk to himself. Not too much, at first, just the occasional word or two, a comment here and there. Gradually, however, various alter egos took over and, after a few weeks, he found himself engaged as orator and audience in long tracts of debate and discussion. He went on about all manner of things and entertained himself with diatribes and discourses from the grand and fantastic, to the small and perhaps even insignificant. He found, one day, that he was talking in loud, determined tones, about head lice. Yes, head lice.

Like every other boy in his tribe, he had long, dark black hair, and this was usually clean, washed and glistening with coconut oil. But now, in his hideaway, he was not keen on washing and he noticed that his scalp would itch like crazy, and that he would, on giving it a good scratch, find dead or dying lice under his fingernails. It became habit to pop them into his mouth, pinch them between his incisors. He wondered how small he could crush them before having to swallow. This gave him hours of entertainment, and he started to think of how best one could cook lice.

Raw - with chilies.

223

Boiled - with chilies.

Fried - with chilies.

Baked - with chilies.

Mashed and diced, with maize - with chilies.

Grilled, marinated in seawater dusted in coconut - with chilies.

He created, in his head, what he considered the best possible recipe for head lice: diced, chopped and mashed, then sprinkled on starfish, with a splash of chilies, accompanied by fresh morning dew straight off the leaf. Yummy!

Jaxxa would do anything to take his mind off his family. He slept all day sometimes, and lay awake gazing at the stars at night. With heavy sighs he wondered where his sister and mother were.

Were they all right? Had they survived? What was the afterlife really like? And was he really going there one day? He was a believer, but he was young, and had so many thoughts blasting through his juvenile head.

He considered the sacrificial ceremonies. He reflected on the blood. All those dead bodies. What happened to them? Where did the souls go? What really happens when you die? Jaxxa was, of course, asking all the right questions, quite normal for a boy of his age. But he had no answers. And it was whilst in one of his *I'm not getting anywhere with this* phases, that he made up his mind. It came to him clear as daylight: He was going to become a Temple Frog Priest, just like his father.

He had spent weeks and months in his own wilderness, and, finally, come through the ordeal with the realization that he was born to be a Temple Priest. It was his destiny.

Excitedly, he gathered up his meager belongings: a coconut shell, a bent stick and a lovely, perfectly smooth, white stone. He set off back to the city.

"Hey, where've you been?"

"Where'd you get to?"

"Great to see you."

"Missed you, Jaxxa!"

"Good to have you back."

"It's great to be back!" cried Jaxxa, and he jumped and ran about like a dog with two tails. "I'm back!" he exclaimed, and people who knew him were happy.

And indeed, Jaxxa was back.

It was easy for him to climb the ladder to the top of the Temple Priest tree. He was a quick learner, and the trade was in his blood. He started off polishing and scrubbing, then accounting and recounting, then brandishing and bullying, then sharpening and grinding, then cutting and gouging and finally ripping out the hearts of countless captives. He was a natural.

There were several, smaller Frog Temples around the city, and Jaxxa displaced other, well-meaning, but perhaps lesser-equipped Priests. It didn't take too long for Gamboa to hear of the ambitious young man who was making a name for himself. He was flamboyant, and brandished the sacrificial knife with a flourish. He had the crowd cheering. He had a flair for engaging the masses, and the people down below felt involved in the ceremonies. It really was for *them* that the hearts were flying, and they cheered and roared when Jaxxa got to the altar. They even chanted his name on occasion, which didn't do him any favours with the other Priests, but did do his ego the power of good.

"I'd like to meet him," said Gamboa.

"Very well, Master."

"Today."

"Yes, Master."

Gamboa was intrigued. He'd been around for centuries and had rarely heard of a Temple Priest rising through the ranks so quickly.

He must be something special, this young man, he thought to himself. *Time to meet.*

Late afternoon came and the insects buzzed like mad, then slept, then roared, then dozed, then buzzed and roared, then dozed again. The noise rose and fell at random intervals. Gamboa sat in his garden. It was hot and he ordered fresh water for himself and his imminent guest.

"Master," announced a servant, "the new Temple Priest, Jaxxa."

Gamboa didn't get up.

"Very well, show him in," he said.

The servant disappeared. He returning shortly, followed by a slim, quiet young man.

Jaxxa approached and gave a very deep bow, almost touching the floor.

"That's not necessary," said Gamboa, smiling. "At least, not quite so low. You're a Temple Priest."

"It's an honour," said Jaxxa, feeling that perhaps he had made a mistake.

"Yes. I'm sure it is. Would you like some water?"

"It's very hot. Yes, thank you."

"Help yourself. It's on the table."

Jaxxa looked around the beautiful garden. He saw a jade goblet and a water carrier standing on a stone tabletop.

"Thank you," he said, pouring himself a generous cupful.

Gamboa indicated a chair opposite. "Sit."

There was a slight pause as Jaxxa found his footing in Gamboa's

presence.

A few seconds passed.

"Now, young man," started Gamboa "tell me all about yourself."

Jaxxa was caught a little off guard and really didn't expect such a direct question. He found his head emptying fast.

"Well," he blustered. "I'm not sure . . . I . . . erm . . ." He stammered to a halt.

"Not sure of what?" said Gamboa.

"Well," tried Jaxxa "I'm not sure that I'm terribly interesting or that I've got anything to say that you might find of value. I . . ."

Gamboa raised a hand.

"Jaxxa, you are a Temple Priest. How can you NOT be interesting? How can you NOT have something to say that will keep my attention?"

He looked straight at the young Priest.

"You stand at the top of your Temple steps and chop people up for a living. How can you be ordinary and uninteresting, hmm?"

He smiled.

The tension seemed to subside, but Jaxxa still felt a little insecure and not wholly convinced he was in the right place. But then, thinking that this was his big chance, and that if he blew it he might regret it for the rest of his life, he mustered all his courage and decided to jump in, with both feet.

"Right. Of course," he said quickly, staring right back at the Chief Temple Priest.

He nodded to himself, fixed a most serious expression on his face and, after an infinitesimal pause, launched into his favourite subject.

"Are you familiar with head lice?" he asked.

Heartbeat!

"I beg your pardon?" said the Chief Temple Priest.

"Head lice."

"Head lice?" Gamboa asked, squinting.

"Yes. Tiny little bug things that get in your hair."

"Yes, I know what they are," said Gamboa, tetchily, "but what have they got to do with anything?"

Jaxxa breathed one of the deepest breathes he had ever breathed. It was now or never. He could sense the irritability in the Chief Temple Priest's voice, and teetered on the edge of fleeing. But he girded himself, drew to his full height, threw his head back and delivered his opinion on the best way to cook head lice. He spoke at some length, and with what he considered to be some authority. When he came to the end he felt he had done a really good job and mentally patted himself on the back. His principal recipe of diced head lice, chopped head lice, mashed head lice, sprinkled on starfish, with a splash of chilies, accompanied by fresh morning dew straight off the leaf, he felt, had hit the spot.

"Yummy!" he couldn't help blurting out at the end of his speech.

Gamboa just stared in total silence.

Finally, he said, quietly, menacingly, "Do you take me for a fool, fool?"

Jaxxa's face drained of blood.

"No, no, of course not, your highness. No . . .."

"Shush, idiot," and he caught Jaxxa with the most terrible aspect in his eye. He folded his arms and stood to his full height. He looked down at the young Priest.

"Don't you know, that the best way to cook head lice, the best *best* way, is by crushing them between two stones, leaving them out to dry for three weeks in the mid-day sun, bake them in banana leaves, then mash them up with baby coconut, finally garnishing with a sprinkle of fresh, ocean seaweed?"

A second passed.

229

Then another.

Then, as the pressure was about to blow, they both exploded into belly rolls of laughter.

Gamboa leant forward, and shook Jaxxa firmly by the hand.

"At last," he said "someone with a sense of humour!"

And from that moment on, they became great friends.

PART THREE

Cities

"Can I take your cloak, sir?"

"Yes, thank you."

"And your hat?"

"Yes."

"What about your cane, sir?"

"No. I'll hang on to that, thanks."

He walked through the elegant foyer and made his way up the thickly carpeted stairs to the relative quiet of the sumptuous red boxes.

"Good evening, sir."

"Good evening, Johnston."

"Pleasant evening, sir?"

"Yes. Pleasant enough Johnston, pleasant enough."

"Would you like a programme sir?"

"Yes, thank you."

"Drink sir?"

"Yes. Usual thank you."

231

"Very good sir."

He relaxed with a sigh and sat down, relieved. It had been a long day and he had walked all the way from Mayfair, quite a stretch. He was ready to put up his feet, enjoy his night out and, for a couple of hours, forget about the world outside.

He loved the theatre: the glamour, opulence, the sights and sounds and general hubbub of the dramatic and musical clamour. He shuffled in the plush blue seat, played absent-mindedly with his bow tie, checked his fob watch and surveyed the flow of noisy aficionados. Actually, he was far too intelligent to imagine that people were there simply for the stage. Aficionados? Far too splendid a word to describe these customers. It was true, yes of course it was, that perhaps some of them were genuine fans but, equally, he was sure that half the audience were there simply to be seen. London had fast become the fashion bonanza of northern Europe, and, as an economic powerhouse, there were lots of people with lots of money to spend. They should be seen spending it. It was the right thing to do.

The Savoy Theatre, on the Strand just down from Nelson's Trafalgar Square, lay smack in the centre of London. With its spanking new, world-beating electric lighting, yellow and gold decoration and luxury seating, it was the perfect medium to attract the emerging moneyed classes. They appreciated the fact that, unlike the old music halls, all seats had a great view of the stage, and with exits on all four sides of the building, and the use of fire proof materials, they were in for a night of fun and revelry without fear of being burnt alive. The theatre had been reopened for seven years, and had a growing reputation for putting on classy, if not exactly highbrow, theatrical fare. The owner, Richard D'Oyly Carte, was intent on promoting the Savoy as a flagship venue for Gilbert and Sullivan comic opera, and tonight was the opening of the famous pair's new work, *The Yeoman of the Guard.*

The place was abuzz. All around him fancy peacocks strutted and pecked. They preened and pruned and generally got in each other's faces. A night at the theatre had become the new breeding ground for the novo-glitterati to wheeler-deal, broker contracts and sell off daughters to the highest bidder. But all that came at the interval, and the after-show dinner parties and drinks. For the moment, business was on the back burner, simmering nicely thank you very much, whilst the milling congregation had a grand time of it, parading frocks and jewelry.

"Your drink, sir."

"Ah, thank you Johnston. Just the ticket."

"Right you are, sir. Enjoy your evening."

"I will. I will."

"Sir."

Alone, his head floated with the opulent glories of the Savoy. It was a fine, new gem, representative of a London built on the back of slavery and the more burgeoning, and perhaps only slightly more legitimate, international trade in stocks and shares. Britannia certainly did rule the waves - if entertainment venues were anything to go by. He was staggered at the frippery and flamboyance on display in the private boxes, and beneath him in the stalls. Here was Britain's new power: the middle classes. Or, at least, they thought they had power.

He couldn't help but smile to himself as he watched delighted faces and gloved hands greet friends and strangers alike, with genuine pleasure and enthusiasm. Some, warmed by the challenge of being friendly to absolutely everyone, and no doubt charged by a nip or two of pre-show aperitifs, boomed and swaggered in salutation as they ballooned from one milieu to another, collecting handshakes. Some, however, red necked, perhaps cursing an impetuous overnight get-rich-quick investment, were clearly to have a long, hard evening ahead, and their hands remained firmly pocketed.

People fascinated him, and he was held, mesmerized. He was intrigued by the fatuous displays of the peacocks and foxes vying for attention, feathers and fur flying in all directions as secret notes, codes and messages were passed between lovers and mistresses. Heavily made-up eyes shadowed real intentions, but from his elevated position, he saw, quite plainly, the long lingering looks, the body language, the physical nuances, which gave away the clandestine dalliances being played out.

The door opened.

"Early tonight?" enquired the newcomer.

"Yes. A bit."

"Everything all right?"

"Yes, fine."

"Good."

"Drink?"

"Got one thanks. I saw Johnston on the way up."

"Ah."

"Hmm . . . Full house by the look of it."

"Yes. Full. New show."

"Yes."

A pause was filled with the background chatter and buzz of nonsense. The clink of their champagne glasses tickled the air.

"Cheers," said Gamboa.

"Cheers," said Jaxxa.

The two men drank in silence and caught each other's eye just the once. It was enough, enough to communicate a million books' worth of questions. The look said it all: *How on earth did we get here?*

Cavalcade

A giant storm raged, furious. Rain lashed the sodden ground and a roaring wind shrieked in undisguised wrath. Manic black clouds yawned across the deathly sky, and mountains lurched up like colossal tombstones into the billowing hysteria. Trees, bent and crooked in the mayhem, moaned as the gales yanked on their twisted branches, flinging anxious boughs into wretched, tormented knots. Earth's wreckage zoomed, lethal weapons in the hands of the hurricane.

The storm, stopping to ponder its next move sat angrily brooding, fitful, agitating on its throne, all-powerful, supreme in its intensity. Then its destructive footsteps strode toward the outcrop of farmhouses.

In the darkness, broken by the flashing crash of lightening, a young girl lay on a crude bed of straw, exhausted. Her thick hair, a tangled swelter of grease and dust, stuck to her adolescent brow and she panted, breathless. Stinging sweat clouded her vision, and she grimaced in torment, fighting her solitary battle. Alone and afraid, she cried out, her little body, wracked with pain, close to collapse.

For hours she had toiled in silence but now, approaching the end, she implored her God for help.

The storm converged on the outhouse, the baying torment heaving and thumping on the big doors. It rattled the beams and rafters, unhinged joists and shutters, and threatened to shred the timbers of the ramshackle barn into matchwood. Rushing wind whooshed with fearsome power as the eye of the hurricane focused right over the roof where, underneath, the young girl trembled in dread. The black, twisting finger pointed its fury down into the bowels of the earth, and the poor girl's heart bled in trepidation as the ground shook and pitched out of control.

The contractions were endless, and in a desperate plea for it all to be over, she screwed up her innocent features in a frantic prayer. Then, through gritted teeth, panting close to collapse, she gave one final, almighty push and with a gush of agony her baby arrived. It erupted into the world in a flood of blood and screams, and plopped helplessly between her legs, a mess of blue and red. The girl, primeval instinct taking over, reached down as best she could and lifted the newborn to her breast. The infant, soapy scarlet, squirmed then puckered its brand new lips and sucked at the nipple. The girl wept tears of joy. She marveled at her achievement. Her angel. Her own miracle.

Then her world diminished, as the internal bleeding of ripped and torn flesh sapped her strength. She closed her beautiful, triumphant eyes, and began to drift into the greying ever-after. Quietly, she slipped away, content and happy, her baby lapping at her dying breast.

*

The caravan was a motley crew, an intoxicating mix of exotic nationalities, each practised in rare skills bordering on the supernatural. Telepathic astrologers, acrobats, herbalists and architects of potions both wicked and divine, they wandered the world as entertainers, as magical conjurers, charming whoever would take the time and patience to listen to them. Indian, Turkish, Armenian and Greek, they plied their mystical trades from rickety wagons, and creaked into towns vowing to astound and amaze. Tricks and magical illusions had naïve audiences wide-eyed. They gasped in disbelief. Awe and wonder filled the air as the travelers, confidently executing their routines, amused and regaled spectators, then disappeared overnight, leaving a flabbergasted wake of marveled bewilderment.

Used to being able to find their way in the dark, they'd been traveling overnight and were tired and hungry. At the sight of a small village, no more than a hamlet really, they rolled sluggishly to a halt, the horses neighing in approval. Not much stirred, save for a few twittering birds and a skulking dog or two. The sun, not yet at its zenith, shone in honey tones, and insects, buzzing about between wild hedgerows and lush green leaves, announced a drowsy welcome.

The small collection of wooden farmhouses showed no signs of life, their big gates leading to the inner courtyards firmly closed. There were no tell-tail wisps of smoke from the wobbly chimneys, and a forlorn cart lay idle. The place seemed abandoned.

"Hello," he shouted out.

Seconds passed. Nothing.

"Hello," he repeated, louder. "Anyone home?"

Silence.

A cat stretched and scooted under a broken fence.

"Not much here."

"No."

"Deserted if you ask me."

"Looks like it."

"Let's move on. There's nothing here."

"No."

"Yes. Let's go."

He whistled, and was just about to give a giddy-up tug on the reins, when a faint cry weaned through the air.

"Stop."

"What?"

"You hear that?"

"What?"

"That."

"What?"

"There, again. A cry. It's a baby."

The others froze, listening. There it was again, faint but most definitely there.

"Yes, a baby."

She dismounted the wagon aiming for the weak cry. Honing in, she made for the farthest of the houses. She banged on the door. No answer.

"It's inside. I can hear it."

"Come on. It's no use. There's nothing here."

239

"It's inside, I tell you. Don't just sit there. Come on, help me."

He got down, ambled over and put his shoulder to the wooden gate. His Greek features groaned as he heaved. Finally, it gave way. She shoved passed him, squeezing through the gap. The yard was empty. She walked over to the living quarters, a stocky, sturdy wood and limestone edifice with a finely carved verandah. The door stood ajar. She went in. She wished she hadn't.

She gagged, breathless, and lost her footing. Flailing about she grabbed at her throat. Through a thick blanket of flies, vacant eyes stared at her and swollen tongues choked out in a bloating purple. She counted two adults and six children. All the necks had been slashed.

Hercules found her.

"Come on," he said "let's get out of here."

"Oh my god," she gasped. "Oh my god."

"Let's go. Come on, let's go."

He hurried her out, but she clung on to an instinct.

"But the baby," she said. "I heard a baby."

"Come on. It's no good. We shouldn't be here. Come on."

He tugged at her.

"No, the baby. I heard a baby," and she struggled free.

The infant cries again broke the air and Sabrina, her bangles and bracelets jangling, rushed to the barn.

Frantically, she shoved open the huge doors. She went in. She zoomed in on the young dead mother and her baby, and with a sad yelp of undisguised pity and grief, scuttled to the pathetic, bloody scene in the hay.

She bent down, her heart secretly exploding with joy and disbelief. She picked up the newborn. Its little mouth yawned in a hungry wail and Sabrina, her soul screaming out in crooked agonies of maternal desire, held the child to her breast. She sat back on her heels and rocked and rocked, and rocked again. Then, with the well of her soul overflowing with gratitude to the Gods, she wept. Sabrina wept as she'd never wept before, and her heart sang a song of total joy.

*

Sabrina had always wanted children, and each night she consulted the cards and looked into the depths of her crystal ball. But with the passing of the years, a nagging concern was beginning to grow, and she wondered what she had done to warrant the barren frame starting to sag beneath her. She was starting to question her clairvoyance, and distrust the reliability of the visions of happiness she saw for herself. She yearned for the day she really would have her own child. Deep down in her heart, her doubts and fears were welling up, and with each fleeting day a sprig of despair threatened to blossom, out of control. But now it had happened. From out of the blue the gift of motherhood had been bestowed upon her, and she thanked the Gods for her good fortune. The uncertain anxiety that had lurked unbidden, unwelcome, dissipated and Sabrina breathed a new life.

"What shall we call him?"

"He's big."

"Yes . . ."

"And strong."

"Hmm. But that's hardly a name is it, 'Big and Strong'". She raised her eyebrows in mock desperation.

"How about Goliath?"

"No," she protested. "Too ugly."

"Well, he's got the lungs of a lion. How about Daniel?"

"Daniel was not a lion."

"He was in the lions' den."

She thought.

"No, don't like it. Too soft."

"Daniel? Soft? He defeated the lions."

"No he didn't. God defeated the lions. We want a name that will reflect his *own* defiance, his *own* strength. Not God's."

"Cyclopes."

Sabrina looked at Hercules. "Are you deliberately being stupid?"

"Well," he replied "you wanted suggestions. And we do need a new act in the show."

"He's just a baby, and, if you hadn't noticed, he's got two eyes."

Sabrina hugged the child to her breast and Hercules smiled.

They fell into a quiet repose. The horses, plodding along in regular rhythm, snorted once in a while, or shook their heads in private conversation. Insects buzzed. Birds tweeted. The countryside, its hypnotic aromas embracing the travelers, nursed them on their way. The sun shone, the trees wafted in a gentle breeze and Sabrina and Hercules, wrapped in their own thoughts, honeyed up to the idea of finally being parents.

Slowly the miles disappeared, and after a long day the convoy stopped and set up camp. Sitting cross-legged on a richly coloured carpet, Bulut and his wife, A'isha, smoked a hookah. The pungent, vanilla smoke, poured aromatically over the darkening campsite, and Bulut, his baggy trousers and big white shirt billowing about his slim, but muscular frame, looked every inch the Turk. His magnificent mustache, piercing blue eyes and beaming golden grin, furnished him with a magnetic character worthy of a magician, or mystic. Indeed, he was billed as the Alchemist.

His wife, a gentle, intelligent woman, puffed on the pipe. She blew concentric rings up into the cooling air. Her greying hair, braided in one long train down the strait of her back, was ornamented with glorious wild flowers of yellows, indigos and reds, and her oval face carried the concentration of one who cares, but does not worry. Her tender eyes, darkly framed by concerned wrinkles, gave the impression of a deeply focused meditation - a soul who has seen perhaps too much, but who shares the load with a greater being. As the Alchemist's wife, she prepared the oils and potions of antiquity, spending hours wandering the fields hunting out the ingredients for the ancient prescriptions and recipes. The elixirs her husband peddled had their roots going back to the ancient Egyptians, and the Alchemists guarded their secrets closely.

Each new place they visited, Bulut managed to pull out new products from his chemist's hat, claiming to have cures for all manner of ailments; colds, flu, blindness and deafness as well as seizures, and a multitude of life threatening diseases. Conditions of the heart and chronic respiratory sickness were guaranteed to be cured by the Alchemists' restoratives. Bulut and A'isha wandered the world enhancing human kind's quality of life wherever they could, and A'isha, in a great display of self-belief, claimed to be over one hundred years old. Perhaps this was true, but Sabrina did overhear Bulut wishing his wife a happy 56th birthday . . . but one year ago!

Hercules sat contentedly, watching the baby asleep in his wife's arms. The fire crackled.

"You very happy," said Bulut, nodding in Hercules' direction.

"Yes."

"I see," said Bulut.

"Yes."

"Sabrina also very happy," he said.

She smiled. "Yes."

"What you call him?" he asked.

"Nothing yet," said Hercules.

"'Nothing Yet?' What kind of name that?"

"No, that's not his name," said Sabrina. "We haven't called him anything yet. He has no name."

"No name?"

"No."

Bulut scoffed and shook his head.

"The boy must have name. You call him name. He must have good name."

Hercules shrugged his shoulders. "Yes. Soon."

A'isha put in. "Leave them alone Bulut. They think of name soon. Good name. Name for strong boy. Good looking boy." She smiled over at Sabrina and they exchanged a knowing glance which only women can.

Bulut drew long on his pipe and offered it to Hercules.

Behind them, the Indians practised contortions. They were a large family and Hercules often lost count. Mrs India, (Hercules, along with the rest of the western world, couldn't pronounce their real name) appeared to be perpetually pregnant, and each town they came to, there seemed to be more of them. The Incredible Little Indians, as they called themselves, featured the entire family, with, of course, the exception of Mrs India, who, after giving birth to hordes of Little Indians, could barely bend down, let alone flex into the twisted shapes demanded by her choreographing husband.

At each new venue, Mr India would announce that the Incredible Little Indians would perform never before seen mindboggling acts of acrobatic distortion. The crowd would cheer. The children smile. But Hercules wondered at the convulsions the young children must have suffered in order to perform their amazing contortions. Now and then, in the dead of night, he would hear the most heart-rending screams escaping their wagon, and then not see several of the children for many days. They would eventually reappear shuffling in pain, and Hercules did pause at the impossibility of some of their gut wringing maneuvers, maneuvers demanding unnatural dislocations. But the Incredible Little Indians were a big attraction, and they pulled a good crowd who marveled at the strange and wonderful shapes the rubbery children cooked up.

Mr India yelled out.

'Tighter. Higher. Harder. Lower. Smile. Not so slack. Bigger. Smaller. Hold On. Smile. Use your head, your head. Look what you're doing. And smile, for goodness sake, smile."

The tower came crashing down.

"Oh my goodness me. You're hopeless. I'll beat you. I'll beat you."

Mr India was a bit of a disciplinarian. He left the children in a pile of broken bones and wandered over to his wife. She'd waddled up from the river where she'd been washing the dozens and dozens *and dozens* of children's clothes, leaving them to dry on the bushes.

"Hopeless. Absolutely hopeless. I'll beat them. I'll beat them."

"Now, now," said his wife. "Don't be so tough on them. Give them a chance."

Bulut smiled, shaking his head. "They just children. They do their best."

"I'll beat them. They're hopeless, hopeless," was all Mr India could say. "I'll beat them."

Hercules looked at Bulut and they both smiled.

"Try some hookah," said Bulut.

Mr India glared at him. "Filth, filth," he said.

"It'll calm you down," offered Bulut.

"Horrible. I don't know how you do it," said Mr India. "It's disgusting."

Bulut pulled long on the pipe and relaxed.

Hercules, the World's Strongest Man, looked at his wife and child. He sighed with a profound satisfaction. Finally, finally he had a child. He and Sabrina could now settle down. Well, not settle in the way others might with a proper house and a proper job, but be a family, a real family. He felt warm inside and a tear came to his eye.

Sabrina caught sight of him and smiled. She loved him very much and now, with the new baby, she had everything she had ever wanted. On cue the infant struggled and shuffled, letting out a cry for dinner. Sabrina looked over at Mrs India.

"You ready Mrs India?" she said.

"Yes, my dear," she replied. "Always ready."

Mrs India, heavily pregnant yet again, bulged with milk, and had been feeding the new arrival for the past few days. She took the child from Sabrina, and undid her blouse. They all looked at her and marveled. It was a miracle, a miracle that only God could have wrought.

The Little Indians came limping down to join their parents.

"Mummy?" said one Little Indian.

"Yes my dear."

"Is he my brother?"

"Well, I'm not sure about that," replied Mrs India.

"Yes, is he our brother?" put in several other Little Indians.

"Well," said Mrs India, wincing as the baby's gums pinched "why don't we ask his mother?"

Sabrina and Hercules shared a bit of an anxious look.

"Well, Sabrina, is he their brother?" asked Mrs India.

Sabrina and Hercules, a shaft of unspoken consideration electrifying the air, beamed.

"Yes," said Sabrina "of course he is. Of course he's your brother," she said to the children. "He's your wonderful, baby brother."

The Little Indians yelped with glee and they all clapped and laughed out loud. The Littlest Indian, five years old and capable of getting her elbows into her armpits and knees into the middle of her back, chirruped gaily, then fell silent.

"What's wrong, small one?" said Mr India.

"Well," started the Littlest Indian "I like having a baby brother, but what do I call him? He hasn't got a name."

Sabrina sat up.

"Ah, well, we were just talking about that, and I think I've got just the name for him."

Hercules, Mr and Mrs India, Bulut and A'isha all looked at Sabrina. The children held their breathes. Sabrina got up, walked over to Mrs India and caressed the head of the small baby as it suckled.

"My son will grow up to be a fine man, tough and strong like his father." She looked at Hercules. His chest grew with pride. "But," she continued, "the poor child almost died before having his chance in life. His mother, torn from this world, couldn't help him, and it was God who led us to save the child. We brought him back from the brink of death. Therefore, I have decided to call him," she paused, looking at the expectant faces "Lazarus. He was raised from the dead."

Smiles and nods of approval greeted the news, and the Little Indians ran around in squiggles of delight, chanting *Lazarus, Lazarus, Lazarus.* A'isha looked at Sabrina and saw there the love and compassion of a mother. She was happy for her, and couldn't resist getting up to embrace and kiss her.

"Lazarus," she said. "That's a good name. A strong name. He'll grow up to be fine boy."

Sabrina looked at her friend.

"Yes," she said. "A fine boy."

And between them, the joys of motherhood flowed in scented ecstasies.

Sabrina and A'isha shared more than they ever talked about, and each knew what this baby meant. A new life, with new possibilities and the long awaited fulfilment of womanhood. But as they bathed in the happiness of their good fortune, both knew that this baby had come at a cost, and, unspoken, each woman thought of the child's real mother, the young girl who had died in childbirth. Who was she? How did she escape the carnage and slaughter? What unimaginable pain and suffering had the young girl endured in her solitude? And who was the baby's father?

As the two women held each other, these and many other questions echoed, unanswered. The fire crackled, and the moment lapsed into a pause for longer reflection. In the distance a lone wolf howled.

The spell was broken by Hercules.

"Time for a celebration," he cried.

He got up, went to the wagon and brought out from under a pile of planks and blankets, a box. He opened it, took out a bottle.

"A drink. A toast. A toast to Lazarus,' he said.

"Where did you get that from?" asked Sabrina, a wry smile fidgeting at the corners of her mouth.

'Saving it for a special occasion my dear. And I can't think of a more special one than the naming of my boy.'

He produced a series of small goblets, and filled them to the brim.

"My boy," he said handing out the drinks. "We must drink to my boy. A toast. A toast," he shouted.

They all smiled, and even Mr and Mrs India, who normally scoffed at the mere mention of alcohol, took a glass and raised it in salutation to the new family, and the naming of the baby Lazarus.

"To Lazarus," said Hercules.

"Lazarus," they all chimed. And the Little Indians rattled and sang again, *Lazarus, Lazarus, Lazarus.*

*

A biting wind whipped across the steppes of Mongolia, skittering clouds in long smudges across a blue-rich sky. The flat plains stretched for miles, and very far away, in the great distance, a brace of hills nudged themselves into the folds of a mountain range far beyond. Snowy white peaks licked into the horizon like uncut diamonds, and the sun sparkled in crystal clear slashes. It was a beautiful day. A day for riding.

The two boys raced to the paddock. They launched themselves into the air, landed with a thud and a yowl, and screamed as their horses charged into the grasslands, their tails lashing in the wind. Galloping lunatics, bareback they surged in crisscross lines. Left and right they dodged and skidded, the horses snorting in excited tempest. With their manes flashing, nostrils flaring and eyes ablaze with the thrill of the chase, the horses, necks bobbing and stretching, blasted their way across the vast open spaces, and thundered on, with the boys howling in delight.

Fearless scoundrels, the riders shrieked in mock battle, hurling pretend arrows and javelins at an invisible enemy. They tore round in circles, cheering, beating the air in victorious glee as their enemies fell, piled in a mound of death. The boys pulled up their mounts, jumped to the ground and finished off the wounded and injured. *No prisoners,* they shouted, driving swords, daggers and spears into the defeated enemy. *Die, dogs,* they called out, as the blood spurted into the air and the dying begged for mercy. *Die,* they yelled.

They heaved in great chunks of the fresh, cold air and laughed as they embraced, celebrating their victory with a toast to the eternal spirit of the plains. Their mangled hair flapping in gusty wisps, ruddy cheeks aglow with the clash of fearless combat, the boys were invincible. They were Mongolians, warriors, afraid of nothing. Their eyes shone and they knew they would live forever . . .

As Temujin stared into Jamuka's eyes, he knew the end was near. Their friendship would never survive this breach. Jamuka had gone too far, broken the bond of the fellowship. Now, Temujin was faced with no alternative. Jamuka would have to die. There was no way out.

As youngsters they had killed thousands in pretend wars and fake battles, but this was all too real, the sharp end of adult, bloody conflict. They both now knew that they would not live forever, and that no matter how strong or brave they were, they would, in the end, die. But how they died was important.

Temujin looked into his blood brother's eyes, and could see the pain of defeat. For one long moment, they held each other's gaze and relived the years of friendship, the good times; of innocence and childhood, and growing up. And Temujin decided: No torture. No blood bath. Jamuka would be treated honourably. A quick, final blow, and a decent burial.

And only one man would now be left to carry the flame, to continue the struggle, to unite the tribes and create a nation rising out of the steppes of Mongolia. One man who could convince the warring families to come together, to live together, to fight together to create an empire, together, the mightiest empire ever seen. A man whose name was no longer Temujin, but the greatest name of the greatest general of all time.

And for years, the name of Genghis Khan drove fear into men's hearts.

The grizzly men sat close to the fire as the cold mountain air crept up their backs. They had ridden all day, and were tired. They wanted to eat and sleep.

In a lumpy bundle, a man lay cringing on his side. Taken captive for no good reason, he was terrified, yet somehow resigned. He knew he was going to die. There was no other possible outcome to his circumstance.

He had no idea why he'd been taken captive and not murdered with the rest of the villagers. At first he'd lived in some hope of salvation, that maybe he was to be used as a hostage, ransomed off, traded for some unknown item of value. But he was a farmer, a simple man, poor and in the eyes of the world, worthless. What could these men possibly want from him? No. He was going to die. It was inevitable.

From his skewed position on the floor, he looked at his captors. They were tough, hardy men, unflinching in their cruelty. Their long hair couldn't disguise the harsh features and each carried a steel glint in his eye, a cold-hearted instinct of survival at all costs. Many were scarred. They carried long gashes, ugly smears daubing their faces with the trophies of past conflict. Between mouthfuls of meat, they growled in sputters, incomprehensible grunts, spitting out gritty, unintelligible sounds by way of communication. Primitive and dangerous, they lived on the edge of the world.

Left in the wilderness, they were the last, terrible vestiges of a lost empire. They had no country and no reason to live. Adrift between kingdoms they found themselves without a patron. They had no-one to fight for. The great leaders they once served had gone. The generals and commanders, the governors, were all dead, killed by the day's new military order. Unwanted, the men felt betrayed by history. Wretched and vile, they reverted to the only thing they knew, the thuggery of their ancestors. Predators and murderers, these vicious drifters held no allegiance to anyone or anything. They simply took what they wanted, and killed at will.

The prisoner closed his eyes and said a prayer. He was an Orthodox Christian, and knew how to petition his God. He mumbled his supplications, then called out, his prayers echoing around the campfire. He struggled hard against his bondage, his wrists bleeding. He'd been beaten throughout the day and his head ached from the blows. Dried blood crusted on his forehead and he winced as his broken ribs grated in his chest. Again he cried out. Earlier that day he'd seen his family slaughtered, and all he wanted now was to be with them, to be in Heaven with his wife and children. He called out to his God.

For years the homeless brigands had roamed Asia, and now they had slaughtered their way into Eastern Europe. They were descended from Jamukha and Genghis Khan, the originators of the Mongol empire. Ancestors of a warrior tribe, they were fearless, but were now outcasts, feeding on the scraps left behind by the defeated armies of the Khan dynasty. Spurned by society, they had lost all sense of pride and dignity, and with each passing year grew more barbaric, losing every trace of self-respect. They were no longer warriors, but thieves and cold blooded killers.

Ruthless in their attacks, they chose to take out their frustration on the unsuspecting, the innocent and gullible. They came like ghosts, deadly phantoms, intent on only one thing, murder. Picking on isolated villages and hamlets, they brazenly attacked in broad daylight, slaughtering all in sight. The scourge of the innocent and meek, they left a trail of blood and death stretching from China to the gates of central Europe.

The Mongol killer threw what was left of the bone and fat on the fire. He belched, wiped his mouth with the back of his hand, and stood up.

"You going to make that noise all night?" he said.

The man carried on with his prayers.

"Hey, you. I'm talking to you."

The man on the ground ignored him.

"I said, stop your whining."

The prisoner continued his conversation with God and, if anything, increased the volume.

"I said, shut up," said the Mongol. "Shut up. You hear me? Shut up."

The mumbling prayers carried on loud and clear, and the murderer, a huge man by any standards, strode to where the Christian lay, dragged him into the light of the fire and spat into his face.

"Shut up."

The man, however, dug deep into his soul and found the strength to carry on praying.

At this, the Mongol assassin drew out a knife, slashed it across the man's throat, and let him drop to the ground.

"What d'you do that for?" asked a voice from the dark.

"I told him to shut up, and he wouldn't."

"Oh."

It was just one more meaningless murder in a world in turmoil.

*

Hercules and the carefree band of travelers, unburdened by the worries of the world, worked their way deep into the undulant pleats of the Carpathian Mountains. With breathtaking beauty, soaring peaks and roaring rivers punctuated their journey, and alpine forests coated the rising foothills and massifs a soft, yet spikey green. Huge slabs of rock erupted grey, black and white against the crystal blue sky, and tremendous monoliths daubed the jagged horizons, their trumpeting peaks blaring in triumphant majesty.

And as they journeyed, the family rejoiced in the happiness brought to Sabrina and Hercules. Like all parents, they fussed and pampered, and worried themselves sick over the slightest thing. The baby cried when it was hungry, woke up every night and demanded attention all day long. Sabrina was exhausted and Hercules did his best to be supportive, to be there for her. Their lives had been turned upside down, and at times they really didn't know what they were doing. But Mrs India was ready to lend a hand, and of course, everybody helped baby-sitting when it was simply getting too much for the new parents.

A'isha was particularly fond of the child, and spent hours rocking and singing him to sleep. Bulut immediately fell in love with new arrival, and nattered and chuckled with him as he lay in his cot. He was convinced that the infant could understand everything he said, and so would tell Lazarus endless stories about fairytale buildings which had magical powers. When she found out about this, Sabrina wasn't too sure it was a good idea. But Bulut's hypnotic voice lulled little Lazarus into a sleepy somnambulism, and so she didn't complain.

One day, Mr India took everyone by surprise. His wife had been suckling the infant and when she finished, Mr India carefully picked up Lazarus and cradled him in his arms. Then he started to gently rub his back. At the same time, he massaged every part of the baby's body, the arms, the legs, all the boy's ten fingers and toes, and neck, and chest, and back and head. Even the ears and the tiny nose came in for a gentle caress. Mr India then recited a poem. And in no time at all, Lazarus was fast asleep and ready to be laid down.

"Where did you learn that trick, Mr India?" asked Sabrina.

"As a baby," he replied.

Sabrina frowned.

"A baby? You remember that?"

"I remember everything," said Mr India.

They all looked at each other. It was unexpected and indeed, a strange thing to say. Even Mrs India was surprised, as she had never heard her husband make such a claim before.

"Everything?" said Hercules.

"Yes, everything. From the day I was born."

"You kept that quiet," said Mrs India.

"I've only just remembered it," said Mr India.

An odd silence drifted over the whole family and then a great big smile broke across Mr India's face.

"Just joking," he said. "I can't remember anything."

And they all laughed. They'd never heard Mr India make a joke before. Lazarus had indeed brought joy into their lives.

But it wasn't all plain sailing. There were moments of panic and fear too. Moments which threatened to breach the walls of the travelers' friendship.

Sabrina had searched the wagon from top to bottom. She was beside herself.

"Lazarus," she shouted. "Lazarus. Where are you? Lazarus."

She had laid the child in his cot and gone knocking on a farmer's door in search of bread. By time she came back, the boy had gone.

"Lazarus," she screamed. "Lazarus."

Hercules came running from the copse where he'd been collecting firewood.

"Sabrina. What is it. What is it my love?"

258

"Lazarus," she cried. "Lazarus. He's gone."

Hercules tried to calm her.

"Well he can be far," he said. "He's only a baby."

"Hercules, he's gone. I know he's gone. I can't find him anywhere."

"Well he must be somewhere," said Hercules. "He can't just disappear. He'll be in the wagon somewhere."

"I've looked. I've taken everything out. He's not there. I tell you Hercules, he's gone."

"He's a baby," said Hercules. "Where could he go? Babies don't just get up and walk away. And they don't vanish into thin air. He must be in the wagon."

Sabrina lashed out in a terrified sob.

"Where is he? Where is he, Hercules?"

A'isha and Bulut were drawn to the commotion. They made all the necessary noises of comfort, but Sabrina was inconsolable.

"He's gone. He's gone," she repeated over and over.

A'isha put her arms around Sabrina's quivering shoulders.

"Now-now, my child," she said. "He's somewhere. He has to be somewhere. We'll find him. Don't you worry. We'll find him. He can't be far. He's just a baby. Come on, we'll find him." And she wrapped Sabrina in an embrace which took the full force of her despair.

"He's gone," cried Sabrina. "My baby's gone. He's gone. My baby. Lazarus has gone."

In a clearing behind their wagon, Mr India and all the Little Indians had been practicing their climbing and tumbling. They came rushing up when they heard Sabrina's cries.

"Oh my goodness," said Mr India. "Whatever can be the trouble? What's happened?"

"It's Lazarus," said Bulut. "He's missing."

"Missing?" said Mr India, eyebrows through the roof of his head. "Oh my goodness me. My *goodness* me." And he immediately set all the Little Indians to work, searching for the lost baby.

Hoping that by some miracle his wife had simply not seen the child, Hercules was halfway into the wagon when Sabrina, in her chaos, broke away from A'isha. She ran about, frantic, shouting.

"Lazarus. Lazarus. Where are you? Where are you?"

A'isha tried to rescue the situation but it was no use. In her frenzy Sabrina scrambled under wagons and charged in circles, and shouted and shouted, raising the heavens with her agonized yells. Her hair flew wild and her eyes cried out in despair.

"Lazarus," she shouted. "Lazarus."

Hercules tried his best to get hold of her but it was no good. She wriggled and fought like a tiger, desperate in her loss.

It was then that Mrs India came sauntering up from the brook by which they had camped. She held in her arms a small bundle of soft cotton. Sabrina caught sight of her, and knew straight away. She flew to

Mrs India.

Snatching the baby up in her arms she cried, "Lazarus. Lazarus. Baby. My baby boy."

She smothered the child in kisses and held him fast to her chest. She looked at Mrs India.

"Thank you. Thank you, Mrs India. Where did you find him?"

"Find him?" said Mrs India

"Yes. Where was he? I went out and when I came back he'd gone."

"Gone?"

"Yes," said Sabrina.

"But he wasn't lost, Sabrina," said Mrs India.

Sabrina looked at her.

"My dear," said Mrs India. "The poor thing was crying, so I took him for a little walk. He's fine now. I think he needed an extra feed. He's fine."

Sabrina stared in disbelief.

"You just took him?

"He was crying. The poor thing was crying. Yes."

Sabrina stared at Mrs India, and a very public explosion silently blew up between the two women. The broken second lasted an eternity.

A'isha could see where this was headed.

"There," she said. "All's well now. Baby Lazarus is safe and sound. See?"

Hercules was also aware that a rift had opened up between Sabrina and Mrs India. He stepped in.

"Sabrina," he said, "he's fine now. Look, he's perfectly well. Mrs India was just looking after him. He was hungry, that's all. He's perfectly alright."

A stony silence held sway for a brief moment, and then Sabrina burst into tears.

"I was so worried. So worried."
"Yes, my dear. I know. I know," said Mrs India.

The men exchanged glances of relief and the women huddled together.

"All's well now Sabrina. All's well," said A'isha. "Baby Lazarus is safe. Come, why don't I make us all some tea. Come."

Sabrina held tight to Lazarus and yielded to Aisha's kindness. A tentative smile found its way to her lips and she finally relaxed a little.

"Sabrina?" said Mrs India. "Tea?"

Sabrina's anger and frustration melted, and through the panic she began to understand the pain of motherhood. She'd made a mistake. She'd left the child unattended. From now on, the agony of constant vigilance would never leave her. She looked at Mrs India. She had done what came naturally to her, and simply taken the child to look after him.

But Sabrina had failed, and she felt terrible. Her face said it all.

"Don't worry my dear," said Mrs India. "It's not easy. You have to work at it." She smiled. "You have to think for three now."

Sabrina lowered her head in shame.

"I failed," she said quietly.

A'isha tutted, "Don't be so hard on yourself. It was a simple error of judgment. Easily done. And anyway, didn't it prove a point?"

"What?" said Sabrina, puzzled.

"That we are all here for each other, and we will all look after one another."

She smiled again, trying to lift Sabrina's spirits.

"Safety in numbers," she added with a finality.

Sabrina's head rose and there were tears in her eyes. She nodded.

"Maybe, yes," she muttered. She looked at her friends. "Thank you," she said. "Thank you."

"That's what we're here for," said Mrs India. "We're a family," and she, too, beamed.

The three women hugged, their smiles turning to joyous laughter as the relief of safety in numbers and the security of family embraced them.

Mrs India looked over at the men.

"No idea," she said, shaking her head.

Sabrina looked at her.

"What?"

"Men," said Mrs India. "No idea."

A'isha looked at her husband and nodded in agreement. Sabrina's shoulders quaked as she grinned.

"No," she said. "No idea."

And the women laughed even more.

Lazarus ate up the months and years, and soon enough he was scampering about on all fours. Then he was walking. Then he was running and racing. Then he was yelling and screaming and generally having a whale of a time. And he was tall and strong, intelligent and charming, and he knew how to get what he needed. He had a tremendous smile and magnetic charisma, which Sabrina and Hercules could hardly resist. They found it difficult to deny him anything.

"You'll spoil that boy," said Mr India. "You have to learn to say "no"."

Hercules laughed.

"He's my son. Look at how strong and clever he is."

"That's not the point," said Mr India. "You'll spoil him."

"Nonsense. He's fine. Just fine."

"Suit yourself. But mark my words. That boy will be spoiled."

Mr India wasn't really serious, but there was some truth in what he said. The boy could do no wrong. And, generally he did get his own way. But his behavior was tempered by the love of A'isha and Bulut, who steered him onto the unselfish path of thinking about others. And playing with the Little Indians, many of whom were bigger and could out-fight him if they really needed to, fostered an admirable humility in Lazarus,

264

which, as he grew up, he wore with some ease. Sabrina and Hercules were proud of their boy, and didn't care one bit if they were laughed at for doting on him. He was their special child.

Seasons came and went. The sun scorched in summer, and in late autumn, as the promise of freezing snow and ice crept up, the band headed south to warmer climes. Down through the Bulgarian plains and into Greece, the travelers relished the milder weather and over the course of the years, they established a routine, a pathway where they regularly stopped at the same towns plying their trade.

Spending their winters in Athens, they all enjoyed the opportunity of rubbing shoulders with the ghosts of the ancient Greeks. There was a magic in Athens, an enchantment they all felt, and as they approached, their spirits lifted, as if the mythologies of Homer and the legends of the past were calling to them, welcoming them into their fables. The Parthenon, magnificent atop the rocky table of the Acropolis, gleamed in its crumbling majesty, and Hercules in particular, felt a proud connection to the splendor of the ageless monument, and the city below.

Trundling through the tangle of dusty roads, they would stop at squares and market places, anywhere where people gathered. The Little Indians would quickly fall into tumbles and shapes and sizes of all kinds, while Bulut sold potions and remedies for ailments both real and imagined. Hercules broke rocks and bent iron rods, and Sabrina looked into the future. Meanwhile, of course, Mrs India had lots more babies, and the family continued to flourish.

Years passed and with them Lazarus grew. His shock of jet-black hair Sabrina braided into a magnificent mane, the long plait tapering to a finely honed point. His wonderfully dark eyes, mellow, yet brilliant pools of intrigue, shone out, intelligent beacons below his superior forehead and temples. His fine straight nose and noble chin gave him an aristocratic air, but his tawny complexion, picked up by his years on the road, gave him a down-to-earth, approachable outlook, and the boy exuded a streetwise confidence.

Hercules was intent on giving his son the best possible start in life, by passing on to him the only skills he knew. Each day would begin with a solid work out of running and bodybuilding. The sessions ended with pushups and weightlifting, and each evening before supper, Hercules would finish the day's education by wrestling with the boy, teaching him everything he knew about self-defense.

"Hercules," Sabrina would say, "what are you doing?"

Hercules, puffing and panting as Lazarus darted here and there, clearly getting the better of his father, would smile proudly.

"Teaching him how to survive. He's my son!"

Sabrina would grin at the sight of them tumbling about and inwardly glow with contentment. Of course, with his brothers and sisters, the Little Indians, Lazarus also got a thorough coaching in contortionism. He learned how to twist and turn his body almost inside out and could imitate all kinds of shapes and images. He would often wait till nightfall, and practise on his own. With his silhouette thrown up by the fire against the wagon's canvas, Lazarus made animal outlines and even the configuration of the stars. He'd shout out to his father, "Look. Orion's Belt," and Hercules would smile, ear to ear.

Mr India, very impressed with the boy's progress, even allowed Lazarus to join in some of the public displays, but was very careful not to let the young boy have too much limelight, as he tended, unwittingly, to expose some of his own children's weaknesses.

But Lazarus's education was not restricted to gymnastics and combat. There were also special days out with A'isha. As a very young child, he often scampered at her side as she went into the fields searching out the spices of her trade.

"So," she would say, "now you've finished learning how to strangle people, perhaps you'd like to learn how to save them?"

And they'd evaporate into Nature's thin air.

The scents and sounds of the ancient landscapes sent A'isha into an empire of her own. She shared this with Lazarus, and she and the young boy regularly disappeared in search of rare herbs. Her vibrant, multicolored skirts bundled about her, she nosed into flowers, weeds and roots, digging out the tried and tested. But occasionally she also found excitingly rare ingredients for her potions, and carefully explained to Lazarus the efficacy of each fresh species.

For her, time evaporated into a heavenly chore, and she would vanish for hours at a time, with Lazarus wandering in her wake, poking his head into ditches and weeds. At the end of the day, as dusk spread its cool whispers into the nomads' camp, they would reappear, willful hair a chorus of tangles, and scratched arms heavily laden with sheaves of exciting new fragrances. Withdrawing into the wagon, A'isha would instruct Lazarus in the concoction of fresh salves and unguents for an unwell world, and as he got older, she taught him the secret trade of brewing potions and tonics.

A'isha's husband, Bulut, content to sit back and slowly roll with the wagon wheels, experimented with new flavours for his pipe, and Lazarus, frequently caught downwind, found himself drifting in and out of the day, floating on a cushion of heady petals. Bulut, a master of facts and figures, chatted quietly to the boy, instilling in him an urgency for understanding his universe, a sense of history and time. He also instructed him in mathematics and architecture, and Lazarus found himself looking at the world through newly stimulated eyes. Together, Bulut and A'isha opened the door to a deftly sophisticated scholarship, a world of understanding and technical comprehension.

Mrs India frequently gave birth to her own new miracle, then promptly got pregnant again, and the Little Indians ran feral through the long grasses where they chased rabbits and leapt about like lunatics, happy not to have too many broken bones for a change. Hercules and Sabrina, basking in their new roles as Mum and Dad, went very seriously about being responsible. Hercules, ever the proud father, looked at his son and imagined great things while Sabrina, growing more beautiful by the day, couldn't contain her angelic euphoria. Theirs was the happiest family in the world.

The small, compact coterie of entertainers, blissfully content with their good fortune, wandered from village to village, hamlet to hamlet, and only stopped to perform if they wanted to. They lived off the fat of the land and together presented a formidably resilient clan.

*

One spring, on their way north, Hercules pulled up the horses.

"Time to feed and water these beasts," he announced, and the three wagons ground to a halt by a small, tidy brook. The horses, pleased to be free of the heavy harnesses, downed gallons of water, and after munching on fresh green grass, wandered off to find the cool shade of a tree. They gently lifted a hind leg and settled down for an afternoon nap. It wasn't long before the humans followed suit, and soon only insects and twittering birds broke the silence.

Sabrina, hypnotized by the sound of babbling water, wondered at her good fortune. She thought about the family she and Hercules now headed: Mr and Mrs India, and all the Little Indians, A'isha and Bulut, and, of course, their very own Lazarus. They were all private, in their own private way, and they had all made incredible journeys to this quiet little spot of unknown riverside. They each had a story to tell, a history, but they never broke the unspoken vow of secrecy bonding them together. They never told of their struggle and pain. But she knew. Sabrina knew. None had told her, but she knew all their secret stories, their trials. Sabrina could see everything:

A'isha, daughter of a famed apothecary in the heart of Cappadocia, came from a long line of mystics whose ancestry stretched back into medieval antiquity. But her father, prey to the angry whims of the local potentate, failed in his efforts to turn silver into gold. As punishment A'isha had been taken into slavery, a concubine in the harem. There she met Bulut, a eunuch, an educated man of numbers and letters, a mathematician and architect held captive in the Sultan's entourage. They struck up a great friendship and dreamed one day of escaping. The Sultan, in his quest for a son, called on A'isha each night, and, inevitably, she fell pregnant. She delivered a baby girl. The child was killed and A'isha thrown out onto the streets. Bulut, risking everything, fled the palace, rescued A'isha and together they made for Istanbul, from where they boarded a boat bound for Odessa.

Mr and Mrs India, as two youngsters wrapped up in forbidden love, had dared cross centuries old boundaries of caste and religion. Ostracized, rejected from their own communities, they had fled Agra in the Mogul Empire, and ran for their lives. They were taken in by a grey bearded, mountain yogi, who taught them the secret power of contortionism. For two years they relished the peace and quiet, and studied hard learning the tricks of the ancient practice. One day, they woke to find the yogi had gone. All that remained was a small pyramid of magnetic filings, and his beard. A wind came and swept the zealot's residue into the clear mountain air, and Mr and Mrs India were alone. Except that they weren't alone, for, by now, they had a baby to care for.

They made for Bombay, where they eventually set up stall as entertainers and purveyors of the physically incredible. Fearing they would be discovered for who they were, however, they jumped on a trading vessel bound for Oman. From there they went up the Persian Gulf to Iraq. Joining a caravan bound for Istanbul, they eventually found themselves on the Bosporus where, after seeing a maharaja and his train on a grand tour of Europe, they panicked again, and boarded a boat heading to . . . Odessa.

Sabrina saw herself, born to a dead mother on the stroke of midnight in a year that no one could recall. As her tiny cries punctured the darkness of the small

270

Armenian peasant shack, the black sky showered a streak of blazing shooting stars in welcome, and she was gifted with an inner voice and insight. This gift took her to the depths of despair, however, as she was bartered and traded by her father for a promised fortune which never came his way. As a savant and child bride, Sabrina was beaten and bruised into infertility by her cruel husband. She was dying. Hercules, a Greek mercenary, a Major in her husband's private army, came to Sabrina's rescue. It was a murder they never spoke of. Leaving Yerevan, they rode horseback for several days, till they reached Trabzon on Turkey's northern shores. From here they took a boat to Istanbul heading for Hercules' homeland and the Christian orthodoxy of the Greek islands. But there was no boat to Greece. The only vessel they could find was one heading for . . . Odessa.

The storm came from nowhere and the band of refugees hung on with all their might. In the guts of the yawl they were thrown about, cracked and battered. Desperate, they clambered up on deck to find that the crew had abandoned ship and they were headed for a barely visible landfall. Lightening flashed, gale-force winds and rain lashed the boat. Then, with a mighty wallop, they ran aground. Splintered wood, beams and masts flew through the air and with canvass billowing, ropes wet slashing and giant waves crashing over the broken vessel, they were swept off the ruptured deck.

Frantically clinging together, they screamed and howled with the hurricane squalls, and in one crush of terrifying foam, they smashed into the sands, sprawling, floundering, gasping for life. The black clouds, gigantic, oppressive, thundered in greeting and then as if conducted by a divine maestro, peace broke out. The wind subsided. The blackness dispersed. A blue sky

271

painted the heavens. The sun, a benign face in a cloudless sky, shone in smiley atonement. It was a glorious day on the coast of Wallachia. And Destiny sat back, its job well done.

Weeks and months went by and as they turned their powers into a source of entertainment and income, it became apparent that the desperados had a gift for survival. They could see and bend, configure and twist, turn and contrive. Their brews, potions, psychic calculations and equations confounded belief. Astounded crowds were all too eager to part with hard earned coin or goods and services, in return for the magical medicines and predictions.

As they travelled, setting up shop in each township they encountered, the gang of exiles quickly grew to depend on each other, and a family emerged, a vibrant dependency never spoken, but theirs nonetheless. They meandered from town to town, generally heading west from the Black Sea coast. One day, one morning full of sunshine and hope, they entered a quiet hamlet and heard the cry of a baby . . .

Sabrina awoke, not with a start, but a gurgled cry. Into the present her head reeled, in a red blur, as the dagger cut deep into her slender throat. There wasn't so much a pain, as more of a numb shock. Her senses rallied in valiant protest but it was no use, the damage was fatal. The blood that should have gone to her head, was, instead, pumping in scarlet jets up into the summer air, falling in glorious fountains on the grasses beside her. Pathetically, she tried to stem the flow and pushed useless fingers into the gash. Sticky and hot, the blood gushed though her fumbling hands, and in no time at all she started to drift into unconsciousness. Above her, she could see a scarred, expressionless face, but couldn't put a name to it. She choked, gagging, and coughed thickly.

She managed one terrible rendition of *Hercules,* but it didn't make any sense. Her vision rapidly faded, and she blinked like mad, as if that, somehow, was going to save her. Then the reality really hit her, and she panicked as she realized she was going to die. And she did, in the end, understand what it is really like to be a mother, for her last, earthly thoughts, were of Lazarus. Lazarus, her child. Her life and joy. *Please don't take my boy,* she thought. *Please. Not Lazarus. Not Lazarus. Please.* And then she floated. Gliding in a weightless mist, she levitated above the ground, her matted hair trailing in a red mop. Then, quietly, without herald, Sabrina sailed away on a scented breeze. She was gone.

The bandits had planned their attack to perfection. Hercules, fast asleep, his head resting on a bale of straw, never saw the axe as it heaved into his bare chest. His ribs splintered, he caved into a dead stare, his heart stopping instantly, speared by a shard of breast bone. A'isha and Bulut, lying blissfully hand in hand, smiling at a pale pink cloud, never stood a chance as the spears lanced their torsos. The last thing they remembered was the disappearing smile of their love, as the black veil of death blanked them out. Mr and Mrs India, spared the horror of seeing their children murdered, also fell to the brigands' blades as they snoozed, imagining even more babies to add to their brood. The children, now awake and screaming, were herded, manhandled, and then slaughtered like pigs, their howling, pathetic echoes in the empty field.

The brook babbled. The birds flew off. Insects buzzed, out of tune. They had come from nowhere, and left with everything.

Survival

Lazarus kept perfectly still until he knew it was safe. Then he sat up. Then he stood. He looked at his mother and father. His head reeled and he clutched at his chest, an empty chasm echoing with the pain and loss. He choked back the tears but the floodgates soon opened, and he cried his young heart out. His shoulders collapsed under the weight of his grief and the tears rolled unhampered down his cheeks. Everything felt heavy. His head, his hands, his whole body, the world pressing down on him. And the universe compressed Lazarus into a tight, heavily condensed, ball of sorrow. He dropped to the floor and caressed Sabrina, her face, her beautiful face. And he cried and cried.

And through his tears he could see A'isha and Bulut, their pale, dead stares monumental, cold. And Mr and Mrs India, bloody, glued together in a spent waste of breath, their bloody expressions horrific in the stillness. Then he saw all the Little Indians. All dead. All of them.

A mesmeric gawp of incomprehension darkened his features, and his young spirit disintegrated. He collapsed. Lazarus collapsed.

When he came to, night was pressing its black fingers into his head and he felt a heavy, thick mist clogging his senses. It took some seconds for his reality to hit, then the full force of realization came like an overpowering wave to torment him in one tremendous punch. He gasped, clutching at air, hopeless. Heaving and panting, he retched into the silky darkness. His pulse raced, and in a terrifying innocence, Lazarus screamed at the sky.

And a deep furrow of change ploughed its way through his veins. Stretched and swollen with the ire of his hurt, his temples throbbed in a conflict of dissent, and his eyes splayed, bloated orbs wriggling red and orange. His limbs trembled, and he felt the earth beneath his feet disintegrate, fall away as he dropped, a dead weight sinking into the crust of the planet. And then he swam in nature's dry clay, and ground out a trough, a conduit, through which he crawled, dragging his dead weight behind him till, finally, spitting out death's decay, he rose up. He was new. Different. No longer a boy. His anger knew no bounds. And he had no idea of how to control it.

In a rush of red, senseless bloodlust, he morphed into the darkness, becoming trees and grasses, the river and bushes. He disappeared and reappeared and reshaped into almighty rocks and rushing floodwater. Then he became creatures and nocturnal beasts salivating. Then cringing prey and reptiles crawling, creeping out of every crevice. He snarled and roared and hissed and barked, and his tortured soul transmuted into an otherworldly entity. Jagged and sharp, then smooth and round, he leapt with ease through tree-trunks and the granite rocks of the hills. Visions filled his young head and he contorted, shifted and spawned new fields of poppy and thorn, then drifted up into the clouds to come swooping down, a dozen hawks like shooting stars, rifling the sky. He sought out every creature of the night and tore, shredded limb from limb, each life he found. His yearning for blood and vengeance knew no bounds. He was lost, out of control, his features a contorted jangle of shape and form. He wanted to kill and maim. Such was his pain, Lazarus saw no rules, no boundaries for his anger and grief, and he tore into nature with a vengeance not of this world.

*

In a hushed swivel of feathers, an eagle owl calmly, deliberately, rotated its head through 360 degrees. From its vantage point high up in the braches of the soaring spruce tree, nothing moved or breathed without the predator's knowledge. Its saucer orange eyes looked down on Lazarus, and blinked once.

*

He was making his way west. He had no great plan but he felt that traveling into the sunset was the best thing to do. During the day he slept, searching out dark recesses in which to hide. He came out at night as the sun was sinking below the horizon and he sought out the moon, which soon became a companion, his inspiration to carry on. He felt better at nighttime - an affinity with the nocturnal world. He felt there was a spirit guiding him, a hand steering him towards some unknown goal.

After the shock of the attack, he was left traumatized, wrapped up in a veil of despair. He'd wept and wept and wondered at the cruelty of the world. His family had meant everything to him. He loved them so much, so, so much. But he was alone now, adrift in a violent world without justice.

With his bare hands he'd done his best to bury the dead. And with each handful of soil, he wondered

277

why *he* hadn't been killed. Why had the killers missed him? How come he hadn't met the same fate as the rest of his family? Standing by the shallow graves, in his mind he replayed the gruesome attack.

He'd been lying close by Sabrina, lazily tracing patterns in the big blue sky. The day was peaceful, and as he drifted off into his daydream, he felt himself dissolve, like melting ice into the wafting grasses. The heady mix of herbs and scents floating on the pollen-filled breeze, had him hovering, thawing yet blending in with the greens and pastels. In a flux of evaporation, Lazarus had felt himself merge with the pasture, sharing a solid coherence, a oneness with the meadows and fields. He felt the beat of the world as it breathed and lolled under the heavens. He remembered the sensitivity of every living creature and experienced the pulse of nature throbbing with the slow rotation of the earth.

Yes, he remembered. He remembered blending into the earth. The colour, the texture. He had become a primary, yet sham ingredient of the elements surrounding him. He looked at the indentation where he'd been lying, right next to his mother. And a dawning of realization illumined his head. They hadn't seen him. *They simply hadn't seen him!*

*

Lazarus made the forest his home. He grew into a lean, muscular young man, and each day he thanked Hercules for the training and discipline he needed to survive. He could climb and run and skip and jump, and launch himself over ravines and the most dangerous of fissures. And he had no trouble climbing the highest of rocks to survey his territory. The skills his family had given him, he employed with keenness and dexterity, allowing him to take his place in the hierarchy of the timberland. He knew his way around the flora, and understood exactly which roots to forage, and which herbs to ingest for best effect. He became a master of camouflage, disguising his physique as a rill, a stream or stem, a frond, a fallen tree or moss-covered rock. He merged with the woods of the primeval forest, and fell invisible with the cascading waterfalls, diving deep into the hidden pools of the wilderness. With a falcon's eye for detail, and the instinct of a lynx, he thrived as a hunter. He learned from the wolves the importance of the pack, but was at once a solitary predator, alone in the great cycle of life and death.

But his early days in the forest were not easy. He was a child. Barely a teenager. He had just lost his entire family and he cried. He was too young to know if he was crying out of anger, sadness or just plain old loneliness. He didn't know and he didn't care. But of one thing he was sure, he wasn't afraid. Even when he was alone at night, the cloying darkness did not make him fearful. Rather, the nocturnal cadences of the darkness lulled him to sleep, serenading him with their rhythms, their raw intonations and jarring, creative melody. He felt at home, where he belonged.

But, eventually, the hours and days of grief caught up with Lazarus. From nowhere, there would well up in him such profound pain that he felt his heart breaking, crumbling with the ache of loss. He would go into a blinding daze of mourning, which had him numbly stumbling about the undergrowth, stubbornly crashing against a rock, or aimlessly drifting, in and out of the trees, ending up in the cold of mountain streams wondering how he got there. Sometimes he thought he would never feel anything ever again. And it was in these moments, that he came to understand the true meaning of grief. He needed to mourn, and he cried and howled with pain. And the wolves howled back, sharing his tormented sadness.

But somehow he managed. He survived. And there developed in Lazarus a synchronicity, a oneness with his environment, the thread of survival which ultimately saw him thrive as a human being. Out of the depths of his despair, he grew strong and he saw his place in the world. Although unsure of where life would take him, he was convinced there was a purpose, a reason for everything that had happened to him, and he sought the solace of the stars, and consulted with the Gods of the forest. In his solitude, he realized that he was not alone, and that something, somewhere, was watching over him. He had not been rescued as a newborn babe to die a pointless death. He realized that now, and each day became a wondrous challenge, a voyage of self-discovery and enlightenment. And this journey became pivotal in his lust for life and his thirst for knowledge, and it was these yearnings which eventually drove him out of the forests, towards a distant, beckoning civilization.

He zigzagged up and over the great Carpathians and headed towards the plains of northern Europe. Although keen for human communication, after so many solitary years he was wary of people. He foraged a living on the outskirts of towns and cities and was careful when meeting strangers. He was aware that he was different from other people, and somehow instinctively knew that his being separate, a different species almost, may spell trouble for him. A simple smile, a spoken greeting and a passing gesture were all that he could manage in the first instances. But gradually, he grew more confident and could eventually recognize a friendly, accepting face when he saw it. He came across languages and tongues he barley understood, but found that he had a natural instinct for communication, and could see past the obstacles of words and sounds into the soul of meaning. Sabrina had done her job well.

He traversed westwards, following the sun, and one evening, after a long day's walk, he saw the orange glow of fire, warm and bright in the distance. It was accompanied by the smell of life. As twilight turned into the thick cloak of night, he cautiously approached the amber light, and as he got nearer he heard voices, the general din of human activity. Silently, he stole from tree to tree, bush to bush, and he crept up on what he could now clearly see was a caravan of wagons.

He moved around the site, quietly, guardedly vigilant lest he be discovered.

In the shadows thrown up by the fires, he saw groups of people hunched in conversation. Every now and then a burst of laughter cracked the air, and a general uproar cackle out into the night. Shouts and cries shot across the fields where they camped and Lazarus, not a little jealous, thought of Sabrina and Hercules, Bulut and A'isha and all the Little Indians, and he wondered.

He saw children playing, chiding each other, joking and giggling and fooling around as they ran about, carefree, untouched by a troubled world. He smiled to himself as he recalled his own childhood, and he envied the children their innocence. But he had the good sense not to turn the reminiscence into a maudlin sadness, and with a contented smile on his face, enjoyed watching the children. He moved in closer.

There were huge pots suspended over fires and the smell of cooking made his mouth water. He saw adult faces, glowing red, their black, vibrant shadows dancing between flames. And even though he was hungry, he was very cautious, aware that not everyone would welcome a stranger arriving in the dark.

The caravan had settled down for the night by a shallow river, and as he moved around the wagons, Lazarus could see a lazy line of horses tethered nearby. But, further into the darkness he also saw great shapes and monstrous silhouettes which were foreign to him. He couldn't make out what these were, and the smells and noises had him curious. Curvy, dune-like outlines overlapped with great, gray-black cutouts, and the collective orchestral snorting and munching pinched at his imagination. What were these creatures? And so big!

Then, from deep within, a dawning realization hit him, and the unusual noises and odors, the wavy forms and gigantic outlines of the unfamiliar, came into focus in an exciting lucidity. He had stumbled across a circus.

Despite the buzz of adventure filling his head, Lazarus kept control of his excitement and resisted the temptation to go trailblazing into the camp, proclaiming to the world that, with his extraordinary powers, he belonged there. He was ready to propel himself into the jagged circles of firelight, when a bout of common sense kicked him in the ribs. It was dark. It was nighttime. *Dark*. And he was a stranger.

He reined himself in. He knew that it made sense to wait until morning. For the moment, he would find a secure spot, bed down for the night and on the morrow cautiously announce his presence. That was a much better idea.

After years of wandering he felt, at last, that here was an opportunity.

*

No one knew how the fire started. Perhaps it was an errant spark, ambitious and pushy, a fanciful flame keen for attention. Or the powers of combustion, eager to impress the world with their ruthless ambition. Or maybe it was simply accident, the collision of fates igniting the imagination of a quiet night, innocent, blameless, a happenstance of coincidence.

No one knew, or, in the heat of the moment, really cared.

The tiny squirt of flame grew, nurturing itself on the clear night air. Nibbling on the stiff corpses of summer grasses starved of water, the juvenile flicker began to gorge, force feed itself into a corpulent, fiery sprout, and multiply, spreading a ghastly, scorched blanket across the meadow. Seasoned on tinder and the dry lumber of broken trees, the fire, eager for stardom, crept up on the encampment. As it reached the outer fringes, in cahoots with a fanning breeze the cunning fire mellowed and ripened, avidly maturing into the promise of a fat catastrophe.

And the circus people, wrapped up in their dreams of glory, slept, content and unaware.

An instinct of survival, primeval, honed to perfection after millions of years, alerted the animals to danger. Ever wary of threat, even in sleep, their territorial sense of self-preservation protected them from peril. And that night, as a deep slumber enshrined the camp, there stirred in the bones of the wild creatures, a warning, a cautionary sign that all was not well. They stirred. Not much to begin with - a raised ear, a shuffling hoof, a claw clenched and unclenched, a tale wafted in trivial annoyance. But gradually, with the tiny disturbances on the still air, there arose in the animals a reflex, a base impulse hinged to an ingrained desire to flee danger. They could sense it. They could feel it. They could smell it. Smoke.

The enormous elephants, mountains of corrugated flesh, railed against their chains, heaving in muscular tugs. Heralds of doom, they trumpeted screams of alarm, loud blasts of cautionary warning, a forecast of death and destruction. Camels and llamas spat in defiance, their insolent faces clouded with scorn as, hobbled like convicts, they fought against their bondage. Tall and scared, giraffes, oddly inelegant, tossed their heads in panicky hoops, and yanked and jerked, their instinct to flee held tight in constricting tethers.

And in the wagons, a slow commotion arose. A concerned turning and tossing. And as the trumpets cut short their dreams, the people awoke, a dawning of consternation falling on their sleepy faces. They rubbed and blinked their eyes, and listened as fierce elephant calls rent the air. Something was wrong. Had to be. They got out of bed.

Fumbling in the dark they dressed. Mismatching their clothes and rooting for shoes, they became more concerned as the calls of the wild grew in intensity. Uneasy, but not too alarmed, they stretched and yawned, and parted the flaps of the wagons. Petrified, they froze in horror. Unable to believe their eyes, they stared into the throat of Hell itself. For the one thing they all feared,

284

they all dreaded with all their heart and soul, was there, right there in front of them. Fire.

Moving quickly, the fire had brashly eyed-up the wagons and was attacking without shame or remorse. The grasslands were alive with flame and licked the wagons with giant, fiery tongues and in an instant, rabid cries went up, crazy and hoarse: FIRE! FIRE!

It took only seconds for the whole caravan to wake, for people to arm themselves, to charge about with water and shout in demented orders. They ran and rushed, and fled for their lives. With shocked, harsh white faces, mothers sprinted, screaming as they scooped up their babies. Moaning, sleepy-eyed children, confused by the chaos, were torn from their beds while infants bawled, vexed into irritated knots of confusion. Shoved and jostled away from the flames, the women and children corralled down by the river. Their innocent offspring herded to safety, the wives and sisters joined husbands, fathers, brothers and sons, together forming a chain to fill the buckets. They toiled and sweated, expunging the blazes in sizzles. But the canvases roared, purple and red, the coaches devoured by the torment. They'd rescued their loved ones but stood helpless as the raging torrent, flame after flame ate wagon after wagon.

Avaricious and hungry for flesh, the fire zoomed in on the animals, the innocent wild creatures unable to escape the scorching lashes of its violent temper. The trainers were losing the battle, their pathetic efforts lost in the heat of combat. A fight too big to be won, they screamed for help.

The horses, thank God, in an intelligent frenzy, had somehow freed themselves and galloped off into the night, neighing, braying, a union of liberty, announcing to the world their timely reprieve from death. But the big cats, the lions and tigers, a parody of metaphor, roared, whined and cringed, ablaze in their own skins. They scratched and clawed, yawning roars of fearful panic, as the intense smoke coiled, billowing deathly black about their cages. Cowered, curled up in futile defence, the doomed animals wept and cried out in defeat, heart-breaking wails of forgiveness for whatever sin had condemned them to this scornful death. Roasting in the din of a crackling inferno, their hair and skin torched to blackness, they prayed to whatever God the beasts of earth call upon in times of trepidation.

Chimpanzees squealed and hooted, riotously hurling themselves against the bars, banging and barging, creating a havoc of noise in their desperate attempts to escape. Bears and wolves paced like banshees, barking, yelping, their bare teeth clenched in useless revolt. Gnashing at the iron staves, their bloodied gums flashed in red, angry torment. And stuck in their grilled cages, the exotic and terrified squealed, as the orange tongues licked at their pens, the wooden coops and crates of captivity. Peculiar birds, tropically florid, outlandish in confettis of feathers, smashed against the confines of the metal ribs and squawked and squawked, discordant, a horrible chorus of dread. And reptiles in tanks, scuttled and slithered in their quiet and silence, crawling at windows, their reflections in flame. And dogs ran about, in outraged conundrums, their hackles raised up in fistfuls.

Water. Water. We need more water. Save the animals. We need more water. The animals.

Clowns and jugglers arrived, fighting blindly against the rage, beating with cloth and spade. Troubadours flung shovels of dirt in pathetic showers of earth, sparking crackers, as blades of wayward grass ignited in miniature sputters. Daredevil acrobats vaulted onto cages, but singed and burnt, they quickly leapt off, tumbling in smoky stumbles unable to release the condemned animals.

In pointless attempts to quell the flames, buckets and buckets went from hand to hand, and flings of water slashed the furnace, never more than splashing in ineffective spits which hissed in short stammers. Waves of heat baked the late night air, and the would-be rescuers were driven back, a wall of heat peeling their eyeballs in a terrifying vision of hell. One or two risked the scalds and smarts of the flames, but were thrown back again and again as the firestorm leapt in jagged, lacerating pitches, shelling out red and orange against the night sky. They screamed and charged about, adrift in the dire inevitability of a lost cause.

In the inexorable face of defeat, they retreated, their precious cargos lost to an act of nature, the most primordial of all elements. Beaten and bruised, the firefighters lost heart, and slowly each one dropped away from the cauldron, falling to his knees, defeated and drained. Tattered and torn they keened and howled with the creatures they mourned, and their souls flew, scattered, strewn in the windswept ashes which twirled, twinkling, fairy lights up and up into the blackness. All lost, they sobbed, dripping tears down their dirty faces.

The stink of burning meat and bone filled the air, and the wild cries were dying out as each breed in turn faded, diminished, resigned to a wretched, unheroic demise. The crowd, silent, watched tearfully, helpless in the face of such crude power.

Fire. They had no chance.

Lazarus bedded down for the night. He was comfortable with the thought that the morning would bring with it a brand new start, another beginning. He'd wake up, go and introduce himself and thus embark on a fresh chapter in his life. He was excited. Here was an opportunity. His time in the wilderness was over. He'd made a makeshift mattress out of the dry, summer grasses. He closed his eyes and drifted off, a contented, benign smile decorating his handsome features. And it wasn't long until familiar faces and pictures flooded his dream-world; his parents, A'isha and Bulut, Mr and Mrs India, and all the Little Indians. He relived moments from his childhood and chatted to Sabrina and Hercules about all manner of things – *and then we went round and round in circles running and playing and jumping and falling over and building castles and pulling each other over and tumbling and climbing and Mr India came and shouted at us and told us we were doing it all wrong and that we should do it this way and we all laughed then fell over again and again until Mr India shouted again then we started again and we climbed all over each other and made a great big tower and I climbed all over the others to get to the top and then we all came crashing down again in a big pile and Mr India shouted again and we laughed and then . . .*

From deep within his dream, his electric instincts erased the pictures and rocketed him to the world of the present.

His eyes shot open. He could smell it. The one enemy all creatures of the forest are afraid of. He could smell it.

FIRE.

In a flash he was on his feet. He headed for the enclosures. He knew the animals would be terrified and unable to escape. They had been tied up for the night and their keepers long gone to their beds. There was no time to lose. He had to act now if he wanted to save them.

He started with the elephants. Humming the mantras of the forest he calmed the huge creatures as best he could, and unchained them, releasing them into the night. They trumpeted, and thundered off in great clouds of dust, their monstrous shapes hurtling into the dark. Next came the camels and giraffes. His gentle caresses eased their frightened spirts, and with the sweet sounds of his melodious voice, assuaged their fears, persuading them into the safety of darkness beyond the fires.

Then Lazarus moved on to the caged animals. He freed the monkeys, the primates, the gorillas and chimpanzees, the orangutans and chittering little marmosets, shooing them in troupes out into the shadows and trees. He climbed up onto the cages of wolves and bears, and undid the bolts and catches, the levers and locks and hinges. Jumping down into their midst, he lifted the dying animals, coaxing gently, calming their terror with a gentle word and carefully laid hands. He raised them up, their heads lolling on his shoulder, and placed them, breathless and burnt, on the ground which he had doused with fresh water. He spoke to them, and breathed into their blackened ears, their poor mangled heads slouching in a barely perceived nod of acknowledgement.

His face pock marked with the arrows and stings of flying cinders, Lazarus now set off for the big cats. He soused himself in water, flung a soaking wet blanket over his head and walked straight into the fire. By now he'd been spotted and the crowd shouted out in warning.

No. It's too late. You'll die. It's too late. Don't, they chanted.

But there was no stopping Lazarus. He climbed the cage, opened the hatch and dropped down, down into the tigers' lair. Surrounded by flames and greeted by fearful, twisted snarls, he spoke. A tender, compassionate supplication, an appeal for trust and faith.

"Come," he said. "Come with me." And he put out his hand.

And the almighty beasts roared and roared, confused in their fear. Their tails whipped madly, their ears darted flat back against their heads and they shook their coats, alive with flame.

"Come," repeated Lazarus. "You have nothing to fear." And again he stretched out his hand.

The tigers of the night, scared, fretful, lost in the flames of Hell, looked at Lazarus and they held each other in beams of silent conspiracy. And in the raging blast, an island of mutual understanding rose up, kindled by a tacit, unspoken bond, drawing them together, a preternatural coupling of trust and comprehension.

The tigers, meek, fell into submission, the temperate measure in their eyes betraying the dawn of confidence in their saviour. And Lazarus, ignorant of the pain and torment of the heat, his hand melting as he wrenched the bolt, opened the gate and let them out.

Baked red hot in the furnace, Lazarus staggered from the cage.

He could hear the weakening roars from the lions' den and turned, determined to rescue the sad beasts. But his legs gave way and he fell to his knees. Amazed that he was still alive, others ran forward to help, suddenly heedless of the flames. Falling backwards, Lazarus collapsed into redeeming arms, which gathered him up and rushed him to the cool shade of a tree, far away from the charred chaos.

A mosaic of burns, Lazarus lay dumb, barely alive.

The disfigurement to his face was horrific. His jaw worked a slow motion of awkward mechanics, but he couldn't speak, his lungs choked, his tongue and throat thrashed, lashed by the incendiary cutlass of the fire. His fingers gnarled, bitten off by the vicious teeth of the blaze, Lazarus lay dying.

But in the broiling mire of his devastation, he managed to smile. Not outwardly (he didn't have the lips for that) but in his heart, in his breast, his blistered breast which caved in and out with rapid, shallow breaths, wheezing in brief, wispy groans. He felt his soul rising, climbing, elevating to the heavens, and he knew he had done his part. Fulfilled his duty. He had given his all. He had walked into the fires of Hell and come out the other end.

And a great calmness came over him. A wonderful sense of completion, a destiny satisfied.

*

Like everyone else, Lazarus couldn't help but be amazed by the circus. It ignited his imagination, his fancy. There was something magnetic, tantalising, something which appealed to his sense of entertainment and adventure, and he couldn't resist the fascination, the magical attraction of the nomadic life of the artistes. He was drawn to the colour, the noise, the general clamour and excitement of huge wagon loads of the weird and wonderful rolling into towns and cities, and the excitement of children yelping, gawping, screaming with

291

delight, thrilled by the decorated caravans pulling into fields and setting up camp. With each stake driven hard and fast into the ground, and the raising of the massive canvas temples of diversion, Lazarus thrilled to the allure of the festive extravaganza.

The theatricality and danger of the performances held him spellbound. The fearless leaps and jumps of acrobats, the gymnastics of trapeze artists and the antics of high wire entertainers, all performing without the reassurance of a safety net, made him giddy in admiration. He was fascinated by the impossibility of sword swallowers, fire eaters, a man who put his head in a tiger's mouth and a very pretty young woman who sat beneath a massive elephant's foot. He was amazed at the prospect of one mistake, one error, one tiny misjudgement, and the enormous calamity that would most certainly follow.

And Lazarus was not alone in this. For, besides the wonder of absurd physical spectacle, and the sad delight of animal tricks, people were also drawn by the macabre possibility that there may be an accident, a fall, a slip, a roaring hunger that may snap shut a lion's jaws. They were on the lookout for the mouse that frightens elephants. The sweaty palm which drops young girls. The tired rope that shreds at its zenith. The baby's cry which triggers stampedes. The audience were there to be diverted from their humdrum lives, to be thrilled, for that is what they paid for.

But besides the daredevil, fearless escapades in the big top, Lazarus was also fascinated by the circus fayre, the traveling side show. Rather than a display of gymnastic dexterity, the fayre was an exhibition of perhaps the more interesting peculiarities of the human form. These side shows or stalls contained not the demonstrations of man's physical prowess exactly, but his historical eccentricities, his legendary and mythical idiosyncrasies. It was a travelling exhibition of fable and saga, and its curiosities held Lazarus spellbound.

*

For months he had lain isolated, unconscious. Unaware of the outside world, he had stewed, prostrate, gathered up in a medicinal cocoon of herbs and unctions. Unable to speak or communicate, his spirit had gone into a deep, dead pool of numb insentience. His heart pattered softly, quiet, a slumbering yet hectic clock, ticking away the critical hours. He had lost several fingers and toes in the fire and his face was a mess, cindered to an unrecognizable blur; nose, lips, ears and brows, all gone in the blaze. And, perhaps most painful of all to a man like Lazarus, he had, of course, lost his eyesight. This terrified him more than anything else, and he had to fight, almost daily, not to fall prey to the panic that lay in his breast.

He would never see again. Ever. He was blind. Blind.

Despite his unconsciousness, he felt the unpredictable rocking of the wagon, and the uneven rumble of the wheels. And every now and then a tender hand would settle on his brow, and cooling words fall in individual cascades of reassurance.

"All will be well. Do not worry."

And the voice would carry him to another place, a place of wonder and supreme joy, not a reckless, unbounded place, but a tranquil, peaceful place where each care of the physical world dissolved in an

293

extinction utterly complete. He had never felt such kindness, such aching understanding and benevolence.

He tasted the sweet balm of security, and was unhindered by the preoccupations of time. A warm glow of compassion embraced him, and, strangely, he revelled in a depth of quietude he had not felt for a very long time.

Captive in his blackness, Lazarus resigned himself to the fact that he would never again see dawn break, nor the sun set. In his despondency, he nourished his soul on memories, and meticulously pieced together the jigsaw of his life. He recalled people and places, events. He went as far back as he could remember, and painted each memory with vivid anecdotes and tales as best he could recall. He relived his young life and agonized, as he had so many times, over the death of his family. Time and again he thought of his mother, his real mother, lost to him yet by his side every day. He thought also of Sabrina and Hercules, his parents. He loved them all and their places in his heart would never be usurped. Yet, here he was, lost in a black world, the recipient of such care and attention. Such love. He had no idea of how to cope.

The creaks and rickety groans of the wagon kept him company, and reminded him he was still alive. He could hear voices, unfamiliar, in tongues strange and wonderful, but couldn't communicate with them. With the inhalation of the flames, his lungs had been scorched, and his powers of speech shredded. He was quite aware of the world but couldn't connect with it. He knew his nurse, but had never seen her face. Never talked to her. Her gentle voice poured encouraging words on his ailing spirits, and held him, embalmed in a mesmeric state of healing.

"Hello," she'd say softly. "My name's Kitsune. I'm here to help you."

At every opportunity she would sit with him, her soothing words caressing his injured soul. She would sing, in unknown languages and recite what he understood to be poetry, and he would drift, wafted on clouds of compassion.

She applied lotions and sweet smelling oils to the scorched flesh, tenderly massaging his burns. But, tight as a drum, his taut, brittle frame at first resisted the creams and unguents, the herbal remedies applied so longingly to his embattled body, and only gradually, with the grudging passage of time, did a degree of suppleness return.

And Lazarus found that his senses grew unusually sharp, picking up nuances and details like pin pricks gently prodding at his consciousness. Secure in his safety, he nestled down into the bundles of pillows and cushions, the exotic fabrics clouded in fabulous scents and perfumes, and glided with the hypnotically swirling fumes of incense. A fragile melody infiltrated his breast, lifting him up beyond the mundane world of man's tortured journey, to a serene domain of beauty and wellbeing.

And then, after weeks of careful, tepid application, Kitsune began to knead and mould, manipulating his limbs, more forcefully coaxing the blistered skin and rigid joints back to life. The hours and hours of concentrated work were gradually rewarded, as slowly a restoration was wrought, and Lazarus began to feel the suppleness return to his rigid skin. More than a nurse, Kitsune, a doctor and surgeon, charmed his body out of its torpor and a new, fresh garden of hope began to appear. Under the scabby, black crusts of death, a fresh undergrowth began to show, a virginal membrane, delicate, eager for cultivation.

He couldn't frown, for he had no eyebrows, but in his heart, growing stronger each day, Lazarus queried this incredible development, and a realisation hit him that he was in the hands of a Goddess - or something like one.

Carefully, his physician nurtured the spores of regeneration, feeding them on exotic herbs and intoxicating spices, encouraging a brand new evolution, a fantastic rebirth. The fingers and toes miraculously began to sprout afresh, budding with vigour and flexibility, yelling out for attention. And from the blackened, stunted nubs, sprung a young vitality, original and buoyant, keen to make its joyful mark in the world.

Lazarus wiggled and pressed, and worried away with his new digits. And he felt a tingling of nerves rifle through to his hands and feet, travel up his legs and arms, embrace his torso, his chest, his back, his neck and head. He felt a vibrant, electric pulse of sensitivity course through his body, touching every organ and bone. His face tingled with rejuvenation as first his brows, then lips, then nose and ears filled with the juice of resurrection. And Lazarus rose from the ashes, fully formed, whole again.

And one day, one miraculous day, the teeniest trickle of light crept up under the silk bandage and ever so slightly, but so, so slightly, tickled the corners of his eyes. And the gentlest of astral kisses caressed his cheek and Lazarus, after months and months of darkness, was led into the light.

And he sat up. And he wept.

He dressed and descended from the safety of the wagon, into his new world.

*

The first time he saw them, he was appalled by the inhumanity, the carelessness with which the poor unfortunates were wheeled out, gawped at by a paying public, exploited for profit. He was no stranger to the fantastic and fanciful, but he was shocked at the calculating abuse of human oddity. He took big breaths of indignation as he watched them, staged, posed, presented as freaks of nature. But was taken aback, a harsh contrition strangling his chest, as, in a moment of enlightenment, he realised that what he perceived as forced bonhomie, the strained laughter of affected, exaggerated expressions of happiness, were, in fact, genuine. Through all the ridiculousness of the dramatic postures, there was, underneath the masquerade, a great sense of camaraderie, an overwhelming manifestation of belonging, of family.

There were midgets, the smallest people he had ever seen, smaller than cats and dogs, who sat under stools and climbed onto tables all vertigo and devil-may-care attitude. And giants, the biggest people he had ever seen, as tall as small giraffes, scraping the sky, head in the clouds, lost in the mist. There were people with long arms, short arms, no arms. No legs, three legs, four legs. People with no noses, big noses - but BIG noses like nothing he had *ever* seen in his life. And people with big flappy ears and claws for hands, wooden and cleft, like goats' feet. And people with spines like vines all creepy and bowed, twisty and back to back. They crawled and scuttled and edged and inched, excused and entreated, arching and barging like creatures fresh out of the sea.

Lazarus, measured, coherent, soon came to realise that he had a lot in common with these circus folk, and that he of all people, with his powers of invisibility and transformation belonged here, to this hotchpotch of oddballs, this mélange of physical mavericks.

In the fayre next to the Big Top, amidst the mishmash potpourri of extraordinary life, there were the classical, historical exhibits, legitimate attempts to educate a population still in thrall at the dusky end of the Enlightenment. In fact, it was a signature feature of the circus generally that they hailed from the murky past of legend and myth. They played on the fixation with things Greco-Roman, promoting a festival atmosphere of neo-classicism, riding on the back of the latest fashion for poets and artists to emulate the resplendent age of the classics. Indeed, the very name was enough to alert customers as to what to expect: *Plato's Incredible Roman Circus,* a cocktailed sobriquet if ever there was.

In a lilac tent, trimmed with silvery silk pompoms and tassels, artefacts from the sagas and fables of ancient Rome and Greece held the audience in a trance, an abstraction of mystery and imagination. The show people, adorned in wigs and the make-up of pomp and grandeur, milled and marched about in their finery: the gowns of governors and emperors, princely togas, historical tunics of conquering Generals and the everyday livery of Greek sages, literary giants and soldiers. Rubbing shoulders with mock philosophers, statesmen and intellectuals, the paying public were treated to recitations of poetry and great speeches from towering figures of the past. Theatrical dramas of tragedy and comedy, conflicts and wars and the heroics

298

of combatants, all were brought to life in a vibrant, carnival pageant of celebration.

Many painted in the azure of the Aegean and Mediterranean Seas, several wagons were also colourfully decorated with the Gods and mythical characters of legend. Together, they formed not just a side show, an appetizer before the main event in the Bog Top, but an impressive spectacle in their own right. Each carriage held several attractions, designed to cast spells of wonder and amazement. Once unhitched from their teams of horses, the coaches, with retractable panels, created natural stages from which entertainers could perform and display their wares.

And on a circular podium, authentically dressed in a floor-length toga, topped off by an oversized laurel wreath, stood the chief barker himself: Plato. In a high pitched, yet gravelly voice, he persuaded even the most sceptical of onlookers that what they were about to see (for a small fee of course!) could not be seen anywhere else in the world, and that this was the one and *only* chance that they would *ever* have to see the *absolutely undeniable, irrevocably verifiable, magnificently stupendous,* specimens from history.

"Captured and tamed," he shouted, circling to address the gathering crowd, his huge, black-waxed handle bar moustache completely at odds with his classical bearing "these inexplicable brutes of nature will stupefy and spellbind. Leave you flabbergasted, speechless in the face of veracity; have you captivated, fascinated and," after a beat or two of mesmeric glowering "hyp-no-tized." He scowled, defying the audience to contradict him.

"Brought into captivity after life-threatening bloody struggles, these unnatural beasts, spoken of by

Homer, Ovid and the poets of yore, now sit bagged, netted and safely in bondage for you to muse upon in wonderment."

The barking orator, in a gesture of true magnanimity, chose to single out the resourceful hunters, the hardy representatives of the circus who pursued and chased down the prey, the quarry which now awaited the eager crowds behind the closed curtains of the wagons.

"With little respect for their own safety," he went on, furrowing his brows in serious confidentiality "our very own huntsmen ventured into the wilds of the ancient lands, tracking for weeks, sometimes months, sometimes years, and snatched from the jaws of history, these fabled beasts. Often seized in titanic battles, on the highest of the most rugged cliff tops, the deepest of the darkest, most dangerous valleys, the thickest of primeval forests where the forces of prehistory still roam unfettered, bloodthirsty and cruel, these wonders of the ancient world are alive, living and breathing entities desperate for their freedom."

The crowd was, by now, eager to part with the few pennies that would draw back the curtains and reveal the wonders of the world. They shoved and pushed and dropped their hard earned coins into the boxes.

"This way. This way," shouted Plato. "This way to the wonders of the ancient world."

He directed the audience to the line of wagons, and twisted and curled his moustache as he heard the clunky thuds of coin.

'This way ladies and gentlemen," he shouted again and again. "This way to the wonders of the world."

The people rushed and flooded in, pouncing on the first of the exhibits. With incredulity they peered at Medusa, her head alive with squirming snakes, hissing, launching fanged attacks at nothing in particular. She sat there, stoic, unconcerned by the poisonous conundrum about her ears. The crowd panted in wonder. Then, hard, sharp breaths were drawn in, when, exposed from behind a blue velvet curtain, a Chimera, half throttled, crashed its lion's head against the bars of a cage. Its chained, goat torso, twisting in obstinate revolutions, flashed its scaly green dragon's tail, round and round in whisks of angry temper. The children gushed in awe at the magnificence of such a creature. Their parents, howver, seeing this as the work of the Devil, shied away, dragging their children with them. But the crowd, hungry for more, churned in swirls of frightened delight, horrified, yet irresistibly drawn to the terrors of legend. With each unimaginable exhibit stretching the limits of credulity, the crowd eased uncomfortably, yet compellingly, from one fascination to the next, until, finally, they were ushered into a small marquee.

Illuminated by dim candlelight, the packed pavilion was thick with sweat, animal odours and an awkward smell of blood and dead flesh. Curtains hung at one end of the tent and a heavy expectation hovered electric, pregnant in its suspense. The mumbling crowd fidgeted, twitching in anticipation. Crushed in unpleasant proximities, they breathed into each other, the reek of bad breath stifling the torpid air. Chattering, they grumbled and moaned and pushed for space until a voice sang out, a triumph of acclaim.

A woman had climbed a pulpit. At least, it *should* have been a woman, judging by the skirt, the shapely lace bodice and the bouncy rings of long blonde hair spilling down onto her shoulders. But it wasn't, or, at least, there was room for doubt. For, in contrast to the feminine attire and luxurious golden mane, her face was adorned by a wreathe of curly black hair, coils of wiry dangles stretching down to her breasts. Her voice, clearly that of a female, a clarion call to the island of Lesbos, rang out loud and clear, but the facial hair had the crowd rumbling in quandary. Was it a man, or a woman?

"The Cyclops," the Bearded Lady shouted, "is thousands of years old. He was born on the island of Crete where he was trapped and then captured, and brought into the light of civilisation."

She raised her voice in competition with the congregation's babbling prattle.

"This poor creature," she went on "this aberration, this abomination, this outrageous, wretched soul, spent years and years alone, unwanted, uncared for and left to fend for itself in the labyrinth of tunnels and caves left over from the glory days of the ancient Greeks."

She heaved a breath. And with that, on cue, the curtains parted.

The crowd cooed and arghed, and pressed forward for a better look. The creature sat scrunched up in a heap, a mountain of bearskin and muscle. It groaned and grunted, a misery of grizzled hostility. Filthy, tangled hair draped down over its temples and with its head hung in a shame of torment, its one eye was kept firmly concealed.

Show us your eye, someone shouted.

Yeah, Cyclops, show us your eye, joined in another.

302

And before long the restless crowd were yelling in a chorus of agitation: *Show us your eye! Show us your eye!! Show us your eye!!!*

The Bearded Lady sensed a riotous thrill pass over the throng, and although pleased to see the place packed, was, nonetheless, aware of the danger.

"Ladies and gentlemen," she shouted above the uproar, "please don't get too near the cage. Please. The Cyclops is a dangerous creature. Don't get too close."

But it was no use, the press of bodies was hot and out of control and the crowd squeezed flat against the bars of the cage.

The creature, upset into a nervous restlessness, began to stir and shifted on its bed of straw.

Your eye. Your eye. Show us your eye, they shouted.

The Cyclops unwound its hefty legs, its thunderous thighs and calves flexed in a powerful display of brawn and muscle. And slowly, but oh so slowly, it undid the knots of inactivity, and gradually, painstakingly, it stood up. Its torso flexed, in clenches, as it breathed in barrow loads of air, and its ribbed diaphragm rippled and contorted as the beast stretched, reaching up high into the top rafters of the cage. Its arms and mountainous shoulders rolled in exercising windmills, sending a broadside draught across the heads of the onlookers.

Up to its full, overpowering stature, the Cyclops began to growl, a towering, brute force of unadulterated ferocity. It barked in wild, crazy stabs. Then it snarled and shook its head from side to side in a threatening see-saw of intimidation. Its hands, clumsy fumbling clods, clawed at the cage and a roar of unbelievable magnitude reverberated through the tent. The Cyclops howled and cried and the people winced at the enormity of the rage in the beast.

And then, as it drew close, unrelenting against the bars, the creature threw back its head. The hairy veil, the screen of matted brown hair, flew back, and as a volcanic rumble echoed from its gigantic chest, in one immense cackle of fury the Cyclops crashed its head against the bars, revealing its one, tremendous eye. Its filthy visage, covered in the stains of inhumane captivity, looked emptily out between the bars. The crowd gushed in awe.

The beast's one eye beadily stared in a cold, unfeeling beam. And the teeming crowd, wary but far too curious to take care, surged even closer to inspect the one-eyed giant.

"Ladies and gentlemen," cried out the Bearded Lady "behold, the Cyclops of ancient Greece."

On seeing the full majesty of the creature's horrifying ugliness and fearsome reputation, the shrieking crowd applauded wildly, thrilled by the spectacle.

"Ladies and gentlemen," cried the Bearded Lady again, "please take care not to go too close to the cage, for the Cyclops is not to be trusted. He is a freak of nature, a mutant, a misshapen coincidence of mixed blood hailing from the darkest corners of history. I must warn you that he is a predator, a hungry carnivore. Ladies and gentlemen, boys and girls, the Cyclops is a dreaded enemy of humans because . . . (and here she paused for maximum effect) . . . he feasts on . . . flesh . . . human flesh!"

Wild cries of horror went up and down and round again. The crowd, outraged, gasped, falling over themselves, taking clumsy but determined steps back, away from the iron bars. Parents clasped youngsters to their breasts, grimacing as the beast picked up and gnawed on what looked like a human leg, "ARGH", shooting spittle and flecks of flesh into the front rows of the open mouthed spectators.

"Yes, ladies and gentlemen, in defiance of all God's laws . . ."

But the Bearded Lady didn't finish the ejaculatory bombast, for, from right in front of the cage, a small boy, no more than seven years old, his face a wrenching agony of torture, screamed in a high pitched slash of pain. Too shocked for tears, his innocence savagely implored the crowd for help. From his shoulder, a gushing root of flesh and shattered bone, squirted a sickly red jet, showering the audience in a fountain of blood. Squeals of disgust and palpable fear were soon accompanied by a crazy panic. People ran, leapt, scrambled and scurried, bouncing over each other in a mad blitz of terror. The Cyclops munched on the boy's severed arm.

Stupidly inquisitive, the boy, a small scamp of a thing, had snuggled up close, put his arm in the cage and saw it snatched up and chewed off, midway between the elbow and the shoulder. Screams of revulsion and shock ensued, and the Bearded Lady, helpless in the stampede, threw up her arms in defensive surrender, a look of horror turning her pallid face even whiter as the gross reality hit her. The boy fell to the floor in a pale faint, a minor lake of blood flooding out over the sawdust. Lazarus tensed, wary and ready to invade, to rescue the boy. He was just about to jump over the onrush of escaping bodies when he felt a gentle pressure on his

305

arm. He looked down. Petite, slender fingers peeped out of a silky smooth cuff, the sleeve of a shimmering sea-green kimono. They patted him, comfortably, a reassuring gesture of confidentiality. He wondered. And the world stopped turning.

His eyes traced upwards and he stared into a different universe of understanding. Coal black hair, cut to the line of a sweeping velvet jawline, framed an oval face of such serenity his breath caught in his chest, and he could have sworn his heart stopped beating. Captured beneath an ebony fringe, two eyes swallowed him whole, pulling him in to a marvellous peace, a heavenly wellbeing worthy of the afterlife. He dived in, deliciously heedless of caution, the raucous din and confusion of the horror gone in an instant of serenity. Almost imperceptibly, the woman shook her head and smiled.

The marquee was empty, silent, save for the hungry grunts of the creature and the little boy's miserable whimpers.

"You can stop now," said the woman.

The boy's pathetic wails still filled the vacant canvass.

"I said, you can stop now. They've gone."

The boy, curled up in a tight ball of mock pain and despair, stretched out and extinguished his cries. The woman unclipped her beard, wiped the perspiration from around her neck and sat down.

"Cor, this is itchy," she said.

The creature removed the prosthetic glass eye from the centre of its forehead, pulled off the gauze padding across its eyes, and yawned. The boy got up, brushed off the tails of straw stuck to his trousers and laughed.

"Can I go play now, Mum?"

His mother smiled, gave him a warm nod of the head.

"Go on then," she said, adding quickly "Don't go gettin' into trouble."

The boy grinned. The creature winked at his son. And the boy ran off. Lazarus look about him. The kimono had gone. The Bearded Lady gave him a smile and a friendly wave. Her husband, the Cyclops, offered an encouraging grin, a gesture of greeting and welcome into their secret. Lazarus nodded in return. He felt a solidarity of companionship, and his heart fluttered.

He felt fabulous. The enormity of the confidence trick had him reeling with pleasure. And he laughed, a great big laugh cutting through his self-consciousness, releasing the tension that had built up between his shoulders. He threw his head back and guffawed. He felt a terrific sense of relief, with no little wonder and quizzical intrigue as, in that brief moment of exposure, he pondered the bizarre world on the threshold of which, he now stood.

How wonderful the world was, he thought, how simply astonishing. And he shook his head in amazement and disbelief, and then, with a broad warm smile creasing his lips, he wandered out of the marquee into the reality and bright light of a beautiful, sunny day. It was great to be alive, and he stretched out his arms, embracing the daylight and the heat of the sun.

He wandered in a happy trance, thoroughly engaged by the medley of peculiarities on view. A reptile man full of scales and spiky, shared a stage with a woman with three breasts. They chatted and nattered away like it was all perfectly natural, and, indeed, it was, for them, perfectly natural. Why not?

Enchanted, Lazarus couldn't help but smile and he nodded in a friendly *hello* to a tree man who had branches sticking out of his head and shoulders, and a man whose hands had petrified, been turned to stone, his fingers jutting out like stalactites. There was a woman who could fold herself into a container no bigger than a jar of pickles. Amazing! He was captivated by magicians and alchemists who turned water into wine and paper into gold. He was staggered by the audacity of the show. He loved the verve, panache, the relish with which all the circus people went about the business of entertainment. They had an energy, a dynamism and vitality which he found irresistible, and he longed to be a part of this magnificent family of misfits.

Following the throng, the excited whoops and hollers of children led him to a field. There, tethered to a post in the middle of a small paddock, was a man-beast. It had the body of a huge, muscular bull, bold, physically imposing, and the head and torso of a man, angular, unafraid and strikingly defiant. Fierce, undeniably wild, the beast strutted about, its hooves sloshing, stamping in the muddy-muck ground. Its tail swished in arrogant flashes and the sturdy legs kicked in rebellion against their ropey arrest. It snorted and raged and wallowed in its angry captivity, throwing its head skyward in harsh, insolent bellows. Livid, thick drools of slaver lashed around in silver lassoes. Its eyes, crude, violent symbols of ferocious revolt, bulged glassy black, marbles, stranded islands in blood shot half-moons. It moaned in guttural thunders, the air steaming with its torrid magnificence.

The crowd loved it. Lazarus grinned. And one shiny, bald eye caught his attention, and the slightest suggestion of a smile flittered across the beast's face.

Encouraged by the keepers, adults and children alike purchased cabbages and turnips and rotten potatoes, and hurled them at the sad creature, erupting in peals of laughter if they scored a hit by landing a vegetable on the horns of the great beast. And the beast throttled and grunted, straining at the leashes, threatening to break its bondage. The crowd applauded in howls of enjoyment at the creature's discomfort, and Lazarus, now privy to the secret, laughed again. He could enjoy the day and he felt a truly brilliant sense of not just relief, but also belonging, for he too, was a chameleon, a changeling who could cheat and defeat nature by bending, becoming what he was not.

He turned away, and as he mingled, squeezing his way between noisy voyeurs, excited true believers and one or two rather unpopular sceptics, he passed another raft of stalls packed with the most amazing collection of museum pieces, icons and relics, bizarre and beautiful artefacts of days gone by. He was invited to shoot arrows from the very bow used by Cupid, the Roman God of love; to drink from the very goblet used by Dionysus, the Greek God of wine; to dig a hole with the very spade and pick axe used by Hercules to clean the Augean Stables; to brandish, and make a wish with the very wand used by the patroness of witchcraft herself, Hecate. Lazarus passed these wonders of the world and, wide-eyed, wondered himself at the veracity of the relics. He was familiar with the myths and legends of yesteryear and frowned in suspicion at one or two of the claims. But there was no doubting the confidence with which the pieces were presented, and the enthusiasm of the crowds was, indeed, palpable. In a glass casket he saw a lock of hair from Aphrodite. In another, high up, suspended from a beam, feathers from the wings of Icarus and his father Daedalus. And sticking up, out of a barrel of water, proud, erect, stood Neptune's trident, its pointy fingers directing the paying customers heavenward.

At the end of this row of magical objects, the climax to an odyssey which could be bought for only a few pence, was the Golden Pavilion. Here, in a roofless trellis of finely worked wrought iron, the sun's energy was annexed, its light directed by giant mirrors and lenses onto a podium. In the centre of this, raised on a purple platform, Lazarus saw the apex of the fayre's show, the zenith, the fantastic pinnacle.

Neither effigy nor sculpture, bold and bronzing in the sunbeams, shone a brightness, a warning to mankind, a reminder of sin and the overpowering urge to fall into the iniquity of greed.

Artistically captivating, but utterly desolate, the magnificent showpiece was a testimony to man's unwavering devotion to avarice. It mesmerized, transfixed and bemused onlookers who pined with the painful heartache of gluttony and loss. For there, in the spotlight of the heavens, mute, for all to see, stood the daughter of King Midas, golden and dead.

The crowd, reverent but aghast at the value of such a prized spectacle, whispered in astonishment. Reflecting the sun's rays in rainbows of blinding colour, the statue blazed intrigue and fascination.

Poor thing.

Terrible.

How could he do that?

Dreadful.

Poor, poor thing.

Must be worth a fortune, whispered some.

And about her shoulders, nesting, basking in a shared glory, Jason's Golden Fleece kept the unfortunate Marigold wrapped, safe from the weight of the world in her brazen tragedy. The priceless sheep skin, its threads and curls brilliant in the sunshine, were labelled as the original, the one and only, the singularly authentic Golden Fleece. Handed down from generation to generation, but eventually lost to mankind, it had been rediscovered and brought into the light by the intrepid circus adventurers, who had trekked into the heartlands of the ancients, and dug with their bare hands to unearth the Fleece, and deliver it up to enjoy the fame it so deserved.

And Lazarus nodded. And then he left. And as he exited, he turned to look at the Golden Pavilion. His mind awash with intrigue, he smiled, his kind eyes narrowed in a warm satisfaction. *How wonderful to be able to see,* he said to himself.

And the circus became his saviour and protector, delivering him out of the obscurity of a lonely, solitary existence, into the arms of a new family.

*

With his fabulous powers and a natural gift for entertainment, Lazarus fitted in perfectly with the circus. He soon headlined. As the spectacle set up camp on

311

village greens and the open fields adjacent to towns, Lazarus became the main attraction. But he was no fool, and he was careful not to ridicule his new hosts. He could out-lift and out-run any athlete, and outwit any magician, or confound all readers of fortune, but he wisely kept his powers in check.

He clapped with the crowds, and joined in their revelry. He recognized the courage of high wire acts, and nodded admiringly at the death-defying trapeze artists, unashamedly smiling at their nerve. He applauded enthusiastically when acrobats flew through the air rolling and falling, cartwheeling in tumbles of joy. He laughed with the clowns and guffawed at their slapstick, appreciative of the timing and practice it took to make people smile.

But his heart sank, however, when he considered the plight of the animals. He had saved them, but saved them for what? Perhaps the lions, poor things had been lucky, to die in the flames. All the animals he had rescued, released, had been captured, and the tigers nursed back to health. Lazarus was pleased with that. But he felt their despair as they were forced back into the painful routines, mechanically begging and balancing, skipping and jumping through hoops, their wild natures beaten out of them. He did his best to soothe the aches and pains of the ill-fated beasts, and he would speak to them in an effort to console their fear, their unhappiness. But ultimately, he knew, they were doomed. They, and all the caged animals, would never escape their drudgery. His heart sank.

Healing

The circus made its way across western Europe. There didn't seem to be any real plan as to the route they were taking but Lazarus knew they were headed for Amsterdam. He didn't know exactly where that was but it didn't matter, he was quite happy. The travellers had made him feel at home. He recognised the camaraderie and love he missed so much from his own family, and he took great care to be respectful and courteous.

Of course, at the beginning he found it difficult. He still hadn't fully recuperated from the horrendous injuries sustained in the great fire, and he could barely speak. His throat had been rasped raw and his lungs seared, almost to cinders. His new hosts greeted him with kindness, and no little gratitude for saving their animals, and he wanted to join in, to share their geniality, the celebratory nature of their thankfulness. But he was frustrated by his incapacity to express himself, and he felt inadequate.

They all knew him, even on that first day as he'd wandered from one exhibit to another in a dumbfounded daze, astounded by the trickery and deception. For months they had followed his progress, and listened to Kitsune as she presented them with updates on his recovery. And they had all paid their special patient a discreet, yet patently busybody visit, to see his progress for themselves. Oh yes, they knew who he was, and they had all voiced their admiration and gratitude. And Lazarus, overwhelmed by the attention, wanted to tell them how much he appreciated their concern, their care and devotion to his wellbeing. Without a voice however, he found this somewhat challenging. But, with a smile and an open expression of honesty and friendship, there soon developed and prospered a mutual understanding, a genuine companionship.

As a stranger and hero, he was, of course, a natural target for the children, and they milled about his feet chattering and generally getting in the way with their endless questions and laughter. Lazarus, glad of the energetic company, didn't mind this at all, as it reminded him of the Little Indians and his own childhood. Also, he wasn't slow to realise, that here was an opportunity to reciprocate the generosity of spirit, unreservedly projected by the circus people.

So, one day, after only the very briefest of deliberations, he decided to treat the children to a display of magic. Real magic. As the caravan pulled up to make camp for the night, Lazarus, with an extravagant wave of his arms, gathered all the youngsters together. Knitting his brows, he gestured that they concentrate really hard on his face. The children, excited and mesmerised by the charisma and magnetic charm of their idol, did as requested, and poured their youthful energies into their hero's startling eyes. They stared and stared and then, to their utter disbelief, in a minor whirlwind of dust, Lazarus disappeared.

Wow, they chimed. *Wow.*

He had them mystified, scratching their heads in bewilderment.

Wow, they screamed in delight. One minute he was there, standing right in front of them, the next, *whoosh,* gone. The children were amazed, thrilled and consumed by wonder. And they were even more

314

impressed when they turned around to see Lazarus standing knee deep in pasture some twenty metres away.

Wow.

And it didn't take long for word to spread that the circus now had in its midst, a new magician, a miracle worker who, in the blink of an eye, could contort and disappear, only to reappear in a field half a mile away. Incredible!

Lazarus soon found himself part of the family, a new addition to the clan of happy circus people, and he basked in the splendour of belonging.

And, slowly, he was getting his voice back. Conscientiously, every day, he ingested Kistune's medicinal potions and brews. And with the steady passage of time, the curative elixirs worked their balanced magic, healing the internal damage caused by the blast of the flames. His confidence returned, his frustrations diminished, and before too long Lazarus was chatting away to Kitsune, expressing more than just his eternal gratitude for saving his life. He would hold her hand, and tell her his deepest secrets, his feelings and emotions, and how he felt about her. And she, after months of nursing him back to health, would melt in the security of his strength, his mystic enchantment, his passion. For she had fallen for Lazarus and could not resist the raw attraction. They revelled, exultant in their happiness, and praised the Gods for their good fortune. Tragedy had drawn them together, but their love was fuelled by the magnetism and divinity of destiny.

The circus went west, then north, then south, then west again, and Lazarus sensed the general progression towards a setting sun. He would look ahead at each new horizon and wonder where life was taking him. He'd been orphaned as a baby, seen his adopted

315

parents murdered, lived with the wolves of the forest, been blinded and was now in love, working in a circus. It was all a dream. But it was a wonderful romance, a terrific story which one day he looked forward to telling his children. He dreamed of that. One day.

As the cavalcade marched on, he would most often than not, walk by the wagons briskly stretching his legs, enjoying the exercise. Sometimes he would take advantage of the wide open spaces, and wander off, sniffing out the herbs and spices secreted beneath bushy outcrops and fern covered boulders. He'd drift off in remembrance of A'isha, the hours and days passing as he conversed with her spirit. Then Sabrina and Hercules would come smiling, all arms and kisses, and he'd embrace them in huge hugs and great heaving sobs of happiness. And Mr and Mrs India, and all the Little Indians, would converge on him, everyone running around like rabbits, hopping about in glorious, carefree abandon. While Bulut, careful Bulut, would nod sagely, and grin in beams of pride, as his student grew in stature. The days were not unpleasant, and Lazarus always had that ability to recall, in the most infinite detail, all and every aspect of his lost family. Except they weren't lost. They were never lost, not now. For he carried them in his heart. And he could see them. Oh yes, he could see them very clearly. For, ever since his blindness, things had never been so lucid.

And he had one person to thank for that, the one person who had penetrated his soul, had opened him up to a new vision of life, his love, the love of his life, Kitsune. The woman who had cured his blindness.

She was beautiful. Wonderfully beautiful. Petite yet grand, innocent yet all-knowing, she was a paradox, a beautiful, young Japanese paradox of royal decent. Ageless, fabulously gifted, and endowed with a

316

supernatural comprehension of the world she inhabited, Kitsune was truly an astonishing person. A doctor, surgeon and sage, she harboured an encyclopedic knowledge and understanding of all things natural and scientific. Her abilities as a physician and healer were incredible, and she drew on the collective teachings of both traditional and modern medicine.

She had studied and meditated with the mystics, the ageless priests of the past. She had prayed with Druids and worshipped with Pharos, and communed across oceans with the seers of the world. She had soared with eagles and swam with fish, and knew the spirits of enchanted forests. She had learned the mantras of shamans, and conversed with the echoes of jungles.

With the physicians of lost worlds, she had raised the dead and cured the dying. She had questioned the perplexities of the world, its conundrums, and composed a bounty of divine remedies for its ailments. She was fully conversant with mummification and the preservation of cadavers, and she knew how to chant, to charm and tease diseases, the sicknesses, out of the ill and needy. And she knew how to heal with her bare hands, and accepted the power of belief.

She'd spent years and decades pouring over ancient scrolls, ever refining her comprehension of how to treat the world's untreatable maladies. And she had an inherent, intuitive creativity, and with her cerebral inquisitiveness, she puzzled over how to merge, to synthesize the practical and ethereal, the spiritual and physical.

She could speak without talking and listen without hearing. She could feel without touching and see without seeing. And she was over 5000 years old, but didn't look a day over twenty-five. Impossible? Of course. Except that this, was Kitsune!

*

They finally arrived in Amsterdam. The circus was a huge attraction, and for several days the show stunned and bemused, even managing to dazzle the Jewish diamond dealers who packed the tent with their families and friends. With their long beards and big hats, these rich, gemstone merchants were not easily fooled, and the circus acts had their work cut out to convince the crowds of their magic. Lazarus played his part and enjoyed popular success as, in the big circle, he disappeared in a puff of smoke, to reappear with a clash of cymbals high up in the rafters of the giant marquee. The audience applauded madly, and Lazarus ignited their belief in the impossible when he stood by a trumpeting elephant, turned, and walked straight through it.

"How d'you do that, Lazarus?"

"What?"

"You know what."

"What?"

"You know - walk through an elephant."

"Oh that."

"Yes, that."

"Hmm. Well."

Pause . . .

"So?"

"So what?" She was getting frustrated. "How d'you do it?"

"Ah well, my darling . . ." he started and looked off into the distance.

"Don't 'Ah well my darling' me then ignore me. How do you do it?"

"It's a trick," he said patiently.

"No it isn't. And you know it."

"Hmm," he hummed, nodding his head.

Kitsune stared into the grey, misty eyes.

"It's not a trick, and you know it. You can actually do it. I know."

"I know you know," he said.

"Well then?"

"Well what?"

"Oh, for goodness sake Lazarus," she blurted, exasperated. "How d'you do it?"

Lazarus shrugged his broad shoulders, leaned over and kissed her gently on the lips. "Magic," he whispered.

"Oh you, you're maddening," she said, and pulled him closer.

"Yes, I know. Really mad, almost crazy," and he laughed.

*

After the fire, Kitsune had insisted on taking him back to her carriage. Along with several others, it lay towards the end of the line, close to the river, and by sheer good fortune had manged to avoid the blaze. Everyone thought Lazarus was dead. *He must be,* they said. His clinkered body showed no signs of life, and onlookers shook their heads in dismay.

Poor man, they said. *Poor thing.* No one knew him, nor recognized him - such as was left to recognize. *Who is he?* they asked. *Where'd he come from?* The stranger had come from nowhere and walked into the fire. Like a madman he had walked into the tigers' cage and simply invited them to walk out. And they did. No-one could believe it. It was a miracle. *But who is he?*

Kitsune didn't care who he was, nor where he had come from. She just knew she had to save him. Quickly, she instructed the acrobats, the strongmen and jugglers to forge a passageway, and bring the burnt man to her wagon. She ran ahead and briskly made a nursing crib on which to lay her patient. She shooed and fussed the eager assistants away, and busied herself delving into the draws and cupboards, the secret alcoves and crannies of her carriage. She sought out the medicinal herbs and curative lotions of her trade, and spared no time in mixing up a fusion of recipes. The man's eyelids had been scorched off, and Kitsune knew that there was no time to lose if she was to save his sight. And his life.

Carefully, she cradled the man's head on a pillow. Then, puckering her lips, she spat into the palm of her hand. With an experienced rhythm she mixed into the white saliva, a cocktail of floury grey powders, which she then made up into an oily salve. With delicate precision, she oozed the greasy ointment into the man's eyes, leaving a thick layer of damp, gooey mud on the exposed orbs. Next, she cut away the clothes and the blanket which had welded to the man's scalp. Meticulously, she went over every inch of the body, slowly applying an even mould of medicinal cream, a sludgy balm smoothly spread, eased into each tear and flap of blackened skin. She sat back in a prayer of supplication and then, in a flurry, rummaged through a series of cases, mumbling in a language she had not used for many, many centuries. She finally found what she was looking for, a small, yellow box filled with tightly woven incense cones. She selected several and strategically placed them at the entrances to the wagon. She lit them, closed her eyes, and in a mantra of healing, began the purification of the chamber.

Hours and days went by, and Kitsune didn't waver in her devotion. She kept a vigil over her patient and each tremor, each shiver and quake of the burnt body she addressed with ointment and a prayer. Thick with incense, the air reeked with perfumes and scents, the balmy essences of her remedies. Lazarus, as he lay unconscious, cossetted in this ghostly tomb, knew nothing of his surroundings, nor the undying attentions of his surgeon.

The circus, of course, was crippled, and for several weeks, repairs were undertaken to fix the destruction caused by the fire. Animals were recaptured, doctored and healed, and the badly damaged wagons restored and mended as best as possible. It was during this time that Kitsune, pale and drawn, emerged from her wagon. She hadn't eaten for many days and she almost

321

fainted as she descended the steps. But, strong willed and determined in her intentions, she simply asked for more water, then silently disappeared again into the darkness of the chamber.

Eventually, it was time to move on, for the circus was a working entity and needed to earn money. By a happy coincidence it was about this time that Lazarus moved, not just a tic or a minor twitch, but a shift, sideways, a genuine fidget of discomfort. And Kitsune knew. She knew in her heart, right then, that the man would live.

The circus packed up, and moved on across Europe. And with time, and assiduous care and attention, Lazarus got better. His skin grew afresh, an Eden of good fortune and the product of miraculous nursing and faith. He could stretch and wiggle his toes and fingers, and as the months went by he learned to love the voice that ministered to his injuries. He could hear but not speak. Feel but not see. And he relished the angelic tones which transported him to another world where he felt safe, secure in the knowledge that all would be well. And he knew that an angel had kissed his brow. And he knew that one day, he would see her.

*

Kitsune and Lazarus were naturally drawn to each other, and with their good looks and magnetic personalities, they quickly became a formidable partnership. With her jet-black hair, easy manner and oriental charms, Kitsune reminded Lazarus of A'isha, and he found it difficult to resist her company. They had

322

a lot in common, but neither offered much about their backgrounds, preferring to trust in the moment and enjoy what they had discovered. They knew they were special, and reveled in the marvelousness of it.

For Lazarus, it was a homecoming, a new beginning and he understood the significance of this fresh chapter in his life. He regarded Kitsune as his equal, and only teased her about his own abilities because he realized he had found someone exceptional.

She had saved his life, brought him back from the very brink of death and delivered him up anew. In his blindness, he had fallen in love with her, and when he saw her for the first time, he knew exactly who she was. Her gentle tap on his arm had opened a door, and he walked straight in.

They both knew they had found a soul mate on whom they could depend, and soon the whole circus troupe realized what a great romance was unfolding before their very eyes.

Lazarus had been lost, but perhaps didn't even know it. And Kitsune, for over five millennia, had travelled the world and absorbed its wonders and mysteries, and she knew everything she needed to know about everything. Except that she didn't know how Lazarus walked through elephants. And that annoyed her.

"You're impossible," she said.

"Yes, I know," said Lazarus, smiling.

They had fallen in love, and the world lay at their feet.

*

The honey bee, having spent the day lost, flitting about the riverside, was snoozing on a decaying, weathered log. It wasn't particularly bothered by the traffic on the busy waterway, but, when a gust of late afternoon wind rushed off the channel, the bee woke up, took off, and was swept up into the leaves of an old oak tree, whose branches stretched achingly but securely abroad, creating vast pools of cool shadows in the prevailing heat. The late afternoon sunshine, skittering through the willow trees, reflected off the gently drifting water, and the bee, wrapped up in its own insect kingdom, dozed off again without a care in the world. As it dreamed, its little body tweaked now and then, but otherwise it sat immobile, not even watching the world go by.

Underneath, a family sat enjoying the remains of a picnic. They were celebrating a grandchild's first outing into the great big world. The proud mum and dad, and fussing, rosy grandparents, catered to each gurgle and thrilling squeak the child made, and, as the infant clenched and grasped and groped and chuckled, quivers of delight dappled the air. The happy family, elated by the small miracle crying in the shade of the giant oak tree, thanked God for their blessings. And their God, perhaps in league with other Gods, decided to send a woodpecker to hack and chip away at the trunk of the old oak tree. The vibrations worked themselves into a minor frenzy, and sent seemingly insignificant tremors, minute pulsating throbs right into the green stem where sat the honey bee, napping. The bee, disturbed from its contemplation of nothing in particular, woke up, annoyed. At the very same time the infant, fighting against the restrictions of its new, itchy bonnet, struggled to free itself. In its effort to express its irritation, the baby, in a worm-like wriggle, penguin arms flapping in frustration, opened its mouth in a wide preamble to yelling out its little heart.

The bee, seeing an opportunity for solitude, dived straight down into the gaping hole. The baby, in panic, snapped shut its mouth and the insect, realizing its mistake, stabbed with all its might into the very first thing it could feel in the pitch blackness. The soft red tissue, of a soft red throat. The baby screamed. The bee ejected itself into the welcoming air and the parents cried out in horror. The baby went into anaphylactic shock and within seconds was dying.

Lazarus and Kitsune, taking advantage of a break between performances, idled hand-in-hand along the banks of the River Amstel. It had been a busy afternoon show and they were enjoying the unmeasured laziness of a carefree walk. They had been in Amsterdam several days now and it had crossed their minds that perhaps, just perhaps, they should do something different. The circus was a great life but they were free spirits, and they felt their powers were being wasted. Kitsune bamboozled the multitudes by speaking in several tongues at the same time, and she held court with her universal knowledge of just about everything that had ever happened. This was not such a great feat really, as she had actually been there and so never had to learn or study these facts and figures, just recall them. And Lazarus, still rendering the crowds speechless with his acts of physical impossibility, was beginning to tire of the shallow entertainment and yearned something more vital, more elementary.

He was just about to suggest that he and Kitsune might consider setting out on their own, when shouts and

325

screams echoed over the water. Up ahead, they could see a small gathering of people agitated, alarmed, rummaging under the arms of a big tree.

"Wonder what that is?" said Kitsune.

"Don't know."

The screams grew louder.

"Sounds nasty," said Lazarus.

"Yes."

They quickened their step, then began to trot, then ran as they realized that something very bad was happening. By the time they arrived the baby was blue, and its throat the size of a yellow melon. Kitsune dived into action, grabbing the choking baby from its mother's arms. The father protested wildly and the mother clung on for all she was worth but Kitsune, with a look of mesmeric hypnotism, froze the adults into submission.

"Lazarus, quickly. The herbs, quickly," she cried. "The child's dying."

Lazarus twisted, and, in a blur, scoured the riverbank for the curative roots and ferns. Within seconds he had the antidote, and the juicy extractions he poured into the baby's clogged throat. Kitsune held the infant fast to her breast, and recited the Japanese sutras of the ancient healing Buddha Akshobhya. She called on him and chanted the incantations reserved for the healing of children. She rocked and swayed and with her eyes blinkering, she soothed the baby's congested screams. The child calmed. The swelling subsided. The parents stood spellbound, gratitude tumbling from their quivering lips.

Kitsune handed the child back to the mother and smiled. The grandparents, tears rolling down their sallow cheeks, offered up thanks to their God, and the old man, a trembling, frail creature, embraced Lazarus like a son. He hugged him tight and long, and muttered in an unfamiliar language, the ageless words calling on Solomon and David to protect and safeguard Lazarus and Kitsune. He held on for some time, and Lazarus felt a little embarrassed as the old man kissed him on both cheeks and patted him on the back. And just as Lazarus thought the old man had finished he started again, took him to his breast and held him close. They stayed like that for what Lazarus thought to be an age, or at least a very long time.

Strangely enough, there were no passersby or spectators that afternoon. The incident passed without witness or fanfare. The wood pecker, giving up on the hard trunk of the oak tree, flew off into its own obscurity, without even a backward glance to see how its thumping had changed the course of history. The honey bee, exhausted by its will to survive, fell, dead. It was now the target of a line of dedicated ants, cleaning up nature's debris on their way to a nest made beneath an ailing cherry tree. The family of Jews went home and the two heroes, job well done, meandered back to the circus.

*

The clowns did what they did best, and had the audience laughing in uncontrolled glee. The monkeys, chuckling and chattering like madmen, swung and rattled around on ropes and fell over themselves leaving the children in stitches. And as Lazarus stood at the

327

ringside, awaiting his grand introduction, he casually put his hand into the pocket of his velvet waistcoat. He frowned a bit as he felt a small, but nonetheless significant, lump of material. He thought it might be a neatly folded handkerchief, or a tiny wad of herbs long put away and forgotten. But as he pulled it out, he saw it was neither of these. It was a red, silk bag, a very tidy silk bag with a purple drawstring. His curiosity wouldn't wait and despite being onstage in the next few seconds, he undid the bag and turned it upside down. And there, sparkly in the smelly, oily candlelight of the big top, tumbled out into his palm, a glittering drove of diamonds.

"What on earth . . .?" was all he could muster, as the master of ceremonies hailed the next act as the most incredible in the history of the universe.

Wolfman

He set off late one blustery afternoon, as dusk settled. All day long the sun's rays had failed in their attempts to burst through the covering of low cloud. Now, as nighttime beckoned, he thought it funny that, for a tribe who held the sun in such esteem, to find themselves in a country where it had such difficulty in shining, all rather amusing. He laughed. Well, he smiled to himself, at least he hadn't lost his sense of humour.

A blancmange of grey and white gusted overhead. A flock of crows had difficulty keeping direction in the bracing squalls and Gamboa, head bowed against the wind, wrapped his coat tightly about him. There was a sniff of rain in the air but it was dry for the moment. He was aiming for London, or at least in that direction, going west from Wetheringdon. Some time had passed since his conversion back to human form and he was enjoying the walk, stretching his legs and feeling the fresh air against his face. He wasn't really sure where his destination lay, but instinct was leading him upriver, towards the metropolis, and he had the rainbow bird's words echoing in his ears, Wolfman, Utopium, Limehouse. He had no idea what this meant, but he was being drawn along the riverbank, towards the city.

As he walked, his thoughts inevitably turned towards his wife Tsok, and their son. Chatlan's words rebounded in his head, *Still killing children?* He felt a cold stream of conscience dampen his spirits and he stopped. Turning his face up towards the darkening sky he mumbled the incantations of his youth, the ancient prayers and petitions he'd recited thousands and thousands of times. He knew the rites of his religion to be the true avenues to Godliness on earth, and he recalled the sacrifices and blood offerings that had for years delivered rain, fertility, harvests and prosperity. He had been chosen and nurtured, cultivated to become the great Leader, and he'd led his people into the light of divine worship and holiness. He had been instructed by the Frog God, the great *Wo-sak*, to extract the beating hearts, and deliver up to the deities the souls of virgins and the innocent. Through his devotions he had made sure the tribe of Suxx followed the divine pathway to universality, and he was sure that an everlasting paradise awaited all the devotees of the true way.

Yet he could not shake off the feeling that somehow, something was wrong. For, ultimately, the human sacrifices had failed. His city had died and only he and a handful of Priests had survived. Despite the blood and the sacred submissions, Suxx had died a dry, parched death. They had killed thousands and thousands of people, the indentured and free, the old and young. Yet nothing had worked. He'd thought about all this before, but had quietly put the discussion to the back of his head as he felt inadequate, almost afraid, to analyze the notion further.

But a deep ember of doubt burned in his soul, and he could no longer deny that he had misgivings, no, stronger than that, fears, genuine fears, that everything he had been doing was somehow wrong.

"But I'd been instructed by the Gods, " he said out loud. "How could I deny them? How could they be wrong?"

*

He'd been hungry. Not for food, blood. He'd gone out on his own, stalked the small farmhouse and stealthily crept in while the family slept. He killed the parents first, left them bleeding to death. He didn't want them, didn't want their contaminated blood. He wanted the children, their innocence. He started with the girl. She could have been no more than nine or ten years old, perfect. She slept so beautifully, so sweetly, her blonde hair spayed across the pillow, her soft lips pursed in a gently slumbering kiss. He leant down and almost lovingly sunk his teeth into the delicate flesh of her neck. The incantations revolved in his head, and as he drank he worshipped the Gods he adored, the Gods who had saved him and given him divine instructions to take human life. This was his religion, his transubstantiation.

The little girl died quietly. She knew nothing of her death. Gamboa kissed her brow and thanked her, blessing her for the ultimate offering, her sacrifice. He turned to the boy, older, perhaps wiser. He bit into his throat searching out the life giving blood

*

Now as he walked, he recalled his wife's words, the look of contempt on her face as she hovered, floated, holding their son's hand. *You broke my heart.* He looked at the heavens. He felt small, insignificant. Had he been wrong? Had he been wrong his whole life?

He couldn't contemplate this, otherwise he had to admit his very existence had been a waste of time. His

331

connection with the Gods, Wo-sak himself, would have been false, futile.

Of course he'd done the right thing, of course the Gods' message had been correct, *and* he had followed instruction to the letter. But he could not now confess the years of obedience as being a giant mistake, a massive error of judgment. He had been doing this for thousands of years. No, he couldn't reject his faith in the Gods, the Frog God who had saved him. His faith was the bedrock of his and his nation's salvation. He was their leader, their spiritual guide, inspired by the Gods. He couldn't simply deny his faith. He had to believe that his life had not been wasted, and that he was following the path chosen by the almighty Frog God, *Wo-sak* himself.

And yet, at the same time, he now began to struggle, painfully wrestling with the notion that killing children was somehow perhaps, well, not quite right. Could the Gods have been wrong? The spirit of his own son had visited him and forced him to confront his beliefs. He couldn't turn his head away from the reality that he had killed his own offspring, and indeed, didn't want to. He knew, he knew in his heart, it had been the right thing to do. And yet.

He began to feel a measure of doubt, then guilt, a horrid, awful feeling which had him cringing, screwing up his face in consternation. Had he been right? Had he? Of course he had! The word of the Gods is righteous and true, and to follow them is to walk in the path of goodness, leading to everlasting life in Paradise. Of course he was right to sacrifice his own son.

Then the image of his wife's face seared like a flaming arrow, her spirit shooting fire and brimstone into his head. And everything ground to a dead halt. The earth stopped revolving. The clouds clung, like huge, sodden sticky lumps of clay, in an unmoving sky. The roof of the world stood still, oppressive, lifeless, frozen in time. And in that instant, as birds fell silent and rivers lay dormant, Gamboa, in his stillness and solitude, realized an amazing truth. A truth so astonishing that he gasped for air. His hands trembled, his heart beat like the thumping of a big bass drum and his sweat-drenched body shivered, shuddering in uncontrollable quakes. His gaping eyes agog, he stared icily, a dry swollen tongue failing to conjure up not even a drop to moisten the anxious roar in his throat. He realized. He saw. He knew.

He knew that he did not have to kill children any more.

He had choice.

Yes, he needed blood, there was no getting around that fact, and he needed human blood in order to survive. And yes, he had to kill people. But he had a choice. He could *choose* not to kill children. The Frog God, in his infinite wisdom, had given him the ability to choose.

He didn't understand everything, but he saw the Frog Gods' plan and comprehended that it had been a stepping stone, and that now he didn't have to kill innocent children anymore. Yes, he needed blood to live, and yes he would kill people to satisfy that need, but the sacrifice of children could stop. *He* could choose, but it would be in the name of the Gods. He knew he was in *their* hands. He was their vassal to do with as they pleased. And he praised *Wo-sak* and his soul emptied of pain and the grit of doubt. The Gods were telling him that it was time to change, and that now he'd been resurrected, there was no need to kill any children. No need.

He felt this in his soul and he shouted at the heavens. He needed blood to live, but from this moment on, he would never again drink the blood of innocents.

*

The big waterway, now at low tide, lay quiet, and the usual trading vessels ploughing up and down the river were nowhere to be seen. Polluted grey and black mud lay exposed on the shallow riverbed, and the smell was rising. Gamboa was appalled by the rubbish sticking up out of the quagmire of sludge and muck, and he wondered how people could do this to the very water they depended on. He shook his head in amazement, that he and his fellow Priests had survived as long as they had in the filthy marshes. But he was glad to be alive and he knew that his faith had been rewarded.

He left the river's tow pathway and came to a fork in the road. A sign indicated Limehouse off to the right. He followed it. He didn't know exactly what he was looking for but he followed the route anyway. The narrow lane changed into a road of sorts, then opened up into a main highway leading into a town. Limehouse. *Welcome*, he said to himself.

It was a spillover from the bursting city and alive with traffic. Wagons and horses clattered about and people trekking to and fro humped, fetched and carried, and generally paraded in front of him the busyness of their day. He wondered how, in the chaos, he was going to find something called *Utopium*. There was mayhem on the street and he couldn't work out which way he was supposed to walk. In the end he gave up on the noise and turmoil, and turned down a side street.

He passed various tall, red brick buildings and a couple of open yards filled with sacks, wheelbarrows and stacks of wooden boxes piled high. He turned right into a crowded, cobbled alley. He wandered along, avoiding being knocked over by barrow boys and heavily laden packhorses when, low and behold, miracle of miracles, he saw a small, shabby door with a discreet sign hanging from a rusty wrought iron scroll. The word *Utopium,* etched in a tatty, faded yellow on a deep mauve background didn't exactly jump out at him, but it did suck at his eyeballs.

"Well, well, well," he said.

He tapped on the door. No answer. An old woman, bent double with rheumatism and blessed with one crooked, tobacco stained tooth, brushed against his arm.

"Just go in dear," she said. "They won't bite."

Gamboa wondered what the old woman meant, but no sooner had she spoken than the door creaked open, just a smidgen. He gave the woman's screwed up face a nonchalant shrug of his shoulders, nodded his head and went in. The windowless room was small and dusty, crowded with colossal, misshapen boxes. A highly polished, solid oak counter, its chunky legs carved with precise geometric patterns, seemed to grow in size as Gamboa squeezed between it and the door, which slammed shut as he entered.

In the middle of the table's smoothly buffed surface, stood a bird, a little brown sparrow, dull, unassuming. On seeing Gamboa it perked up and announced in a cheeky, cockney accent: *Welcome to the Utopium.*

Gamboa gave the bird a wry smile. It put its head on one side and smiled back. Then to Gamboa's surprise, the sparrow's straight, rather ordinary, short brown tail, became a tantalizingly sharp swishy thing, tapering to an exquisitely dangerous point. Before Gamboa's disbelieving eyes, the bird then grew thick, magnetic fur. Two extremely pointy ears popped out of its small, round head and with the teeny-weeniest of a tiny clatter, the sparrow's petite pointy beak dropped off, skittering across the counter's shiny surface. Its eyes grew into enormous plate-sized orbs, and in a moment of amazement, Gamboa saw, there, right in front of him, the grinning, round face of a barrel-fat cat. Despite the darkness of the room, its teeth shone like pearls and its lips, precise red splashes of lined, self-importance, creased into some kind of unbelievably believable, feline greeting. Its florid pink eyes and heart-shaped nose glowed brilliantly, and Gamboa could clearly see two fluorescent crenelated eyebrows, arched in curiosity. The cat's shrill, orange and red stiletto stripes, jiggled a provocative dance, tracing snappy slashes about its chest. Its paws, wrapped like bandaged presents, padded silently as it eventually stood up, failed miserably to stretch its tubbiness, and stood stark still, looking into the depths of Gamboa's soul.

"Wow," said Gamboa, somewhat taken aback.

"Yes," said the cat, yawning. "Wow."

And with that, it circled in two dozen or so concentric loops, curled up and fell fast asleep, purring like a new-fangled steam engine.

Behind the counter, floor to ceiling shelving units held drawers baring labels of extraordinary

336

intrigue. They were arranged alphabetically, and starting at "A" Gamboa's attention was drawn to Abyssinia: pollen, a cure for dull aches of the heart. He noticed "L", Lapland: spruce sap, a cure for melancholy memories. Finally, his eyes dropped to "Z", right down in the bottom right hand corner. Zululand: juice, a restorative for the lackadaisical.

Gamboa stood puzzled.

"Hello," he called. "Anyone at home?"

No answer.

He looked around some more. He felt that he was perhaps in the right place but maybe the wrong time. It seemed abandoned, forlorn, not to mention extremely odd. There were five doors in the room, which was an impossibility, as there was only space for three.

Gamboa, bold as brass, decided to venture forth. He chose the green door at the end. The one after Z for Zulu juice. He pushed his way in. He gasped, amazed. Trees. Rivers. Blue skies with puffy white clouds. A sun, toasting the hills and valleys with beams of golden honey. Birds and bees and funny furry things hoping about in bunches of happiness. Gamboa, no novice when it came to miracles and wonderment, nonetheless took a few breaths to clear his head.

To his left, a stream silvered in tinkling spate. At his feet a pathway meandered off into the distance. He started walking. He headed towards a wooded area dense with brambles and privet. He then veered left, back towards the water and Gamboa was about to follow the gravelly route when his feet, independent of thought, took him right, straight into the thickest of blackberry bushes. He struggled as his scratched legs surged through the undergrowth, but he found, to his most

337

pleasant surprise, that there was no pain as the sharp needle points of the bushes scratched and scraped at his skin.

There was no way through the thickets, but somehow he was making headway. He gave up fighting it and found that the more he gave in, the faster he went and, as if by way of making his intrepid lurch through the undergrowth more inviting, enormous, shiny ripe blackberries sprang up right before his eyes presenting themselves to be eaten.

Then the bramble thicket opened up into a small orchard, filled with raspberry and gooseberry bushes, plum, apple, pear and cherry trees. This led to a grove where he saw arcades of tropical fruit of all kinds: guava, rambutan, papaya, kumquat, lychee, paw-paw, fig, durian, mango and pomegranate. Coconut and banana plantations fringed by pineapple, jackfruit, lime and grapefruit stretched as far as the eye could see, and the orbs of blood oranges hung in auburn clusters like armfuls of weighty jewels. There were constellations of fruit he had no way of recognizing and he wondered at the sweet, sensual aromas.

After this, a wild, crazy paddock of herbs and spices grew uninhibited, random and rambling yet with a rhyme and rhythm of natural harmony, sending reckless perfumes smoking through his head. Framed by a barrage of glorious sunflowers, protective, yet smiling in welcome, he saw crowded tumbles of pepper, cardamom, sorrel, vanilla and sage. Chives, licorice and fennel cozied up to yellow and white mustard while paprika, thyme and dill sprang up in concord supported by cumin, garlic, ginger and kava. A glorious symphony of scents and flavours whisked Gamboa away to another world, and he reeled in the pungency of myrrh, eucalyptus, lavender, frankincense and mint. There were plants and flowers from Africa, India, Australasia and the Americas and he floated, cast into a saffron dream boosted by nutmeg and coca leaves, his body disappearing on the invisible wafts of aniseed and poppy.

He couldn't believe his eyes and they crackled, expanding, filled with the cornucopia of exotic bounty.

"I see you found my garden."

Gamboa's swirling, drunken senses, skidded. Before him hovered a creature of immense beauty.

"It's alright. You're welcome here. In fact, we've half been expecting you. Or at least, someone like you."

"Who are you?" he asked.

"Don't worry, I'm a friend. Come."

Kitsune took his hand and stared into his eyes. She saw the trip, the journey, the hundreds and thousands of years and the blood. She saw the pain of loss and joy of victory.

"So, what can I do for you?" she said.

"I'm looking for Wolfman."

"Wolfman?"

"Yes."

"Ah, the Wolfman."

"Yes."

Kitsune smiled. "So, you want the Wolfman? Everybody wants the Wolfman."

"I want to see him. Do you know where I can find him?"

She rang a bell. A gentle smile embraced her delicate lips.

"If you could help me, I would really appreciate it," said Gamboa.

"You look like you've travelled a long way," said Kitsune. "You need a break from life's tedium. I'll get you something to melt away the agony of human waste and degradation."

She turned a slow arc.

"Come on," she said, and he followed her scent through a door at the base of the sky where it met the horizon.

He walked into a dimly lit room, fragranced red candles throwing out a soft warm glow. He was directed to a low bed. It was draped in a crimson velvet throw, its tassels tickling the wooden floor. At the head, next to a plush yellow pillow, stood a small, highly polished table, on which were placed an ivory pipe and a pale blue and white porcelain teapot. A small cup decorated with the purple of foxgloves, waited by the side. A Chinaman appeared.

"Hong will help you," said Kitsune. "See you at the other end," and she turned away.

"But what about the Wolfman?" said Gamboa.

"Oh, don't worry about him. He'll be around somewhere," she said. And she left.

The Chinaman, neat and small, his long greying pigtail adding to the oriental air of the place, invited Gamboa to take off his jacket and shoes.

340

"You lie now," he said.

The mattress was hard but welcome after his long walk, and he took a big breath and sighed. Hong said nothing as he prepared the pipe. The Chinaman, his smile an intriguing mystery, meticulously primed the bowl, then lit it. He offered the long shaft to Gamboa. He inhaled and almost immediately his mind grew wings, lifted off and soared skyward. His relationship with the physical world diminished to a pinprick, and, as he inhaled a second draught, his head melted. His body shrank and any thoughts he had of sensible conversation swam up through the gaps in the rafters above the bed. The opium wormed its way into the tinniest of Gamboa's brain cells, and took him on a wondrous, intrepid journey. A journey he'd been longing to take for some time.

The room in his head had two large windows. Through each one he could see the ocean. Fish swam, sailing boats cruised and the sun shone a burning yellow. On the back wall his homeland stretched in a tropical panorama. He swayed with the warm sea breezes and walked on the beach, his toes dryly squelching in the sand. He could taste the fresh salty air coming off the sea and hear wavelets lapping on the shore. Chirruping birds skittered about, and Gamboa's body thawed, melting into leaves, twigs, branches and the roots of palm trees fringing the shoreline. He could feel Nature's heartbeat and the rhythm of the planet beating in the core of the earth. He traveled the crests of time and saw his whole life played out in ultra-slow replay, each detail in rapturous multi-dimension. Through every pore he soaked up the euphoric ecstasies of birth and death and rebirth. But then he looked up and saw the faces of frogs, angry and threatening, yet smiling and consoling. And from a bitter recess in his mind a sudden panic set

341

in as he realized that he couldn't escape the room. His doubts grew into a giant, angry gnashing, and his body coursed in sweat.

He saw the door and stretched out an arm. He couldn't reach it. He was trapped. He was trapped in a room with only one door and his body was transmuting. Dragon claws, a sharp swishing tail and enormous wings cluttered the chamber, and he began to suffocate, unable to breathe in the shrinking space. Claustrophobia quickly gave way to alarm and a rising panic, then a freezing cold, followed by a burning fever. The raw talons of paranoia burned into his soul and he trembled, a quivering wreck, in dread of an eternity of obsessive terror. The frogs sneered, jeering in ridicule and he fretted as the floor, a cascade of diamonds crisscrossed in a maze of triangular black holes, threatened to suck him under. He was drowning in horror. His tattered senses, frayed and shredded, stabbed at his hysterical mind, and as the frogs morphed into fuming devils, the walls crept in and in. His throat, clenched and strangled, bleated out throttled cries for help and he readied himself for everlasting purgatory.

"Mister," the dragon said. "Hey mister. You smoke now. Smoke more now. You get better."

The chasms of hell opened up. He stood stammering, tottering on the brink of infinite blackness. He felt his shoulders shake. A sprinkle of water splashed his face.

"Hey mister. Mister."

Gamboa felt his head lifted from the wet cushion.

"Bad dream. Here, you smoke more. You get better. Very bad dream."

342

Unconsciously Gamboa inhaled. The smoke wormed its way into his bloodstream and he melted again.

He flew high above the Atlantic Ocean, his brain floating on a cloud of delicate pastry. He looked down at himself, swimming with giant yellow and green spotted leatherback turtles, and singing love songs to killer whales who pirouetted, curtseyed and bowed to each other as seahorses applauded their elegant footwork. Penguins winged in attack formation and swordfish, sabres swishing, fenced off the advances of feverish electric eels. Zooming down from the heavens, Gamboa skimmed the water's surface to scoop up frothy wavelets, spouting them out in orange fountains, from which drank handsome unicorns and vibrating humming birds. All this accompanied by an octopus, who recited poetry while performing magic tricks with its arms and legs tied behind its back. Gamboa drifted on through vague mists of mango and pomegranate juice, until he finally came to a plodding halt, mired in a porridge of fog. His feet dragged in the sticky sludge, then sleep overcame him, and he disappeared.

Two days went by, then another. Gamboa lost track of time but he did know he was in the right place. After all, outside it did say *"Utopium - Limehouse"*.

The Chinaman returned.

"Tea sir?"

Gamboa couldn't move. His arms and legs were nailed down, his torso crushed to breathlessness. Through the numbness he could vaguely feel a hammering on his temples but it shifted to a gentle tap tapping on his arm.

343

"Tea sir? Tea. It's time for tea. You must drink something."

Gamboa tried opening his eyes. A slurry of custard muddled his brain, and yellow gooey stuff messed with his mindscape. Insensitive to the real world, his head felt dead. It wouldn't follow instructions.

"Tea sir. You want tea?" persisted the Chinaman.

Through parched lips he mouthed a silent, "What?"

"Tea sir. You must drink now."

With an almighty effort Gamboa managed to open his eyes. A squid stared at him, its face narrowing in and out of focus.

"You here now."

The squid's sticky tentacles searched Gamboa's body and tentatively lifted him up.

"You here sir. You here now."

Gamboa conjured up a twisted smile. "Hmm," he managed.

"You drink now sir. You drink."

Gamboa swallowed. The Chinaman poured again.

"You drink," he said.

Gamboa shifted his weight to lie on his side. The world tumbled, slipped into a ditch, then righted itself. Well, almost. He lay, numb, adjusting to the slanting earth. The Chinaman again lifted his head and held the cup to his lips. He sipped.

"How long?" he asked.

"Very good days, sir."

"Hmm. How long?"

"Very good days."

Gamboa looked at the Chinaman. "Yes, good, but how long?"

"Maybe three days, sir. Three days."

Already feeling the effects of the tea he roused a little and stretched his eyes wide.

"Three?" he said.

"Yes sir. Very good time. You have very good time."

It might have been two in the afternoon or four in the morning.

Gamboa had no idea. The Chinaman was clearly used to this.

"Afternoon, sir. Five o'clock."

"What day?"

"Friday. Friday afternoon sir."

On the table he noticed a small package.

"What's that?" he said stretching.

"What sir?"

"That package."

"Man left it for you."

"When?"

"When you were away."

"Away?"

"Yes, you know," and he closed his eyes and wobbled his head a bit.

"Oh right, 'away'," said Gamboa.

He blinked but still found it hard to focus. With the Chinaman's help he sat up and sipped more tea.

"Who?"

"Who what?"

"Who brought it?"

"A man."

"What man?"

The Chinaman shrugged. "A man."

Gamboa gave up, put the cup down and picked up the package. He unwrapped it and found there, quietly unassuming in its paper bed, a vial. A vial exactly like the one he had lost, the one the old man had given him many, many years ago. The one he had thrown in the river.

"A vial," he said.

He looked around.

"Where's the man who brought this?"

"He gone," said the Chinaman. "Long time gone."

"What did he look like? Who was he?"

"I not know. I not see him. He gone now."

Gamboa frowned, finding his senses beginning to function.

Wolfman? he thought to himself. He grounded this consideration, and as he did so, his eyes snagged on a dog sitting in the doorway. A black and silver dog. A black and silver dog with one eye. It winked at him, or blinked, sneezed, turned around, pattered towards a wall and walked straight through it.

"Hey," he shouted. "Wait."

But the dog was gone and Gamboa, way too slow to catch up, was left puzzled.

"The one-eyed dog," he said. "The one-eyed dog!"

"Can I help?"

Gamboa turned towards the voice. "Sorry?"

"Can I be of assistance?"

Gamboa stared. Languidly stretched out on a purple chaise longue was a man with a long thin nose. He was dressed in a red velvet smoking jacket, navy trousers and a rather unusual hat.

"Pardon?" said Gamboa.

"Assistance. You seem to be having some kind of trouble. A one-eyed dog."

"Oh no. Not really."

"A one-eyed dog," said the man raising a pipe. "Interesting. There's something elementary about a one eyed dog. Most interesting."

"Yes," said Gamboa hurriedly, not wanting to get into a long discussion with the stranger. "I'm sure."

"Oh well," said the man with a sigh. "Pity, though, I could have got my teeth into that."

Gamboa nodded, not really listening.

"Well, if you do need help, here's my card, just in case. Best of luck," and he blew rings of dark interesting smoke high into the room, turned over and started to hum Mozart's violin concerto No 3 in G major.

Gamboa, far too preoccupied, absent mindedly put the card in his pocket. He headed for the door. To his surprise, on passing through its portal he found himself back in the shop with the shiny table. Gone were the gardens of herbs, the trees and bushes, the orchards, rockeries and flower beds. And the sleeping cat had gone and in its place the little sparrow had returned. He pushed around the counter and went out onto the cobbles of the small alley. Setting off at a brisk pace, he walked up the road retracing his steps home, to Wetheringdon.

He patted his waistcoat pocket, wherein the vial lay snug and safe, and as he did so he remembered the card. He casually took it out. Unfortunately, the top line had been smudged, the writing illegible, but in the middle, typed neatly in italics, was an address:

221B Baker Street, London. Gamboa sniffed, pulled at an earlobe and put the card back.

Strange fellow, thought Gamboa. *Funny hat.* And off he went.

An Evening Stroll

Gamboa liked to walk, alone. He frequently went out after dark, wandering the lanes and byways of the countryside east of London. He used his solitary meanderings as a time to think, to ponder, to reminisce and reflect on his life. His had been a wondrous journey. He couldn't explain it and perhaps he wasn't supposed to. Maybe there was no need to seek explanations. But he did think about his voyage, his flight through time itself. It was incredible what he had achieved and it was only natural to look back, to examine the details of the past. But, more often than not, he failed in his attempts to understand the great *why* of it all, and his mind would blank in awe as he saw himself a small cog in the great universal wheel.

Perhaps it was enough, he thought, just to be grateful to a beneficent God that he had survived, transcended time and found himself alive.

And as he trod his private path, rational explanations simply would not surface, and he was left only with the glorious comfort that the Gods were in charge, and that he was their vassal, compliant in his servitude. There was no place for justifications, his universal itinerary had been preordained by a power much greater than he.

Just what the great *Wo-sak* had in store for him, he had no idea, but he was absolutely sure that there was a plan, a strategy in place which had him at the centre. He chewed this over a lot as he ambled across poppy fields, sauntered through a tightly knit copse or tramped in the old grooves of a farmer's cart. He liked to sit, to take in the moon, the stars. He wondered, struck that the universe he had known as a child, was the same one he now encompassed as an adult, except that his place in it had changed. For some reason *he* had been chosen, and had travelled thousands upon thousands of miles and an untold, vast expanse of years. He, Gamboa. Out of all the people in the world, the Gods had chosen *him*.

He marveled at this. But what was the plan, and how did he fit into it? His past. His childhood. The visions. The infant sacrifices. The blood. And now here, walking anew in a strange, alien world. He'd started off life as an orphan. A little lost boy, shifted, shunted from pillar to post then left forlorn, but not helpless, on the fringes of society. He'd seen himself elevated to God-like status and led a mighty people. He'd killed but never murdered, and he was a good person. But he knew in his heart, now, right here in this new land, that things had to change. He frequently came back to the same theme, and reassured himself that the decision to stop the child sacrifices was the right one. He didn't feel guilty about the past, but he did know that from now on things had to change. And they already had. He no longer sought out the blood of children.

Each new day he went out, Gamboa saw as a bonus, an opportunity. He was so glad to be alive, to be a breathing, vibrant being again. He loved the very air he swallowed, like silver spoon-fulls of golden, clear honey, and relished the smell, the bouquet, the nectar of the crude yet fabulously sophisticated countryside.

He would set off during the day and walk for miles and miles, his sojourns eventually stretching far into the night. He relished the nocturnal fragrances, and his heightened senses made him especially aware of

351

small animals scurrying about, hunting, mating, their rude sounds carrying him back to his childhood, to his stick-rough shed. He bathed in the longing. And he could hear the grasses chatting, growing, and the leaves of trees spreading gossip as their veins stretched in their deadly slow expansions. The fizz of baby fireflies made him smile, reminding him of his distant home, and he watched as their little flame torches skittled about in silent slashes of light. A bird, perhaps disturbed by a crafty predator, would occasionally crash through the branches of a looming tree and Gamboa's nerves flew with it, on edge, his keen eyes drawn to the fluffed muttering of feathers, and an alarmed squawk and cackle. He could feel the earth. It's beating was as his own heart.

He was here, on earth, but he was aware that there was another place. A place he knew existed high above him. A place inhabited by the Gods. And his wife and son.

*

Gamboa enjoyed the company of the other Priests, but there was a limit to his civility. He tired of the chit chat, and the rehashing of the same stories, and the ever increasing embellishments in efforts to make the old, familiar tales, fresh, entertaining. All the Priests were getting edgy. They missed the old ways, the customs, the traditions, the food and drink. It began to cross Gamboa's mind that what they needed was a club. Yes, a club. The house, Wetheringdon, was fine, but what was really needed was somewhere the Frog Priests could go out for an evening. They needed a club house.

Now, just where they were going to find that was a problem to which Gamboa was prepared to give considerable thought. As usual, he went out for a walk.

He'd been to the *Utopium*, spent perhaps a day or two there (he couldn't remember, exactly) then decided to walk to London, the city. He walked all the way from Limehouse, in the East End, to the centre of the great metropolis. Not too long a jaunt but the rain had made it unpleasant. It had been a clear, crisp early evening when he set off, cloudless skies and stars just beginning to peep out. But it had become cold and wet after an hour or so, the wind getting up, blowing in a change of temperature and mood. His coat, too thin for a blustery November night in London, wasn't nearly enough protection from the strong gusts and huge, pelting rain drops, which heralded the onslaught of winter proper. But, to his delight, the cobbled streets, slippery and glistening in the gaslight, were deserted. He could meander without fear of distraction or interference from the gangs of thieves, robbers and ne'er-do-wells, which usually thronged the byways after dark. London, dangerous enough during the daytime, was perilous once the sun went down, and although he could look after himself perfectly well, he didn't want the fuss of interference. He was simply out for a walk.

Vaguely following the Thames, he had taken his time sauntering through the overflow of growing towns and industrial communities to the east of London. He was intrigued by the variety in architecture and buildings, but wasn't particularly impressed by the overcrowding and squalor he could see, hanging onto the riverbank. As he passed the warehouses and wharfs of the docks, he wondered at the idea of empire, and speculated as to where all the ships had come from. He was aware of his place in the world, but he had no idea if his ancient civilization was now part of the extensive trade routes being ploughed by this new, economic kingdom. He thought of how so much had changed in his life. So much. But he stepped headlong into the rain, and for the time-being put the idea out of his head. The past was gone.

Drifting away from the riverbank, he eventually found himself pottering along The Strand. He had negotiated a somewhat protracted meander through a no-man's-land of nondescript heath and outbuildings, finally to come across the more substantial mortar of the city, with its spires and banks. He decided to head north, approaching the lights and glamour of Covent Garden. He hadn't been there before and was surprised by the bustling activity. It was almost ten o'clock and there were people and carriages coming and going and young girls, even at this time of night, selling flowers. A couple of barrow boys were still flogging roast chestnuts and he noticed, of course, the usual supply of prostitutes, blatantly advertising themselves. He couldn't help but wonder at the eternal hopelessness of such depravity, and inwardly cringed, as a tawdry woman sidled up to him, flashing an ankle.

"What about it dear?" she said, her eyes screwed up in a twisted grin. "Five minutes for a copper or two?"

"Not now," he replied.

"Come on dearie. Just five minutes."

"No thank you," he said firmly. "Not now."

She placed a claw on his arm. "It'll put a smile on your face."

He raised his voice. "Not now, I said," and he pushed her away, firmly but without rancour.

"Alright, alight," she said, cackling through a mouth full of broken teeth. "No need to get rough." And she made off to the other side of the street.

He shook his head, despondent. *Some things never change*, he thought to himself.

As he cornered the old fruit and vegetable market, he saw what all the fuss was about, and why there were so many people thronging, even in this inclement weather. The Theatre Royal, Covent Garden, a large, illuminated building with magnificent columns, had finished its evening performance. It was belching lights and well-dressed multitudes onto the street, where cabbies and private carriages waited with drenched horses. As each horse-drawn cab became occupied and left, another took its place. It was busy traffic as fresh passengers popped up out of the heat and brilliance of the theatre, piled in their transports, and went off, clip-clopping into the night. Despite his interest, he had no inclination to linger in the rain, and so moved-on, deciding to walk back in what he thought was the direction of the river. In fact, he was lost, simply wandering the streets, soaked.

As he plodded along, he was passed by a splendid coach, pulled by a fine team of black horses. The street was straight and narrow, but ahead lay a dogleg bottleneck, twisting to the right. The coachman slowed down. As they approached the curve the horses suddenly reared up as an old wooden barrow shot out from a narrow passage. The horses neighed and whinnied, the coachman pulled and tugged and yelled out a severe "Whoa" as the carriage jerked and rocked in the sudden stalling. In the confusion, three men quickly ran out into the road. At first, it seemed like they were set on helping settle the horses, but, as one of the men climbed onto the barrow, it soon became clear what their real intentions were.

"Stay where you are," he shouted at the driver, the rain pouring down his face. "Hold the horses steady, an' if you know what's good for you, don't say a word."

At the same time another man was yanking the carriage door open.

"Get out. Now," he roared.

The third man, a lookout, stood furtive and menacing, as two figures began to exit the carriage descending into the wet street.

"Everythin' out of your pockets," the second man demanded. "Now, come on."

One of the figures, an elderly gentleman with a very bushy, very white moustache and extremely large lamb chop sideboards, raised a hand.

"But we don't have any money. Take what you want, but we haven't got . . ."

At that, his assailant pulled out a gun.

"Do as I tell you, or you'll get this," he shouted.

The other figure, slim, meagre in the wet light, interrupted, pleading, "But we don't have any money."

"Shush, my dear," said the old man, putting a hand on what was very clearly a young lady's slender arm.

"Oh, spikey tart you, aren't you!" shouted the thug. "Shut your mouth and get your necklace off. And let's have those rings an' all!"

"Is that really necessary?" offered the old man.

"Shut up! I told you, you'll get this in a minute."

"But really, this is outrageous . . ."

BANG!

The crumpled figure fell to the ground clutching his chest.

"Grandfather!"

"I told you. I told you what would happen," and he was just about to strike a blow to the young lady's head, when a whoosh of air filled the empty space between the roadside ambush and the hefty foundation stones of a building opposite. Two bodies came crashing down, their necks breaking and their heads splitting in resounding cracks on the cobbles.

"What the . . ." gushed the man with the gun, but he didn't have time to finish, as he was lifted high off the ground and hurled against the wall. As he fell to the pavement, a foot trapped his gun hand, crushing every bone, and a fist went into his windpipe. He choked for air, as his nose was then pummeled and spread like cream cheese across the rest of his face. The powerful force of the blow carried on into the man's brain, and darkness fell over what expression he had left on the red mush where his features used to be.

"Are you alright?"

"My Grandfather. He's been shot. There's blood."

"Yes. He needs a hospital."

"No, we have our own doctor. If we could just get him there."

"Not a hospital?"

"No, we have our own doctor in Kensington," she insisted.

The old man was conscious, just.

"Thank you. Thank you," he managed before passing out, his head lolling in his granddaughter's hands.

"Grandfather," she gasped. "Grandfather."

She fussed and bothered and searched for a handkerchief to wipe the old man's face.

"Grandfather."

Desperation and fear blasted through her as she rocked to and fro in the cold rain.

*

He was thinking over the past. So much had happened. So many incredible things. He smiled to himself in disbelief. Here he was, the universal man-God, walking the streets of London. How had *that* happened? His mind travelled back over the centuries. He glued together a picture of the one-eyed dog, the box and the old man. He replayed the thousands of sacrifices, and felt the pain, the death, the murder of his wife Tsok. He'd seen his tribe, his empire, destroyed. He'd carved himself into an amphibian and survived. He'd spent hundreds, perhaps thousands of years, buried beneath the ground. He'd killed his own son and now drank blood to stay alive. He'd inherited an alien world, a changing world so foreign that even he, Gamboa of Suxx, a God on earth, found his head spinning with the incredulity of it all. He belonged nowhere, yet everywhere. He was a living God. A living God in Victorian London.

The gunshot shattered the window of his daydream. He saw a young woman being brutally attacked. Primeval instincts kicked in. He moved quickly, invisibly. In the blink of an eye he covered the fifty yards and savagely killed the three thugs. Now, he dealt with the fallout. He leaned forward and placed a well-practiced finger on the old man's neck.

"It's all right," he said. "He's still alive. But we must get him off the street."

"Grandfather, please."

"Come on, let me help," said Gamboa, and he gently lifted the injured gentleman into the carriage.

The young woman climbed in and made a pillow of her wrap. "Grandfather," she whispered "Grandfather, please don't die.

Please don't die. Please."

"He's losing a lot of blood. He needs a doctor. Driver," shouted Gamboa "take them straight away, as fast as you can. Kensington, the doctor's. No delay."

"Yes sir, straight away sir."

Gamboa stuck his head in the carriage window.

"Will you be alright?"

She didn't reply.

"Madam, will you be alright?"

She looked up, tears and rainwater running down her soft cheeks.

"Please, come with us," she said. "I can't manage on my own."

It took only a split second.

"Very well." And with that he jumped in.

The horses raced at a fine pace, and now and then the old man groaned in his unconsciousness, but he didn't move and his granddaughter kept close attention by dabbing a wet handkerchief at his forehead.

"Here, have this," said Gamboa, taking off his silk scarf.

She looked up, caught his eye, and for the briefest of infinitesimal moments the crisis disappeared and they looked at each other. He couldn't be sure exactly what it was, but he knew the world had shifted.

The moment passed, the miniscule silence broken by the clatter of wheels and hooves.

"Thank you," she said.

He nodded.

She held her grandfather's head on her lap and mumbled her prayers. Gamboa sat silent. London rattled by outside.

Eventually the driver yelled out. They'd arrived.

"I'll get him out, you go wake up the doctor," said Gamboa.

"Righto," shouted the driver.

Within minutes they were all inside. The doctor directed them to his surgery.

"Put him on the table, over there."

"Will he be alright?" the young lady asked, desperately.

"We'll see. We'll do our best. You two wait outside. I'll see what I can do."

"Can't I stay with him?"

"No. You wait outside." He looked at Gamboa. "Take her outside, please."

The rain battered hard against the windows. The wind howled. Gamboa and the woman sat hushed, wet and shivering from the November cold. The young woman stared at Gamboa, her lips tightly wrapped in despair.

It wasn't a particularly large room, but the ceiling was high, the cold only just kept at bay by the embers of a small fire left to settle for the evening. A large, ornate clock ticked loudly on the mantel piece, reminding them that time was passing far too slowly. He looked at her.

"Are you alright?"

She nodded.

"Try not to worry," he said.

She didn't move.

"It'll be alright."

Still she didn't move.

Gamboa crossed to the fireplace, prodded and jiggled with the poker and threw more coals into the grate.

"Come, sit by the fire," he said.

She sat down.

"There, you'll soon be warm and dry."

She didn't say anything, just stared into the fireplace with a grim expression.

"Will he . . ." she said finally, falteringly. "Will he be alright?"

"I'm sure the doctor will do his best."

"Yes. Yes, I suppose."

An expansive silence settled on them and they both occupied themselves with thoughts of the evening's events. The rain. The gunshot. She sobbed into her hands.

"How could this happen?" she said.

"I know," offered Gamboa. "I know."

"But *how*? We just went to the theatre."

She broke off in tears and Gamboa moved a little closer. He wanted to comfort her but he was a stranger and he felt awkward.

"Yes," he said.

She looked up at him through blurry eyes.

"If you hadn't come along . . ."

"Don't think about that now," and he wanted to take her in his arms.

She broke down and he could resist no longer. He stooped to comfort her. The tremor of her heaving sobs seeped into his shoulder. Gradually she quieted until she said, in a soft voice, "Thank you."

"It's alright now," he said "you're safe."

And the clock ticked.

*

For some unknown reason, not a single policeman was drawn to the gunshot, and the rain continued to pour down onto the three crumpled bodies lying drenched on the pavement. Water gushed from a broken drainpipe, forming murky, shallow pools in the cracks between the uneven paving stones, and a casual eye would have seen nothing out of the ordinary. Apart from the three dead bodies on the ground, of course. Except that there weren't three dead bodies on the ground. The bodies had long since disappeared and left not even an outline of where they'd been.

But in the pools of water, a keen inspection would have resulted in the observation of three rather unusual faces. They stared out of the grey-brown liquid, appearing to grin and almost smile. The way frogs do. The small, neat red face, looking up from the watery stone with a watery stone expression, nodded knowingly. The tidy, turquoisey-blue face, with wet circular damp eyes, gave a shrewd wink, or was it a blink? The last face, a compact, stoically confident, speckled countenance, affected an almost undetectable bow.

"There," they all seemed to be saying. "Job well done."

Then it stopped raining, and in a flash all the water drained away and the frogs disappeared. Gone.

*

The door opened. They stood up. The doctor, a severe expression on his pasty face, was wiping his hands on a bloody cloth. He looked at the young woman and shook his head.

"I'm so sorry," he said. "I did all I could."

The girl broke down in a wail of tears.

"He was an old man and the shock was too much for his heart. There was nothing I could do."

Gamboa reached for the girl in an effort to comfort her, but she shrugged him off and cried pitifully into a handkerchief. The doctor, wringing his hands, walked over to Gamboa.

"I'm sorry, have we met?"

"No, no," said Gamboa.

"Are you a friend of the family?"

"No, not really. Well, not at all. I just . . . erm well, I was just passing by and helped out a bit."

"Oh," said the doctor.

An uncomfortable quiet shrouded the chamber.

"My dear," added the doctor. "I am truly sorry. Truly, truly sorry. He was a great man. If there's anything I can do?"

She shook her head, barely acknowledging the words.

"Well," said the doctor, looking at Gamboa "I have the paper work to finish off. Please stay here for as long as you want. I'll have the maid bring in tea."

"Yes, that would be nice, thank you," said Gamboa, not really knowing what to do next.

The doctor left. The room suddenly didn't seem quite so welcoming. Gamboa took a big breath and wondered. *What was this all about? How did he get here? What was he supposed to do? The girl was inconsolable and a complete stranger. What WAS he supposed to do?*

He poked the fire. A trivial flame chuckled its way out of the embers and belly-danced up towards the gaping chimney. It curlicued and twisted, cavorting in the void of air sucking up into the empty roof of the fireplace, and as Gamboa looked at it, it looked straight back at him.

"Lazarus," it said.

Gamboa blinked. "What?"

"Lazarus."

Gamboa hit the roof.

"Of course," he said out loud. His eyes narrowed and he shot out the door.

The girl, bundled up in her grief, hardly noticed him leave and she sat, huddled, her heavy tears etching weighty stains down her face.

Gamboa strode purposefully into the surgery. Ignoring the doctor's protestations, he snatched up the body and made for the door.

"Hey, what're you doing?" cried the doctor.

"Saving him."

"He's dead."

"Exactly."

He put the body in the carriage, whipped up the horses and set off. He left the house in a clatter of hooves, twisting and turning as he threaded through the narrow streets. He wasn't too sure which way to go, but he knew it was east - where he'd come from.

The rain poured down and through the thick, black clouds, lightening rocketed, forking its shocking tongues from one horizon to the other. The horses snorted, and Gamboa, screaming and shouting in the teeming wet, rolled with the carriage as it rocked from side to side.

In the murky dark, he could just about see the towering Monument to London's Great Fire, its orb, a spikey golden urn, fighting to burn in the soaking rain. He charged the horses aiming for the giant pillar. Running parallel to the Thames they galloped, pulling with all their might, streaming with fury. In the empty boulevard they sped like demons, their iron shoes clashing, hammers on the cobbles. Gamboa was intent, a furious concentration on his face as he steered, lashing at the horses to go *faster, faster*. He stood, then sat, then stood again, straining to find a landmark, anything to help him find his way. Then, out of the gloom, he saw the great dome of St Paul's Cathedral. In a flash of lightening it loomed in a terrifying majesty and Gamboa cracked his whip in a thrilling surge of grim determination. The manic horses tore into the ground, bolting, their eyes on fire.

They flew past the ghostly Temple and Gamboa, at last, had a sense of where he was. He aimed for the

Tower of London, its walls and Keep a landmark, a signpost for his violent journey. The horses, tongues flapping, valiantly kept charging and Gamboa, knowing all was a race against time, hollered again and again to keep going. *Faster. Faster.*

The haunting skeleton of Tower Bridge came and went and he rattled away from the city, heading out on the highway east. Lonely candles glimmered in houses, but without the street lights it was almost impossible to see ahead. He dared not slow but it was crazy to race in the darkness. The horses stumbled and lurched, faltering in the torrential gloom. Creaking, and wrenched at every turn, the carriage whiplashed, splashing up cascades of water as it slooped through the rain. They hit a sodden pot hole and Gamboa, jolted from his seat, flew up high into the air. He came crashing down, barely hanging on in the chaos.

And then, a miracle. In the lightening, he caught sight of a signpost: Limehouse 2 miles. He cried at the horses and they pounded, a new found energy pushing them on.

They rounded a corner and Gamboa, eyes flaring, roared out. A fallen tree blocked the road. In a slalom, the carriage lurched left then right, the giant wheels only just gripping the gravelly surface. They slewed in the soggy wet, clawed up a steep embankment and smashed down again. The horses, hooves grappling, shrieked wildly but on they went, heads craned forward.

A deafening crack of thunder exploded overhead and Gamboa shuddered in the blast. But it wasn't far now, and he knew he could make it. Steaming hot, the horses were beginning to flag but Gamboa was unforgiving. He whipped them up again and again, and finally the carriage clattered into the main road leading

367

to Limehouse. It was dead, only a few, isolated gaslights fighting off the storm. He turned the horses into the side street but pulled up sharp realizing they would never fit down the alleyway where the house lay. He tugged on the reins and the carriage skidded to a fretful stop. The horses, close to exhaustion, caved in and out as their chests heaved, nostrils flaring in a desperate bid for air.

Gamboa jumped down, retrieved the old man's body and ran along the narrow passageway. He kicked at the door.

"Lazarus," he shouted. "Lazarus. It's me, Gamboa. Lazarus."

The door opened. Kitsune stood there, a gentle smile igniting her inscrutably angelic face.

"Hello, Gamboa," she said calmly. "Come in. We've been expecting you."

*

After his induction at the *Utopium*, it didn't take long for Gamboa and Lazarus to strike up a friendship, establishing an easy routine where they would often sit together on one of the many ornate verandahs. In companionable silence, they would settle into soft comfy armchairs, sigh big sighs of contentment, and drift off into their own cloistered thoughts. Hong the Chinese would fill, and refill, their cups with an eccentric blend of mixed herb tea and they would drink, contentedly. Words didn't come too easily, but that was not a problem for the men, as they shared much more than a clumsy alphabet and the awkward phonetics of human communication. They understood each other.

Beyond them, undulating dunes rose in obtuse silhouette against a twilight sky, and the blood-red sun, held in a tropical abeyance, would do what it always did in the *Utopium*, stay exactly where Kitsune had put it, shyly peaking over the distant horizon. Time held no boundaries for the men and they wandered the bottomless pools of their own private universes, safe in the knowledge that there would be no disturbances to their deep meditations.

On Gamboa's very first visit, Lazarus had been eager to make sure his new guest felt welcome. He went out of his way to ensure that Hong lavished a careful attention on him, and Lazarus recognized in Gamboa an unusual spirituality, which he found attractive. He was keen to nurture a friendship, and sure enough, it didn't take long for the two men to become close.

Lazarus knew all about the Priests. Of course he did. He'd been in England a long time now and any newcomers found it hard to slip in without his notice. The *Utopium* was a living, breathing entity and Lazarus and Kitsune quite literally felt anything new prickle and tingle in their sensitive fingertips. The two of them had grown so close, they shared heartbeats and felt the same pain and pleasure. Their symbiotic existence helped maintain a resistance to the horrors of the nineteenth century, and protected them from the intrusions of industrialization. But they were, nonetheless, realists, and understood that perhaps they needed something more, something other than a common heartbeat to counter the threat of an encroaching, increasingly ugly world. The *Utopium* was their fortress, their bulwark against a menacing nineteenth century. But they also needed the comradeship of fellow human beings and saw

369

in the Priests an opportunity not just to converse, but to grow, to exchange lifetime experiences in an effort to comprehend an incomprehensibly violent world. By a miracle of cosmic coincidence, the Frog Priests and Kistune and Lazarus, found themselves in exactly the right place, at exactly the right time.

*

After discovering the diamonds, Lazarus and Kitsune left the circus, jumped on a boat destined for London and sailed away into a setting sun. They crossed the lower reaches of the North Sea, then went up the Thames and landed at St. Catherine's dock. From here they went back along the river, and found a perfect spot to build their perfect home. Standing alone in its own space with a duck pond and lilies, it was a simple, red brick affair with two floors and a flat roof. Fields stretched out in all directions, and Lazarus and Kitsune enjoyed the lazy peace and quiet of rural England. They indulged their curious common interests, but also disappeared into their own, personal, spiritual worlds.

Lazarus bent into the contours of the landscape and swayed in his own breeze, eddying this way and that, thrilling to the symphonic melodies of the peaceful setting. He rode the backs of wild deer and zoomed in cavorting hula-hoops with swifts and swallows. He conversed with the breeze and learned new bird song. He nested in the abandoned homes of tiny wrens, and burrowed in the soft brown earth with rabbits and hares. He grew with the heather and blossomed with the apples and pears. The thick English sky became his mantle, his palette, his vast sketchbook of vision and astonishment.

He painted his world a vitality of wonder, a spectacle, a marvel of creation.

Meanwhile, the magnificently ethereal Kitsune, a serine smile decorating her velvety Asian lips, searched for the world's ancient magical flora. Her head spinning in a natural chapel of harmony, she wandered for hours and days and weeks, tracing ancient hedgerows, and glossy, mossy outcrops. She closed her eyes and followed the magnetism of the earth's core, purposefully drifting, migrating across dale and barrow gently sniffing, aware of the delicate nuances of a primitive, undisturbed earth hiding the roots and tubers of a lost, curative homeopathy. With an air of determined bewilderment across her rare beauty, Kitsune spoke to the earth, teasing out her best kept secrets. In barely whispered directions, she was led far into the recesses of the planet's undiscovered grottoes, its hush-hush corners and caves. She softly plucked and dug gently deep into the face of the good earth, and thanked the planet for her generous bounty.

Together, Lazarus and Kitsune lived an idyllic, heavenly life and were very, very happy.

But that was before the industrial overflow from the city converted the simple, rural community, into a congested jumble of warehouses and factories. With unregulated expansion, the small, quiet village of Limehouse soon rattled with the rumblings of manufacturing, commerce and industry. By comparison with the neighbouring workshops and warehouses, the house diminished in size, and Lazarus and Kitsune found themselves squeezed into a brick sandwich. They simply disappeared into the morass of nineteenth century iron and dust. Their idyllic bubble had burst.

As their external world contracted, however, they looked inward, and with concentrated effort expanded each room, each cubbyhole, each chink and crack. A cupboard became a paddock, a room a field, a stairway hills and mounds, a shelf a plateau and walls the steep slopes of mountains. Horizons knew no limit and it grew and grew. Kitsune planted her oriental gardens. She introduced fabulous new species of fruit and plants, and grew the remarkable rare spices of her trade. And, recalling A'isha's careful training, Lazarus helped her. They worked together, toiling in the internal fields, digging and excavating, hoeing and planting, pruning and cropping until they had cultivated and nurtured in every space, in every room, topiaries of the exotic and medicinal. And the house that Lazarus built, became a magical monument to nature.

But, as the landscape expanded, so did their withdrawal from the outside world. They never went out. They had no visitors. They saw no-one. Despite the joy and love they experienced in each other's company, a certain unwelcome tetchiness entered their lives. They didn't speak much, and silences often stretched out for much longer periods than they were prepared to cope with. Life was almost . . . well, dull.

They were not quite frustrated, and certainly not falling out of love, but they were both well aware that they had more to offer.

One day, they were sitting down at opposite ends of an enormously long table filled with plant cuttings. Wrapped up in their own worlds, they were going about the general horticultural business of the day, inspecting roots and leaves and stems and things. In the hushed quiet, completely un-orchestrated, they both stopped what they were doing, looked up at each other and, at exactly the same time, said, "Let's open a shop."

And they did.

Reviving their roots in the entertainment business, they decided not to open just any old shop, but a *Utopium*. They didn't need the money. No. They simply wanted to offer the world the benefit of their skills and experience. And Lazarus, his sense of showmanship powering forth, set about creating a Temple to the trade of illusion. Shunning the grey-brown dirt of the city, the house now glistened with rainbow stripes and zigzag outlines. Repetitions and crisscross designs were broken on the front by giggling windows, planed to an orange and purple distortion. On the sides, hundreds of regular windows collided oddly with the diminishing perspectives created by the green and yellow rays focusing on the middle of the building. All lines wiggled, all wiggles bent, and all bends curved. Nothing was straight. And nothing ever seemed to be the same from one day to the next. The only consistency appeared to be one of *in*consistency, which Lazarus fought hard to maintain. Perhaps most interesting of all, though, was the rooftop. It could be anything it wanted to be. It all rather depended on who was looking at it.

When it opened its doors to the public, there was a drip, then a trickle of clients. Perfect. As word spread, they came from near and far. The rich, the famous, the good, the bad, the curious. Lazarus was selective however, and the house was designed in such a way that the unscrupulous, the devious and unprincipled could not actually find it.

A sturdy, polychromatic door wedged itself beneath the fizzy red sign announcing to the world that this was, indeed, the *Utopium*. Except, of course, that the world couldn't see it. It wasn't that kind of sign. In fact, it wasn't that kind of building. What the world saw was a small, shabby door with a discreet sign hanging from a

373

rusty wrought iron scroll with the word *Utopium,* etched in a tatty, faded yellow on a deep mauve background. It could only be seen by those who really needed it. The lost and frightened. The forlorn and desperate.

And, of course, it was ideal for the Priests. Gamboa's initial experience had convinced him of this. As he walked away, down the alleyway after his first visit, he looked over his shoulder, and there, blazing in bright colours was a splendid building and an even more splendid sign, *Utopium,* in luscious gold lettering. How come he'd had trouble finding it? It was huge, a great big flamboyant building. He shrugged. *Oh, well.*

But it wasn't until after several visits that he suggested to his compatriots that they should, perhaps, accompany him. They did. It was an instant success. Kitsune and Lazarus welcomed them with warmth and generosity. The Frog Priests felt they had come home. And indeed, in many respects they had. After their epic journey, feeling lost in an alien world, the *Utopium* gave them a sense of belonging. They had a place where they could go and drift away, to melt into the mystical, return to their homeland. They could experience the blissful universe in a transcendence befitting their aristocratic priesthood. In the *Utopium,* they had found an earthly gateway to a nirvana of enlightenment. They loved it.

When there, as they tended to be with increasing regularity after the initial introduction, the Temple Priests' imaginations turned the *Utopium's* roof terrace into a tropical beach, with multicolored palm trees of tangerine, turquoise, pink and yellow. They saw florid fish splashing about in warm, blue waters and a boatman about his catch. Buttery sand, with rosy pink and green speckles, led to the steps of a Temple, with a golden zenith reaching high up into the navy blue heavens. The

Priests felt very comfortable, which was the whole point of the business.

In an effort to make guests feel even more at home, Lazarus allowed the house to project their images and portraits in the windows. The Frog Priests, although now in human form, were proud to see their own amphibian faces adorn the *Utopium* and posed, wearing jazzy clothes, imagining their homelands.

Rather comically, the whole structure appeared to be about to fall down, except that in designing the house, Lazarus had employed Bulut's finest architectural secrets, and it could withstand any natural disaster in earth's arsenal of destruction.

The Frog Priests' home remained at Wetheringdon, but, increasingly, they spent more time at the *Utopium*. Days would pass when they lost track of where they were, and their new realities. Hong was kept busy with the tea pot and pipe, and the Priests spent so much time there that Kitsune one day suggested they take, as their own, an entire suite of rooms. Here they established miniature Temples, and Frog God idols, carved from the smooth stones found on the banks of the Thames. They worshipped and prayed and renewed their vows of dedication and servitude to *Wo-sak*. Lazarus was easy going with this and he preferred not to ask questions when the Priests disappeared each new moon for two or three days. He knew what they were up to but preferred not to know the details. The Temple Priests were his best customers and rapidly also became his friends. He struck up a frim, close relationship with Gamboa and he and Kitsune felt a camaraderie they had missed these last few years.

*

Lazarus knew of the unrest in Gamboa's soul. When they had first met he had felt a magnetism and similitude, an invisible bonding with the complete stranger. And he knew this to be reciprocated by Gamboa. They shared the same space and recognized a brotherhood, a mutual existentialism crossing all boundaries. The two men relished an exhilarating love of life, but also knew the grief of having lost family. And this common element in their backgrounds drew them together, if not exactly as soul mates, then certainly as emotional warriors. Their friendship brought out an instinct for honesty, and besides anything else, they actually enjoyed each other's intelligent company.

Late one afternoon, as the darkness descended, Gamboa, sitting crossed legged between the arms of his favourite leather armchair, described to Lazarus his wife's visit, and his son's words permanently echoing in his head: "Still killing children?"

Lazarus was a patient listener and he sat, rock steady, as Gamboa told him of his life, his role as leader of the once vibrant Suxx empire, and the demise of the noble race. He talked of the Gods and how *he* had been chosen. Shockingly, of course, Gamboa had told him of the sacrifices. The child sacrifices. They had talked at length about Gamboa's religion, his beliefs and his conversion into a frog then back into human form, and Lazarus was made speechless as even he, a contortionist of universal proportions, had to admit to being astonished by the supernatural nature of Gamboa's survival.

"Are you still killing children?" asked Lazarus.

376

"No," replied Gamboa, the simplicity of his response disguising the turmoil in his heart. "No," he repeated. That's all finished."

"And what about the blood?"

Gamboa breathed deeply.

"We cannot avoid that," he said. "We shall die without it. But," he added quickly "we have agreed that from now on we only drink the blood of the evil, the deadly, the ruthless, the wicked and corrupt. No longer shall we prey on the innocent and fair. We shall protect them. Protect them from the injustice of the world."

And Lazarus looked at his friend and his heart marveled at the magnitude of Gamboa's amazing soul.

*

Kitsune led Gamboa round the back of the counter and through the smallest of the five doors.

"This way," she said.

As he entered, Gamboa was hit by a pungent scent, a fragrant wall of perfumes which sent his head circling in a hypnotic gyration, designed to anesthetize, to quell anxiety. He felt giddy, yet strangely calm.

"Put him here," said Kitsune, clearing space on a bed of red and white oleander leaves. "He needs the poison to counteract the shock of the bullet's death blow."

"How did you know he's been shot?" said Gamboa.

"You told me."

Gamboa frowned.

"When? I've only just walked in. I haven't told you anything."

"Oh," she said. "I could have sworn you did." And she smiled.

Lazarus put a hand on Gamboa's shoulder.

"Don't worry Gamboa, Kitsune knows what she's doing."

The old man was quite dead. He lay stone cold on the bed.

"I'll be back in a second," said Kitsune. "Take his clothes off," and she disappeared back into the shop.

After a hectic rummaging and opening and closing of drawers, she returned.

"Here," she said, holding up a cylindrical box with *Lazarus* written on it in faint, ochre lettering. "I haven't used this in some time, but it should do the trick."

She opened the lid and from such a tiny container leaked drops, then pints, then gallons of liquid, which didn't run anywhere but stayed exactly where she put them. She covered the whole body.

Then she inserted her hands into the thick, heavy syrup, laying them on the man's heart and, closing her eyes, began the lament, a moving dirge, which changed into a hopeful hymn of uprising, then a triumphant fanfare of victory as she leant down and breathed into the man's mouth. His chest heaved in ancient undulations and the empty cheeks puffed in and out like bellows.

"There," she said kindly. "He's fine now. You can take him home."

"Is that it?" asked Gamboa, apprehension in his simple question.

"Oh yes," said Kitsune. "All done." And she extended a smile so peaceful, so benignly humane, that Gamboa felt his own spirit lift and launch into a new comprehension of what true compassion really is.

"Thank you, Kitsune," he said.

He felt Lazarus's hand on his shoulder.

"See, all done," said his friend.

Gamboa looked at the old man. He was stable, but weak.

"Can he travel?"

"Yes."

"Good."

Together they dressed the sleeping man in a thick cotton smock, and got him out into the carriage.

"Thank you, Kitsune. Thank you," said Gamboa.

She smiled the smile of angels.

He was about to set off when she called out. "Who's the girl?"

"What girl?"

Kitsune and Lazarus looked at each other.

"There's always a girl," they said in harmony.

Gamboa raised his eyebrows. "Is there?"

379

Lazarus laughed. "Take care Gamboa," he shouted.

"I will."

And with that the carriage set off back to the city.

*

It was still dark and spitting with rain, but the storm had long gone. He was in no hurry, but he didn't dawdle. He got back just as it was getting light. Pulling up outside the Doctor's he jumped down. The old man, conscious but unaware of his whereabouts, needed help getting out of the carriage.

Gamboa rang the doorbell. The Doctor opened.

"What the devil d'you think you're playing . . . My God," he said. "What on earth.? But how?"

"He's weak but all right. He needs a lot of rest. Can you see to that?"

"But how? What?" The Doctor was speechless.

Behind him the girl stood, ashen.

"Grandfather?" she gasped. "Oh my goodness." And she fainted.

*

"His wife and son died of cholera in 1831. They'd only been married a couple of years and their son was just a baby. Tragic. But so many died at that time. A terrible disease. Killed thousands and thousands. He was heartbroken of course. Didn't know what to do with himself. So he left. Went to Africa. Stayed there over ten years and came back rich. So much money he didn't know what to do with it. Ivory. Bought this place, but hardly lived in it. He was a different man, so they say. So he's told me. He couldn't settle down. Never remarried and never had children. So sad."

A cat was nestled on her lap, and as she gently stroked its back, it reared up, did a carousel turnaround and settled itself back into exactly the same snuggly spot.

"He went to South America," she continued "and made even more money, mining. He went all over. Uruguay, Bolivia, Argentina. All the way down to Tierra del Fuego and then up through Chile, Peru, the Andes. He sailed up and down the Amazon. Spent some time in the jungles of Brazil, then settled for several years in Central America. Mexico mainly."

Gamboa frowned. "Forgive me," he interrupted "but you call him Grandfather. How is that possible if his wife died and he never remarried?"

"He's not my real grandfather," she replied. "I'm adopted."

Gamboa looked at her and his world turned over, a tumbler falling into place.

"You're adopted?" he said.

"Yes. He found me in the ruins of a deserted Temple in Mexico." She paused.

Gamboa was intrigued and sat forward in his chair next to the fire. "He *found* you?"

"Yes."

"In Mexico?"

"Yes."

A couple of beats passed into a longer silence and Gamboa couldn't resist it. "Where exactly is Mexico?" he said.

She frowned. "You don't know?"

"My geography's not very good," he offered, and, in as much innocence as he could muster, "I've lived a rather sheltered life." He smiled.

Of course, he knew, more or less, where Mexico was but he'd never actually seen a map. He was curious.

"You don't know where Mexico is?" she said.

He shook his head.

The cat yawned and stretched and Charlotte, more than a little intrigued by this stranger said, "Gamboa. That's an odd name isn't it? Where's it from? Asia?"

"No."

"Oh? Where then?"

"Oh you know, around. You know."

"No I don't know. Where?"

"I'm not sure. Just around." He hesitated. "It's a bit unusual but I'm used to it."

"Yes, I'm sure you are," she said. "Gamboa. Not English, I don't think."

"No. I don't think so," he agreed.

The fire crackled and a flame or two rocketed up the chimney.

"Mr Strange Name," she said deliberately, with some humour.

"How very interesting."

She got up. She gently shooed the cat to the floor. She walked over to a ceramic and wrought iron globe which, besides giving vital information as to the whereabouts of oceans, nations and empires, also happened to house, in its core, several bottles of expensive spirits.

"Come," she said. "Look."

Gamboa got up and peered at the end of her index finger. He saw a smudge of green and brown, and next to it a large expanse of blue.

"This is Mexico," she said.

"Oh," he said, with some curiosity. "And where are we, now?"

"Here," she said, indicating Europe and then England. "Right here," she added, pointing directly at London.

Gamboa looked hard and with some consternation. "Hmm," was all he could manage.

They looked at each other. Despite himself, he couldn't help but stare at her somewhat dark features and terrific, thick back hair, her almost almond eyes and the almost certainly exotic complexion. He smiled again. She felt his eyes bore into her and she cut him short before he could say anything.

"Where are you from?" she asked with a more determined curiosity.

He looked away not really knowing what to say, but he mustered his wits and put forward the best he could manage.

"Down the river," he offered, trying to sound absent minded.

"Down the river? What's that supposed to mean?"

He hunched his shoulders.

"Well," he said "if you go down the river, you'll eventually come to where I'm from."

She twisted her mouth. "What kind of explanation is that?"

"It's the only one I have," he said innocently.

"Hmm!" was all *she* could manage.

The door opened. It was the Doctor.

"Charlotte, thank you for being patient. Just had to settle him in. Check on a couple of things. You know what doctors are."

"Yes, I know," said Charlotte smiling. "Thank you Doctor. I don't know what we would have done without you."

"Don't thank me. Thank this young man here." He looked at Gamboa. "I don't know how you did it, but you saved that man's life. A miracle." He shook his hand.

Gamboa had the good grace to look slightly embarrassed but he genuinely didn't know what to say. What could he say? The truth?

"Thank you Dr Watson," said Charlotte. "You've been really wonderful."

"A pleasure my dear. You can go on in if you like. But don't tax him too much. He's an old man now you know, and this has taken a lot out of him."

"I won't," said Charlotte.

The Doctor bade farewell, and left.

Charlotte made for the door leading to the bedroom.

"Shall I come?" asked Gamboa.

"Of course. That's why you're here. He's asked for you especially. You're the hero."

"Hardly that."

"Oh yes you are. Believe me."

Gamboa shrugged, a little self-conscious, but followed her anyway.

*

After returning with the old man, Gamboa felt the weight of the night about his shoulders. Daybreak would soon splinter the urban shadows, and he needed to go home, to rest. He walked down quiet streets and blind dead-end alleys, then found himself following a busy line of wrapped-up people heading for what he perceived to be a hole in the ground. Engulfed in mufflers and winter coats, what turned out to be London's new breed of commuters were heading for the entrance of an underground train station, Kensington. He had no idea what this was, but was tempted to follow the crowds down the hole. But his nerves got the better of him, as he considered that not once, but twice, he'd been entombed underground, and so thought better of it. He ploughed on wandering the streets and followed a gentle slope, which he hoped would take him back to the river. And sure enough, just as he was about to give up, he saw the masts of tall ships trading up and down the waterway. With a renewed vigour he conjured up the spirits of his resurrection, and in no time at all was outside the gates of Wetheringdon. Home.

*

Having slept all day and most of the next, Gamboa had, eventually, roused from a deep slumber. He was preoccupied and his sense of honour told him that he needed to visit the young lady and her grandfather. So off he went, purpose in his step, but an odd concern in his heart.

He arrived at the Doctor's. He knocked on the door.

A maid answered. "Yes."

"Oh, forgive me," said Gamboa, "but I came here with an old gentleman, some time ago now, and I was wondering if . . ."

"Oh," interrupted the rather plump, ruddy face "you mean Mr Trentham."

"Yes, that's right. Mr Trentham," he smiled. "Mr Trentham."

"He's gone."

"Oh?"

"Yes, he left this afternoon." The maid bustled, taking in Gamboa's fine features. "But the young lady left a message."

"Really?'

"Yes. She left this card for you actually."

"A card?"

"Yes. Her card, or rather, Mr Trentham's."

She fumbled at the occasional table next to the door. "Here it is. She said for you to drop by any afternoon this week. About tea time."

"Tea time?" said Gamboa.

"Yes."

"Right."

"Is there anything else?" asked the beaming face.

"Er, no. No thank you. That's about it."

The busy, round housemaid, looked into Gamboa's eyes for a half second too long, then closed the door. He was left with a card.

*

They entered the bedroom.

"Missed by miles," the old man announced, sitting up.

"Oh Grandfather. You could have died."

"Impossible. Too tough."

"Too stubborn, more like."

"Ha! Maybe," and he laughed.

He looked at Gamboa. "Young man," he said. "I owe you my granddaughter's life. And my own of course."

Gamboa managed to look suitably abashed but he had to admit he felt a certain pride at being acknowledged.

"It was nothing," he said.

"Nothing? Three dead men? That's not 'nothing'. And *I* was dead! How did you do that? What are you, God?"

Gamboa humphed and allowed himself a smile.

"Grandfather, please you're embarrassing him."

"Nonsense."

The old man stuck out his hand and they shook warmly.

"Well, no matter. I'm here now. Thank you," said Trentham. "Thank you from both of us."

Twenty minutes later they were still going over the details of the attack, until Charlotte had had enough and suggested tea.

"Yes, good idea," said Trentham and he changed the subject.

"So, Gamboa, where do you live?" adding quickly "strange name by the way."

Charlotte made a funny face.

"We've already been into that. He doesn't live anywhere, at least, not that I can work out. As for his name?" she said shaking her head "don't ask."

"Nowhere?" said the old man.

"Well, not exactly nowhere," said Gamboa. "But..." he drifted off.

Trentham thought briefly. "Well, we can't have you living 'not exactly nowhere' can we. You can live here."

A pause and stammer did not faze the old man and he steamrollered Gamboa.

"Good, that's settled. Now, more tea anyone?"

And that was that.

*

And so it was that in London, the glorious capital of England afloat on the filthy Thames, Gamboa had climbed not just one rung of the social scale, but a whole scaffold, to find himself the recipient of generosity unbounded by greed, jealousies or skin colour, and access to a world he could never, ever, have imagined.

Suspicions

The lights went down. The audience chatter tapered to a dim rustle of frocks, and seat backs creaked and squeaked under the stress of fat cats adjusting their fluffy posteriors. Finally, as the overture commenced, appreciative attention, genuine or otherwise, was given to the evening's entertainment. Spotlight: Gilbert and Sullivan's, *The Yeoman of the Guard.*

Gamboa sat comfortably, his opera glasses at the ready for the opening act. Although he had a great seat, with an excellent, uninterrupted view of the stage and performers, he always liked to use the glasses. For he could get that much closer to the action, and he would, at the same time, surreptitiously scan the audience noting the early snorer, the compulsive fidget, the bored brainless "must be seen at the opera" types, and the one or two real fans who knew the score of every comic opera ever written, and were dead keen to lap up this new musical feast.

By time they got to the interval, however, the real aficionados were asking some very severe questions:

Where's the big opening chorus?

But how can you start with a solo?

But she's all alone on stage. Why?

That's not Gilbert and Sullivan.

Where's the chorus?

Yes, where's the chorus?

That's not *Gilbert and Sullivan.*

The snorers, of course, enthused:

Great show eh?

Yes, marvelous idea for a story . . . and the singing - marvelous!

The fidgets chipped in with nervous in-between comments:

Yes, well, I don't really know you know.

I mean, it's, you know, sort of, well, you know.

Yes, yes of course. Yes.

Yes, well . . .

While the must-be-seens avoided everyone's eye and made straight for the bar:

Large gin and tonic, please, plenty of ice.

Gamboa and Jaxxa had a champagne refill and stood, stretching their legs.

"What d'you think?"

"Not bad."

"Hm."

"Could be a little colder."

"No, the play. The show. The musical."

"Opera."

"Alright, op-era."

392

Pause.

"Well?" said Jaxxa.

"What?

"What d'you think?"

"About what?"

"Gamboa, don't be obtuse. You know what I'm talking about."

"What?"

Jaxxa looked at his friend. "Gamboa?"

Gamboa gazed out over the auditorium. He was elsewhere and Jaxxa knew it.

"What is it?"

"Hmm?"

"What's wrong?"

"Nothing."

"Don't give me that. I can see you're miles away."

Gamboa took a big breath and smiled a thin, unpersuasive smile. "Maybe."

"What is it?"

He shook his head. "Nothing much."

"Really? That's not very convincing."

The two men shared so much, and they knew each other so well that it was pointless trying to keep secrets.

Gamboa swallowed. "It's Charlotte."

"What about her?"

"She isn't Charlotte."

"What d'you mean?"

"She isn't Charlotte. She's someone else."

"What, you mean adopted? Yes, we know that. You told me."

"Yes, I know. I know, but there's something else."

Jaxxa shook his head. "What?"

Below them the volume of inane conversation rose to cackle level, and Gamboa turned away from the stage, sitting on the circle rail, his back to the milling crowd beneath.

"Did you know she's from Mexico?"

"Charlotte?"

"Hmm."

"Mexico?"

Gamboa sipped his drink. "Yes."

Jaxxa sat down. "Mexico?" he said.

"She's not what you think, Jaxxa."

Jaxxa hunched his broad shoulders in an unspoken question.

"She knows," said Gamboa.

"Knows what?"

"About me."

"About you?"

"Yes."

"How? How does she know?"

"I told her."

"You told her?"

"Yes."

"Why?"

"Because she already knew."

"What? What d'you mean '*she already knew*'?"

"Jaxxa, she's not who you think she is."

Jaxxa knitted his eyebrows. "What d'you mean?"

"She knows everything. Always has."

"Everything? How could she?"

Gamboa took a big breath. "She knows. She's always known."

"But how?"

The five-minute bell rang, and the audience began to fill their seats.

"She knows," said Gamboa, with finality.

The two men didn't exchange another word. They sat quietly, each wrapped-up in his own fantastic, bloody world. Hundreds and then thousands of years whizzed by in the silence separating them, and for all their great friendship, they might well have been a million miles apart.

The lights went down. The curtain went up. Act two commenced.

A Sense of History

"Burn it. Burn the lot."

High up on his stallion, Hernan Cortez, brandishing a sword of the finest tempered steel, surveyed the Aztec capital, Tenochtitlan.

"Destroy it. I want it destroyed," he said deliberately.

It was a magnificent city, filled with fabulous carved stone citadels, huge complexes of brilliantly decorated Temples, sacred pyramids, distinguished glossy palaces, and beautiful, wide avenues allowing for trouble-free perambulation, the taking of fresh air and easy-going, comfortable conversation. Waterways and canals provided efficient and comprehensive transport systems connecting all sectors of the vast, urban metropolis. The population, numbering over two hundred thousand, was housed in stable, sturdy accommodations, some made of stone, others out of wood and loam. Food was plentiful, or at least had been until the Spanish blockade, and the Aztecs of Tenochtitlan lived a secure life, knowing that despite challengers, they reigned untouchable in their world. Their enemies did not exactly quake at the name, but they knew that the Kings of the mighty Aztecs of Tenochtitlan, could call on thousands of warriors, and that any confrontation would be fatal.

But all that changed with the arrival of the Spaniard, Hernan Cortez, and what came to be called his Conquistadores.

"Raze it. I want nothing left," he declared.

They had arrived in the Gulf of Mexico in the spring of 1519. By November they were outside the gates of the fabulous Aztec capital. Having made an alliance with the Confederacy of Tlaxcala, Cortez sought to defeat the defenders of Tenochtitlan, first through a slight of diplomacy, then with force. But in 1520, he was sent packing after the Aztecs threw him out of their city, killing many and taking hostages, both Spanish and native. King Cuauhtémoc, a successor to Moctezuma II, thought the Spanish defeated, but he was mistaken, and in May 1521, Cortez ordered a siege of the city.

The Spanish had come loaded with guns and horses and swords. But they didn't need them. For at the end of the siege, the people were not only starving, but also falling prey to the ravages of the most lethal of all weapons of mass destruction, smallpox.

After more than seventy days with little water, next to no food and dropping like flies to the deadly disease, the sick Aztecs of Tenochtitlan, had no option but to surrender. And with this surrender, came the ultimate decline and final destruction of their culture and religion. Through the forced abandonment of the ancient Gods, the Aztecs' beliefs and traditions of worship were erased, and Christianity, (the driving force of the invading zealots which veiled the real motives - the expansion of the Spanish empire and the search for gold) was thrust down the throats of the indigenous peoples.

The wanton destruction of the great city dealt a final, fatal blow to the noble civilization. So much was lost forever as the churches rose up over the graveyard of the dead, crushed Aztecs. The Temples and palaces were dismantled or reduced to rubble. All the houses easily demolished. All remnants of the Aztec Empire ground into dust. The very stones of the great pyramids themselves were used to construct the Spanish cathedrals and government offices. Destruction on a mass scale, it compared to anything history, both ancient and modern, could throw up. Backed by a brutal religious ethos responsible for the murder of thousands and thousands of people in the old and new worlds, the Spaniards patted themselves on the back for having wiped out eighty percent of an indigenous people, practicing what they, the Spanish Catholic Church, perceived to be a barbaric religion.

But, as the Spanish should have known, it takes more than murder and destruction to eradicate a God.

*

Chaltexla, the beautiful Goddess of Water, waited patiently. She sat on her universal throne, high above the earth, draped in a cape of green mosaic. Her glistening proud head, thrown back in an arrogant torque of superiority, radiated, adorned with a terrific headdress of seashells and the skin and bones of sacrificed children. She lived in the heavens, but also existed in the earthly veins of the Aztec people. And this symbiosis of the worldly and spiritual, lay at the very core of the Aztec creed.

398

Their civilization had grown out of the lost ashes of the long dead past. And Chaltexla knew of the fabulous first empire, an empire led by a charismatic man-God. A man like no other, who had been chosen. He had led his people to magnificent glories, and then seen it all destroyed. She knew that there had been a hiatus, a break, a schism in time when the great religion of the prehistorical past had been lost, destroyed by drought and tsunamis, taking with it the people and all trace of their antique civilization.

Chaltexla was a Goddess of Water, a new conduit, created by the new tribes of central America, a thread linking her people to the history of their former glories. She knew the chronicles of this nation, this enormous congregation made up of pious individuals who respected the Gods, and worshipped them with virtue and holiness. This new world was fresh and vibrant, but based on the old, unwritten testimonies of the lost, forgotten world destroyed by drought many thousands of years before.

And now, here she was, Chaltexla, the Aztec Goddess of Water, awaiting the renewal of earthly vows. She was aware that her privileged position relied on these ancient people's fidelity and servitude. Without her ardent devotees, she would cease to exist. Yes, here she was, now, ready to refresh her place again in the hearts of the living, and rule as an everlasting Goddess. She was ready. Ready for the restitution and rejuvenation of her people's faith.

For centuries now she had been revered, respected. Her subjects paid homage to her greatness, her beneficence. And each year, as the complex, astral alignments fell into place, she settled with expectation, as the sacrifices were offered up in her honour. She needed this devotion. Without the praise and tribute of her subjects, she, like all other Gods, would fade into obscurity, and disappear.

With the rise of the new Aztec empire, Chaltexla's fortunes had prospered and she thrived, her image carved in stone, adorning the Temples and pyramids of the great city. She was bowed down to, admired as an illustrious benefactor. And she repaid the Aztecs' devotions with life-giving water. And today, yes, today, was a very special day indeed. For today, Chaltexla was to be given a princess, a beautiful young girl, whose whole life had been a preparation for this moment, the day when she would proudly sacrifice herself in the name of the God she loved. And this royal sacrifice would guarantee Chaltexla's place in the pantheon of the Aztec Gods.

This was *her* day. Her big day, when she would receive the blood offerings allowing Chaltexla, in acquiescence, to replenish the seas and rivers, to keep storms alive and ensure brimful, chattering streams. This day, she had seen the hearts of slaves and captured warriors beat openly in the afternoon sun. She had witnessed mutilation, decapitation and bloodletting on a massive scale. But now, *her* time had arrived. The time when the Aztecs bowed down in supplication to *her*, and her alone: Chaltexla, the Goddess of Water.

Chaltexla's effigy was placed high on the topmost altar of the great Temple and the people, by now delirious after hours and hours of bloody pandemonium, swayed in the tumultuous cacophony of sound and blinding, garish colour. They chanted and chorused in the disharmonies of bloodlust, as the young princess, dressed divinely for the divine occasion, appeared on the supreme altar, as if out of the heavens. Her parents, beaming with the pride that only parents can know, stood hand-in-hand, heads held high, basking in the fame and honour of the occasion.

The scarlet wet hands of the Temple Priests guided the delicate girl to the sacrificial stone. Her young eyes betrayed no fear, no dread. Only a serenity of purpose as, like a sweet somnambulist, she gazed out over the glorious empire of the Aztecs. Her beauty fanned out deep, velvet waves of poised tranquility, high above the chaotic storm way below her.

She was giving her heart willingly to the Goddess, and Chaltexla, a victorious attitude of wellbeing cruising through her frame, raised her arms in salute. This was it, the bloody finale to the day's celebrations and praise. The ultimate act of fealty and devotion. The crowning glory of an awe-inspiring rite. Chaltexla was pleased, very pleased, and she smiled.

The princess lay on her back, untethered on the stone. Her slender arms and legs dangled out longingly from the already wet, blood-red killing plinth. She had prayed her devotions to the Goddess of Water, and this was her jubilantly youthful day to join the eternal ones in the hereafter. This was her day to ensure the Goddess Chaltexla was appeased, and the city would have water for the coming year.

With one last look at her devoted parents, the girl prepared for eternity. Her parents glowed in the magnificence of it all.

The knife was held aloft, and the drums battered out a crescendo of staccato stabs in readiness for the final cut. The Temple Priest, eyes through the roof of his head, wavered, then brought the blade swooping down to the Princess's naked, delicate abdomen. The obsidian flashed a blister streak of blood. The knife sliced through the child's fine layer of pubescent stomach fat, digging

401

deep into the as yet still infant diaphragm. The girl let out the faintest of whimpers. This was her day and she was not going to spoil it by cries of anguish or pain. *This was her day!*

The knife then veered upward, towards the chest, clearing a path for the Priest's hand. The crowd, silent for the briefest of moments, gasped in one collective breath of expectancy, their keen anticipation heightened by the sweet stench of the glistening blood on the Temple steps. Drum beats and music stopped. Time itself took leave, and the moment stretched into eternity. Chaltexla leaned forward, her heart thumping, her head swimming in the frothy, crimson tides of adoration.

This was her day too. Her moment.

But something wasn't right. Something was out of rhythm. Something Chaltexla couldn't quite put her finger on. But she knew. Oh yes, she knew. Somehow she knew that the day wasn't going to work out. And indeed, somehow, by some miracle of malcontent, it all went horribly, horribly wrong.

The robes of the Priest were too itchy brown and uninteresting to flash, his stature too small to make an impression. He was dull, unimportant, a small, grey bearded dull man of no significance. His name would not be remembered, his face, unpainted for posterity, never hang on a museum wall. He would be unknown to history. But despite his anonymity, his facelessness, what he did in the next moment, his one awful act of sacrilegious vandalism, created a whole universe of cataclysmic consequence.

The heavy, iron cross flew in a somersault of crucified anger. It struck the Temple Priest's head as he prepared to thrust his hand up into the naked, heaving

402

chest of the young princess. The cassock-clad priest, black Bible in hand, yelled out in a pious exhortation.

"In the name of the one true God and His Son Jesus Christ, I defy you. I cast you out. I call on the true God, of the one true faith, to condemn you to Hell. For you have broken His word: 'THOU SHALT NOT KILL'."

A perplexed stupefaction swept up the Temple steps and on to the high altar. The Temple Priests stood frozen in their mystical trances, warriors swapped confused, unbelieving glares, and the masses below, incredulous, gawped in astonishment.

The Jesuit, taking advantage of the silent bewilderment, picked up the bloodied cross and again struck the Aztec Priest. He then turned to the girl and gathered her up in his arms. With her steaming intestines spilling out onto the altar floor, the Jesuit shouted to the heavens.

"Forgive her. Forgive her. She knows not what she does. She knows not what she does."

Then, as the realization hit home, the Aztecs exploded.

The crowd, until that moment dumbstruck, surged forward up the Temple steps, yelling thunderous expletives at the ridiculous Spaniard. By the altar, the girl's parents, furious in their disappointment, screamed their outrage. Temple assistants, and the King himself, Moctezuma, broke their paralyzed horror and vented vile abuse as the intruder continued the sacrilegious defilement of the ceremony.

"Forgive her. Oh God, forgive this poor wretch. She knows not what she does. She knows not what she does."

The girl's pitiful expression, louder than any drum, struck hard into the hearts of all onlookers, and the inevitable pandemonium served only to destroy what slim chance there might have been of completing the ceremony. Warriors furiously belted up the Temple steps, while high above, the anguished Priests stood frozen in despair. Assistants and novitiates fell over themselves in vain attempts to try to get at the Jesuit, who was now descending the steps with the dying girl in his arms.

A lone archer loosed arrow after arrow, but failed in his attempts to kill the Spanish maniac. Tripping and falling, one young Temple Priest launched himself from the top of the altar, only to go helter-skeltering way off the mark, tumbling head over heels into the irate, charging devotees, who saw only calamity ahead.

"Forgive her. Oh God, forgive her," continued the Jesuit, uncaring of the hellish chaos he had created.

Finally, a warrior, seething with hate, caught up with him, yanked him by the hood of his robe, and with one almighty blow of his stone club, smashed the Jesuit's head in two, the brains belching out in a confetti of grey and brilliantly dark red splatter.

The girl fell. She tumbled, broken and torn, into the crowd.

Cries went up.

"Her heat."

"Her heart."

"Get her heart."

"We must have her heart."

A young Temple Priest, the first to reach her, shoved his hand into the gaping crevasse and pulled with all his might, tearing out the small, neat heart. He held it high, high enough for all to see. The Aztecs craned their necks.

Then the hot air cooled and a murder of jet black birds, circling, united in one last clatter of beaks delivering a deafening, solitary screech of despair, before deserting the wretched scene in a flurry of inky cloud.

Far away, waves froze at their crests and the seas turned to stone. Inland, the wet arteries of streams and rivers stood still in their watery tracks, petrified, and the parade of life simply stopped, for one very long heartbeat.

For the girl was dead. Her heart, it did not beat. She was dead.

The girl was dead.

Silence!

Chaltexla watched, livid. How could this happen? How could this be? This was *her* day, *her* sacrifice. The child was prepared, sanctified. All was ready, awaiting the final act of devotion. The heart. Where's the beating heart? The Spanish. The Spanish with their wretched crosses and Bibles were to blame.

She boomed out in a monstrous cry, and the trees bowed in terror, the seas roared at her anguish and rivers and streams wept themselves dry.

Chaltexla would not be denied. But what could she do? There was no heart. No heart, no life. What could she do?

*

Moctezuma immediately ordered the banishment of Cortez and his allies from the city. Several were incarcerated or killed, but most left. Not long after, the siege kicked-in, and with that the end of the Aztec city of Tenochtitlan was but seventy-five days away.

*

The Water Goddess Chaltexla, ethereal without human dimension or scale, soared the heavens, leaving scorch marks in her wake. Shooting stars rained down on the Earth, and meteors the size of small nations zipped through the atmosphere as the Goddess's cosmic skids ripped up the sky. She was facing the end.

With no one to worship her she would die. Her very identity would disappear and she would be left, forgotten, a faded memory no one was interested in. Without worship she had no purpose. Her very existence was void. She would end her reign in the darkness, roaming the far reaches of the bleak universe, petering out until she disappeared altogether. What could she do?

Damn the Spanish invaders with their stupid Bible and their stupid religion. Damn them. Damn them all!

For a million years she flew to a million worlds but found nothing. No new peoples to impress. No new congregations to worship her. No beginnings to mould, no living enterprise awaiting her glory. Through star systems and distant galaxies, she jetted back and forth searching, hunting everywhere for signs of life. But it was useless. She was alone.

The other Gods could not be found and had abandoned her, for they, too, were already beginning to fade, losing their powers without the human adoration of the Aztecs. Alone and in the dark, she had no choice. She had to go back, back to Mexico. It was her only chance of survival.

When she returned, flowing inconspicuously as a tributary river, only a short time had elapsed in the Aztec astral calendar, and she watched, as the famine and disease began to decimate her flock of followers. Heartbroken, she vowed to have her revenge. She hated the Spanish. And she hated their Bible. She would survive and she would rise again. And so, she planned.

Refuge

"Simply wonderful, darling. Wonderful."

"Yes dear."

"Divine. It's just so Sullivan. So, so . . . Sullivan."

"And Gilbert my dear."

"Oh darling, it's so wonderful isn't it?"

"Yes dear, wonderful."

"The costumes, the singing, the story. My goodness, who'd have thought it of Sullivan?"

"And Gilbert, my dear."

"Yes of course, and Gilbert. Simply wonderful."

"Yes dear."

"Wonderful."

"Yes dear."

"Divine."

"Yes dear."

The curtain down, the house lights up, the audience was in the throes of rapture over the rather surprising turn of events on the stage. What they were hearing was a radical departure from the usual Gilbert and Sullivan musical fare, the topsy-turvy nature of previous works thankfully left in the dressing room. A relieved Sullivan had, reportedly, been over the moon, that Gilbert had rewritten the original libretto, and eradicated the nonsense of multiple marriages, confused identities and happy-ever-afters, thus giving the composer something with which to work, other than the usual fantastical, banal coincidences. He had something to work with, finally.

"Marvelous. Simply marvelous."

"Yes Dear."

Gamboa was getting a bit tired of the monotonous, sycophantic expletives, and suggested they take a breather outside.

"Right behind you," said Jaxxa.

Any expectations they had of fresh air, however, were quickly dispelled, as they hit the Embankment, inhaling the toxic aromas of the Thames, a fish sauce factory next to the theatre and the violent pungencies of a perfumery up the road. The reckless olfactory assault was staggering. They did, however, take not the slightest notice, as they had things on their minds.

"Cigarette?"

"Thanks."

They lit up, smoke vanishing in the chilly wind, the Thames ferrying its filthy cargo of human waste only a matter of yards away.

"What are you going to do?" asked Jaxxa.

"I don't know."

"Is it a problem?"

"It might be."

"So, who is she?

Gamboa told him.

*

Ten kilometers to the north of the capital city, the early Aztec pyramid of Acatitlan rose out of a sandy, slightly gravelly, earth. Not a mighty Temple, such as found in Tenochtitlan the capital city, it was, nevertheless, an important ceremonial site, and hosted religious rituals in honour of the great Gods. Chaltexla made her way there in the hope of finding comfort and solace. But all she found was a frightened people, awaiting the onslaught of the Spanish. But the Temple Priests, tough and resilient, were disregarding an edict from the conquering invaders that all human sacrifices must stop, and were preparing a final homage to all the Gods, Chaltexla included.

Two young girls were in the final stages of preparation, being painted and made up in readiness for the sacrifice. On a smaller scale than in the city, the ceremony's quite low key ambience was accompanied by muted drums of a somber nature, beating out a sad, final rhythm of retreating defiance. The Temple Priests of Acatitlan were, however, no less pious in their devotions, and all care had been taken to make sure the sacrifice went according to plan. In the circumstances, the ceremony was as sanctimonious as could be expected. Lookouts had been posted at the entrance to the main square, and a small band of warriors stood at the ready should the Spanish attempt to interfere.

The girls were escorted up the steps. The drumming increased in tempo and the Priest, after calling on all the Gods, and raising his knife to the heavens, steadied himself for the killing cut. The sun caught the blade in silhouette. The gathered crowd chanted incantations and the knife dug deep into the child's stomach.

At the same time, however, there was a gun-crack. It sent a wave of panic through the congregation. The bullet went straight through the Priest's eye socket, taking yellow-grey brain and gore with it as it hit the stonewall behind the altar steps. The Temple Priest, no time to react, fell backwards leaving the knife erect, sticking vertically out of the girl's abdomen.

More shots rent the air and the Aztecs, still not accustomed to explosive firearms, fled in terror. Yet again they had been thwarted.

But the girl, the flint still upright in her stomach, was alive. The blade had missed all organs and she was breathing, as was the intention.

This time, Chaltexla was not to be cheated and, like a torrential waterfall, swooshed into the wound, up into the child's chest and embedded herself in the beating heart. If the heart were not to be offered up in sacrifice, if she could not *own* the heart, then she would *be* the heart itself, and live. Yes, she would live. She would be the heart of the child and survive.

A Spaniard came bounding up the steps to the high altar and took the infant in his arms.

"Help. Here. Up here. Help," he shouted.

Others came tearing up the steps to assist. Aghast at what the Aztecs were about to do, the

411

Spaniards quickly attended to the girl's wound, delicately removing the knife, applying pressure and soaking up the blood. A crude dressing was made, and she was taken down the Temple steps to the shade of a tree, under which a Jesuit made the sign of the cross and read from the Bible.

"My child," he said "My child. You are saved."

Gunfire echoed in the distance as the Spanish routed the warriors. The Temple Priests were arrested and the population dispersed. The young girl, in severe pain but safe, was taken and looked after by the Spanish. The girl's family was ridiculed by the soldiers and prevented from ever seeing her again.

Years passed and the girl grew up, not as an Aztec, but as a daughter of the Spanish invasion.

*

Chaltexla lay in the youngster's heart, waiting and waiting. The years came and went and came and went. The girl grew up and married, and had children of her own, and Chaltexla passed into the heart of the eldest daughter of each generation. Patiently, she lingered, abiding her time, knowing that one day she would be free again, and rise up as the Goddess she once was. Her day would come again, and she would rule the world as an Aztec Goddess. Oh yes, her day would come.

Three centuries passed. The Aztec empire had gone, consigned to history. Mexico was born and Chaltexla lay stagnant, trapped in a human heart. For decades she had passed from one generation to the next,

412

trusting that the little girl in whose heart she lay would live well, and long enough, to get married, have children and so allow her to pass onto the next generation. Year after year she waited, until one day she found herself in the arms of a man whose tongue she did not understand. Neither Spanish nor Aztec, the man was kind and generous, and picked her up with love and tenderness.

"You're safe now. Safe."

He cradled her in his arms, holding her close to his chest.

"Safe," he said. "You're safe now."

*

Trentham, a keen amateur archeologist, had been travelling through Central America for several years. Leaving Caracas, Venezuela, he had charted a boat captained by a Dutch renegade gunrunner working out of the island of Curacao.

He sailed around the northern coast of South America, calling in at Maracaibo, where, unfortunately, he contracted a particularly nasty dose of malaria. Holed-up in a grubby, cockroach infested hotel, Trentham did, after a few weeks' recuperation, set off again, to Barranquilla. And then Cartagena in Colombia. His destination was Mexico. He was intent on hunting out Temple pyramids and lost civilizations. The Dutch captain assured him that the best way was to sail up to the Yucatan Peninsula, and from there, trek his way through the interior, all the way to Mexico City. Trentham, however, being a man of his own devises, insisted on travelling up the River Coco on the Honduras/Nicaraguan border, and from there go overland, aiming for Tegucigalpa. The Dutch captain warned against this idea but Trentham was no man to argue with.

"We're going," he announced.

And that was that.

They traced the coasts of Panama and Costa Rica, eventually, after many days, finding the Coco estuary. They sailed up-river as far as they could. Trentham thanked the Dutchman and paid him off. He then hired an army of local Indians and set off for Tegucigalpa, and the fabled Mayan ruins of the Gulf of Mexico.

After Honduras, he travelled west to El Salvador, then north to Guatemala, where he spent over a year searching out the best sites, collecting artifacts and keeping a detailed journal of his adventures. The malaria kept retuning though, and at one point he thought he was going to die. A local medicine man, however, came to his rescue with a mind altering concoction which, if not curing the disease, at least made his symptoms bearable.

From Guatemala, Trentham made his way northeast to Belize and the Yucatan Peninsula. Here, he rested and gloried in the pyramids and ruins he was searching for. He trekked into the heartland of Mexico proper, and was amazed to discover that Mexico had been populated, not by Mayans, but by Aztecs. They had built huge, giant Temples and pyramids, and had left acres and acres of ruins, which he spent months exploring.

It was on one such exploration, approaching a quiet archeological site some ten kilometers north east of the great metropolis, that he was intrigued to hear a child's crying. He and the porters, a new contingent from the Mexican capital, stood silent as the desperate sobbing echoed around the Temple ruins. The plaintive, heavy sighs tugged at the men's hearts, and Trentham, puzzled and concerned, was determined to find the source of the distress. He followed the sound and traced it to the rear of the half destroyed Temple and there, at the foot of the ramshackle steps, was a young girl, no more than two years old, alone, forlorn. There was no one in sight and the neighbouring town of Santa Cecilia was some distance away. Where had she come from? Who was she?

As he approached, he saw that the girl, scantily dressed in only a filthy skirt and a few scraps of bangles around her wrists, was sitting next to what appeared to be a body. Yes, it was a body, a woman by the look of it. Trentham kneeled down. He saw there, the grief and sadness of a terrible scenario. The woman, clearly the girl's mother, was dead; her throat cut, head lolling in an agony of despair. The young girl clung on to her mother's hand, the tears running like tiny streams down her small, dirty cheeks.

"What on earth has happened here?" said Trentham tenderly.

One of the porters came over.

"She bad woman. Bad woman."

"What do you mean?" asked Trentham. "What could she have possibly done to deserve this? And the child? Who could have done this?"

But he got no answer, as all the porters had disappeared, gone in a fit of dread.

Trentham took out a handkerchief and dabbed at the girl's tears. His heart went out to her, and he could see no alternative. In his mind's eye he saw his own child hit by the ravages of cholera, and his wife, cold, dead on the slab in the hospital's morgue in London.

"There, there, child. There, there," he said.

He picked her up.

"You're safe now. Safe."

He cradled her in his arms, holding her close to his chest.

"Safe," he said. "You're safe now."

Abandoning the boxes of supplies and personal effects, he carried the girl to the nearest town, Santa Cecilia, and sought out a doctor.

The town, a rather out-of-the-way sort of place, boasted one clinic owned by the one doctor. Of Spanish descent, he was a gruff, impatient man who had little time for indigenous peoples. He thought of them as barbarian and not worth the bother of his medical expertise. He greeted Trentham without charm or warmth.

"She's Indian."

Trentham looked at the doctor. "So?"

The doctor shrugged.

Trentham went on.

"I found her out by the old Temple site. She was lying next to what I presumed to be her mother."

The doctor shrugged again.

"The mother was dead," said Trentham.

The doctor had the decency to look up.

"Well?" said Trentham.

"Well what?" replied the doctor.

"Can you have a look at her?"

"She's Indian."

Trentham gave the doctor a cold stare. 'So?'

The doctor sipped at his coffee, crossed his legs and picked up a medical text.

"I don't treat Indians."

"What do you mean, 'you don't treat Indians'?"

"What I said. I don't treat Indians."

"Why ever not? You're a doctor aren't you? This girl needs attention. Help her."

"Nothing I can do. She's all right anyway. Look at her."

Trentham could not quite believe his ears.

"I found her out by the ruins, her mother's throat has been cut and the poor girl is alone. God knows how long she's has been there. She needs attention."

"So, attend to her," the doctor said.

"But you're a doctor."

"I don't treat Indians."

Trentham realized he was getting nowhere, picked up the girl and went in search of a hotel. Down the dirt road he found a hostel. He half expected the same response as at the doctor's, but he was pleasantly surprised to be offered a room, which came with a bath and two beds. Amazing.

He checked in and took the girl upstairs. He laid her on the bed. "There," he said. "Let's get you better. You're safe now."

After he had bathed and fed her, he put the little girl to bed and went downstairs to the bar. It was empty. A lone waiter, wearing a grubby white apron, polished a glass.

"Cold beer please," said Trentham.

"Coming up," replied the waiter, amicably.

Trentham sat at the bar and mulled over the day's events. His beer arrived.

"There you go, one cold beer."

"Thank you."

"Pleasure."

The barman returned to his polishing then nonchalantly looked up at the stranger.

"So," he began "where'd you find her?"

"I beg your pardon?" said Trentham.

"The girl. Where'd you find her?"

"Oh, right. The girl. Yes," he stumbled. "Out at the ruins."

"Ah," said the barman with a knowing nod. "Out there."

"Yes," said Trentham.

He drank his beer. A few flies occupied his attention for a second or two, but otherwise he was miles away. He thought about the girl upstairs. What was he to do with her? But in his heart, he knew the answer.

The barman interrupted his thoughts.

"One of two possibilities," he said.

"Hmm?" said Trentham, roused from his reverie.

"The girl's mother. One of two possibilities."

"What?"

"Well, she's either a prostitute and it's all gone wrong, or she's a sacrifice."

Trentham gulped. "A sacrifice?"

"Yes. Still get them around here you know. But they don't rip their hearts out anymore. Just slit the throats. Nasty." He went on polishing the glass.

"Sacrifice?" repeated Trentham.

"Oh yes. Now and then. Specially out there, at the ruins."

Trentham breathed deeply. "Sacrifice?"

"Oh yes," said the barman, a serious shadow coming over his very swarthy features.

Upstairs Chaltexla settled down for a long, well-deserved rest. She was almost there. She felt it. This was her way out. This man, this foreigner would help her, she knew it. He had to be the one. She rejoiced, nestled inside the girl's heart, and imagined her incredible future. She would break free and she would take her rightful place as an Aztec Goddess once again. Oh yes, it was coming, and she knew it. All she needed was a beating heart, and a ritual.

A change of heart

London's streets were filled with fresh food, the plentiful supply being added to daily as the unwanted, the abandoned and discarded, drifted into the metropolis in their hundreds and thousands. They came from the provinces and the countryside, in search of something better, only to find that the streets were not lined with gold and that life was not just hard, but miserable and unforgiving. Sadly, these poor unfortunates, without prospects or hope, were easy prey for the unscrupulous and uncaring. Those adults and children who could find employment were, more often than not, worked half to death in the factories. And having little or nothing to go home to, it was no surprise that they took to alcohol, in an attempt to ease the pain of a life spent in drudgery and filth.

The homeless slept where they could, on the street, any dreams of a life other than misery, dashed by the grinding, merciless nature of unbridled industrialization. Others, perhaps crammed ten to a room could, at best, hope for a short life to end the misery of a wretched hand-to-mouth existence. Terrible living conditions, unemployment and sickness were the rule for most, and those with an eye for evil-doing were treated to a ready supply of resources. Crime was out of control. The meager, untrained police force was stretched beyond its capacity, and the fabric of this new, exploding population, threadbare in terms of human dignity. For the unscrupulous, the opportunities were infinite. The haves had loads, the rest, nothing.

The Temple Priests picked their meals carefully. Disease was rife and they were very aware that not everything was edible. They had a natural inclination to avoid infected meat, sensing the putrid, the rotting and the contaminated either by smell, sight or natural aversion. Cholera and tuberculosis were rampant still, and smallpox, heart, liver and kidney diseases, particularly common ailments among the under-classes. Late nineteenth century London was not a nice place, and the Priests harvested their prey with great care. But of one thing they were meticulous, no more children. Gamboa had made that quite clear.

The two Priests stood watching the crowded bar. A million miles from home, they were in awe of the stupidity of this new race of people. They seemed to have no sense of pride or wellbeing, no appreciation of life itself and, with destructive disregard for self-preservation, thought nothing of drinking untold quantities of alcohol, then falling over in a dead pile in the street. Malcontents, thugs and murderers had no trouble picking them off, as the semi-conscious and drunkenly incontinent, left licensed premises staggering, crawling their way into the night.

In silence, the two men waited patiently, the cold, clear night keeping them alert. Through the frosted glass of the pub's windows, they could see the smoked filled rooms crammed with late night drunks, singing and cheering as a pianist bashed out popular music-hall tunes on a broken piano. They seemed to be having a good time.

The door of the bar crashed open. Smoke poured out and a brawl fell into the street. A tangle of angry men and a pair of tough, painted women tripped over themselves, throwing punches and hurling expletives into each other's faces. Too drunk to do any real harm, they did, nonetheless, land a few hardy blows and scratches. But the fight didn't last long, and the tumble broke up, some returning to the pub, others reeling incapable, weaving a path down the street.

One of the women, her large, scarlet face intoxicated into a badly weathered punching bag, zigzagged and lurched like a ship in a storm. She crossed the road, just, eventually falling over, head banging into a cast iron gaslight. "Ow! Bugger me."

From out of the shadows, between the public house and a building site, came a figure.

The Priests, watching intently, nodded to each other.

"Him."

"Yeah."

The woman, by now sitting up, keenly rubbing her head, was helped to her feet by the stranger.

"Let me assist you, madam."

"'Eavens above. Banged me 'ead there alright."

"No matter madam, allow me. Please, take my arm."

And that was all it took.

The woman on his arm, the man gave one shifty look up and down the road, and escorted his new companion into the night. The Priests followed.

*

The Temple Priests had gathered in the ballroom of Wetheringdon. Despite the glow from a crackling fire, the huge room was cold, and as candles threw shadows up the heavy curtains, the men stood in pensive silence. They knew something was up, for they had been called to a meeting, the first time this had happened since their conversion back into human form.

Gamboa, sitting in a large, wing-backed armchair next to the fire, folded his hands neatly on his lap. He stared into the flames, a measured, determined expression clouding what was usually an open, quite welcoming face. He knitted his eyebrows above the bridge of his nose, and took a big breath, lifting his head as he did so.

He spoke.

"It has to stop," he said quietly. "This cannot continue. We can no longer kill the innocents and drink their blood. It must stop."

On cue, a minor explosion hissed from the fireplace, and a purple flame danced, searching out the chimney.

"It must stop," he repeated.

"And why must it stop?" someone asked.

"Because it's wrong," he said.

"It wasn't wrong before," came the reply.

"Yes. It's what we've always done," said another. "It's who we are. It's what we do."

"Yes, it's what we do," echoed another voice, perhaps older, more determined. "Why must we stop? It's how we survive."

"It's our tribute to the Gods," a voice from the back chimed in. "It's who we are."

"Oh please," said Gamboa "spare me. This is not tribute to the Gods. It must stop. We're not serving the Gods by killing children. All we're doing is drinking the blood. We don't rip out their hearts and we don't have the ceremonies. We've changed. There is no need to kill children."

"Why? Why must it stop, Gamboa? I don't get it." A gentle voice spoke up, searching for more explanation.

"Because it's not right," Gamboa replied. "That's why."

"What d'you mean 'it's not right'? I don't get that. It's what we do. It's what we've always done. Back in our own land it's what we do."

"Did."

"What?"

"'Did', you said 'do'."

"But the blood of the children must be shed in order for the Gods to be satisfied," spouted a gravelly, determined voice.

A crumb of frustration, threatening to overflow into anger, crept into Gamboa's response.

"But we're not there anymore, are we? We don't have any harvests any more. We don't have droughts and crop shortages. And let's face it, the weather here's so bad we hardly ever see the sun, so it's pretty difficult to offer it the hearts of children. We live here now. We have to change."

"So what? It's our religion," pleaded a mature voice.

Gamboa could see where this was going.

"We don't change our religion," he said. "We change the sacrifices. We drink the blood because we have to. We'll die without it. We know that we *will* die if we don't. We kill our prey because we have to, in order to survive. But we can no longer kill the innocents. It's not right." He raised his voice. "And we will stop!"

There was general clamour in the room and voices grew loud, some in anger, others not quite so volatile.

Gamboa stood up. He called for silence.

"I am your leader, and I'm telling you that we must stop. We have to drink human blood, otherwise we'll die. We know that. But we cannot keep killing innocent children. We cannot."

Jaxxa looked at his friend and he could see that he was serious, and that something had happened. He didn't know what it was, but he knew something profound had taken place.

"Friends," said Jaxxa "please, let's give Gamboa a chance here. There is some truth in what he says. We no longer grow crops. That is true, and in truth we don't even eat the same food anymore since we changed. We just drink human blood."

One or two heads bobbed in agreement.

"We no longer suffer the agonies of drought," continued Jaxxa. "And yes, for better or worse, well, there isn't much sun here, but that doesn't mean that it doesn't exist. Clearly it does, and probably has done since, well, forever, with or without our sacrifices."

At this, one angry outburst rose above all the others.

"Then it's only because *we* have been sacrificing *our* children. It is the blood of *our* children that keeps this place alive. And it was you, *you* Gamboa who instructed us to do this, and showed us the way. *You* sacrificed your own son. I remember, I was there. I saw you do it. We all followed you. We all killed our own sons. We did this for you."

Gamboa stood his ground.

"And that's precisely why you can trust me now. You must follow me and listen to what I'm saying. Killing the children and the innocents is wrong. And it is not necessary here. Things have changed."

"Are you saying that our very religion is no good? That we must change our beliefs?"

Jaxxa looked into Gamboa's face and he thought he understood. "No comrades," he put in. "Listen carefully. I think I know what

Gamboa is saying. Our religion is sound. We have our Frog Gods and we can worship in the way we should, and always have. But the deaths of children are no longer necessary. Killing our sons on the sacrificial stone was not the answer."

"Then who do we sacrifice?"

The bomb had exploded.

427

"No one," said Gamboa.

Silence.

"No one?"

"Yes. No one," repeated Gamboa with finality. "We don't need it anymore. It is enough that we drink the blood of humans. The Gods we have served for all time will reward us."

"Then how do we . . .?"

But Gamboa wasn't listening anymore. All he could see before him was his son and wife: *Still killing children? You broke my heart.*

"Enough," he shouted. "I have spoken. It stops. It stops today!"

*

"No matter madam, allow me. Please, take my arm."

And that was all it took.

The woman on his arm, the man gave one shifty look up and down the road and escorted his new companion into the night. The Priests followed.

The man steered the woman down the alley. She protested a little, but really, she was in no condition to remonstrate, and in truth, she was quite prepared to make a few bob out of the encounter.

"Where we goin'?" she slurred.

"Just down here my dear. A little privacy."

"Oh, yer want privacy do yer?"

"Madam, privacy is a most valuable commodity."

He held the woman firm, and guided her feet to a secluded yard, where one single gaslight tried vainly to throw its yellow haze onto the cobbles.

"'Ere, where you takin' me? I don't live down 'ere."

"Madam, just a little further, then we'll have all the privacy we need."

"Don't know what we need privacy for. Where you taking me?"

At this point the man realized that the woman was becoming not just wary, but beginning to fetch up an attitude. She tried to get away and shoved and pushed against the restraining hand around her waist. The man forced her against the wall banging her head with a crack.

"Ow! That 'urt," she wailed.

"Stop it, whore. Or I'll kill you right here."

She froze.

He violently put a gloved hand over the poor woman's mouth and reached into his coat. He brought out a long, surgical knife and put it to the woman's throat.

"One more word out of you," he hissed "and I . . ." But that was as far as he got.

The blow, when it came, was so fierce that it broke the man's neck in two places. The top three vertebrae of his spinal cord crunched in a snap of splintered bone, and he fell to the ground in a silent heap. The follow up blow twisted the neck to an impossible angle and the man lay perfectly dead.

"Please don't hurt me. Please don't hurt me," the woman whimpered, pleading, her wet face a picture of terror.

"Go home," said the voice.

"W . . . w . . . what?'

"Home. Go home. You're finished. This is your lucky day. Go home."

"Home?" she whimpered. "Go, now," insisted the passive, but firm voice.

The woman, finding her senses, gathered her wits and set off towards the lights at the end of the alley. Her heart beat wildly. She couldn't believe what had just happened. And instead of going home, as the voices had suggested, she went straight back to the bar, where she sat down, slouched, a vacant expression on her rouged face, and drank herself into oblivion.

The two strangers dragged the body further into the murky corners of the yard. One stood watch, while the other bent down and meticulously, greedily, drank from the broken neck. Wiping his mouth on the back of his hand, he stood up.

The lookout spoke. "Good deed for the night, eh?"

"Yes."

"No children."

"No."

"Good."

Then he too, knelt down and drank his fill.

The Heart of the Matter

Mary was just turning in for the night when there was a tap on the door. Drunk on gin she shouted.

"Not now dearie. I'm all in."

There was the shortest of pauses then another tap.

"Not now," Mary repeated. "Didn't you hear me?"

Outside there was a shuffling and grating of shoes.

"Oh laws," she muttered half to herself. "Give us a rest will you".

She took a big breath, turned her head toward the door and called out. "Go away." And with that, slumped backwards on the bed, watching the room swirl in and out of focus.

It was Friday, way past midnight, and Mary had already serviced a pile of customers. She was tired, three quarters drunk and really did not want the bother of yet another late night punter. The room twisted and turned. There was another tap at the door, louder and more insistent this time.

"I said, go away. Not tonight. Go away!" She closed her eyes.

Then a voice sounded.

"Mary."

A stranger.

"Mary," it repeated.

She opened her eyes, looked at the door and couldn't help frowning. New customer? Maybe. Old one from the past? No, she thought. She didn't recognize the voice. No way. It was mysterious, mellow, a baritone, quite attractive really, almost magnetic. She had to admit she was a little intrigued.

"Mary," it said again.

She frowned, wondering just who it could be. It certainly wasn't one of her regulars. The room took another turn and she considered getting up. She ran a grubby hand through her long, brown hair, and swung her feet over the side of the bed. Yes, it was late, and yes, she was really tired. But business was business and, as usual, she needed the money

"Who is it?" she asked tentatively.

"Mary. Please. Let me in," the voice replied.

"Who are you?" she insisted.

"I just want to see you," the voice responded. "Can I just see you? Please. I'll make it worth your while. Please?"

It was the gentle pleading in his voice that convinced Mary to open the door. She was used to a far more aggressive approach, and wasn't in the least bit shocked by foul language and the crude, if sometimes exotic demands, made by her clients. This, however, sounded different.

She got up off the bed, straightened her clothes as best she could, caught a quick glance of herself in the cracked mirror above the fireplace, then swayed over to the door.

"Do I know you?" she asked.

Silence.

She placed an ear closer to the door.

"You still there?"

A tight expression formed around her sallow features.

"Hello?"

She could hear some slight breathing beyond the door, and was still in two minds about the whole thing, when intoxicated curiosity took over. She opened the door a crack, and peered into the foggy night. A courtyard gaslight shed a diluted, yellow misty glow across the cobblestones, and she saw, silhouetted against the damp night, an unfamiliar shape.

"What d'you want?" she inquired sternly, but not without inquisitiveness.

"You know what I want, Mary."

"Yes, well it's a bit late and I'm done for the night," she replied, half expecting the man to give up and disappear.

"You can't be that done, otherwise you wouldn't have opened the door now, would you?"

Mary was quite fascinated by the voice, and found herself drawn to this insistent, quite mysterious man on her threshold.

"Who are you?"

"That doesn't matter," said the voice. "Can I come in?"

"I'm not sure," she said, hesitating. "I don't know you."

"Oh, that doesn't matter. We both know what you do Mary, so let's not kid ourselves. I'm a customer, and I can pay well. Please, just for a while. It won't take long."

Mary prevaricated a few paltry seconds, then opened-up the door and let the stranger in.

"Well," she said, "as long as it's quick."

"Oh, it will be, don't worry," said the man. And he eased past her into the middle of the room.

It was a rather shabby lodging, but she was proud of it. Unlike a lot of her colleagues working the streets, Mary had the place to herself. She was lucky, and she knew it. But she was poor, and had little alternative to her life of prostitution propped up by alcohol. But at least she had a roof over her head. Yes, she was lucky.

The bed stood opposite the door in the corner. Its yellow sheets reeked of the business of passing trade, and what meager personal effects there were reflected the paucity of taste and money. A small fireplace sat cold and bleak in the candlelight. Grey curtains hung at the window, and an inadequate, threadbare carpet covered a small square in the middle of the floor.

"This is nice," said Mary's visitor.

"Thank you."

"Very nice."

Mary stood with her back to the door and looked at the man. He was tall, well over six feet. He wore a long, dark green coachman's cloak and a squat, top hat. His feet were encased in large, shiny black boots, and he had a walking cane gripped in his right hand. Clearly very athletic, the man gave off an aura of confidence and superiority, which left Mary quite breathless. She had never had a client quite like this before.

"Well, you're a fine one aren't you," she said, taking a step forward.

Still standing, the stranger inclined his head but said nothing.

"Oh, gone quiet now, have you? Well, we'll just have to get you relaxed a bit. Come on then, let's be having you." And she started to undo her blouse.

"Slowly," he said.

"What?"

"Slowly. Take your clothes off slowly."

"God, aren't you the one. Look I haven't got all night. And it'll be payment in advance, if you don't mind. Come on, cash on the mantel piece and we'll get down to business." She stared at him.

"There's no rush, Mary."

She paused. She stared up into the limpid eyes. And God what eyes; deep as pond pools. Mary felt she could have dived in and drowned. No, she really had not seen this man before. She would have remembered him all right.

She caught her breath.

"'Ere, how d'you know my name?"

"I know everyone's name Mary."

"What d'you mean, 'you know everyone's name.'"

She looked into his face and saw something very odd indeed. The eyes. Something about the eyes. They were changing. How odd. First, slightly almond and a dark shade of brown, they now seemed to be almost round and black.

"Who *are* you?"

She was beginning to regret having let the stranger in.

The man smiled, but Mary felt no comfort. Something in his face wasn't quite right. Not quite sincere. She was used to men, but this was like no man she had ever met. He was too smart, too well presented. Too much a gentleman. She now realized that this man, this presence in her room was unwelcome, and her fingers started to fidget, nervously, giving away the unease she felt.

"There's no need to be frightened, Mary," the man said. "There's nothing to be afraid of. You know me."

"I don't know you," she insisted.

"Yes you do."

"No I don't."

"Oh, but you do. Don't play games. You know exactly who I am. And you know exactly why I'm here."

And in that moment, alarm bells exploded in her head, and all trace of intoxication left her in a flash. She *did* know who this was, and she knew *exactly* what he wanted.

Too late, she made a lunge for the door. The man caught her by the wrist, swung her round and threw her on the bed.

"No more games Mary."

He knelt beside her, covering her mouth with one hand and with the other drawing from his inside pocket, a green, jade knife.

"Know who I am now?"

He smiled, and in Mary's last moments of life, she almost thought the whole thing a joke, as she could have sworn, yes, most definitely could have sworn, that she saw not a man leaning over her, but what appeared to be . . . a frog.

As the knife slashed at the young prostitute's throat, a fountain of blood sprayed across the room. Mary stared incredulously as life itself left her.

*

George Baggster Philips was the first doctor on the scene.

"Lord help us!" he exclaimed, as he made the sign of the cross.

"God in Heaven. What kind of a . . ."

He broke midsentence as he took-in the full intensity of the bloody slaughter before him. Experienced as he was, even he, Baggy Philips as he was known, could not quite believe what he was looking at. It was a slaughterhouse. The walls were covered in blood spatter, and the bed a mass of matted guts and gore. The doctor took out a handkerchief and held it to his nose.

"I've never seen anything like it," he said. "Not in all my years, never."

Inspector Abbeline nodded his head and blinked.

An hour later the two men stood outside the house. Baggy Phillips broke the silence hanging between them.

"No organs. None. None at all. All removed. Eviscerated, entirely."

Abbeline nodded. "Yes."

"How can anybody do that?"

"I don't know," the detective said.

"Poor girl."

"Yes."

Baggy Philips looked at Abbeline. "You'll have my full report in the morning."

"Right."

"Right."

The Doctor started to leave then turned back to face the detective. "Get him, Inspector," he said grimly. "Get him!"

"Hmm,' said Abbeline taking out a cigarette. "Oh, I will, don't you worry. I'll get the bastard. I'll get him."

As the Doctor set off the Inspector called out. "So, Doc, is it the same bloke? The same one?"

Baggy Phillips coldly stared at Inspector Abbeline. "Oh yes," he said. "It's the same one alright. No doubt about it."

And with that, he was on his way.

Abbeline faced the house, lit his cigarette, and girded himself for a last look at the crime scene. He finished his smoke and stepped firmly, yet with a heavy heart, inside. Inevitably, his eyes were drawn to the bed. On it, lay the remains of Mary Kelly. Her face, mutilated beyond recognition, rested cushioned on a blood-soaked pillow, with her head twisted at a despairing angle. The eyes had disappeared in a mash of tissue and bits of cheekbone, and her neck, a gaping, dried, black-red gash, silently betrayed the killing thrust and yank of the blade.

"Hope it was quick," the Inspector said to no-one.

He saw again how the young woman's breasts had been savagely hacked off. How her lower stomach had been sliced open, the intestines and all organs taken out. And how the upper thighs had been primitively chopped at, baring bone and gristle. He stepped back and looked around the small room. A torture chamber.

"I hope it was quick, girl," he repeated.

Of course, the papers the next day were full of it. Nothing attracted an audience more than a murder, and this one was especially gruesome. Headlines scorched across the tabloids, and London was abuzz with the latest in a string of brutal killings. Leaked details splashed on front pages, and somehow the press had got hold of the fact that all the poor girl's organs had been ripped out and scattered about the room, and that there had been a small fire made, as evidenced by the embers of the victim's clothes in the grate. Speculation grew as to why the killer had burnt his victim's skirt and undergarments, but left her blouse and brassier neatly folded on a chair. The cold-bloodedness of the atrocity filled the pubs and bars with gossip and dread in equal measure. But there was little doubt in the minds of Londoners, that the perpetrator of the latest murder was indeed, none other than . . . Jack the Ripper.

The public, however, was denied access to one detail. One detail that even the hacks of Fleet Street couldn't buy.

The police searched everywhere. Went through every scrap of blood and gore and mess of intestines in the room. But no one, *no one*, not even Inspector Abbeline himself, nor George Baggster Philips, could find it. They had taken the place apart, scoured it inch by inch, but to no avail. It was a horrifying mystery. A mystery which struck terror into the very soul of everyone who knew. It was a mystery which had Abbeline and Baggster Philips shockingly puzzled. For, after hours and hours of painstaking deliberation of all the evidence, the investigators realized, that there wasn't a trace anywhere, not a smidgen nor blood drop, of the one organ which had kept Mary alive for all her young years. Not one single sign of poor Mary's dead, unbeating heart.

441

Savage Hearts

The room, clothed in gothic orange and yawning, cavernous yellow shadows, blushed, stabbed by the knife edge flames of a blazing fire. Its walls, crowded explosions of Victorian overstatement, heaved with dead heads. Wildebeest, baboon, mandrill, hyena, wild dog, lion and zebra, once proud African game, were now nailed to the walls, crucified, clinging to their lost dignity in a last desperate gesture of defiance. Impala, leopard, hippo and rhino vied for corners of space as stuffed vultures faked their scavengers' hunger, with large beady eyes eyeing up the rigid trophies. Skinned mamba, viper and cobra, their mouths stiffly ajar, gaped in silent hisses, while their python cousins stretched out, prostrate in mute homage to two giant elephant tusks, one either side of the colossal, marble fireplace.

A splendidly posed crocodile, corrugated skin polished to an industrial sheen, sat guard at the hearth. This prehistoric charlatan, its mouth, a snappy, deceitful smile littered with chiseled, glossy white teeth, invited collusion in a sham mockery of friendship.

On an onyx table, a single rhinoceros horn stood erect, sad and lonely. Two black, leather gorilla hands, palms up, awaited ash. While six pygmy skulls, straggly hair draped in thin, knotty strands, stared in bewilderment at their alien setting, wondering at the stark, static African mortuary surrounding them. Rich, Arabian tapestries hung next to thick, crushed red velvet curtains sucking up fumy, mesmeric oriental incense. Aromatic curls wafted, in hypnotic trances towards the majesty of a brilliant, diamond chandelier. Suspended from heavy gold chain in the centre of the vaulted ceiling, this refracted the jigsaw light rays into miniature iridescent rainbows, a sparkling meteor storm across the chamber.

All this was observed by a pair of stuffed flamingos, a taxidermist's delight, their elongated pink necks elegantly stretched, supporting curious beaks in an oddly angled salute to the shocking carnage.

"Did you bring it?" she asked.

"Yes."

"Show me."

He put the neat box on a small, oak table.

"Here," he said.

"Open it."

He did.

Charlotte bent over and looked inside. A sharp intake of breath, an unsuffocated gasp, accompanied the perfect 'Oh' of her lips. And the ebony pupils, dilated in the white expanse of her radiant eyes, greedily swallowed the object of her divine hunger. There, inside the box, resting on a bed of cream silk, lay a heart.

A heart.

She breathed in deeply, her chest heavy in expectancy, the palms of her hands suddenly wet. Her mind could barely cope as her soul sang in exaltation, her pulse racing out of control. All the years, the hundreds of years she had waited, waited in despaired patience for this moment, this one moment, now became as seconds as the plots and plans, the hopelessness of decades lost in the wilderness, were about to be hurled into the murky past, forever.

Charlotte, clothed in an ocean-green, taffeta floor length gown, smiled to herself. Sensing her imminent victory, she laughed, a quiet, rather personal laugh at first, almost private, even girlish. Then, as the realization of her dreams ignited her consciousness, she let out a purr of exquisite delight. Her eyes began to flare and her cheeks flush and Charlotte, hands quivering in testimony to the nervous electricity surging through her veins, suddenly boomed a volume of self-satisfaction. Her head flew back in ecstatic triumph, her mouth opened into a cackling chasm and she roared, snarling an unearthly screech which tore into the very fabric of the building. And finally, in an ear splitting eruption, she bellowed a barking shout so loud it awoke the dormant, sleeping demons in the very depths of Hell itself.

The foundations of earth and Heaven shook in fearful awe and trepidation, and the Gods of ages past and present began to weep at the terror about to be released into an unsuspecting world.

*

The two men walked in silence. They decided not to take a cab, instead following the Embankment towards Westminster on foot. One or two late barges grunted upstream against the tide, and gaslights could be seen piercing the darkness on the other side of the water. The trivial events of the theatre were soon left far behind, and the men, lost in thought, plodded on morosely. It was Jaxxa who spoke first.

445

"She's a Goddess?"

"Yes."

"But how?"

"I don't know. I don't know it all. She didn't say. But she's waited years and years to be released. And I fear she may be on the verge of succeeding."

"Is that a problem?"

"I don't know, but I have a feeling that it isn't right."

"Why?"

Gamboa stopped, a consternation shrouding his features.

"Things are different here Jaxxa. This isn't our homeland and we are strangers. We cannot . . ."

His last words were lost in the earthquake, the prehistoric rumbling shaking London to its roots. The perambulations of late night passersby were thrown into confusion, and fearful screams and shouts shot out across the darkness. On the water, boats rocked and expletives punctured the air, as men were thrown overboard into the black, sloshing waters. Slate and brick fell, smashing to the ground, and cabbies struggled frantically, in desperate efforts to calm terrified horses that reared up, panicked harbingers of the apocalypse, their strangled whinnies and blood red eyeballs proclaiming the end of the world. A wind, scooped up out of nowhere, swept leaves, dead trees and debris in chaotic tornados, rifling up and down like mad banshees. Then, luminous, blood-curdled clouds lit up the horizons to the west as a golden sun, long set, made a brief reappearance, firing scorched rays across the megalopolis. The capitol, swathed in scarlet shards, was blinded, raped of its nocturne.

The two men looked at each other, horrified.

"It's too late," shouted Gamboa.

*

Charlotte replaced the top on the vial. One drop was all it had taken. One drop, enough to revive the dead heart. One drop of life-giving elixir from Gamboa's vial.

Did he think she was stupid? She'd known about the vial all along. Ever since he'd moved into the house in Mayfair she'd kept tabs on him, his movements, his habits. She'd suspected from the first time they met, on that wet night in Covent Garden, that he wasn't of this world, and she knew in her soul that he was very different. It was in his eyes and she recognized it immediately. Yes, she'd been upset at Trentham's being shot but her senses, ever alert, had registered that the stranger, just like herself, was not what he appeared to be. He came from nowhere and he had the strength of a titan. In the blink of an eye he'd killed the attackers and then later disappeared with Trentham's dead body. He'd returned with the old man . . . alive. How was that possible? There was only one conclusion and she knew, she just knew.

After Trentham invited Gamboa to live at the house she had kept a careful watch on Gamboa. He was polite and good company, and knew when to laugh, and compliment, and indeed he was most charming in a very masculine way. But Charlotte wasn't fooled. She knew

447

he was from another world. Her own experiences told her that. When they looked into each other's eyes there was a bottomless pool of intrigue, a knowing yet an unknowing at the same time. Charlotte became increasingly aware that the man who had saved her, was also her enemy.

After dinner one evening she challenged him.

"So, Gamboa, where are you really from?"

He raised his eyebrows. "I beg your pardon?"

She laughed. "Come on, Gamboa. Let's not fool ourselves. Where are you from, really?"

They were sitting by the fireside, alone. Trentham had gone to bed.

"What d'you mean?"

She breathed deeply. "Do I look like a fool?"

He slowly uncrossed his legs and shuffled upright in the big leather armchair.

"No," he said, a smile ringing his eyes.

"Good," she replied. "I'm glad we respect each other, at least."

Gamboa raised a hand to his mouth and brushed his lips with his fingers.

"Well?" said Charlotte.

Gamboa didn't know what to say. He knew she knew. He could tell by her confidence that she'd seen through him. Perhaps she didn't know everything, but she certainly was aware that he was not just a man from down the river. That was clear by her question. But he also felt, and understood, a primeval connection between the two of them. Theirs was not an ordinary relationship, and they both recognized an ancient synergy locking them together. Their destinies seemed conjoined, and Gamboa felt his pulse beginning to race as he realized that his secret was no longer. He was also beginning to question just what had led him to rescue this woman from the street, and why he had been there at exactly the right time. *What forces were at play here?* he asked himself. What was it that had placed him at exactly the right spot to save the old man and this young woman? Was it simply coincidence or something much bigger, something much more spiritual than simple earthly chance, happenstance? He thought back to his roots. He was special. He knew that! But what had placed him here? What grand design was on the table which he hadn't yet seen? He was puzzled, awkward. Who was this woman? Or better, *what* was she? He knew she wasn't a simple peasant girl. No, that was impossible. She was far too astute. Her good looks were undeniable but behind this also lay a wealth of knowledge and perception. She was no ordinary refugee salvaged by a do-gooder. Here was a profound energy at work, a spirit not of this world but another, ethereal and provocative. He felt the danger and was troubled. He knew this was going to end badly.

"Why is it important?"

"What?"

"To know."

"About you?"

"Yes."

A second passed. A second when Gamboa could have sworn he felt Charlotte's breath breeze down his spine.

"It isn't important, well, no, not that." She paused. "I just want to hear you tell me about yourself. Where you're from, who you are, what you do. I know nothing about you."

She stopped and stared at him. A cold transmission triggered between them and Gamboa, unnerved by the power of this woman had to admit a degree of fear.

"I'm no-one, from nowhere," he said blandly.

She laughed.

"No-one from nowhere? Well, that's rich, I must say," and laughed some more. "Mr No-one from Nowhere!" She clapped her hands. "Well done Gamboa. You have just confirmed my deepest suspicions."

"And what are they?"

"That you are indeed a very attractive man of mystery."

She got up, blew him a kiss, and left the room.

But Gamboa knew it was not that easy. Charlotte was neither smiling nor laughing. She was a most dangerous adversary and he would have to be very, very careful. Very careful indeed.

But he'd not been careful enough. She knew where he kept the vial and had been waiting for this moment. This one moment.

The drops of liquid seeped into the heart.

"Are you sure she was a prostitute?" she asked.

"Yes."

"Good." She smiled. "My mother was a prostitute. Did you know that?"

"No."

"Oh yes. My last mother."

Charlotte moved away from the table, her job done. All that remained now was the ceremony, the ritual, the spilling of blood and the raising up of the sacrifice in her honour. She nodded. It began. The invocations and sacrificial chants called on the ancient spirit of Chaltexla, the long hidden deity, starved of worship.

A God can only live on through worship and sacrifice. But no ordinary mortal can excite a phantom of the past. It needs a sanctified Priest, a Temple Priest of the ancient order, to perform the rite. And Chaltexla had finally found her supplicant, her acolyte. She had a willing servant to elevate and breathe life-giving air into the waning flicker of her existence.

The disciple reached into the box. He withdrew the heart and raised it, high, the coagulating blood slowly running through his fingers and down his forearms.

"I worship you. You are the one true Goddess," he said. "I serve you. You are the light and the darkness and all that brings life to our world. You are the Goddess of Water, of Birth and Renewal, and it is you I serve. I call upon you, here and now, to reveal yourself to the new world awaiting your magnificence. I offer this blood tribute to your power, your supremacy, your everlasting dominion over mankind. I promise to obey your commands, and to keep the blood flow constant in your name. With this heart I summon your true image. I call upon you to reveal yourself."

And with that, the supplicant closed his eyes. He lowered the beating heart to his lips then bit, hard. As carefully as he had removed it from Mary Kelly's breast, he now savagely tore, his elongated canines shredding the meat. He swallowed the dripping, raw muscle, piece by piece, and with each mouthful Charlotte faded, bleaching away, finally disappearing into a powder of ash. In its place, the flushed outlines of a harsher, swarthy, yet fantastically beautiful woman appeared, her antique aquiline features of a distant world, mocking the earthly confines of the room. A torrent of air, first cold then boiling hot, rushed in, curling swells around the metamorphosing figure.

The ceiling disintegrated, fracturing into a jigsaw of falling rubble, and lashings of sharp stinging rain pelted down, drenching the room. Thunder cracked, discordant claps deafening in the billowing red sky. Visions of ancient Temples with their scarlet sticky altars and bloody, mutilated dead, cannoned off the walls, and the hearts of the hundreds and thousands of victims, stretched out to eternity.

Chaltexla's face discharged a terrible beauty. Fine, exquisite lines accentuated her fierce femininity, her delicate frame at once small, fragile, and yet grand and imposing, demanding. Her heavy, tar-black hair, braided in silver rills about her head, shone a burnished ebony, glistening under a superb headdress of bright, kaleidoscopic feathers. A pale green shawl, with deeply woven thread tassels, fell about her shoulders, and she glowed with the vivacity of the cosmos. From her jade skirt, flowed an emerald river whose waters swirled in spate, eddying in a zig-zag rushing tide, an uncompromising wave sweeping all before it.

Bejeweled in an array of gold bangles and semi-precious stone amulets, Chaltexla raised her arms, closed her eyes and prayed to the heavens. She had almost made it.

Finally, she thought, a Goddess again.

Her powers restoring, her rightful place in the pantheon of deities virtually secured, she now stood supreme, unimpeachable. The only living God left from a destroyed civilization, she would rule alone, omniscient and dreadful, for within her heart beat and thundered a hatred of mankind, a hatred of the Christian world which had thrust her into the darkness for hundreds of years. The invaders had destroyed her world, her church, her whole religion, and now she would seek revenge. No longer a caring, tender Goddess ensuring the protection of the innocent child, she would seek out those who had destroyed the Temples, the altars and the books of her ancestors.

The ignorant savages from across the seas would pay for their sacrilege and disrespect, the destruction of her very own people and her followers and devotees, who were ridiculed and driven out of their homes and religious centres. The Conquistadors would pay.

"I want the hearts of all their children. I want to see the faces of the innocents, pale and drawn, their blood pouring, cascading in infinite scarlet waterfalls. They will pay. They will pay with their dead. I want their children, their wives, their newborn infants freshly bloody from their mothers' wombs. I will not cease till I have rid the world of the conquistador infidels. And you," Chaltexla pointed at the prostrate figure, "you will bring me all I ask. You, my devoted Temple Priest will serve me and deliver what I demand. The innocents. I want the innocents. I want their hearts."

With that, Chaltexla hurled her head back and roared a vengeance of almighty proportions, the vibrations rocking the earth sending shock waves from pole to pole.

The Priest's head reeled with victory. He was sick with the stink of triumph. He too had made it. He had achieved his life-long ambition. He, the Apprentice who had once been scorned, driven from his home, forced to live among the corpses, denied his birthright and rejected by his family and friends, now, right here, was on the brink of Godliness. For he had been chosen. Out of all, Chaltexla had chosen him. She had plucked him out of the mire to be her aide, her tabernacle servant, to enable her to transform from simple moronic human, to the Goddess her destiny demanded.

He was to serve her in the cosmic church. This was his journey's end. He had killed, betrayed and lied his way to the top and no one was going to stop him taking his place alongside the immortals. He raised his head in a simpering leer.

"Your Highness."

Chaltexla smirked in triumphal anticipation of what was to be, and from her jade skirt the emerald river rose in a swirled, eddying, rushing tide. It chopped a frothy course around the room, wrapping Chaltexla in a watery vortex, a torrential wet wall, a liquid throne, defying attack.

She opened her mouth to speak, a jubilant oration, but was violently interrupted when the doors flew apart and in burst Gamboa and Jaxxa. Breathless, the two men skidded into the flooding waters, narrowly avoiding being swallowed by the inundation. Chaltexla was furious. In an instant, she flung a rocket of fire at Gamboa. He was slick enough to dodge out of range, but Jaxxa, slipping on the edge of the torrent, caught the full force of the volley and was sent hurtling through the air.

454

Head over heels, he smashed into the wall. His temple split, ribs cracked, and his leg snapped in two places as he fell to the floor in a crumpled heap. Chaltexla, raucous with the scent of victory, sent a flaming mortar to finish him off. But Gamboa threw himself in front of his friend and took the full force of the blast. He fell and stumbled, shuffling on his hands and knees. His chest ached with a deathly smarting, and his head reeled, but he somehow survived the fiery bolt. Chaltexla sneered, grinding out a cruel warrior chant. Gamboa staggered to his feet, and disregardful of the churning, dizzying water, fearlessly turned to face his adversary. Chaltexla, in violent rhapsodies of grandeur, glared at the him.

As the deafening storm drove him back, Gamboa realized that Chaltexla was very close to full reincarnation, and her powers had almost climaxed. She had come back to rule the world, and there was little to stop her.

And in that moment, he realized why he had been called to this spot, this particular moment in time, and why his God had chosen him. *Wo-Sak* had known. He had known all along that this time would come. And He knew that only an ancient man-God, Gamboa, would have any chance against her.

Above the chaos, Chaltexla could be heard howling in derision.

"You're too late, you fool. Too late."

"Charlotte," shouted Gamboa frantically.

"I'm no longer Charlotte, idiot. I am Chaltexla."

"No, this isn't right."

"Silence, fool. You're too late. You can't change anything. Vengeance will be mine and I will rule the world. I will rule through the blood of the innocents."

"You can't do this. You don't have to do this."

"I can do what I like. I am the Goddess Chaltexla, and it is my destiny."

"But Chaltexla, it's too late for you. You belong to another world, a dead world," hollered Gamboa.

"It is you who belongs to another world. You are betraying your people."

"No. We've changed," shouted Gamboa. "We have all changed. Our world is now ready for a new power, a new domination. We feed on the blood not of children and the innocents, but of the evil and wicked."

Chaltexla jeered at this, and summoning all the power and glory of her ancestors, trained the eye of the gale, sucking and blowing with unbound force, right at Gamboa's head. A booming thunderclap and brilliant flashes of lightening ejaculated across the room, sending ricochets of sound and light whizzing, thundering in all directions. Gamboa lay low, holding fast for his life, his head spinning in the maelstrom. Then rain and shattering hail stones crashed down into the room, and Gamboa felt his head split as the pelting ice cut deep into his scalp.

"Then feed on the Conquistadors, fool," shrieked Chaltexla "and the blood of *their* children. For it was *they* who killed us. It was *they* who defiled our Temples and flattened the cities. The Conquistadors. It is *they* you must devour. You must drain them dry. *Their* children and offspring. *All* of them. *Kill them all.*"

The furious Goddess, her countenance now a malformation of dread, opened her fingers and loosed upon her prey a blazing fire, a belching, megalithic tongue of scorching coals. It belted across the room, shedding daggers of brimstone which singed into scalding steam. In the chaos, Gamboa's instincts vanished him into the vapours, to reappear, miraculously unscathed, on the other side of the room.

But Chaltexla wasn't fooled, and she swiveled, sending spitfires and red hot ash into the now boiling, condensed air.

"Think you can fool me?" she bellowed, and she propelled incendiary forks drilling through the hellfire, intent on crucifying Gamboa to the mantel piece.

"You started killing the children Gamboa, and it was we, the Aztecs, who followed your example and carried on the tradition of human sacrifice. *You* chose to kill the innocents. And we followed in your stead. While you slept, we rose up, and magnificent kingdoms grew out of the disappeared, dried ashes of *your* world. There was no trace left of your empires. The forests and jungles ate up your cities but the spirits lived on, and new towns and cities were built, and the Mayans and Aztecs built new Temples and they thrived. And we, the new Gods, lived in harmony with the new races and ruled supreme."

She spat out rains of sizzling spittle, showering Gamboa in fiery sprays. She went on, in an incandescent rage.

"But then the Spanish came, to what they called the *new world,* and with them the destruction of everything we had. Everything YOU started Gamboa. And so now, *I* must take revenge on *them*, and restore everything YOU started."

She paused in her rage, and Gamboa thought for one mistaken moment that she was receding, retracting as the fires dimmed. But she renewed the onslaught, and the watery furnace steamed in the ferment.

"I'm grateful to you Gamboa. For through your ancient religions, you helped create me. But you have lost your way in this awful, pathetic world, lost in its sour religions. We must destroy them all."

Chaltexla stared straight into Gamboa's very soul. And for one infinitesimal moment she extoled a note of compassion, almost a plea.

"You can help me Gamboa. Come rule with me. Come, and together we can kill these infidels. Kill their children, and restore our kingdoms of paradise, here on Earth."

Gamboa shook his head.

"You're wrong Chaltexla. You're wrong," he said. "That time has gone. It's too late now and we, the Temple Priests, we seek out only the evil and profane, the malevolent and wicked. It is those whom we drain of blood. We are here to purify the world, not resurrect a lost, bloody kingdom."

He was about to expand, to somehow explain, but Gamboa, his attention to physical safety distracted by the futile discourse, was caught, smashed by a crashing wall of water, a wave which knocked him off his feet, sending him tumbling into the murky torrent. His arms flaying, useless against the riptide, he went into somersaults of dizzying velocity. In a blurred mess of chaos and panic, unsure of gravity, he twisted and rung himself into a sequence of warped figures, swilling, spraining into pitching jerks which hurled him further beneath the rolling surf. Gamboa's legs, fighting with all their strength, thrashed out in vain attempts to free himself, struggling against the ferocious currents. He tugged and pulled, belligerent in his fight for survival, a determination to avert the inevitable plastered on his distorted face. Further and further down he went, folding under the weight of the drag, and Gamboa's pulse rocked in fury, his veins swollen in blasted expansion and his head raged, bereft of oxygen. His chest burned in protests as he gasped for air and he swallowed, his lungs drowning. Starved of breath, his strength waned with each passing second, and the rampant Aztec Goddess saw her chance and bore down on the hapless Gamboa. She dived into the swirling whirlpool, deadly, murderous, her hair streaming in strangled knots.

She laughed, sneering as Gamboa's eyes begged her for help.

"You're going to die, Gamboa," she boasted into the wet flux. "Do you hear? You're going to die. Drown. Right now." And she roared again, sending battalions of exploding fiery bubbles, fizzing lathers, sizzling straight into Gamboa's despairing face.

And then the Goddess sped, swimming upwards, spiraling an agitated gyration. Her splendid robes, incandescent ribbons and glorious garlands of sparkly emerald, splayed out behind her, a glittering of scintillating streamers, heroic banners unfurled in celebration, a declaration of supremacy.

She had expunged the one obstacle in her way, and she prepared herself for the dreadful reign which had lain planned and plotted in her breast for hundreds of years. She rose above the waters and hovered, then settled onto a watery throne surveying the genesis of her new kingdom. In wonderful trepidation, thunderclaps of praise sent scurries of darting lightening, shooting electric pitchforks in warning exaltation of the new Queen of the World.

Below her, beneath the vicious sea and angry rivers, Gamboa's heart was giving out. He was too deep. Too weak. He was dying.

But Gamboa had not been brought all this way to die. The Gods would not permit it. It wasn't in their plan. They looked down from on high and determined that Chaltexla would not have her way. And as the terrible calamity swarmed about him, Gamboa felt the Word of his God. He sensed His presence. And he was touched by the divinity of his heavenly father.

And *Wo-Sak* spoke.

"My Son," He said. "Reach into your heart, your heart. Dig deep beneath the layers of prayer and your struggle for goodness and you will find your deliverance. For there, hidden in the dark harbours of your soul, you will unearth an angel, a fallen angel, who was driven out of Paradise for his lies and deceit. He found a home in the secret pockets of man's humanity, and there he lurks, right now, in the eerie coves of *your* heart, waiting and scheming. You must call on this beast, this ghoulish fiend, banished in his black imprisonment, and release him, liberate his wickedness, and use it to save yourself. You must trust me my Son. The beast lies not between the waves and the molten red hot kernel of the planet, but in your breast. You MUST release him. It is the only way you can survive."

Gamboa, helpless, sinking with the violent wet spiral, listened to his Father, and with his final breath gone, and his body achingly torpid in the last throes of life, he frantically searched his soul. He sought out the primitive, original sin which would allow him to unlock the key and release the monster held captive in his heart.

460

A mighty tumult stirred and tore at his senses. It ripped through the tinctured veneer of his civility, and in his torment Gamboa understood man's evil. How he had to tame it, control and manipulate it. How he prayed that it would never take over, plead and beseech that he would never succumb to the frightful, uncontrollable rages that inhabit the soul.

And he turned.

Gamboa twisted, screwed and contorted into a thing so vile he cried in the torturous transformation. His head exploded with the contusions and bruises of ancient combat, and his back snapped, broken. His ribs retched a torrent of pain as he warped, perverted. And he bawled in horror as the realisation hit him that in every man, in every babe and soul there is a mortifying hatred, a terrible evil waiting to burst out, to cavort in the world, free, untamed, abominable.

Inside Gamboa, an asphyxiation of loathing feverishly unwound its coils, fold upon fold, a sputtering of mechanics, the bitter energy of torture. And, in this critical unravelling, in a fiery defiance, surfaced a creature. It blinked, squinted then stretched its bulging, bloodshot eyes afloat in a fetid, sludgy syrup. Coursing down from the sluggish orbs, salty secretions crept like lava-puss, leaking dirt yellow and brown, a slow, all too easy flow of deathly contamination.

Aflame with contempt, Gamboa tossed his clumsy giant's head back, opened his immense mouth and, in a roar fit to split the heavens, clawed at the drenching tomb. His teeth clashed, gnashing open and shut, great random scissors slashing in desperate hunger. His lips curled back in sickly grimace, and he let out a shattering, primitive snarl, parting the torrential waves. His chest, a mountain of veined, purple-black muscle, heaved and quivered as the mammoth claws of his feet dug long and profound into the slime of the inundation. His enormous legs, hammering titanic strength, pounded out a hateful beat in the heat of the conflict and his tail, a train of lacerating spikes and jagged serrations, fanned out in lethal arcs of loathsome disdain.

Reaching up to its full height, the monster extended its arms, its hands splayed in a deceitful gesture of amity. It attempted a smile, a knowing grin of camaraderie, for it knew that Chaltexla was of *its* kind, an evil, mercilessly wicked entity. For one moment, its eyes flickered in respite, almost concern - a remnant of the compassionate Gamboa - but it was lost, gone in an instant, as the fiend let out a magnificent, ogre's battle cry that rocked the world, shook the mountains, made valleys tremble and deflected the vast waters of great rivers. It stood immeasurable in its awful majesty.

And *Wo-Sak* sat back, brooding. And he saw his Son in his nakedness, his evil, the evil inside all men. And he sighed, for he had let loose upon the world the beast from Hell: The Leviathan.

Chaltexla laughed, laughed in the face of evil. She swivelled and swept up to the skies in a stinging, toxic, frothy spool of scorn.

"You can't defeat me," she scrawled in blazing red letters across the sky. "I'm immortal, eternal, undying. I will never be vanquished."

The Leviathan cascaded a horror of biblical mockery on her words, and spat out claps of unholy abuse.

"Thou shalt be killed," it bellowed. "Thou shalt be killed."

Its mouth a noxious chasm of green, toxic bile, it laughed in ridicule, a mocking cacophony of cynical derision, and its clawing fingers cracked in triangular dislocations. The terrifying figure, filled with the hatred of thousands of years' confinement, sped upwards. Up, up towards the Aztec deity the gargantuan flew in loathsome revolutions, surging up out of the water. It targeted the Goddess with a blaze from Hell itself, the fiery javelin tonguing, lapping at Chaltexla's skirts, and she winced as sparks cindered her legs, her arms. She tore to the left, then right, then up and away across the sky, up to the firmament of the heavens.

The Leviathan, the smell of burning flesh fresh in its sprawling, wet-black nostrils, sensed blood and maw - the feast of the damned. It screeched and wailed. It warped and bawled, and launched its gigantic form in a ravenous pursuit. In profanities of ungodly odium, it distorted into chicanes, squeezing its bulbous, clacking green scales into holes between the planets. After aeons of committal, the beast was a poisonous infestation. Septic, yellow boils discharged their thick, bloody puss, and reeking of putrid, decaying ulcers, the stench of the gorgon's rotting carcass sent the cosmos into tilted disgust.

"You will never destroy me," shouted Chaltexla. "Never. I will live forever. You hear me? For ever."

She scowled and zoomed in a concentric vortex, and in one whoosh of divine corruption, hurtled out into the vastness of the furthest star system. She danced and cavorted. She rocketed, burning up the light years of space between her and the beast. She cackled, tossing her head in complete abandon and she radiated, shining in the unadulterated rays of a distant sun.

She swept into an infinity speckled with the blinks of unknown stars. She flew, unfettered, through blizzards of anonymous spheres - severe, brilliant, their blinding radiances igniting a fantastic artery through the corridors of eternity. Blazing in translucent hues of ginger green, she scythed across space, slicing, chopping the measured corners of time into bits of trivial inconsequence. The universe was hers, and she would reign supreme. She would never be beaten. Never!

Finally, she settled on the highest point of the most distant fragment of existence, and rested.

Chaltexla rejoiced in the surety of her safety and chortled in a gleeful repertoire of contempt. Brilliant, silvery green sparks settled about her, and in preparation for dominium, she ingested the secrets of creation. She coiled her slender fingers about her bodice and hugged her aching figure. Slowly she calmed, reassured by the solitariness of her pinnacle. Mistress of all she surveyed she breathed, in scheming respite from the chase. Tranquil, she relaxed, tame.

And in that quietest of quiet moments, a massive darkness rose up behind her, a cloaking, drowning veil, ominous, bereft of goodness or compassion. Chaltexla, a grim foreboding slowly dawning on her drained face, turned, and in utter disbelief, her blood stuck in icy coagulation, stared into the eyes of an eternal abyss.

The Leviathan opened its colossal jaws. A booming silence stilled the universe and worlds skewed to a standstill.

The magnificent Aztec Goddess, shattered, strength sapped by the anticipation of impending death, lowered her head and in one lonely, encompassing gulp, was gone.

To the Leviathan, however, this was not the end, merely an aperitif, a start, the beginning of a sacred vengeance.

The devilish creature, dripping in sin, recalled the darkness of its expulsion from Paradise. It had starved, denied for thousands of years, and it vented its freedom in an orgy of destruction. It began to hunt, to patrol the oceans, scale cliffs and precipices, vault the craggy heights of earth's wonderment and fantastic innocence. And it guzzled and gnawed, greedily feasting, consuming whole races and breeds of nature. It searched out the weak and strong, the rare and beautiful, the ugly and fantastic. It devoured them all. It bent in gyrations, in articulated vaults, spanning the continents and up, up it went, way up into the trembling skies where it looked down in defiance, screeching out a juddering threat, a proclamation that the end of the world was nigh.

And *Wo-Sak* saw. And He spoke. He spoke with the power and dignity of a true God, yet the tenderness of a loving father.

"My Son," he said. "Enough."

Somewhere, buried beneath the profundities of contempt and depravity, Gamboa heard the word. He scratched and clawed at the hollow soul of the Leviathan. He waded, plodding against a blockade of malicious wrath, scraping his way up through the evil, bitter resentment. But, mired in a vengeful, pitiless rancour, the beast fought, beating down on Gamboa's spirit, tearing at his virtue. In base eruptions of hatred, it battled for its freedom and in a curdling, horrid discord of rage, gross in its vile intensity, it growled out a gurgled, clotting menace.

465

And Gamboa's Father, in an embracement of resolve, reached down and quieted the beast. He caressed the peril, the cruelty and threat, and gently eased the torture of the beast's violent cravings into a framework of softer yearnings. The metal of hatred and detestation tempered, quelled into submission and the spiritual rivets of captivity were secured once again, trapping the monster, fastening it beneath the armoury of Gamboa's goodness.

Wo-Sak then lifted his son free of the quicksand of despair, raising him up, up out of the Leviathan's boundless sin and turpitude. And Gamboa grew in strength, his gracious virtue flowering lush, fecund, eclipsing the terror of the beast. And a balanced cadence of reason returned, and he was, piece by piece, restored, the mellow consideration and symmetry of nature blossoming prosperous, rich in the moment of triumph.

And the Leviathan shrank, its profane form diminishing in significance. It withered and decayed, returning to the catacombs of Gamboa's soul where it remained, bonded, a convict denounced.

The worlds turned once more. The heavens calmed. And Gamboa, spent, bled of power, collapsed.

The water gone, dark clouds gave way to the vaulted ceiling and the curtains, smoothly velvet, returned to their uncrushed, comfortable drop. The fireplace sat cozily neat, slight domestic flames licking the insides of the chimney. The trophy heads' glass eyes gawked pacifically, as if nothing had happened. Only the ticking of an old grandfather clock disturbed the crystal silence of the room.

Gamboa came to, fetal, curled, coddled by his own embrace. He found himself lying on the floor, a thick dry carpet, soft-pile smooth against his skin, an earthly comfort under his half-moon form. Not a sign remained of the mad hurricane. He breathed, the even in and out and in and out of life.

From where he lay, he could see Jaxxa, crumpled in a heap next to an armchair. He frowned. His head a quarry of smashed memories, he winced in a simple movement, easing his torso beneath the protective clutch of his arms. Slowly, he pieced it together, the puzzle of conflict, victory, defeat and rescue. He smiled. *Wo-Sak*. His God had saved him. Saved him and the world.

Gamboa looked at his friend.

"That looks bad."

"It's ok."

"You need a hospital."

Jaxxa surveyed the shattered tibia sticking out like two white gateposts. "Later," he said.

"Here," said Gamboa. "Let's get you up."

He lifted Jaxxa onto the sofa. Exhausted, he took the seat opposite. They sat in the soft stillness, each lost in thought. What had happened? How had the Goddess returned?

In the quiet, the flamingos, standing elegantly in their pink suits, offered no explanation. They only stared, vacant, their beaks aloft.

"The attacks," said Gamboa, finally. "In the paper. Not the Ripper. It's one of us, Jaxxa. One of us."

Jaxxa had the energy to nod his head, but that was all. He lolled on the cushion, his breathing shallow. He closed his eyes and passed out.

She must have had an accomplice, Gamboa said to himself. *She couldn't have done it on her own.*

"Don't move."

Gamboa froze.

"Not one muscle, or I'll cut your head off right now."

Gamboa felt a thin, very sharp blade at his throat.

"Put your hands on the chair."

"What?"

"Your hands. Your hands," grunted the voice rapidly. "On the chair. Now."

"Alright, alright. Take it easy."

Gamboa did as instructed. Jaxxa was out cold and Gamboa was alone to face whatever this was. The pain, when it came, was excruciating. He yelled out as stiletto daggers drove hard into the back of each hand, pinning him to the arms of the chair.

His face contorted. He yelled out.

"There," said a voice "now we can all relax. Comfortable?"

Gamboa grimaced. From behind him he could hear hefty, laboured breathing.

"Who are you? What d'you want?"

"Oh, you'll get it soon enough. It'll all come clear, don't worry."

The voice moved around the chair.

468

Gamboa flinched, eyes wide in disbelief as, coming into focus, just inches away, was a countenance so bloody, so hideous that even he, a Temple Priest, used to untold ritual sacrifices, felt the bile rise in his throat.

"Oh, not impressed Gamboa? Not pretty enough for you?"

Where the facial features should have been, there was now only raw tissue, bone, and the straggles of white and pink sinew. The forehead, fleshy cheeks, chin and jaw line were missing, and the nose and cartilage gone. The eyes bulged, unblinking, two squidgy soft boiled eggs beneath naked, gun-turret brows.

The Apprentice had peeled off his face. Only the lips remained.

"The last time I did this, I cut off the lips as well, which made communication rather difficult. So, this time around . . ."

Gamboa was completely lost.

"This time around? What d'you mean, 'this time around'? Who are you?"

The Apprentice laughed.

"Oh Gamboa, Gamboa. You know me. Don't you recognize me? I haven't changed a bit. Look, same bone structure and everything."

The repulsive head turned in profile, posing. "But then again, you didn't pay me much attention in those days did you. Not much for you to remember, really."

"What are you talking about?"

"You'll get it in a minute."

469

"Who are you?" repeated Gamboa. "What d'you want?"

"What do I want? Well now, that's a big question."

The Apprentice eased the blade into a fleshy fold under Gamboa's chin, wiggling it from side to side.

"I'm going to take your face off Gamboa. That's what I want. I want your face. What d'you think about that idea, hey? Take your face off."

Gamboa gasped.

"Look I don't know . . ."

"And then," the Apprentice interrupted "I'm going to take out your heart. Kind of a demonstration really, just to remind you of the old days. You might enjoy it, you never know." He broke off. "God, it's so funny," he said. "If you could see your face. It's a picture. Really, a picture."

And he laughed

Gamboa wrestled against the daggers.

"Don't bother struggling Gamboa. There's no way out of this. You may as well sit back . . . unwind a bit."

The Apprentice then stretched towards the small table, grabbed the rhino horn next to the pygmy skulls, and drove it deep into Gamboa's stomach. The shock and pain were appalling. He screamed. Blood flooded his groin and legs.

"You don't have a clue do you?" said the Apprentice.

Gamboa gritted his teeth.

"Who are you? Why are you doing this?"

"Don't you recognize me Gamboa? My voice? My young voice? The voice of a teenager? Well, perhaps not much of a teenager these days. But you should recognize me. I've been around quite a while."

Gamboa gasped for breath, horrified at the amount of blood pouring from the terrible wound in his stomach.

"What d'you want?"

"What do I want?"

The Apprentice walked around the chair, coming close to Gamboa's ear.

"I want you," he whispered. "No, more than that. I want to *be* you."

"You're mad," said Gamboa.

"Ah, that may be true. But, in a few minutes I'll be you, and you'll be dead."

"You'll never get away with it."

The Apprentice roared.

"Really? I've done it before and you never guessed."

The Apprentice grinned, his lips curdling in a hot, sticky disfigurement.

"You've really got no idea have you?"

Gamboa swallowed, desperate not to lose consciousness.

"Why are you doing this?"

"Well," said the Apprentice drawing up a chair "since you're *that* interested, I'll tell you." He sat down. "You know, I spent years in the wilderness because of you. Did you know that? Years. With the dead and the dying, the corpses. The stink, my God the stink. You wouldn't believe it. Anyway, because of you, I had to fight my way up from nothing. All because of you, the ridicule and the humiliation you piled on me."

"I've done nothing to you," said Gamboa.

"Oh, but you have."

The Apprentice reached across and the scalpel slid some more into the delicate tissue, dribbles of blood running down onto Gamboa's chest.

"And now you've ruined it again. Ruined my big moment for a second time. Destroyed my glory. The moment when I would have eclipsed even you, the mighty, untouchable Gamboa."

"Look, I don't know what this is about, but . . ."

"Not very graceful, are you?" interrupted the Apprentice.

"Graceful?"

"Yes. At least your wife didn't moan and kick up a fuss."

Gamboa bridled. "My wife?"

"Yes, your wife."

"What's my wife got to do with this?"

"Oh, you don't know? Oh, well, you're in for a treat. I thought you knew."

472

Pause.

"It was me."

Silence.

"What was you?

"Who killed her."

"You? What d'you mean?"

"I killed her. Just as she asked me to. Begged me actually, if you really want to know."

"I don't believe you."

The Apprentice took a big breath.

"Only yourself to blame, you know. I mean, after all, you did kill her only son. Not too bright that."

Incredulous, Gamboa's head spun out of control. Despite the agonies, he managed to go back to the night he found his wife, decapitated, her heart missing. They had searched and searched but found nothing. No sign of anyone having been in the house. But they knew that someone had been there, in the bedroom. There was no way his wife could have done that to herself.

"When you're an outcast," the Apprentice continued "a social rat, you get used to moving around unnoticed. It's like you don't exist. It's amazing how people don't even see you. Well, they see you. But, well, you know what I mean."

Gamboa writhed, dumbfounded.

"I could come and go as I pleased in those days. Anywhere I liked. No one saw me and even if they did, they paid no heed to a know-nothing like me. I burned with hatred. But despite my impatience I waited and

473

waited. And then, it was amazing. I couldn't believe it. The almighty Gamboa, Chief Temple Frog Priest actually gift wrapped the perfect opportunity for my vengeance to come crashing down on his head."

Gamboa groaned, his eyes closing. A hand smacked him awake.

"Hey, I'm telling you a story here."

The Apprentice leaned in, red spittle flecking into Gamboa's eyes.

"She was so upset. Sobbed her little heart out. You'd done that. You. She was ruined with grief." The Apprentice smiled. "And I just happened to be in the right place, at the right time. How lucky."

The contorted face did its best imitation of concern.

"She must have hated you. You, the great Gamboa. How very fortunate I was on hand to help the poor woman out." He leaned back. "By the way, the guards at your place, shocking, asleep most of the time."

A brief silence cloaked the room, the wheezing of Gamboa's desperate breathing the only sound.

"Am I boring you? Probably. Well, long story short then. I broke into your house, easy enough, as I say no one sees a rat. Your wife was distraught, in heaps of tears on your bed. There was one of your knives on a table. She saw me. She didn't seem to be too bothered that a stranger was in her bedroom. Didn't even raise the alarm. Anyway, one thing led to another, you know as they often do in life, and before you know it, I'd sliced her open, dug out her heart and chopped her head off. The heart, by the way, was delicious."

Gamboa screamed in fury. "Who are you?"

The face contorted into a grotesque mockery of a smile.

"I'm your reject. Your throwaway." He titled his head to one side. "And I'm the man who's going to kill you."

Gamboa thought back over the thousands of years but still he was lost.

"Yes, it's difficult for you because I didn't matter, did I? I was the trash, thrown out with the garbage, disposed of, dumped by the roadside. Left for the vultures. A nobody."

Pink saliva drooled down the scarlet remains of his chin.

"I meant nothing to you. I was just a kid, another sacrifice, to be slaughtered and forgotten."

"Look," started Gamboa "whatever it is I did to you . . ."

The Apprentice twisted the rhino horn further into Gamboa's stomach. His agonies billowed.

"You're going to die Gamboa. But not before I've filled you in on all the details." He sat back in the chair. "Relax. It's a good story, you'll like it."

He told him, everything. He told him about the aborted sacrifice, how he had killed the old man outright on the altar-stone and been laughed at, scorned and ejected from the Temple. How he had spent years in the death pits piling up the bodies. How his family had rejected him. He finished his tale with the murder of the Priest, peeling off his face and stealing his identity, eventually standing alongside Gamboa in the old regime.

Gamboa couldn't resist an astonished, bloody gasp.

"You?"

"Yes, me. And you had no idea."

"I don't believe you."

"Then you're an idiot Gamboa. I fooled you then, and now I'm going to steal your face and fool the rest of them.'

"You'll never get away with it."

"Why shouldn't I? I've been doing it for years."

The Apprentice stood up, toying with the scalpel, slowly inching it under Gamboa's skin. Angling up towards an ear, the knife painstakingly jig-sawed left and right, gradually creating enough space for a finger or two. Gamboa jerked and shoved his chin into his chest. The Apprentice crashed his fist into Gamboa's nose, releasing a deluge of blood.

"Sit still, damn you."

Gamboa's will began to fade, as he realized that his situation was hopeless.

The Apprentice stood over him.

"And now, what are you? A Priest who only drinks the blood of bad people." He laughed. "Pathetic. Oh, I'm so scared," he shrieked scornfully. He became harsh, deadly poisonous, deliberate.

"You are as nothing compared to the Aztec Gods which we Mayans, yes we the Mayans, created millennia ago." He got close, very close to Gamboa's face, venom shooting out with every word.

"You betray the Gods and insult them with this idea of killing only the bad." The voice spat out a bloody petition. "We need to kill the innocents. Sacrifice the children. It was you who told us to do it and we followed you. And now you tell us we can't? You can't just change the rules like that. It's our doctrine, our dogma, our code of life itself. It's part of *my* soul, the very centre of *my* religion. How can you betray that?"

Gamboa rasped. "It was you, wasn't it?"

"What?"

"The prostitutes."

The Apprentice tossed his head back. "So what if it was."

"Why?" asked Gamboa.

"For the Goddess, Chaltexla. She couldn't be free without a heart. A compatible heart."

"You're crazy. Those days are gone. It's all gone."

The knife-edge shot up close to the eyeball, and the Apprentice shrieked into Gamboa's face.

"Shut up. You know nothing. You're going to die. It's time for you to die, now."

He savagely pulled out the rhino horn and stuck his hand into Gamboa's stomach, poised to rocket it up into the chest and rip out the beating heart. They held each other in a beam of hatred and despair.

The gigantic elephant tusk, used to standing sentry with its twin by the fireplace, travelled at some speed. It entered the Apprentice's back, left of the spine, pried open the ribs and continued into the heart. It

477

crashed out of the chest on the other side, the bloody tip coming to rest millimeters from Gamboa's right eye. A guttural, curdling cry yelped from the Apprentice's mouth, and gobs of blood, spluttering up from the man's throat, sprayed Gamboa's face.

The scarlet countenance of the Apprentice, tendons, sinews and muscles stretched and torn, leaked, juicy, in a hellish torment. The body fell backwards with the weight of the tusk, thumping awkwardly to the floor.

Gamboa, bleeding to death, the skin of his face hanging in haphazard folds, was drifting into darkness.

"Gamboa," said an urgent voice. "Gamboa."

He nodded, barely perceptible. He recognized the voice but it was on the edge of his consciousness.

"Who . . .? " he mumbled.

He lifted his head, twisting as best he could, and there he saw, blurred yet distinctive, Lazarus. Gamboa almost smiled but it was way, way too painful.

"The vial," he whispered hoarsely. "The vial."

Lazarus looked around.

"She had it," managed Gamboa, life slipping away.

Lazarus scoured the room but saw nothing.

"Where Gamboa, where?"

Over by the fireplace Gamboa could see the crocodile. He managed to raise an index finger and pointed to the grinning, triumphant smirk. *Here,* it seemed to say. *Over here.*

Lazarus zoomed in on the creature's mouth and there, dangling from the giant teeth, he saw the vial. He grabbed it.

"Gamboa," he said "pour it on the wounds. Now. You must do it yourself. Now. You must do it. Pour it on the wounds. Now."

But it was too late. Gamboa's eyes were closed and his heart had stopped beating. He was gone. It was too late. He had passed over.

And in his dream he saw his Paradise, its green fields and pastures, lakes and streams and waterfalls, a promise like no other on earth. Peaceful, bequieted, his soul hovered and floated, drifting into the eternal horizon of a deep, blue Heaven. A stillness and serenity overtook his struggle for life, and his passions coalesced into a graceful acceptance of his final destiny.

And as the last vestige of his earthly existence seeped away, from the mists of the hereafter there came to him a tranquil pool of translucent luminescence, a brilliant light, a divinity, a face, an angelic, beatific face. But not the face of his beloved God. No. It was not the Frog God to whom he had devoted his whole life. It was Tsok, his wife.

She smiled. And in the smile Gamboa felt the pain of thousands of years melt and thaw. And in her eyes he saw the love that had never wavered, not once.

He tried to speak, but couldn't.

"Don't," she said, shaking her head "no need. No need to say anything."

She looked into his eyes and embraced his aching body. She read his thoughts.

479

"Gamboa, not now. Not now my darling. Not this time. You have work to do."

Gamboa felt his heart surge, and his soul rolled with the swell of his wife's words. But he frowned, not fully understanding.

"Make it worthwhile, Gamboa," she said. "Make it all worthwhile. You have work to do."

He looked at her longingly, tears welling up inside. She saw it all, the craving that tore him apart.

"Gamboa," she said, ever so gently, so tenderly. "I forgive you. I forgive you, Gamboa."

And he wept the tears of regret and longing.

And Tsok disappeared, dissolving in a mystical vapour, a fog in the eternal cosmos.

And from the precipice of oblivion, Gamboa turned away, his dying heart beating loudly, the blood racing, fueling his fight for existence. He saw the dim glow of Earth's dawning grow, and beckon him across the universe. And he, Gamboa of Suxx, roared back, trailing a blaze of coal and fire.

An explosion of air gushed from his lungs and he gasped as Lazarus pulled out the daggers from his hands.

"Gamboa,' said Lazarus, ecstatic "you can do this. You can do this.'

He placed the vial in his hands.

"Pour it on your wounds and all will be well. Pour it on the wounds. Do you hear? On the wounds. *You* must do this yourself, for you are the Chosen One, not I."

It was hard to concentrate, but he managed to move, enough. Enough to pick up the small object. The vial.

With shaking fingers, he poured the liquid into the gaping hole in his stomach, and then massaged it into the horrible lacerations on his face. Within seconds he began to feel the healing powers of the unction. His vision cleared, his head making sense of his surroundings.

"Lazarus?"

"Yes, my friend."

"You?"

"Of course. Why not?"

"But how? How did you know? How did you get here?"

"Ah, well. Women!"

"What?"

"Kitsune."

"Kitsune?"

"She knew. She knew as soon as the earthquake hit. She knew you had something to do with it. And low and behold, I was dispatched. And here I am."

Gamboa smiled. "Really? Kitsune?"

Lazarus heaved a sigh and shrugged his shoulders. It was the best he could do.

"Gamboa," he said matter-of-factly "does it really matter how I got here? How I knew?"

Gamboa looked at his friend and shook his head. "No, I suppose not," he said. "Not at all."

A bond of profound understanding wedded them together, and Gamboa and Lazarus stoked the fealty which only brothers in arms experience. The moment lasted then disappeared, but it left an inky tattoo of loyalty. They looked at Jaxxa.

"Is he alright?" asked Lazarus.

Gamboa stood up, weary but steady, and made his way over to Jaxxa, still out cold on the sofa. He poured the lotion onto the broken leg and within seconds the injury was healed. A reflective pregnancy filled the room, and the three men knew that something very special had happened. They were men among men, but they knew they were more than that. Destiny had brought them together, and it was destiny that would determine their future. They had defied fate, and were about to take the first step on a very long road. Just where it would lead, they had no idea.

Gamboa broke the reverence.

"I wonder if it had a happy ending?"

"What?" said Lazarus.

"The Yeoman of the Guard."

"The Yeoman of the Guard?"

"Yes, we were at the Savoy."

"Oh," said Lazarus. "Very smart."

Jaxxa smirked quietly. "I wasn't impressed."

"Why?" said Gamboa.

"Well, I mean, how can you have a Gilbert and Sullivan opening with only one person on stage? You need a full chorus for that stuff. A full chorus."

Gamboa raised an eyebrow. "Maybe. Maybe."

He crossed over to the fire, next to which lay the crocodile, stuffed, jaws agape, smiling. And in the sparkling light he was sure he could see, yes, he was sure, absolutely sure he could see, trapped in the beast's eyes, Chaltexla, screaming and howling, beating her fists on the retina of the prehistoric reptile.

"Prima donnas," he said.

"What are?" asked Lazarus.

"Actors, singers. They're all the same. Prima donnas. They only do it for the attention. The applause, the adulation," and he winked at the crocodile.

"Well, I don't know about you two," said Jaxxa "but I'm starving."

"Yes," said Lazarus. "It's been a long night."

"A very long night," agreed Gamboa, rubbing his hands together. "Come on then," he said "let's go. My treat."

And with that, the three men left. They found a quiet tavern, and chewed over events. They talked and talked and then talked some more. Then Lazarus got up and went home.

Gamboa and Jaxxa strode out into the dark streets of London and walked. Gamboa spoke quietly as they headed for the Embankment.

"No innocents," he said, raising an index finger.

"No," said Jaxxa, shaking his head vehemently.

"And definitely no children."

"No," said Jaxxa "definitely no children."

They stopped, looked at each other.

Silence.

Then they beamed.

"You know," said Jaxxa, laughing "I'm really thirsty."

"Yeah, me too," said Gamboa, smiling from one ear to the other. "Come on, let's go get a drink."

And off they went, together, into the cold night air, of a cold, cold London.

A Good Book

Trentham slowly turned the last page of his book. It had been a long night for him too. He had an unquenchable thirst for knowledge and he was on the brink of completing the whole of Darwin's *On the Origin of Species,* in one sitting. Remarkable. He read in silence down to the last word, then gave out a contented grunt.

"Hmm," he said "I do like a good story."

He closed the book, got up from his chair, stretched his arms and yawned. Then he looked at the dog sitting by the hearth.

"Come on boy, let's go."

The dog got up, shook itself awake and with its one eye looked at his master.

"There's a good lad," said Trentham, in his thin, gentle voice. "Keep up and keep an eye out. There's a good lad."

With that, Trentham and his one-eyed dog walked brazenly, yet unhurriedly, straight into the fireplace, straight into the burning orange flames. And they went up, and up, and up, and up even further into the pitch-blackness of the chimney. It was the tallest, the darkest and the scariest chimney, not just in London but in the whole wide world. It was a chimney with no end, a chimney that went on forever, that led to the very soul of the very furthest parts of the universe. And it was into this dread, black hole, that old man Trentham and his one-eyed black and silver dog, disappeared, never, ever, to be seen again.

PART FOUR

Revelations: The Blood of the Lamb

It had been a cold, windy day, with grey clouds dashing across heavy skies, and now, as the narrow streets in the East End began to fill up with the business of the night, a fine rain fell. Heads down, people had their collars up, huddled against the chilly wet. In their search for a good time, they charged purposefully across roads and alleyways. It was Saturday, and the gin palaces of London were filling up with a determined clientele. Alcohol was the main drug of choice for a population fighting the tyranny of poverty. For many, life was, at best, a crushing cycle of appalling work in terrible conditions, followed by the horrors of overcrowding in the city's slums. For those desperate migrants who couldn't find work in the factories, every day was a trial of homelessness and beggary. The streets were filled with vagrants handcuffed to a lifecycle of penury and destitution. And so, having no other choice except to slave in the factories or beg on the streets, what pennies they could scrape together, the under classes spent on gin.

Whatever benefits there may have been to empire, the profits of world domination certainly did not reach down to the engine room of the nineteenth century.

The working classes, a downtrodden, desperate workforce, malnourished and sick, were denied access to the basics of human decency by a rigged system which saw the rich get richer, and the poor ignored. A lack of clean water, hospitals, schools and orphanages was an open wound, grinding the uneducated and dispossessed under the privileged heel of indifference.

It was into this divided, unequal world, that the ancient Temple Priests had been catapulted.

Gamboa stood in the damp shadows under a railway arch. He had watched people come and go for some time. He liked observing this new world close up. He'd been feeling a little out of sorts holed up in Wetheringdon, and decided to venture into the city. He needed to see it. He enjoyed the countryside and the peace and quiet of fields and trees, the hedgerows with their wildlife and fresh air and scented flowers, but he was brimming with questions and curiosity, and thirsted for understanding. True, the Gods had given him, if not an encyclopaedic knowledge of his adopted world, then certainly volumes of information, both historical and contemporary. But this was not *understanding*. He needed to see for himself how this world worked, how its people lived, what beliefs they had and what governed their daily lives. He felt the gaps in his comprehension, and he sensed a profound drive to go exploring, to experience his environment first hand. The magic of his own life needed to be put into perspective, and he also wanted to know what mystique, if any, existed in this place he knew was called London.

From Wetheringdon he'd ambled along soggy, wet country lanes, until eventually his footsteps were guided by the city's spires. Light eventually turned to dark, and in respite from his meanderings, he was now taking advantage of the huge semi-circular apertures created by the new railways that were crisscrossing London. Trains occasionally rattled overhead, and he stood in agitated anticipation, as the noise and thrill of the hissing steam engines approached in mounting screeches of devastating havoc.

But, strangely, he wasn't so impressed by the engines, (although, the first time he heard one he thought Hell itself was erupting from the bowels of the earth) as by the wheels. The wheel. He considered this concept for a while.

My goodness, he thought, *what we could have achieved with that.* His lips tightened and he shook his head. *Oh well, we managed without it.*

As he looked around, his eyes fell on a bronze plaque, and he marvelled at the information it contained. It told him that this was the new London Necropolis Railway line. He'd been gifted an impressive vocabulary, and, as he stood there, still trembling with the thrill of the train overhead, he deliberated on the idea of a necropolis.

"Well, well, well," he said.

Gamboa and his Priests had landed in a London brimming over with dead bodies. The rampant disease and infestation bought about by the poverty, overcrowding and filthy drinking water of the Thames, had created thousands and thousands of corpses, and London had no way of burying them. There was simply not enough space in the cemeteries. And so a railway line had been built to carry a dead cargo to a new, gleaming graveyard in the south western suburbs. What Gamboa did not know, however, was that many of these corpses were destined to be cremated - a rather new, though not yet quite fashionable, form of disposal.

A necropolis, thought Gamboa. *Now there's an idea.*

He reflected that this, perhaps, this be the answer to his search for long term bloody sustenance. But, after some thought, he decided that dead, contaminated meat, really was not what he and his Priests needed. No. They needed fresh blood, something the London Necropolis Railway could not provide.

His interest was definitely piqued, however, and he leaned closer to the plaque for a more detailed inspection.

Narrowing his eyes, he was astounded to see, in circular custom, the outline of a snake swallowing its own tail, and the words, London Necropolis and National Mausoleum Company, stamped proudly along its body. In the centre of the serpent's circle were a skull and two crossed bones - tibia he suspected. He frowned, and looked closer, as he saw engraved beneath the bones, what looked like an hourglass sand timer. Just what this represented he wasn't really sure, but then, after some consideration, came to the conclusion that perhaps it was to symbolise man's limited time on earth, and that it should not be wasted. Or, that it had already ran out?

Just why a company should choose as its symbol a snake eating itself, however, remained a mystery to him, but he warmed to the engraving as it reminded him of the Temples and carvings of his homeland. The skull was reassuring, and he raised a hand to touch the blackened outlines on the tablet. It was then he noticed the words MORTUIS QUIES VIVIS SALUS in big capital letters, embossed on a sculpted sash, or ribbon, below the timer and bones. He wasn't too sure what this meant either, but could guess at a more or less meaning, and translated the words as having something to do with death and life, peace and health. He nodded. Yes, perhaps there was something he could relate to in this modern world after all. He smiled.

As the rumblings of a slow death train chugged into the distance, Gamboa thought he could hear music. Strange music, not what he was used to. But then, that wouldn't be too surprising, for he was from a very faraway place, from a very long time ago. He strained to hear. Yes, he was sure. He could hear music, the blast of brass and drums, and singing. He was curious and followed the noise which was actually quite an attractive tune. It had him humming along and stepping out in time. He wasn't familiar with marches, but he was getting a sense of regulated rhythm, the steady beat and thrum of a regimental tempo.

Walking away from the arches, securely putting one safe foot in front of the other, he turned a corner, then another and finally, after traversing a short alleyway, walked slap bang into the middle of a parade. At least, that's what he thought it was. There was certainly a flag, and a band, and singers and people in strange costumes having a good time. They seemed happy enough clapping their hands and playing their instruments, and Gamboa found himself intrigued.

Who are these people?

It was, after all, Saturday night, hardly the best time for a street show. He followed them for a while, quite enjoying the quirkiness of their behaviour. After a street or two, marching and singing with a fervent enthusiasm, they stopped outside one of the city's thousands of public houses. *Ah*, thought Gamboa, *refreshment*. But, no. To his surprize, they did not go into the pub. Instead, they set up a circle in the street, right outside the smoked-filled windows.

A small, thin man, dwarfed by the big bass drum he was carrying, undid its straps and created a centrepiece by placing the wieldy instrument skin down, on its side, in the road. On top, he placed a thick, black book. He took a step back. Then another man strode forward into the middle of the circle. He was impressive for several reasons, not least for the fact that he boasted a very long, very thick, grey beard. Someone addressed him as General.

Oh, thought Gamboa, *this must be an army. But where are the weapons?*

The General, his thunderous voice booming out like canon fire, burst into a speech littered with curdling rhetoric. For an old man he was surprisingly agile, perhaps not prancing, but jumping and flitting across from one side of the circle to another like a fellow possessed. He moved with the zeal and fitness of someone half his age. His sonorous tones and animated message soon attracted a large crowd, and Gamboa, keen to maintain his anonymity, made his way to the safety of the opposite side of the road. Here he stood, quietly observing. He was fascinated by the pantomime, and was curious to see what would happen next.

At first, the General's words entertained Gamboa, and he inwardly grinned at what he considered to be the old man's naiveté. He talked of the horrors and evil of drink; how alcohol was the instrument of the devil and that gin, the mainstay of a downtrodden class, was a vile, insidious poison which led to indolence, depravity, violence and crime. The General was addressing the crowd and passers-by, but his message was also clearly designed for the drunken customers

492

inside the public house. He thumped the air and railed against the brewers, calling them purveyors of filth and cruel peddlers of terrible degradation.

Gamboa thought this quite amusing as, although he didn't drink much himself, he could appreciate the attraction of the occasional alcoholic excess. But he could also see that the old man was really quite serious in his determination to get his message across. Perhaps, he thought, he has a point. After all, what did he, Gamboa know, a stranger in a strange land?

The General carried on.

"Mend the error of your ways, brothers. Come into the fold and turn your backs on alcohol. Together we can fight the good fight and defeat the Devil. Put aside the bottle and mend your ways. Gin is the work of the Devil and only by rejecting alcohol and tobacco, yes comrades, even tobacco, that too is the Devil's work, only by rejection of these two sinful evils can you be saved and claim redemption. Soldiers of the Lord unite. Unite to fight the good fight."

And with that the band stuck up again, a stirring tune with equally stirring words. The ladies started singing, and one or two in the small crowd, who had by now been given song sheets, joined in.

Gamboa wasn't too sure which Devil the General was talking about, but the energy he put into his words was most impressive. And he liked the idea of fighting a good fight. And the brass band . . . well, he was mightily impressed by the brass band.

Onward Christian soldiers, onward as to war.

The chorus of singers threw back their heads and launched into the song, singing heartily, putting

493

everything they had into the hymn. The band roused the crowd and cornets, tenor horns and euphoniums, kept in check by the strident splashes of a side drum, belted out the melody with a rousing beat. Arthur Sullivan, the great Victorian composer, would have been proud to hear such a vigorous rendition of his inspiring melody out in the open air. With stirring conviction, the ladies emphasised every word, and, as they sang, they scanned the crowd for potential clients, customers, new converts in waiting, ready to be plucked from the Devil's clutches. With determination they targeted the young and old alike, and rallied in twos and threes around those they thought to be in need of salvation.

With the cross of Jesus going on before.

Gamboa didn't have any clue as to the real meaning of the words, and most of the refrains he simply did not understand. But now and then, a phrase stuck out, and he felt an accord, a fellowship of camaraderie with this strange collection of people in the street.

Forward into battle, see his banners go.

Inside his shoe, Gamboa found himself tapping his big toe. He was enjoying himself, even though he had no real comprehension of what was going on. He saw the fervour, the military insignia and felt at home. The costumes, the noise, the cacophony of music and the milling crowds, had him swelling with enthusiasm for this extravaganza, a free show outside a gin palace.

A gust of wind swept down the street, circled the milling ensemble, then scurried up in an uncontrolled squall, unfurled the flag and there, heralded in bold lettering, Gamboa read the words inscribed on the pennant.

THE SALVATION ARMY - BLOOD AND FIRE.

Gamboa's heart beat loudly in his chest.

BLOOD AND FIRE.

The song finished. The General continued.

"You must fight against the evils of gin and beer. You must cleanse your soul of the Devil's poison. Come, brothers and sisters, come and be saved. Kneel, kneel here at the feet of the Redeemer and be saved. Kneel at the feet of Jehovah."

Gamboa was getting confused. Saved? Saved from what? And who was this Redeemer? Kneel at the feet of the Redeemer? And Jehovah, who was that?

It was beginning to dawn on Gamboa that this was not just a rant against gin, but something a bit bigger. He shifted from one foot to another.

As he did so, in a cascade of frothy liquid, a bottle of brown ale twizzled through the night air, smashing into the bell of a trombone. This only gave the soldiers more vigour and they started to play another rousing tune, performed with renewed strength, convinced in their war against the evils of the bottle.

Over this the General blasted out his message.

"Follow us and be saved, saved from the power of the Devil and his temptation. Yield not to that temptation, brothers," shouted the General. "If you want everlasting life come and kneel here at the drum, at Jehovah's feet. Join us in the battle cry of freedom and salvation. Join our Army of the Lord. Onward, Christian Soldiers."

Gamboa stood amazed, hardly daring to comprehend what he was hearing. If he wanted everlasting life, all the had to do was kneel down by this drum at Jehovah's feet (whoever that was!) and join this army. Incredible. He'd never heard anything so preposterous. But he was strangely, uniquely drawn to the festive nature of the rally, as it reminded him so much of the ceremonies at home. The tunics, the headdresses and uniforms, and the chanting, and the super commotion rising in intermittent crescendos through a wonderful chorus of noise. He loved it.

The General and his soldiers wore fine, military attire, bonnets with big bows, caps with shiny peeks, and red jerseys with a cross and stars and swords embroidered in splendid colours across the chest. Stiff, high collars were highlighted by military style badges and crests, and all this, along with the music and drumming, reminded Gamboa of Suxx, the warriors, the Priests and the battle cries.

But the idea of a war against evil was confusing him. Just what was this evil they were talking about? And alcohol? What's wrong with alcohol? Salvation Army? What kind of army was that? And the Lord God Almighty, and Jehovah? And just who was this Jehovah? A God perhaps? There was only one supreme God and that was *Wo-sak*. What *were* they talking about?

"Salvation can be yours if you will give up your sinful ways, give up the gin and the bottle. Come my brothers and sisters join me here. Join these soldiers of the Lord Jehovah. Join our army, the Salvation Army of the Lord God Almighty."

Without warning, a group of drunks came staggering out of the pub. They threatened the soldiers and hurled abuse at the ladies. Gamboa was alarmed by this and considered intervening, but realized he had no right to interfere. And besides, this aggravation seemed to egg on the soldiers, who girded themselves with a zealous armour, and played with renewed vigour in the certainty that what they were doing was right and true. The musicians struck up yet another stimulating tune, and Gamboa was left open-mouthed as he listened to the words being sung.

Are you washed in the blood,

In the soul-cleansing blood of the Lamb?

Are your garments spotless? Are they white as snow?

Are you washed in the blood of the Lamb?

More blood. He couldn't believe it. *Are you washed in the blood . . .?*

His eyes widened as a dawn of comprehension began to sink in - the true meaning of the words. Here he was, thousands of miles from home, and he'd found a tribe of people who believed in the same thing he did. He was amazed, and felt the stirring of great fulfilment, a circular satisfaction running through his veins. He'd been right all along. His Gods were the true Gods and they had led him to this place. Blood, it was all to do with blood!

The General raised the book to the heavens.

"The good book says that only through God can we enter paradise. Only through the blood of Christ can we find salvation and have eternal happiness. Turn away from sin and kneel here, at the drum, the feet of Christ the Redeemer."

One of the thugs dug out a cobble stone and threw it at the old man. It hit him square in the chest and he staggered back, breathless. Several of the ladies

497

rushed to his assistance, but he brushed them aside and as he shook the Bible at his assailant.

"God forgive you," he shouted above the circus. "God forgive you. Brethren, let us pray together. Let us pray together, for the souls of our brothers and sisters who have strayed from the path of goodness and mercy. Who have yet to see the error of their ways."

The old man's voice rose in terrible crescendos.

"Oh God in Heaven, save these poor wretches from the sins they commit. Guide them to see the light. You, oh Lord, are the light of the world and only thorough You and Your light can we be saved from the grip of the Devil's work, and an eternity in Hell. Only through *Your* word, the word of the good book. Oh God, you gave us Your son so that we may live. Oh God, Your son died for our sins that we may be born again, raised up after death, and walk with Thee in paradise. Your son was sacrificed, so that we might live . . ."

Gamboa was speechless. He had given his son? He had killed his own son? He had done this? What was this old man talking about? Who was this God he kept referring to who gave his only son - who *killed* his own son, sacrificed him?

He paused, a quickening realisation growing in his soul, misty, yet nonetheless profound. He shook.

"But that was me," he said out loud. "That was me. I did that."

Gamboa's head whirled in a haze.

He's talking about me. All this is about me. I am the God. I am the living God here on earth!

The whole spectacular pageant was being played out for him, he knew that now. It was all designed to confirm his beliefs. He was a God, the Chosen One, and he was here to lead. He felt the earth tremble and the heavens roar in approval. He had killed his son, washed in his blood and now here, worlds away from his home, he had discovered his true destiny: To rule these people . . . as a living God!

They were here to worship him.

He *was* a God.

The pub door flew open. A fat man with a piggy-eyed head and a huge, wobbling beer belly, came thundering out. His face screwed up in furious hatred, he headed straight for the old man with the beard.

"I've told you before, General whatever-your-name is, you're not wanted here. Now bugger off. Hear me? Bugger off."

He had a bottle in one hand, and he shoved it up close to the old man's face.

"Get out of it. Bugger off with your flags n Bibles an' your trumpets. Go on, clear off, or you'll get this," and he shook the bottle in a very real threat. He was livid.

Every Saturday night, for weeks now, these Salvation Army clowns had struck up outside his pub. He was fed up with them, with their brass bands and singing, and Bible thumping. He was losing money.

"Go on, you hear me? Get out of it. I'll set the dogs on you. Clear off."

The music carried on even stronger in swellings of glory, and the soldier musicians seemed even more fired up. It was God's work they were about, and there was no way they were backing down. The cornets bleated out a melody, while the trombone and euphonium created harmonies and a vibrant rhythm. The women in the circle sang heartily as the fat man threatened and bawled.

A young woman, in tears, knelt down at the drum and wailed as she denounced her drunken sins, exposing her soul to the world. A woman in uniform, a gifted speaker, dressed in a dark navy gown, black cloak and a dark blue war bonnet and bow, encouraged her in a strong, steady voice.

"Come, my child," she said. "Come into the arms of Jesus. He will save you. He will save you from your sinful ways and forgive you. He will lead you to a better life in the light of the Lord. Come, my child, and be welcomed into Jehovah's Kingdom. Give up your life of sin and be washed, be washed in the blood of the lamb."

The fat man snorted a spittle filled expletive and roared.

"What the 'ell you doing down there? Get back inside an' do your job. Go on, get back behind the bar. GO ON. Shift yourself."

The old man, his beard wafting in the cold wind, strode over and, placing a firm hand on the landlord's extremely large shoulder, started to speak. But before he could say anything of significance, the publican clenched his exceptionally podgy fist and punched the old General in the face. Blood flooded from his nose and Gamboa flinched. But there was nothing he could do, it wasn't his fight.

Several drunken patrons came out to see what the commotion was. They laughed and gurgled and, after some jibing and derogatory insults, threw a fist or two. Apart from one young euphonium player, who continued with a doleful rendition of *Rock of Ages*, the soldiers, not shy to engage the Devil's workforce, stopped playing and ploughed into the drunkards. The clatter of brass, and sloppy sprays of beery spit, filled the night air, and the collision of late nineteenth century good and evil played out in enthusiastic dissonance. The ladies huddled together and, undaunted by the scuffling brawl, sang in compassionate harmonies to the mournful melody of the hymn.

Gamboa had seen enough.

The impulse to run was overpowering. Not out of fear, but exuberance. To run. To run like a child, an athlete, a warrior, the wind - not away from, but towards a triumphal battle, one which vanquished doubt and trepidation, and heralded a renewed claim on a profound understanding.

He was right.

He'd always been right. He'd known it, of course he had. But here, right now, in this new world, he was again confronted by the truth of his own conviction: Only through blood was there salvation. His exultant heart sang out in a loud, victorious chorus of rejoicing. He wanted to run, to explode, to extol in jubilant hollers the reaffirmation of his beliefs. He wanted to announce his victory to the world.

He'd been right, of course he had. And here he was vindicated by the words of unknown evangelists thumping on drums and blasting on trumpets, calling on a dirty world to be washed; to be washed in blood. For thousands of years his own civilization had been sacrificing in the name of the Gods, and here, eternities later, the same message pulsated on the grimy thoroughfares of a desperate London.

Blood. He was right.

He turned and ran. A deliberate, excited pace of solid understanding. He'd been right. Blood. Only blood can lead to salvation. Yes, he, Gamboa of Suxx, had been right.

He set off in measured, thumping great strides of confident, righteous virtue, securely taking him away from the street's chaos. He heard the yells and smash of glass fade into insignificance behind him. His head swam with a justified clarity he hadn't felt for a very long time.

He was right. And he ran.

From deep within, a wonderful turmoil of emotions churned his world into broiling wells of comprehension. His mind sprinted, painting in big, black and red swathes, the contours of his faith, his belief slashing to ribbons any doubts he may have had.

He was right. He'd *always* been right!

Each step brought him precious images, the pictures of his childhood. The old man, the frogs, the first sacrifices, the willing faces so eager to give of their lives for the good of his tribe and people, the empire. Each step brought to mind in violent colour, the death of his son, the cut and thrust of the death blow. He could see his child tumbling down the Temple steps, and the glory of personal sacrifice showering his shoulders.

Are you washed, Washed in the blood?

Of course. He had offered his own son and he had been right all along.

Onward he ran, his breath coming in huge dollops, ballooning lungs heaving massive doses of oxygen into his powerful form. He surged through alleys and streets, over shiny gas lit cobbles, down avenues and boulevards of fine, heady houses, high as castles, and across yards filled with factory debris, the carcasses of Victorian dreams.

The City of London's glory faded behind him, and, as he picked up the pace he sped toward Wapping and the Isle of Dogs.

He sprinted, then jogged and loped, and tumbled headlong into obscurity, away from the city.

He ran in shapeless patterns, vaguely following an invisible, weaving thread, an unpredictable tangent to the course of the great Thames. The lights dimmed, then disappeared to an almost darkness down by the waterway, but on he went, trouncing out a beat on the stone road, reaching out, heading east.

The tide was receding, and Gamboa, keen to embrace the elemental forces of nature, dropped down the embankment, and plodded through the muddy slime of the now dwindling waters, slurping and slopping around in its grey, creamy gunge. His rasping lungs burned as he gulped on the sharply cooling night air, but onward he ploughed, undiminished in his celebration and his aching desire to prove himself worthy of his fierce nobility. He was a Priest, a steadfast, religious figurehead but also he had, in his past life, been the leader of a great warrior class.

And so, in an effort to renew, to freshly embrace his vaunted position he forced, pushed himself to the very limits of his physical capacities. In a personal demonstration of divine and practical value, he sought to reestablish, to validate his regal station by going beyond the limits of human endurance. With each staggering step, he crunched his teeth and ground out the prayers of his ancestral home. He tripped and fell in the gluey sludge of the riverbed; logs, trees, the detritus of the city jabbing at his feet in the darkness, but onward he went, his heart thumping in determined resolve.

Sandbanks, grit and shale, littered his furrowed pathway till he passed Woolwich, then Barking. He looped up by the old Tilbury fort then found himself at Horseshoe Bay. Heaving in the moonlight, Gamboa looked up at the heavens and saluted the stars. He'd been right all along, and no one was going to stop him now. Blood had revived him and no matter that the sacrifices had not saved the ancient city, his empire, he *had* been right. Sacrificing his own son had been right, and the blood and hearts of the countless victims of the old nation had not been given up in vain. For here, in this new world, the old beliefs were still relevant: To be washed in blood, to drink blood, was to gain life itself.

He crossed Holehaven Creek, arriving at Thorney Bay, just south of Canvey Island. He followed the waterway till he came to Oyster Creek. Then he waded across marsh land till he saw Two Tree Island across Hadleigh Ray's short waters. Breathless, panting like a race horse, globes of sweat running down his thickly veined neck, he gasped for air. His clothes, torn ragged with the dirt of his trek, hung cloying to his soggy physique. He was caked in clay and mud, and he shrieked in the off-white light of approaching dawn. He belonged to the world and this world, this new world into which he had been hurled, had proven him right. He was a God. He was the Chosen One. The new earth he

504

had inherited was claiming him as the Gods' emissary . . . and he was right.

He looked at the short stretch of black water and couldn't resist. He tore off his clothes, flinging them onto the slight bank opposite. He waded into the shallows emptying into the Thames and wallowed, ducking under the wet undulations of the small tributary.

He bathed, washing away the filth of his flight. His golden torso glistened in the speckled star light, and he cleansed himself, purging his body.

He emerged naked but boiling in the heat of his deliverance.

Far away to the east, the broad shafts of pure, rising sunshine shot through the mists of early dawn, shaking awake the flat, sleeping world with spears of golden lightening. The mystery of night and the deadly patrols of spirits and nocturnal animals were put to rest, and the edge of Europe opened its eyes to a challenging, fresh start. The eastern sky bled, red raw, and pink and orange streaks shot through the wet offing like knife edges. The universe of stars disappeared in Heaven's light blue, and earth's heart, beating stronger with the energy of the sun, luxuriated in a new promise, a promise of rejuvenation and rebirth.

Gamboa closed his eyes and thanked the Gods for his being. He marveled at his own stamina, his ability to outrun, outwit and outlast the ages of time. He walked, a gentle stepping of one firm bare foot in front of the other. He was consumed by his clarity of mind, and a rising sense of security and wellbeing gave an added transparency to the emerging day.

Rekindling his ancient heritage, he'd abandoned his shoes, left the narrow strip of sandy shingle, and headed up a steep rise towards a row of buildings, houses. He scrambled up the hillside, searching out a higher vantage point, his wet clothes clinging, dripping on the grassy mound. He could smell flowers and the clashing aromas of human habitation, but the place was deathly quiet. Dead street lights stood guard as his feet padded silently on the road. He was way past Tilbury and Mucking now, and he had to admit to being impressed by the rising hilly edges of land and the unexpected coastal cliffs, where the river met the North Sea which divided England from the rest of Europe.

He'd left the torrid streets of an overcrowded London far behind, and was now heading toward he knew not what, except that an expectancy was in his heart, and he could hear a grand song, a novel, captivating melody, a rapturously huge sound pulling him towards it. He felt the rhythms of this latest world and a growing sense of belonging slowly taking hold. He felt the pulse of the earth and a cadence, an evolving modulation in the melody of the new day.

The inner peace which had settled on him, was now coupling with original sensations as the first, slight lightening of dawn was breaking into a vibrant day. The ground beneath his feet began to vibrate to a spirited melody, and his washed soul beat out in a purified, rhythmic regularity.

He found himself being pulled, drawn irresistibly away from the shoreline heading inland. His forehead throbbed with melodic pulses, enormous symphonic overtures of song and instrumentation filling the vacuums of his temples. Horns, woodwind and strings joined forces with hundreds of voices, and percussion burst into cannons of metrical explosions.

He marched towards a grandiloquence of sound which had him transfixed, focused, intent. Orchestrations of glorious tenor and pitch lured him, their aural temptations burrowing into his heart. He heard melodies so fancifully wonderful, that his head spun with the ecstasy of their rendition, and volumes of harmonies coursed through his soul, impelling him to question the existence of such beauty. Yet all were real. Each blast of instrument and handsomely baying voice, was very real. He could hear the magnificent sounds echoing round and round, reverberating, bellowing in terrific tribute to . . . *in tribute to what*? he wondered.

He walked past lines of houses, identical, quiet and dull in the rising light. Some seagulls cawed as they swirled in the swing of morning breezes and a sparrow or two twittered on fresh green lawns. A fox nonchalantly trotted across his path, and he was tempted to shout out in greeting. But his head was filled with the consuming music, and he droned on, pulled invisibly by the heat of the melody. It wasn't long before he found himself outside the doors of a huge building, pointed, massive, heavy.

And the music bellowed in his head, majestic. And words. Such words as he had never heard before:

Hallelujah: for the Lord God Omnipotent reigneth

The Kingdom of the world is become the kingdom of our Lord,

And of His Christ; and He shall reign for ever and ever.

King of Kings, and Lord of Lords.

Hallelujah!

Gamboa stood reeling, leaning his back against the broad wooden beams of the giant doors. He closed his eyes. He listened to the words sung over and over again, echoing, banging around in his head.

King of Kings and Lord of Lords. Hallelujah.

How had he been drawn to this place? What was happening to him? His Gods had prepared him for many things but this had him faint, swooning.

Is that me? Am I the God? The King of Kings?

He had never heard music like it and he disappeared into a heady dream.

*

The first, virginal rays of the day's heat beat boldly, reflecting through the stained glass, highlighting in vague focus the outline of the sacred, holy church's high altar. Here the solar fingers emptied their defiant strength, and belted heavenly, yellow arrows, onto a silver cross. In the warming air, tiny flecks of dust rose, dancing in keen draughts, twisting and turning in the curling eddies. The flames of fat cream candles lost their lustre, and the shadows, the blurry giants of tall, grey-white columns, evaporated into daylight. Pews lounged patiently, resting as an exhausted silence reposed, cautious, on their polished wooden benches.

The pregnant aura of belief, now in cessation after the pious rites of the Feast Day, still welled in echoes across the arches of the building. But the suspense, the praise and clamour continued to live its

508

moment. A resonance, the reverberating timbre of the glorious tribute paid to the Saint, continued to circulate in palpable heartbeats in the masonry, the sanctified mortar and brick of a place of worship.

And into this chasm of veneration, Gamboa's feet softly, reverently trod, caressing the cold stone. He walked deliberately, easing away from the fine wooden doors of the Cathedral into the central aisle of the nave. He stood, mightily impressed by the magnificent stone arches soaring up to the vaulted roof. He had never seen anything like it. His eyes feasted on the fierce enormity of the construction, the architecture, the design and beauty, and he felt the power emanating, rising from the stolid foundations. And he knew. He just knew.

"A Temple," he said, breathless.

And his head rang with the overtures of music still bounding and rebounding about this hallowed place. And yet the Temple was empty. Empty. Gamboa looked and looked. It was the music which had attracted him and yet there was no one here. The building was empty.

High up behind the altar, the five perpendicular fingers of leaded glass pointed to three circular windows, the largest of which, in the centre, shot down segmented rainbow orange and green light, piercing through the apse and chancel into the maw of the Cathedral. A brilliant, hazy luminescence filled the Minster, and Gamboa again rejoiced at the continued volumes of music crowding to fullness in every nook of the Temple. He heard the *Hallelujah* of Handle's *Messiah* rain in downpours of melodic thunderbolts, as a choir of songsters chorused in perfect harmonies. The grand pipe organ, vibrating in profound basses, furnished an inspiration, and raced in high counterpart octaves, breathing out expectorations of melodies reveling in the glorification of God.

Hallelujahs rang out again and again and Gamboa's head reeled in wonder. The Cathedral was empty, yet his head was filled with the music of the Gods.

Elevated, towering high above him, the vibrant, jigsaw glass mosaics leapt into Gamboa's eyes and he stared, squinting in wonderment at the picture stories unfolding before him. In a striking multitude of shades of crimson, yellow and the deepest of sea-blue indigo, he saw the outlines of long gone characters, confidently standing proud in their frames, retelling a narrative which had him mesmerized. Faces, expressed in complexions of colours he had rarely seen, portrayed tranquil serenities, along with violent conflict, and yet more compositions of harmony and beguiling beauty which had him catching his breath.

He didn't know who these characters were, or what they stood for, but he was intrigued by the portraits and ensembles, and could only imagine that, as in the carvings in his own Temples, the pictures told histories, tales of wars, victories, successions and great feats of magical renown.

As the sun grew stronger, the splintered rays lanced through the glass windows in hues defiant and brilliant, illuminating the sublime outlines of Saints. And there, in the middle, her soft brown hair framing her delicate humanity, stood a woman with a cross, the cross of her Lord. Carrying her discovery with a universal dignity, she smiled benignly on the vacant church, a charming, all-embracing invitation to the lost host of antiquity, to join in her rejoicing at discovering the mighty cross of her saviour. The weight of a cruel

Roman world hung on her slender shoulders, but a forgiving, compassionate spirit of eternal suffering and benevolence shrouded her in an aura of stillness, a calm tranquility, worthy of great adoration and tribute. And, in a triumphant expression of forgiveness, she called on the violent, turbulent errors of empire to bow down in praise to a new glory.

Gamboa was unavoidably drawn to this woman, and he was eager to know who she was. He approached her, for he could see a name on a scroll of black and scarlet. He walked reverently towards the heavily leaded window. He craned his neck to see the glass sash, and through curious eyes he read the inscription: *St Helena.*

He puzzled over this.

St Helena and cross, he thought. *Hmm, must be important.*

Gamboa didn't know who she was. But he whirled round as the great door, swinging on vast cast iron hinges, suddenly banged shut. A silence boomed out killing the music. He was left alone, stark in the empty Cathedral. Whatever eminence had called him here, whatever power had filled his head with the music of the heavens, had now decided that he must be alone, alone in a deferential silence.

He felt the wet cold of his wet clothes drip cold onto the flagging, pooling on the slabs beneath his feet.

He felt the magic, the splendid aura of mystique and reverent charm. The universal spirits had lead him here to this sacred Temple and he stared, amazed at the wonderment in his surroundings. His mind flew through the millions of empty spaces to his own Temple, to his own divine Church, and he reflected on his own enchantment, his own connection with the great Gods of

511

eternity, and he knew he was in a hallowed place. He could sense the devotion, the fervor behind the creation of such a building. And he considered his own Temples, the care, the piety, the mighty driving force of service which had thrown up the fantastic Cathedrals of his own culture. He pondered on the honouring of the Gods, and he saw the parallels here in this sanctified edifice.

He marveled at the magic of the pictures dancing in the light, and, in his imagination, saw his own Temple of the Frog God, *Wo-sak*; the carvings of stone, the details so lovingly created in the erection of the ancient Temple, and the sacrifices made in the presence of the Gods atop the altars.

He looked in astonishment at the high table and saw there, gleaming, the silver cross. To the side, to his left as he looked at sunlight blistering through the glass, hung a magnificent wooden sculpture. He took a step towards it. Quietly he examined the piece, his critical eye impressed by the high standard of work. He admired the craftsmanship, the dedication to duty, to service. He took in the details, seeing there a man, hanging, bloody, hair strewn downwards in wet tresses framing an expression of hopeful despair. He saw the thorns, and Gamboa, puzzled yet again, examined the pain in the man's eyes and couldn't help wondering who could have done such a thing to him, and, perhaps more importantly, why.

He was touched by the kindness and humanity emanating from the man's countenance, and Gamboa couldn't help being stunned by the craftsman's expertise in creating such a work of art.

"Wow," he said softly.

But he was bewildered by the carving. Why was it there? What was it for? What did it represent? He was

512

clever enough to realize that it held an importance for these people, but he couldn't quite work out why. Then it occurred to him that he had seen this somewhere before, not exactly the same, but similar, yes, definitely similar. He thought.

"Yes," he said. "I've seen this before."

In his mind's eye he pictured the house where he and the Priests had feasted on the children. Their faces, etched on his memory, morphed into a cross - the cross he had seen hanging on the rafter. And yet it wasn't just a cross; it had been a cross with a man on it. He frowned. Yes, he HAD seen this before and, as a Temple Priest himself, knew it had some great import. He nodded.

"Yes," he said quietly.

He didn't quite know what he was saying *yes* to, but he knew he had entered a very special place and he was intelligent enough to respect it.

He looked to his right then, and there he saw a woman, a wonderful woman, crafted in a sitting position, a blue mantle around her head and shoulders. On her lap there lay a man, dying, or dead, he wasn't sure. But he could clearly see that it was the same man who was on the cross; thorns, hair, blood. Again he puzzled to work this out.

The same man.

Stronger than ever, the realization hit him that this man held some very real significance for the people of this world. He was on a cross, and then, here, opposite, in a woman's arms. He looked at her smile, her benign, compassionate, enigmatic smile and he almost smiled with her. Again, he couldn't resist it.

"Wow," he said, shaking his head in an almost childlike wonderment.

He saw the love the woman felt for this man, and he considered for one moment that it was perhaps, his wife. But on closer scrutiny he discovered a different love, a maternal love, an instinctual, maybe even visceral love. And in her eyes Gamboa saw a love which had his heart miss a beat.

"His Mother. She's his mother!" he said.

Once more Gamboa marveled at the artist's skills. He had captured an eternity of love and watchfulness, the tender hands, the quiet curve of her shoulders, the gentlest of petal cheeks and the supreme moment of loss. Her son was dead.

And yet he also saw there a triumph. And, again, he puzzled at this. What was this victory, this joy he detected in her?

Out in the North Sea, the tinniest scurry of wind curled itself up tight into the smallest of cloudy funnels, twisted into a cone of opaque dense moisture, and mutated into a tall, misty wet pipe, whipping round and round in sharp concentric circles. It picked up speed and began to throttle up high, high over the open waves, which now began to accompany the new rage with a frenzy of their own. The swell of gentle undulations gathered pace, and soon churned up into troughs, cresting in threatening rollers breaking, swirling in white-capped walls of water cannoning in wacky commotion. The ensuing chaos challenged the torpor of the deep sea and a great rising and agitation produced a storm, unpredictable and fickle, a capricious tempest sullying the skies and sending up enormous blue-black clouds of water, blotting out the sun and plunging the east coast of England into darkness.

Inside the Cathedral, Gamboa tensed as the windows fell silently dim, inky. The yellowy flaming light of the waxing candles on the altar, regained their lost strength, and giant shadows threw themselves up against the cold-stone walls. Gamboa, primitively aware of an elemental change, stood attentive, quickly organized for this revolutionary transformation.

A gust of grey, dusty breeze crept menacingly under the doors, shot sharply down the body of the church and in ominous coils headed for the chancel and altar above it. In a shocking burst of energy, it blew out the flames and the Cathedral was left in complete darkness. In the cold, silent cavern, Gamboa could hear a breathing, a rhythmic intake and exhaling of air. Nothing stirred and the world was deathly silent, except for the metrical panting. He stood absolutely still, only the beating of his heart and the steady pulse of the deep breathing disturbing the profound stillness.

And in this quiet, Gamboa knew he was in the presence of *his* God, the mighty *Wo-sak*. He had brought him here, transported from his ancient beginnings to this new, strange place. The blackness, cloying in its cold, sticky intensity, gathered about Gamboa's shoulders and he felt the beat of his God's heart, his spirit. He felt the powerful arms of his protector and guide, his divine benefactor, wrapping themselves around his soul. And he knew he was safe. His God was with him. And he *knew* he was safe.

And in that moment the deep, black storm abated, the savage wind and cruel sea subsided, easing nature's uproar back into a more leisurely, logical pace.

515

But it left a dull, grey smudge across the world and the sun, momentarily defeated in its urgency to regain the world, slept, hidden behind a thick veil of murky, concentrated cloud. A vague, not quite sepia light tried, half-heartedly, to fill the windows of the church, but the building was left dull, unimpressive in its ordinariness. The glass pictures had no lustre, no tale to tell and fell mute. The carvings no longer sparkled with artistic intrigue and now looked shabby, drab, the fusty outlines of forgotten, inconsequential whimsies.

Gamboa surveyed it all and laughed.

Another God? Another entity offering up a child in sacrifice?

He laughed.

Who was this God who had killed his own son?

He heard the old General's words anew in his ear and began to reassess them.

For God so loved the world that he gave his only begotten son . . .

He had killed his own son? He loved the world so much he had sacrificed his own son? Well, so had he, Gamboa. Gamboa was a God and he had killed his own son to save his people. There was nothing new in that!

He felt the warmth of his own self-confidence and relished its comforting reassurance. He was a God, a God who plunged his hands into the chests of living people. He was not afraid of anything and his people had worshipped him for thousands and thousands of years. What was this new God compared to him, Gamboa, and the ancient Gods of the past?

516

He rose to his full height and shouted with a mighty vehemence.

"Where are you, God? Where are you? Show yourself, Jehovah."

Silence.

He looked around.

"I thought so."

He turned his back on the altar and walked away.

Out of all the people in the world it was he, Gamboa, who had beaten the ages, and death itself, and been reborn, raised from the dead and given new life so that he may rule. It was Gamboa who'd been chosen. He walked, a glint in his almond eyes. He was right. He'd always been right.

He walked smartly, in a determined, deliberate step, away from the Cathedral. He passed early bird milkmen, heads down against the heavy morning, and he wondered at their normality, their routine.

As the road sloped gently down towards the cliffs and the beach below, the cold north wind died, and the sun peeped out from behind the morass of rapidly disappearing clouds. It was turning into a lovely summer's day. He noticed a bandstand, a Victorian cast-iron lattice work contraption, a mess of painted metal sticking up like a bad thumb out of the seaside lawns. And a big name in big bright letters announced to the world that this was Westcliffe-on-Sea.

A cardboard sign, wired to a stanchion, proudly announced that the next concert was to be given by that extremely popular musical ensemble, the Headington

517

Brass Band, all the way from the city of Oxford. Gamboa noticed with mild interest that this was scheduled for today, 19th August, 2pm. He also noticed a rather weather-beaten, perhaps arthritic man, in a long, ill-fitting miserable brown overall, putting out deckchairs, and, for the briefest of moments, considered spending the day here. But, to his rescue came common sense and a welcome sigh of relief. He turned away: he'd had enough of brass bands for one day . . . and night.

He made his way down through the flower beds onto the strip of beach. His feet welcomed the soft sand and he wiggled his toes taking comfort in the earthy texture. The sensuousness of it reminded him of his childhood, and he thought back to the days of his youth; the innocence, the charm of life and the exotic fantasies of the tropics. He took off his shirt, fell to his knees and, facing the now naked glorious sunshine, began the sacred incantations of his ancient faith. He raised his arms in salutation and faced the risen sun.

He had almost been seduced by a building, carvings, and the trickery of glass windows. He prayed his prayers.

There was only ONE true God of Heaven and earth, and the universe beyond, and that was the great Frog God *Wo-Sak*, and he, Gamboa of Suxx, was his representative on earth.

SPECIAL THANKS

Wolfgang van Hooff (Luxembourg): the beer yogi who started it all in a bar in Beijing.

Reverend Dale Roberts (England): a ruthless reader who turned me away from Disney and on to something much more profound.

Rafael Abellan (Brazil): website designer with a great big beard - extraordinary.

Sophie Lauratet (Mauritius): photography made in Beijing for safe keeping and inspiration.

Terry Hamilton (New Zealand): invaluable encouragement with the early text.

Nomer Adona (Philippines): reliable ideas on photographic reproduction.

Richard Ambler (South Africa): the first critical voice to make an impact - cruel to be kind.

Ryan Pantner (on the island of Jeju, South Korea): a crazy supporter of the impossible.

Lucas and Debbie at Panopus (London): professional scanning like no other.

Beijing World Youth Academy (China): invaluable support from the best small school in Beijing.

Mike Smythe, Chris Walsh, Colin Lilley and Jennie Parker (London): for always being there.

And finally my wife, Cosmina Lascu (Romania): the first and last standing when the bell tolls.

Discussion

Gamboa: a God on Earth. He is the Chosen One. He is immortal. He dies but is reincarnated to lead his tribe.

Twelve Priests: represent the twelve Disciples of Christ.

The Apprentice, Xirqutz Xirqutz: represents Judas. He makes a deal with the Devil (Aztec Goddess Chaltexla), betrays Gamboa and wants to take his place.

Gamboa, Jaxxa and Lazarus: the Holy Trinity. Father, Son and Holy Ghost.

Kitsune: Mary, mother of Christ, a healer and Saint.

Lazarus's family: martyrs, prophets and spiritual guides. Punished and slaughtered for their beliefs.

Gamboa's son: sacrificed. Allusion to Abraham and God's direction.

The Vial: chalice or holy grail.

The Box: Arc of the Covenant, lost at sea.

Magic birds and force of nature: visions and dreams of the Old Testament.

Lazarus and Kitsune's house: search for lost Paradise on earth.

Trentham's resurrection: miracles, raising of the dead.

Destruction of the Beach Paradise: God is unhappy and destroys the world.

Gamboa bathing in the river: baptism.

NAMES IN THE NOVEL

It would have been easy to delve into Mayan and Aztec history and steal names from their past. I don't know about you but I find complicated, incomprehensible names a real pain when reading a story. So, a decision was taken to use modernish names, pronounceable, yet with a flavour of the exotic.

GAMBOA

Clearly this is a modern Hispanic sounding name and I chose it deliberately as the character transcends time and geography. I am aware that he would have had a name perhaps more antiquated (and probably much more complicated) but I wanted a name with which readers would feel comfortable. Should Wo-Sak, The Frog God ever be translated into Spanish or Basque (the true origin of the name) I suppose there will be many who will complain that it is too modern and most unlikely. For the average reader, however, the name serves. Gamboa means "peak" "zenith" or "summit". Either way, it suits the character well enough. He is top dog! (or frog!)

WO-SAK

This is a combination of names of the Mayan Astrological Zodiac.

Wo (Uo): August 15 - September 3

Sak: (Sac or Zak): February 11 - March 2

Both these signs have the frog as their animal totem. Those born under the sign of Wo are gifted with the ability to shift between levels of consciousness and are prone to seek out mystical wisdom and mysteries. Those born under Sak have the frog as a power totem, being adaptable and at ease with change - just like the frog.

522

The combination of these two signs seemed an appropriate name for the principal Frog God.

CHALTEXLA

The Goddess Chaltexla actually exists in a much more ornate fashion as Chalchiuhtlicue. She is the Aztec Goddess of water. Her name means: She Who Wears a Jade Skirt. Clearly the root of the name is evident but for the convenience of the modern reader her name has been simplified. Apologies to the true aficionados of ancient mezzo-American culture.

TSOK, CHATLAN, JAXXA AND XURQUTZ XURQUTZ

All made up names. Any similarity between these names and others in history is entirely coincidental.

KITSUNE

Japanese word for fox. They are commonly found in folktales and have magical abilities.

LAZARUS

Perhaps of Greek origin, it means "God has helped" or "God has been my help". Of course, in the Bible Lazarus was raised from the dead.

HERCULES

The Greek hero Heracles became the Roman Hercules. He is famous for his great strength and fantastic adventures.

SABRINA

In Arabic the name Sabrina is associated with "patience". In Hindi and Punjabi, it means "everything".

BULUT

Turkish in origin, this name means "cloud".

A'ISHA

Popular in various cultures, A'isha refers to "one who lives', is "womanly" and "vivacious".

GHENGIS KHAN

A true historical character who forged one of the biggest empires the world has ever seen.

MARY KELLY

Mary Kelly was the final victim of Jack the Ripper. Her heart was never found. Just who Jack the Ripper was has been the subject of speculation for over one hundred years.

GEORGE BAGSTER PHILIPS

Nicknamed Baggy in the novel, Bagster Phillips was the medical officer on the scene of Mary Kelly's murder.

INSPECTOR ABBELINE

Abbeline was tasked with finding the serial killer Jack the Ripper. To his great frustration, he failed. He was also on the scene at the murder site.

HOLMES AND DR WATSON

Fictitious, but greedy to appear in lots of novels, these two names pop up all over the face of literature - as they do here, albeit very briefly.

HERNAN CORTEZ

This Conquistador was indeed very real. He was responsible for the destruction of the Aztec Empire and near obliteration of their entire culture.

GENERAL WILLIAM BOOTH AND THE SALVATION ARMY

William Booth founded the Salvation Army in 1865 in the East End of London. It still exists today as a religious organisation with a quasi-military format.

SETTINGS, NAMES, PLACES AND EVENTS

The novel opens on a tropical coast somewhere, sometime in prehistory. It could have been just about anywhere but it has, as its future, the rise of the Mayan empire and later the Aztecs. Therefore, the original setting is the Gulf of Mexico. The city of Suxx rises and falls, eventually disappearing with the drought which blights the fictitious city. It disappears, then the real historical Mayans rise, followed by the Aztecs.

Why the Mayans just got up and left their great cities has been the subject of many studies and no explanation has been rendered water tight. The most popular reason given for their demise is drought - this I have used as the source of the decline and fall of the original (fictitious!) city of Suxx.

ACATITLAN

This ancient Aztec site really does exist some miles to the north of today's Mexico City.

ST HELEN'S CHURCH, WESTCLIFFE-ON-SEA, ESSEX

The Catholic church in the novel was founded in 1862 and built in 1867. St Helen (or Helena) of Greek origin, is credited with finding the cross of Jesus.

MUCKING

This small, Essex village sits about the Thames Estuary and has a long, proud history.

SAVOY THEATRE AND GILBERT AND SULLIVAN

Gamboa and Jaxxa go to the Savoy Theatre, London, and see a performance of a new opera, The Yeoman of the Guard. Gilbert and Sullivan did indeed offer up this comic musical at the time of the novel's setting and the Savoy was the first theatre to boast electric lights.

WETHERINGDON HALL

Entirely fictitious, yet based on the many great mansions scattered about London and the Thames.

UTOPIUM, LIMEHOUSE

Limehouse, still thriving today, is situated in London's East End. The Utopium, on-the-other-hand, is entirely the product of the author's imagination - although opium dens did certainly exist and Sherlock Holmes did frequent them.

KRAKATOA

In 1883, the Indonesian volcanic island of Krakatoa did actually explode in a ferocious eruption. Over 35,000 people were killed and weather patterns worldwide were changed for some time afterwards.

RIVER THAMES POLLUTION

It is well documented that during Victorian times in the mid 1800s, the River Thames in London was so polluted with human waste and industrial effluent, that outbreaks of cholera were blamed on its contamination.

Printed in Great Britain
by Amazon